Theirs not to
Reason Why

Theirs not to Reason Why

MICHAEL SAWYER

TATE PUBLISHING
AND ENTERPRISES, LLC

Published by Tate Publishing & Enterprises, LLC
127 E. Trade Center Terrace | Mustang, Oklahoma 73064 USA
1.888.361.9473 | www.tatepublishing.com

Tate Publishing is committed to excellence in the publishing industry. The company reflects the philosophy established by the founders, based on Psalm 68:11,
"The Lord gave the word and great was the company of those who published it."

Book design copyright © 2014 by Tate Publishing, LLC. All rights reserved.
Cover design by Junriel Boquecosa
Interior design by Jimmy Sevilleno

Published in the United States of America

ISBN: 978-1-62854-953-9
1. Fiction / Historical
2. Fiction / Romance / General
14.01.09

Cover composition by Angela Howell Arnold

Picture: The Charge of the Light Brigade
by Richard Caton Woodville

DEDICATED TO

Henry John (Jack) Sawyer
Who gave his life for his country

ACKNOWLEDGING

John for his advice and encouragement

THANKING

Pam for her patience and understanding

THE CHARGE OF THE LIGHT BRIGADE

ALFRED LORD TENNYSON

Half a league, half a league,
Half a league onward,
All in the valley of Death
Rode the six hundred.
"Forward, the Light Brigade!
Charge for the guns!" he said;
Into the valley of Death
Rode the six hundred.

"Forward, the Light Brigade!"
Was there a man dismay'd?
Not tho' the soldier knew
Someone had blunder'd;
Their's not to make reply,
Their's not to reason why,
Their's but to do and die;

Into the valley of Death
Rode the six hundred.

Cannon to the right of them,
Cannon to the left of them,
Cannon in front of them
Volley'd and thunder'd;
Storm'd at with shot and shell,
Boldly they rode and well,
Into the jaws of Death,
Into the mouth of Hell
Rode the six hundred.

Flash'd all their sabres bare,
Flash'd as they turned in air,
Sabring the gunners there,
Charging an army, while
All the world wonder'd;
Plunged in the battery smoke
Right thro' the line they broke;
Cossack and Russian
Reel'd from the sabre stroke
Shatter'd and sunder'd.
Then they rode back, but not
Not the six hundred.

Cannon to the right of them,
Cannon to the left of them,
Cannon behind them
Volley'd and thunder'd;
Storm'd at with shot and shell,
While horse and hero fell,
They that had fought so well
Came thro' the jaws of Death
Back from the mouth of hell,
All that was left of them,
Left of six hundred

When can their glory fade?
O the wild charge they made!
All the world wondered.
Honour the charge they made,
Honour the Light Brigade,
Noble six hundred.

FOREWORD

MY ORIGINAL INTENTION had been to write a historical novel about the Crimean War. However, when I was about to begin I thought; "What about the people who played an active part in the war, what were their origins and how did they come to be there?" Many books, both fiction and non-fiction have been written on the Crimean War but they tend to deal more with notables such as the Earls of Cardigan and Lucan et al. I have tried to show things more from the common soldier's (or rankers as they were referred to) point of view. These men privates and NCO's, were mostly from the dregs of British society. Born in slums, prisons and brothels, they had grown up in workhouses, orphanages or on the streets. Many rankers were in the army because the courts had given them the option of enlisting to avoid being hanged, imprisoned or transported.

While poverty had always existed to some extent in British society it was greatly exacerbated by the industrial revolution which started in the latter part of the eighteenth century. The cottage industries could not compete with the new manufacturing techniques, forcing most artisans to abandon their small towns and villages and migrate to the large towns and cities in search of work. Common land which had been granted by Royal Charters to communities "In perpetuity" through the centuries, was seized and built on by avaricious industrialists. Although villagers, who had no land of their own relied on these commons to graze their livestock, the various governments over a period of approximately a hundred years chose to allow these illegal acquisitions to take place. Losing access to the land on which to graze their livestock forced yet more villagers to migrate to the cities seeking employment. Rich aristocrats who had the foresight to invest in industry, the big mercantile companies and the new upper middle class were quick to take advantage of the huge pool of cheap labor. Among the upper classes an attitude of entitlement existed. They believed that it was their right to keep a large portion of the population in abject poverty thereby ensuring a steady supply of cheap labor for every menial occupation from domestic servants to factory workers. The rich and powerful kept pressure on the government to enact statutes imposing draconian sentences to punish theft, theft usually resulting from hunger. It should be noted that the oppressive legal system that existed during this time in history did nothing to reduce crime. It was not until later when the legal system was overhauled and severity in sentencing was reduced along with a more liberal social structure that the incidence of crime was also reduced.

The rankers that fought in the Crimean and other wars during the empire building period of Britain's history were actually fighting for and taking orders from the very people who were responsible for the oppressive social conditions that caused them to be under arms. What is difficult to understand is how and why these rankers for the most part; fought with such great valor as shown in actions such as the Charge of the Light Brigade.

During the Napoleonic wars the great Duke of Wellington once described his rankers as "Scum of the Earth!" Yet that very scum was the most essential component in the building of a great military/commercial empire. However, these valiant rankers who built Britain's great empire benefited little from their nation's wealth which was gained from exploiting the imperial territories, and were cast aside when they were considered to be no longer of use.

This book is based on historical facts however, I have taken some liberties with times and places and most of the characters depicted are fictional. Some of the more notable characters e.g. The Duke of Cambridge actually existed, and the social conditions of the period are verified in numerous historical volumes.

This book was written as a tribute to the 17th Lancers and its descendants, and to those Victorians who were able to rise from poverty at that time in England's history when glorious imperialism and oppressive poverty went hand in hand.

PROLOGUE

A MAN WHO APPEARED to be in his forties sat at the long bench table in the Royal George Inn nursing a tankard of porter, even though seated his straight back held a military bearing, his hair showed iron grey under his cap and there was a livid scar running down his cheek from the outside corner of his left eye to just below the corner of his mouth. A tall young man who appeared to be in his early twenties sat down beside him uninvited and said, "Hello, I hear you were in the Crimean War." The grey haired man looked up and stated; "That is true, and who are you?" The young man said; "I'm John Beaconsfield but my friends just call me John, I work for The Daily Messenger." The older man looked at him and replied; "I don't think I've known you long enough to be your friend, so why are you bothering me John Beaconsfield?" John replied; "Well sir, my paper is looking to publish an account of the Charge of the Light Brigade in which I understand you took part; and I'd like to hear your story." The older man asked; "D'ye mean someone wants to write about what me and the other poor buggers have to say instead of how the lords and generals tell it?" The older man studied John for what seemed like an eternity then declared; "I could tell you a story that you'd never hear from the likes of Lucan and Cardigan and such, but they bloody lords and their like won't want to read about it, how am I to know you'll be writing it like I tell it?" John replied; "If my editor likes your story you can read it for yourself before we put it in print." The old soldier then began give his account of the charge. As he was recounting his memories of the charge he would frequently digress and refer back to his childhood, of growing up in a workhouse and how he came to be in the army. This John decided would make a great story, far better than just the charge itself which had been written about countless times over the years. He decided then and there that as well as interviewing the old soldier he would investigate his origins and then write an account of the his life, not just the charge. After a while John interrupted the old soldier and said; "I'd like to meet you here tomorrow when we can start working on the story from your beginnings." "Well young man I think I'd like that" The old soldier replied. Then John turned to him and said; "By the way sir what is your name?" The older man looked at him his eyes gleaming; "It's Jack, Jack Spratt." This started John Beaconsfield on a journey that would reveal a tale of man's inhumanity to man, class distinction, privilege and courage.

As John was leaving he put a shilling down on the bar and told the barkeep to see that Jack Spratt got something to eat to go with his porter; he failed to notice the barkeeps knowing grin.

CHAPTER I

PENURY

JACK'S MEMORY OF his origins only took him back to when he was around five years old. John decided that he would try to find out what he could about his birth and early infancy. He determined that the best sources would be the workhouse and parish records. His research and Jack's narrative revealed a harrowing story which was all too common during the early and middle Victorian eras.

Jenny one of eight children, was the oldest daughter of Thomas Spratt a laborer employed on the estate of the Marquis of Chesham. When she reached the age of thirteen her parents decided they would have to find her a "position" girls had to be clothed and fed and on a farm laborers wages it was no longer possible now that she was grown, furthermore Thomas and his wife Eliza still had the other seven children for which to provide. Thomas confided his situation to the estate foreman who in turn relayed the information to the head footman at the manor house. Eventually it reached the ears of the Marchioness who recalled that the housekeeper at their town residence had said she would need a replacement for one of the maids who was leaving to get married. She had word passed down to Thomas who was instructed to have Jenny at the servant's entrance of the manor house at eight o'clock the following morning, where Jenny was interviewed by the manor's housekeeper. Jenny being found suitable was instructed to be back at the manor house Monday morning at six o'clock sharp when she would be leaving for town with his Lordship's coach. Monday morning saw Jenny and her scant belongings loaded on the top of the coach with the baggage, even though the coach was empty a servant girl could not be permitted to ride inside. On arriving at the town house she was interviewed by the housekeeper and informed that she would receive twelve pounds a year to be paid monthly, less cost of board and uniforms. Her hours would be six in the morning till eight at night and she would get one day off each week. She was then told that breakfast in the kitchen would be at five o'clock the following morning after which she would be instructed in her duties by the maid she was about to replace. Jenny who had grown up with hard work settled into her new surroundings and became very efficient in performing her duties; her life became almost idyllic by the standards of a working class country girl until the Young Master came on the scene. His Lordship's eldest son whose formal title was Earl of Dunnington; but who was referred to by the staff as the Young Master had been brought home from school to start a career in the army; his father had purchased him a commission in a "smart regiment". He soon spotted Jenny who was very well developed for her age and decided he would "have her." The Young Master was sixteen and had been constantly aroused by the erotic stories he and his schoolfellows would tell each other, now decided he would "have" a real girl. One afternoon when Jenny was dusting in his bedroom he entered, locked the door then raped her. After he had done with her he said; "If you tell anyone I'll have you dismissed and tell the Beadle that I caught you stealing." Jenny was compelled to answer his summonses during the following weeks for fear of losing her position and being arrested; until he left to join his regiment. Soon after the Young Master had left Jenny realized she was pregnant. She managed to hide her condition by wearing her predecessor's larger uniforms for almost nine months until the housekeeper saw her when she was wearing only a chemise and her condition was obvious, she was made to leave immediately. Jenny began to walk back home which was a days ride by coach, three days on foot. The second day tired, hungry and sick she stumbled into a village which was about half way to her home; she collapsed in the middle of the road and later regained consciousness in the workhouse infirmary. While she was in labor the female inmate who was acting as midwife asked her name, she was barely able to say that it was "Jenny Spratt." Her baby boy came into the world shortly afterwards, then Jenny fell into blessed oblivion. When the midwife told the Beadle Jenny's name he said with a laugh; "Then we must call the boy Jack." Jenny died the following morning and received a pauper's burial. Jack's birth was duly recorded in the workhouse and Parish records: Male born: Twenty Fifth day of October Year of Our Lord Eighteen Hundred and Thirty-two. Name: Jack, Mothers Name: Jenny Spratt, Father: unknown. Jack was handed over to a young girl who had come to the work-house in similar circumstances as Jenny and whose baby had died. She served as his wet nurse until he was weaned; when he joined the other infants in the baby ward.

Somewhere between the ages of five and six he was moved to the boy's ward where he and the other boys slept when they weren't working. The Workhouse Master would wake them every morning at six when they would be marched to the dining hall; there they were fed a watery dish of porridge with a small piece of stale bread to be swilled down with water. After breakfast they were marched to the workshop where they would be employed performing various menial tasks; such as picking oakum. Dinner was at midday when they would be served cold tough mutton or salt pork with half cooked brown potatoes or turnips and wilted cabbage. At six o'clock in the evening they were given a piece of hard yellow cheese after which they were marched back to the ward and told to go to bed.

It was not long before some of the larger boys started bullying Jack and he soon discovered that cowering and crying just encouraged them to bully him even more; so he decided to fight back. He was quick on his feet and he soon learned how to use speed to his advantage. One evening after the boys were back in their sleeping quarters one of the older boys walked over to Jack and cuffed him on the ear saying "That's wot we do to trollop's brats in 'ere." Jack held his hand up to his ear and turned away at the same time pretending to cry. As the bully started to laugh at him Jack spun around and planted his foot squarely between the bully's legs. When the larger boy bent over clutching his balls Jack grabbed the back of his head and brought a knee up into the bully's face smashing his nose. Not content with the damage he had already inflicted; while the bully was bent over with one hand held to his balls and the other to his broken nose Jack kicked his legs out from under him. This all occurred so quickly that the other boys had hardly realized what had happened until Jack was methodically kicking the bully who was bellowing while writhing on the floor. Hearing the commotion the Master arrived wheezing and red in the face exclaiming; "Wot the bloody 'ells goin' on 'ere?" He soon summed up the situation and lifted Jack off his victim with one hand while beating him with the stick which he carried in the other for just such occasions. Jack bit into his lower lip until it bled but he was determined not to cry out. Eventually when the Master's arms were aching from holding Jack with one hand and beating him with the other, he let him drop to the floor. Looking down at the trembling boy he said; "That be just a taste of what you gets if I catches you a fightin' ag'in." After he had left some of the boys gathered around Jack with admiring looks on their faces, the fact that he had not even whimpered during the beating made him a hero in their eyes. Meanwhile the bully was lying on the floor sobbing and bleeding. This incident not only put an end to the bullying but it also caused the younger boys to look up to Jack as their leader from that time on.

At the age of sixteen Jack was moved into the men's ward where he spent his days between being hired out by the parish to local farmers and walking the tread wheel which operated the grindstones of the grist mill. He'd been in the men's ward about two months when one night after he and the others retired following the evening meal he was assaulted. He had hardly fallen asleep on his truckle bed when he felt hands grabbing him, he knew what was going to happen if he did not get the best of his assailant, he had heard about the older men buggering some of the younger lads and he wasn't about to become a victim. When his attacker took one hand off Jack to pull down his trousers he reached out, found his attackers thigh then slid his hand up and grasped the man's balls and squeezed with all his strength. While his would be rapist was howling and holding his crotch he slid off the bed and pulled out one of the loose bottom planks. From the noise his attacker was making Jack took a guess as to where his head was and swung the board with all the strength he could muster. He heard the board crack on the man's head as it splintered in his hands. The door of the ward flew open as the Master holding up a bulls-eye lantern charged in exclaiming; "Oo the 'ell is making all the bloody noise?" Then he saw Jack's attacker lying unconscious on the floor and Jack standing there with the shattered plank in his hands; "Well I'll be buggered, yew be up to yur old tricks ag'in!" The Master made a grab for him but Jack was too quick, he went under the Masters arm and through the door. He ran down the alley to the High St. when he got there he decided he would take the road that he had heard led to town. He walked all night, by morning he was cold and hungry and very tired, as he came into town he was looking for somewhere to rest when he smelled the aromas coming from a bakery. He spied the bakers shop across the street and was drawn to it like a nail to a magnet.

He looked into the bakery window and saw the loaves and buns all fresh and warm from the oven, he drooled. Jack sidled up to the shop saw that no one was inside then reached around the door for the nearest loaf of bread. His hand was almost upon it when he felt someone grab his shoulder saying; "Got ya, ya young bugger," he was spun round and found himself in the iron grip of a very large man with a big florid face. "Now wot ya got t' say fer yerself yew young bugger?" Jack's answer did not evince any sympathy from the Beadle; "I was hungry zur an' I din't mean no 'arm" said Jack." The Beadle expressed his irritation; "'arm ya sez, 'arm, why youse a thief, I'll give ya 'arm!" His captor marched him up the road to a red brick building and pushed him through a large oak door while still maintaining a firm grip on him, Jack then found himself looking up at a white haired elderly man. The elderly man was sat behind a high desk and he slowly looked up from Jack to his captor's face; "What have you got there Bert?" Bert explained; "I cawt this young thief a stealing from bakery zur." "Where's the stolen goods?" enquired the white haired man. The Beadle replied; "I grabbed un fer ee cud take anythin'." "Well now what are we going to do with you young Master Thief?" asked the elderly man. Jack answered; "Please zur I was 'ungry 'an' it won't 'appen agin." "No it won't 'appen ag'in" said Bert; "Cuz yur goin' to jail, then you'll be brought up in court and 'anged or ship'd orf ta Bot'ny Bay." The elderly man looked at Jack and said; "You know young fella I'm going to give you a chance to become someone useful instead of being a thief." Then he addressed the big man who still had a firm grip on Jack's shoulder; "Beadle, take him over to the barracks, maybe they can make him into a soldier." "But wot if they don't wan' 'im zur?" the Beadle asked. "We will address that problem if and when we have to" said the Magistrate. The Beadle steered Jack out of the door and proceeded to march him along the street saying. "You be lucky young'n, that magistrate could have 'ad you put in jail and brung up in court." After they had walked for a few minutes a high grey stone wall came into view, as they rounded a corner Jack saw a gateway about fifty yards along the wall. Against the wall to one side of the gateway was a blue and white striped sentry box in front of which stood a trooper of The Duke of Cambridge's Own 17th Lancers, Jack had never seen such a vision as the resplendent soldier in his life. When Jack and the Beadle came up to him the sentry came to attention and Jack's eyes took in the breathtaking sight in awe. He stared at the dark blue tunic with its white front and double row of brass buttons and the tight blue breeches with a double white stripe down the sides, the spotlessly white gauntleted gloves and black shiny riding boots. All this was surmounted by a white topped lance cap with a white horsehair whisk above which fluttered a red and white pennant attached to a highly polished lance head. "Wot can we be doin' fer you today Beadle?" enquired the sentry. The Beadle replied; "Magistrate zed to bring this young thief to you'ns to see if you can make a sojer out of 'im." The lancer nodded towards a single story grey stone building, "Take 'im to the Guardroom and ask the Sarge, ee'l know wot to do wiv 'im." The Beadle propelled Jack toward the guard room which had a tripod of stacked lances each side of its door. When they entered there was another soldier just as splendid as the one at the main gate sat behind a desk. This one had three silver chevrons on his right arm and exuded authority, he asked; "Wot we got ere Beadle?" "I cawt this un a thieving over at t' bakery, Magistrate zed to bring 'im over and see if you wan' 'im," the Beadle replied. The Sergeant studied Jack; the ragged cap, torn shirt, canvas trousers the bottoms of which ended halfway between his knees and his ankles, calloused bare feet and pinched face. He knew this boy; it was himself twenty years ago. He told the Beadle to wait while he sent for the Orderly Officer. He ordered another much younger soldier with no chevrons to go find the Orderly Officer and ask him if he could come to the Guardroom. When they returned Jack was dumbstruck by the vision of an officer of the 17th Lancers in full dress uniform. Not only did his uniform have all the attributes of those of the main gate sentry and the sergeant's but it was even more splendid. He wore a cloak fastened at the throat by a gold chain connected to two gold lion's heads. His lance cap had white egret plumes instead of the ranker's horsehair whisk, where his blue cloak was pulled back from his left side showing its white silk lining a saber in a polished steel scabbard was slung from two crimson and gold straps. The Sergeant quickly came to his feet and saluted. Then the officer addressed the Sergeant; "D'ye think we can do anything with him?" The Sergeant replied; "Well zur ee needs fat'nin up zum but I reckon we can make 'im inta summat." The officer instructed the sergeant to have Jack taken to the regimental orderly room where he was sworn in and became a member of the 17th Lancers; he was now starting a new life as a soldier.

CHAPTER 2

A NEW LIFE

FTER HE HAD been sworn in a sergeant called over a young lad who might have been two years older than Jack and ordered him to take Jack to the cookhouse saying; "See if cook can put zum meat on 'is bones." His conductor was wearing what Jack later found out to be stable dress. This uniform consisted of a waist length blouse with a single line of brass buttons down the front, and straight blue trousers of the same dark blue material as the other more resplendent uniforms he had seen. Around his middle was a dark blue canvas belt double buckled on the left side with a double white stripe around the center of its circumference, this was topped off by a peak-less forage cap. As they walked into the cookhouse as the men's mess hall was known; Jack noted the long bench tables and the scrubbed flagstone floor. Another soldier wearing no blouse with the sleeves of his grey woolen shirt rolled up and a white apron fastened around his waist approached and his escort informed the cook; "Sarge Woodford said to feed un, I'll be back later." The cook gestured to Jack to sit at one of the tables, "I'll fetch ee zum vittles." He returned a few minutes later with a tin plate which was loaded with the most sumping tuous food Jack had ever seen or smelled. There was a sizzling piece of steaming roast mutton, hot boiled potatoes and crisp kale. The lad asked him if he had a knife and fork, when he said no he went off to fetch the utensils. Jack had ploughed half way through meal using his fingers before he got back. When the first lad returned Jack had finished off everything on the plate and sat with his hands folded on his stomach. His original conductor said; "Look at un ee thinks ee's in 'eaven," then both young soldiers laughed uproariously. When they arrived back at the guard room Jack addressed the sergeant; "Thank ee fer the vittles zur." The sergeant glared at him and boomed out in a loud parade ground voice; "First thing you gotta larn lad is ya calls sergeants and corporals by rank not zur, ya zee these yere stripes he touched his chevrons I'm a sergeant, and that's wot ya calls me, Sergeant." "Now officers an' sergeant majors ya calls zur, an' ya better not fergit it." Addressing Jack's escort he ordered; "Get un over to Quarter Masters and see wot ee needs till tomorrer, but fust scrub the bugger and get rid of 'is fleas." His escort then led him to the front of some stables, stood him outside the double door and told him to take off all his clothes. Jack started to protest when the older boy reached behind the stable door his hand came back holding a riding whip; "We ken do this the 'ard way or the easy way, wot's it gonna be?" he asked, then Jack began to take off his rags. The lad then disappeared into the stable to return in a few minutes with bucket full of water in one hand and a large block of yellow soap in the other. He gave Jack the soap then upended the bucket over Jack's head saying; "Now wash yerself" He disappeared again; then reappeared with the refilled bucket. After giving Jack a few minutes to finish lathering himself he rinsed him off by pouring the second bucket over him. He went off to fill the bucket again but this time he returned with a stone jar in his other hand. He told Jack to close his eyes then poured some liquid from the jar onto his head; "Now rub them turps inter yer 'ed." Jack started to rub in the turpentine when he felt a burning

32

sensation; he bit his lip but was determined not to cry out. Then the lad told Jack to cup his hands then poured some turpentine into them, he then instructed Jack; "rub that round yer balls and under yer arms." "You bugger yer trying ta kill me!" shouted Jack. "No I be killin' yer fleas." replied his escort. When the lad was satisfied that Jack had taken care of his underarms and nether parts, he emptied the third bucket over him then handed him an empty feed sack with which to dry himself. Jack had just finished drying off when he noticed that he had an audience. A group of youths were gathered round him laughing; he noticed they were all wearing stable dress trousers but they were without tunics just grey woolen shirts. He tried to cover himself with his hands but this made them laugh even more. Ribald comments came from the group; "'Ee don't need two 'ands to 'ide wot 'ees got." "Reckon that worm uv 'is aint big enuf fer fishin'." A soldier appeared in full stable dress with two stripes on his right arm, he was older than the others; and he was furious shouting; "You young buggers get back to work right now, if I catches any of ya a fuckin' orf agin it'll be squadron orders tomorrer mornin'." Jack's erstwhile audience hastily disappeared back into the stables their hoots of derision drifting back to his ears. His escort exited from the stables this time with a worn and faded stable dress blouse and trousers. "Ere put these on fer now; we'll have to burn yer rags." Jack dressed hurriedly then turned to the lad; "You gotta name or aint it right fer me to call yer by it?" The lad replied; "They calls me by me nickname Chalky; cus me surname's White." "Ya reckon they'll be a givin' me a nickname?" Jack asked. Chalky answered; "Yeah I reckon we'll call ya Fishy, Jack Spratt." Chalky handed Jack a length of twine and instructed him; "Tie that 'round yer ta keep yer trousers up." Then he led him off to the Quarter Masters. They eventually arrived at a two story building made of the same grey stone as were all the other buildings which comprised the lancer barracks. Chalky ushered him through the large oak door and up to a chest high counter, behind which was a soldier with two stripes on the arm of his tunic. He looked at Jack and asked Chalky; "Wot yer got 'ere White?" Chalky replied; "Orderly Room Sar'nt zed ta bring 'im fer zum kit Corp'." The corporal looked back over his shoulder then called out; "'ey Sarge they sent us a new un wot'l I give 'im?" The sergeant then appeared from a room at the back of what turned out to be a large storeroom. He looked at Jack, shook his head and said to the corporal; "Issue 'im stable dress, a shirt and work boots we'll kit 'im out fully tomorrer." The corporal then took two blankets from the rack behind him placed them on the counter then put the prescribed items on the blankets, before folding them into a bundle he threw two pairs of coarse linen draws with tapes at the waist on the pile. He looked at Jack, "They's ta keep the shit from get'n on the inside of yer trousers." He then opened a large book on the counter, dipped a quill in an inkpot and began to write on a blank page, When he had finished he turned the book around towards Jack and said while handing him the quill; "Make yer mark at the bottom." Jack shook his head; "I don't read er write." The corporal put his finger at the bottom of the page and said; "Put a ex 'ere." Jack made an X where he had been shown then the corporal wrote something beside it. "This ere sez JS2 we already got a JS, so you be JS2 and that be yer mark from now on."

Chalky then conducted Jack out of the Quartermasters Store and preceded him towards a single story building. When they reached the large double doors in the center of the building Chalky gestured for him to go inside. The sight that met Jack's eyes was one of Spartan orderliness. The floor of the barracks building consisted of white flagstones (he was to find out later how they got to be so white), at each end of the building was a cast iron coal stove with a bin and bucket all of which were gleaming black . There was a row of wooden cots along the length of both walls interrupted on the one side by the doorway. Against the wall beside each cot was a four shelf wooden rack each containing various items of neatly folded uniforms. At the bottom of the racks on the floor were highly polished black riding boots or work boots. The racks above the work boots had stable dress uniforms on their shelves; those above riding boots had dress uniforms with everything folded in exactly the same manner from cot to cot with each cot having a large trunk like wooden box at it's foot.. Chalky stopped by an empty cot and indicated that it was to be Jack's and proceeded to show him how to fold his blankets on the cot telling Jack; "The only time yew unfolds these blankets is when yew gets in bed ta sleep, yer kit goes up 'ere," he said placing Jack's items on the shelf and his boots on the floor; "Corp' ull show yer how to do everything proper in mornin'."

The following weeks of Jack's life was one big blur of activity. First he had to learn how to take care of his kit; what uniforms to wear, foot drill, dismounted saber and lance drill and cleaning. Everything in the barracks was constantly being cleaned, painted or scrubbed from the flagstone floor to the men's personal kit, to painting the flagpole and rails around the regimental insignia board at the main gate. Reveille was sounded at five o'clock in the morning; after completing their ablutions they were marched to the cookhouse at half past five for breakfast. At six o'clock they were marched back to their barrack room where they swept, dusted and arranged their personal kit and folded their blankets in the prescribed regimental manner. All this was done with frenetic energy and with junior NCOs constantly driving them and barking orders. Seven o'clock was first parade when they were lined up on the side of the parade ground and inspected by their Troop Sergeant and then by the Sergeant Major; woe betide the soldier whose dress was not up to regimental standards. There were barrack room inspections, work parties, endless drills and parades. Sometimes Jack was assigned to the officer's stables work detail. There he learned how to groom horses, to soap saddles and tack, clean bits and polish bridle chains. He would also have to muck out their stalls and feed them. And here he discovered his love for horses; a love the animals seem to reciprocate.

One time on stable duty while curry combing a beautiful charger he was talking soothingly to it when the corporal in charge of the work detail said; "Yew'll 'ave your own soon and there won't be nobody to take care of it fer ya cos you ain't no bleedin' orficer." The day came sooner than he expected. On the Friday of their eighth week as lancer recruits they were informed on first parade that they would start mounted training on Monday morning; Jack was elated.

On Monday morning after first parade the new recruit detail was marched to the indoor riding school; a large building which had a dirt floor surrounded by a low circular wooden barrier with a gate. In the center of the floor mounted on a bay gelding was a lancer in stable dress wearing riding boots with spurs, he had four reversed chevrons on his right arm. He addressed the group formed up in front of him. "I be Riding Master Perry and you'll address me as zur at all times, d'ye understand? This statement was met by silence from the recruits which elicited a bellow from the Riding Master: "I asked you young buggers a question; I wants an answer." The corporal in charge of the detail shouted out; "Yes zur." "Right, now let's 'ear it from the rest of yew" roared the Riding Master. "From now on when youse spoken; to yew will answer yes zur." They all shouted out in loud unison; "

For the next week they suffered under the harsh tutelage of the Riding Master. They learned how to saddle and bridle; first on a wooden horse then live horses. Friday morning a sergeant appeared together with the Riding Master who introduced him as Farrier Sergeant Woden. The Farrier Sergeant using his own horse showed them how to care for the horses hooves, explained to them what problems to look for and how to take care of simple things like a stone in the foot and trimming the hoof back flush to the shoe. He then emphasized the need to report to their troop sergeant when a horse needed shoeing and any signs of injuries or abscesses in the foot and any other signs of the animal being out of sorts. He ended his lesson by telling them that their horses were the most important thing in the regiment. "The Colonel pays fifteen guineas fer yur 'orses an' none uv yew young buggers be worth a bloody farthin'!"

When they arrived at the riding school next morning they were greeted by the sight of a line of horses tethered to the rail that ran along the length of one wall. The Riding Master smiled to himself at the looks on their faces and then addressed them. "These 'ere be remounts which your goin' to be takin'care of, the corporal 'ere ul tell 'ee wot numbers er yourn then you'll make yur mark by the number." A corporal in stable dress with spurs strapped to his work boots showed each one of them where to make his mark in a large ledger then informed them; "That number that you signed at be on your 'orses front left 'oof, go find 'im, get un 'alter on 'im and bring 'im into the middle of the trainin' floor." They all ran over to the line of tethered horses and began looking for their numbers. One boy got bitten and two others were kicked; each incident bringing curses from their victims and gales of laughter from the others. When they had found and haltered their allocated mounts, they brought them to the center of the floor where the Riding Master ordered them to be silent and had them line up in front of him and proceeded to instruct them. "Now 'eres yur fust lesson ya allus stands on the left side of yer 'orse and ya allus mounts un from that side." Those who were on the right adjusted accordingly and then he ordered them at ease and proceeded to give them further instructions. "Ya never runs up be'ind a 'orse an' riles 'em up, two of yer jes found out why, an' they got a front end too." Looking at the boy who was bitten he said; "An' you'll be 'avin a good bruise on that arm in the morning, if the skins broken put some turps on it, if it goes septic report to the surgeon." The Riding Master then went on to tell them about the horses that would now be the most important part of their lives: They were all bay geldings, bay; because that was the Colonel's preferred color; geldings; "Cus mares goes in 'eat 'an stallions fights wiv uver stallions an' gets randy when they smells a mare in 'eat." He then proceeded to tell them that the horses were all two years old, broken but not trained; training the horses was going to be part of their mounted training. They were then ordered to take the horses to their stalls which were in the stable behind the riding school. Just as they were leading their horses away the Riding Master told them that they could give their horse's names but not to get too fond of them; "One day youse might 'av to shoot un." As Jack led his horse into an empty stall he saw that there were saddles slung over a rail which ran the length of the stable wall; and tack hung from hooks above. The boy in the next stall to Jack's said "wot ya gonna call yourn Fishy?" Jack thought for a moment then replied "I'm gonna call im Nipper." "Nipper!" the lad exclaimed; "'e aint no nipper 'e be fifteen 'an a 'aff 'ands 'igh." Jack replied; "It wur the name of zumbody I yuster know."

Jack's thoughts took him back to the day Nipper was brought into the workhouse. One of the boys that worked at the village livery stable came into the workshop where the boys were picking oakum. He had a dirty ragged bundle in his arms, he addressed the Master. "They told me you'd be 'ere, I found this 'un in the straw at stables." He placed the bundle on the work table which revealed itself as a small boy. The child was shivering and began to cough. "Take un to Matron looks like "e needs to be int' infirmary" the Master instructed him. The stable boy shrugged, picked up the tiny boy and headed for the infirmary. Two days later the Master came into the boy's ward just before bed time showed him to a cot and told him he would be starting work in the morning. Over the succeeding days the boys learned his story. He had worked in a boot black factory in London for a shilling a week where they made boot polish from lard, naptha and lamp black. After the ingredients were mixed in heated vats the mixture was ladled into small jars where it solidified. The children that worked in these factories for twelve hours a day suffered from burns and were subjected to fumes from the vats.

The boy; who because he was so small they named Nipper, came from circumstances that were all too common in the cities at that period in England's history, his father was an unemployed drunk and his mother was a whore who plied her trade in the local ale-houses. When Nipper got too sick to make his quota filling jars; the foreman put him out on the street. Nipper was afraid to go home knowing his father would beat him near to death for losing his job. Not knowing where to go or what to do he started walk-ing, having no sense of his direction he headed eastward, stealing or begging food on his way as he passed through two towns and some villages losing count of the days. Finally he was so sick and weak from coughing he stumbled into the livery stable and col-lapsed on the straw. Because Nipper was so small, Jack became his self appointed guardian, preventing the larger boys from bul-lying the unfortunate waif. Nipper coughed constantly especially at night. One night about three weeks after he had arrived he had a coughing bout which was even more intense than usual. Jack felt his way in the dark over to Nipper's cot and was helping the boy to sit up when he felt Nipper's head fall onto his shoulder and then a rattling sound came from the boy's ravaged body. In his short life Jack had had enough experience of death to know that Nipper's suffering had ended. The following day a small pine box containing Nipper's body was unceremoniously dropped into a hole in the pauper's graveyard.

The weeks following their introduction to the horses were a frenetic period of training of mounts and riders: mounted lance and saber drill, jumping hurdles and riding bareback. All of this while still having to keep their barrack room meticulously clean, uniforms properly folded, other items of clothing laundered and boots polished to a mirror like sheen. One Friday after a particu larly grueling week of practicing review drills the Riding Master gave the command for the troop to line up in review order. When they were formed up to his satisfaction he began to address them;. "Tomorrer mornin' you lot er gonna be on regimental mounted parade, Gawd 'elp us! Order of dress ull be full parade dress an' everthin' clean an' shiny."

Saturday morning after breakfast they were marched to the stables; where after they attended to their horses usual needs, with the exception of food and water "(Colonel don't like they 'orses pissing and shitting on parade)," they put bridles, saddle cloths and saddles on their mounts and then marched back to the barrack room. In the barrack room they donned the full dress uniform of The Duke of Cambridge's Own 17th Lancers. After being inspected by Troop Sergeant Hansen, they marched back to the stables holding their saber scabbards up with their left hands, shouldered lance pennants fluttering in the breeze with spurs clinking; they presented an impressive sight. When they reached the stables the Riding Master was waiting mounted and in full ceremonial dress, he ordered them to stack their lances and lead the horses out. After they led their horses out the Riding Master ordered them to mount and recover their lances; the butts of which they seated firmly in their right hand stirrup buckets. At this point the Troop Sergeant rode up, also in full parade dress. The Riding Master ordered them into line and addressed them. "This be the last time I'm gonna be with you buggers. I'll ride with you today but your troop sergeant ull be in charge. Sergeant Hansen take charge of yer troop." The Troop Sergeant, in his parade ground voice responded; "Yes Sir." The Sergeant then ordered them to form up in review order, he then gave orders; "Troop will turn right in columns of three dressing from the left, at the walk, forward, then he and the Riding Master trotted to the head of the formation.." With the Riding Master and the Troop Sergeant at the head of the column the troop of newly trained lancers proceeded to the parade ground.

CHAPTER 3

ODYSSEY

BEACONSFIELD AND JACK were sitting at a small table near the stone hearth in the George's lounge as they had been doing every week for three weeks. Jack was talking while the young journalist was taking notes. It was about eight o'clock when Beaconsfield said; "I think that's enough for this evening Jack, and I have something to tell you." He went on to tell Jack that he would be gone for a week or two on newspaper business, he did not tell him what the business was. He gave Jack a guinea and told him he would contact him when he got back. John Beaconsfield was about to enter on a journey for which his respectable middle class upbringing had never prepared him.

From Jack's story John knew the town where the barracks were located, so he decided that was the obvious place to start his research. He took a train to London; then boarded another train for his destination. When he got to the barracks, he found a smart young hussar on main gate guard who came to attention bringing his saber up from the at ease position to the carry. The hussar informed him that the 17th Lancers had not occupied the barracks for many years. John walked back to the White Lion

Inn where he was staying, ordered a pint of porter and enquired of the landlord if he knew of anyone that would remember when the lancers were at the barracks. "Well they left them barracks afore the Crimean War; I was just a nipper back then." Replied the landlord. "Would there be anyone in town who might remember anything of when they were here?" asked John. The landlord answered; "There be Bert he yuster be Beadle but we got a Peeler now;" using the term applied to the members of the police force created by Sir Robert Peel. John asked; "Where can I find this Bert; Landlord?" The landlord replied; "well zur, if ya waits five more minutes eel be 'ere, ee comes in eight sharp every night." John waited until a very large very old man came through the door and stomped up to the bar. He made his enquiry; "Excuse me sir, are you Bert that used to be the Beadle?" Bert answered: "Aye that be me, and oo be you?" John identified himself and explained that he was seeking information on when the 17th Lancers occupied the barracks. Bert exclaimed;" that be a bloody long time ago, what d'ye wanter know?" John explained; "I'm trying to get some information about a soldier that was in the regiment; his name was Jack Spratt." The Beadle uttered a surprised exclamation; "Well I'll be buggered! Of all the young buggers I took over to them barracks ee be the only one I do remember, cuz of "is name. Yew remembers the rhyme; Jack Spratt would eat no fat 'is wife would eat no lean?" Bert went on to explain how the Magistrate would send young offenders to the barracks in the hope that they might take them in the army. "'Ee wur a soft old fool; ee didn't like to jail 'em cus then they young thieves 'ud be 'ung or transported, ee wuz a retired major or zummat like that." John ordered a porter for Bert; then said, "The person I'm investigating claims he grew up in a workhouse." Bert shook his head; "Ee warn't from this work'us; I knowed oo allus inmates wuz." "Are there any other workhouses in this area?" asked John. "Nearest un I knows of wur about fifteen miles down the road," replied Bert; he gave the name of a village. The following morning John took the train (a railway had now replaced horse drawn coaches) to the village and began his enquiries. He started at the White Lion; he had learned that pubs were usually the best source of local information. After discovering that the workhouse no longer existed, he enquired as to the whereabouts of the Parish Council offices and presented himself to the Parish Clerk. As soon as he entered the clerk's office he sensed the air of self importance that exuded from the pale sharp faced little man behind the high desk. John thought to himself "I suppose I'll have to kiss this pompous pricks arse." He introduced himself then proceeded with some serious arse kissing. "I have been informed that you are the best person to provide me with some information that I'm seeking. Apparently you have a reputation for keeping accurate and comprehensive records." He could see the clerk puffing up with pleasurable pride and knew he had him eating out of his hand. "I'm looking for information on a Jack Spratt who might have been an inmate of the old workhouse." "What year would that be sir?" "Early to middle thirties I think." The clerk went over to some shelves against the wall and took down two huge volumes with which he staggered to the table by his desk where he placed them with a gasp. "This one is 1801 to 1850 and this ones 1851 till they closed the workhouse. John said, "I think it's most likely the first one." The clerk opened the tome and began turning the pages then suddenly exclaimed; "This looks like what you're after." John came around the desk to the table just as the clerk was saying, "he was born there." John looked and sure enough the record stated that Jack was born to Jenny Spratt October 25th 1832. The clerk looked up Jenny Spratt's name; and informed John that she was recorded has having died October 26th. "Was he from around here do you think?" "I don't know sir but there are some Spratt's' that works on Lord Chesham's estate; about five miles from here." John literally ran out of the office back to the White Lion to get his notebooks. From there he hastened to the livery stable; when he arrived outside; he paused for a moment recalling Jack's story about Nipper. He picked out a sturdy looking hunter and waited impatiently while the horse was saddled and bridled. When the ostler had his horse ready he strapped his note books in one of the saddlebags and mounted hurriedly. It then occurred to him that in his haste he had forgotten to ask directions. After getting directions from the ostler he left the confines of the stable and set off for the Chesham estate at a brisk canter. After about five minutes John realized that the horse could not be expected to keep up the pace for five miles he slowed down to a walk. He arrived at Chesham Manor at about three o'clock in the afternoon; he took in the high grey limestone walls, the gatehouse and the wrought iron gates. He rode up to the gatehouse, dismounted and tied the reins to a hitching rail. Before he could knock a tiny wizened old woman in a billowing black dress wearing a white mob cap opened the door. She asked; "What be your business young gentleman?" John introduced himself then said; "I'm looking for the family of Jenny Spratt." "Well you just found one of 'em she wuz me sister, you better come on in." John ducked his head stepped through the low doorway into a cozy feeling low ceilinged room. She then informed him; "I be Mary James; used ter be Spratt 'for I married, why be you asking 'bout Jenny young fella?" John lied glibly and told her that he thought she might be his grandmother; and that he was trying to trace his family history. "If Jenny were your grandma one of yer parents wuz a bastard." John asked her how that could be. She then told him how Jenny went to work at the town house and was dismissed when she got in the family way. When asked what happened to her afterwards Mary said they had never heard of her again. By now it was getting late and Jack didn't relish the idea of riding back in the dark; so he asked Mary if there was somewhere he could stay for the night. She directed him to an inn about a quarter mile along the road from the manor, informing him that her son was the landlord and telling Jack to be sure to let her son know that she had sent him. John set off for the Black Bull Inn with the intent of having a meal; and after good nights sleep returning to the White Lion, he had no idea of the revelation which awaited him. After introducing himself to the landlord; he told him that he had been directed to the inn by his mother and requested a nights lodging and stabling for his horse. The landlord told him his name was Jed, and then asked what John's business was with his mother. John repeated the story he had used on Mary and was surprised when Jed said "why luv ee zur you should 'ave come to me fust." When asked if he knew what happened to Jenny; Jed stated that he didn't know any more than his mother, but as he didn't live on Lord Chesham's estate in one of his houses he could tell John more than his mother dared. According to the footmen who traveled to town and back with the coach; until the railway came, it was the Young Master (the present Lord Chesham) who had got Jenny in the family way. Jed laughed when he saw the look of astonishment on John's face. "I'll be buggered; you and me might be kin." John thought to himself; "I wonder what Jack's reaction would be to this information?" After a supper of roast leg of mutton, peas, carrots and potatoes washed down with two pints of porter John spent a restful night. He arose at six o'clock and enjoyed a breakfast consisting of a large gammon rasher fried eggs and fresh baked bread with farmhouse butter. John paid Jed and thanked him for his hospitality; then went out to the stable yard where a pot boy was holding his horse's bridle. He mounted the horse and began his journey back to the village, as he passed the manor gatehouse he tipped his hat to Mary who was working in her garden. As Mary responded with a wave he recalled Jed's admonition: "don't tell nobody I told ee 'bout Aunt Jenny, I wouldn't put it past 'is bloody lordship to take it out on mother."

That evening back at the White Lion; John ate his supper while listening to the regulars airing their views about various local happenings and exchanging gossip. However his mind was somewhere else, should he, or should he not inform Jack of what he had discovered? Finally he decided to disclose what he had learned of the circumstances of his birth in the workhouse, but none of the preceding events.

CHAPTER 4

ON PARADE

WITH RIDING MASTER Perry and Troop Sergeant Hansen at their head the troop of newly trained lancers arrived at the parade ground, where they came to a halt at the end of "D" Squadron formed up in review order. Sergeant Hansen gave the order; "Troop will turn left in review order dressing from the right, left turn." Horses and riders turned left as one; their three ranks symmetrical to the squadron on their right. The Riding Master and Sergeant Hansen then trotted to their stations front and center of the troop; as they came to a halt a young officer trotted up to the Troop Sergeant who saluted him and reported; "Troop all present and ready for your inspection sir." The young officer returned his salute then accompanied by the Troop Sergeant walked his horse up and down the three ranks after which they both took station at front and center with the officer in front of the Troop Sergeant and the Riding Master. After the officer had taken his station the Regimental Sergeant Major rode on to the parade ground and called the regiment to attention. As the band struck up three mounted officers appeared from behind the reviewing stand: the Colonel in Chief of the Regiment HRH

Prince George Duke of Cambridge, the Commanding Officer Lt.Col.H.M. Butler and the Second in Command Major R.P. Hawkins. They approached the Regimental Sergeant Major at the walk. After they came to a halt in front of him, the RSM saluted and addressed the Colonel in Chief; "Colonel Your Royal Highness Sir, the regiment is present and ready for your inspection, Sir."

It should be noted that Colonel in Chief of the Regiment is an honorary title usually conferred on former officers of the regiment who have risen to general rank or members of the Royal Family. The commanding officer of a regiment was usually a lieutenant colonel who was customarily referred to by members of the regiment as The Colonel.

After returning his salute, Prince George with the two other officers proceeded across the parade ground to the first squadron. As they came up to the Squadron Commander he saluted them and then fell in with them as they passed along the front rank of the squadron at the walk when the inspecting entourage came to the end of the line the Squadron Commander saluted and his salute was returned before they proceeded to the next squadron. After having his salute returned; the Squadron Commander resumed his station in front of his command. The same procedure was repeated with the other squadrons until they finally came to the trainee troop. The Troop Officer saluted and joined them for the inspection after which Prince George congratulated him on their turnout then rode off after salutes were exchanged. Across the parade ground was a reviewing stand all decked out in the regimental colors of blue and white with the dark blue regimental flag bearing a silver skull and cross bones; with the words "or glory," the whole spelling out the regimental motto "Death or Glory." To the left of the stand was the regiment's band, to the right were seated men in civilian apparel and finely dressed ladies. Seated on the stand itself were officers of various ranks from a variety of regiments creating a riot of color with their different dress uniforms. Prince George, Lieutenant Colonel

Butler and Major Hawkins rode to the front of the reviewing stand and faced the regiment. Mounted; in front of the reviewing stand sat rigidly at attention facing them with his back to the regiment, was Regimental Sergeant Major Royce. After saluting he addressed the Colonel in Chief in a parade ground voice that echoed off the surrounding buildings; "Your Royal Highness, Sir, the 17th Lancers request your permission to pass in review." After returning his salute the Duke replied: "you have my permission Mr. Royce, carry on." The Regimental Sergeant Major saluted the Colonel in Chief again then curveted his horse into an about turn to face the parade, drew his saber; brought it up to the carry and gave the order: "The Regiment will turn right into columns of three and pass in review, advance at the trot; forward." With this he sidestepped his horse then backed up to take his station to the right of the reviewing stand. As the band struck; up the regiment preceded by the color guard bearing the regimental guidon, moved off following a rectangular pattern around the perimeter of the parade ground. As each troop approached the reviewing stand the Troop Sergeant ordered head and eyes right as the officers saluted with their sabers; to which the Duke responded with a hand salute. The civilians applauded; the men clapping their hands, the ladies slapping their folded fans. There is nothing more splendid than a cavalry regiment passing in review, and there was no cavalry regiment more splendid than "Bingham's Dandies."

In the early and middle nineteenth century not only were officer's commissions purchased but regiments were bought and sold. Rich aristocrats would buy a regiment and design their own uniforms, subject to Horse Guards approval (whose office in London loosely controlled the cavalry corps) and spend lavishly on their regiments horses and equipment. The name "Bingham's Dandies" came from when the Earl of Lucan the then Lord Bingham owned the regiment.

The early autumn sun shone on the lance points and sabers; and their accouterments rang seemingly in time with the band.

Jack felt so proud he thought his chest was about to burst. When the regiment halted after coming back to the starting point the Regimental Sergeant Major gave the order; "Regiment will turn left into review order, regiment left turn." The officers and sergeants took their stations in front as the regiment turned as one into three ranks deep. Then the order was given; "Dressing from the center the regiment will advance in review order; at the walk, forward." The band struck up and they advanced their horses to within ten paces of the reviewing stand. They halted still in perfect formation as the band ceased playing, the officers saluted with their sabers and the Colonel in Chief returned their salutes. He then addressed the Regimental Sergeant Major: "Mr. Royce you may dismiss the regiment." The Regimental Sergeant Major then gave the order; "The regiment will turn left into columns of three and march off." When they were in column he then ordered: "advance at the trot, forward." The band played them off; and as Jack's troop came off the parade ground the riding master and troop sergeant reined their horses to the side and the order was given to halt. The Troop Sergeant then ordered left turn into line and the Riding Master addressed them. "Lads yew did good today, now I don't feel like I'bin wasting me time all these weeks, now make sure you remembers wot yew larned; it might save yer life one day. Sergeant Hansen they're all yourn." With that he trotted off towards the stables. In all their weeks of training that was the first time they had received any words of praise.

Sergeant Hansen then ordered them into column and led them back to the stables. At the stables he ordered them to dismount, stack their lances and remove their sabers and headdress. They led their horses into the riding school and walked cool down for ten minutes. After tethering the horses in their stalls they were ordered outside; retrieved their sabers and lances and donned their lance caps. The Troop Sergeant marched them to the barracks where he ordered them to fall out, change into stable dress and reform. He then marched them back to the stables where they fed, watered and groomed the horses. When Sergeant Hansen was satisfied that their mounts were properly cared for, he marched them to the regimental orderly room for their first pay parade. When they were halted he ordered them at ease and informed them that this was the only time they would be paid at regimental headquarters. Monday morning they were to be allocated to their permanent squadrons where all their future pay parades would be held. He then instructed them that when the corporal at the door called their names they were to come to attention and answer here sir. Then march into the office, come to the halt in front of the pay officers desk and salute. When the officer paid them they would take the money in their left hand, take one pace to the rear salute the officer; about turn and march back to their place in the ranks. At the conclusion of pay parade they were marched back to barracks where they were informed that after dinner they would have the rest of the day off. They were to be allowed out of barracks for the first time and the required dress would be patrols. The patrol uniform consisted of a blue tunic with a single row of buttons down the front, white leather belt with brass buckle bearing the regimental insignia, straight trousers with the double white stripe and a pillbox hat with chin-strap. The Troop Sergeant ordered; "Make sure them boots are shined and fall in out 'ere for inspection when yur dressed."

After dinner they got dressed in their patrols then fell in out-side, where Sergeant Hansen inspected them. When he was sat-isfied he told them to fall out and proceed to the guard room in an orderly manner; where they were to report to the Provost Sergeant. Provost Sergeant Deeks was a large imposing figure who ordered them to line up in single file and inspected them minutely. They were then ordered into the Guardroom one by one when they were inside he ordered them to state their name which he wrote down, then told them to fall in outside and wait. When he had taken all the names and they were lined up outside once again he addressed them: "Now you young buggers; you be goin' inter town with money in yer pockets and gawd only knows wot's in yer minds. Let me tell yer this; if yew comes back drunk or if the town patrol brings you in you'll be locked up till Monday when you'll be up on orders. Don't be fuckin' no wimin you picks up in taverns unless you wants to get the French pox, and report back 'ere afore 'alf past ten, and if yer thinkin' about getting drunk Think about church parade tommorer mornin'" The Provost Corporal standing at the side of Sergeant Deeks remarked; "'ow many times 'ave yew said that and 'ow many times 'ave I 'ad ta the bring the buggers in?"

Jack and the lads headed for town at a brisk walk and one of the boys said that he'd heard that the Crown was a good place for getting girls. Jack had never had anything to do with women; but he knew that some of the boys who came to the regiment from the courts and jails were experienced. When they got to the door of the inn he turned to one of the boys who had joined the regiment by way of Newgate Prison and asked; "wot be the French pox?" He was told; "It's wot yew gets when yew fucks a dirty 'ore." Jack then asked; "Ow d'ye know if she's dirty or not?" The lad told him' "I can tell by just lookin' at 'em." Inside The Crown on one side of a large room was a long table with bench seats on either side. On the other side of the room were a number of small tables with chairs at which people were drinking and eating. At the end of the room was a bar where a barkeep was busy filling tankards and mugs and placing them on trays. Two barmaids with dresses that exposed most of their breasts would move around with the trays delivering the customers orders. Most of the men when their drinks were delivered would make lewd suggestions to the barmaids and slap them on the rear. The girls would giggle and make half hearted protests while somehow managing to evade the men's attempts to grab them. There were a number of women sat at the bench seats and tables; some with male companions and some with other women. It was not long before the unescorted women were fawning over the young soldiers, one came over to Jack saying; "Come on dearie sit down 'ere with me and Molly and 'ave a drink." She guided him to a small table where another girl was sitting and as they sat down a barmaid placed a tankard of porter in front of Jack and a mug of gin in front of the girl. The girl took the mug, put it to her mouth, slurped noisily then put it down and wiped her lips with the back of her hand. She then turned to Jack and said; "Me and yew can 'ave some fun tonight but if you wants Molly as well yer gonna 'ave to buy 'er drinks too." Even though Jack had had no physical experience with women he knew what she was talking about. He stood up and said; "I gotta go talk wiv me mates." He walked over to the long table where four of the lads were sitting with some more girls and spoke to the rusty haired fugitive from Newgate; "Eh Ginger wot 'appens when you gets the French pox?" As Ginger looked at him he exclaimed; "Lord luv us don't yew know? Yer dick goes rotten then it drops off." Jack ran out of the tavern throwing a sixpence for the drinks on the table where is erstwhile companion and Molly were seated, he could still hear their laughter when he was half way down the street. Jack slowed down and started to walk then turned right down a cross street. As he was passing the entrance to an alley he heard a commotion; he turned his head and looked into the alley and saw a girl struggling with a soldier who had her pinned up against a wall. The soldier had a pillbox hat similar to Jack's but was dressed in a red blouse with black trousers, Jack heard him say "c'mon luv give us zum, yew know yew'l enjoy it." The girl was struggling frantically and kept shouting "NO! NO! NO!" When Jack reached them he spun the soldier round by pulling on his left epaulette, he then grasped the right one and crashed his forehead into the bridge of the soldier's nose. The soldier brought both hands up to his nose as the blood started to gush, Jack then drove his right fist against the would be rapists jaw then kicked him behind the knees bringing him to the ground. Meanwhile the girl stood a few feet away her eyes wide with fear and astonishment. Then her attacker groggily picked himself up off the ground groaning and muttering "Wait till me and me mates catches up wiv yer, we'll beat the bloody shit outta ya." Jack laughed and said; "Not if me mates er wiv me, now fuck off!" The bloodied soldier staggered away towards the street still muttering empty threats. Jack turned to the girl who seemed to have recovered from her ordeal and said; "er yew gonna be alright Miss?" She looked him straight in the eye saying; "I thank you greatly sir, but I prefer you not use that kind of language in my presence." He had not been around many girls in his short lifetime and the few he had known were not refined like this one. He just stared at her with his mouth open and she started to laugh; "What's wrong has the cat got your tongue?" Jack started to speak but found himself momentarily tongue tied, while she continued to laugh at him. Finally he regained enough of his composure to apologize; "I be sorry Miss, I dint know yew was a lady." She drew herself up indignantly; "Oh! So what did you think I was?" Jack started to stammer and she began to laugh again; "Enough of your awkward apologies what is your name?" Jack started to say Fishy then caught himself and told her his name was Jack. "Do you have a surname?" "Yes Miss it be Spratt." She started to laugh again and quoted the old nursery rhyme; "Jack Spratt would eat no fat his wife would eat no lean." Jack ignored her teasing and told her he would walk with her to the street to make sure her attacker was gone. "Jack, would you walk me home please?" she requested. "Yes Miss if that's wot yew wants." Jack replied." She then said; my name is Margaret but everyone calls me Meg; so you can call me Meg from now on." Jack was curious as to why she was in the alley and she told him she had been to her uncle's bakery and had left by the back door. As they were walking along the High Street they passed the front of the bakery and Jack realized that this was the shop he had attempted to rob. He considered telling Meg but dismissed the idea. After they had walked the length of the High Street they crossed a green which brought them to a large red brick house surrounded by a low wall with a wooden gate. Meg opened the gate and beckoned Jack in, they then proceeded along a flagstone path to the front door. When they came to the door she told Jack to wait; then lifted the latch and entered. After a few minutes she returned and told him to come into the house. Jack remembering what he had been taught at the workhouse about entering the houses of the farmers he had worked for; removed his hat and placed it under his left arm and followed her down the hallway into a large room. Jack had never seen a room like this and stood just inside the doorway dumbstruck. "Jack you may sit here" said Meg pointing to a large overstuffed leather chair. Jack had just sunk into the chair when a tall imposing figure strode into the room; Jack's military training brought him to his feet immediately; standing to attention. The tall man addressed him; "You may sit down young fella; I understand my Meg and I owe you a great debt." "No zur," said Jack; "it wer nuffin." "Nothing you say? You saved my daughter from being ravaged by a scoundrel, and you call it nothing?" Jack started to stammer and Meg's father smiled and said "I know you meant no offence please let me shake your hand, Jack rose and shook his hand. "I see you are with the 17th Lancers, damned fine regiment." This brought an exclamation from Meg, "Papa, please mind your language!" A smile came to Jack's face which Meg's father saw. "I see she's already told you to control your tongue." As Jack replied; "Yes zur" he was already beginning to like this distinguished gentleman who talked like an officer but had a kindly air about him. While Meg's father was addressing him he glanced at her, she was illuminated by the setting sun from the window. He had already acknowledged to himself that she was pretty, but now he thought to himself "She's bloody beautiful!" Then he looked up with a start wondering if her father had read his mind. Meg's father then said; "It's about time we had some introductions; my name is Jonathan Langsbury formerly of John

Company (a nickname for the British East India Company). Unfortunately Meg's mother died so I retired and brought Meg home, India's no place for a man to try and raise a young gal on his own." Jack started to rise but Jonathan held up his hand saying; "Please don't stand." From deep in the overstuffed chair Jack stated that he was Private (the rank was changed to Trooper later in the century) Jack Spratt of the 17th Lancers. Jack thought he detected a slight smile at the corner of Jonathan's mouth but he did not laugh however, Meg did. Jonathan turned quickly to Meg and said; "Now who needs to watch their manners young lady?" Meg looked downcast saying; "I'm sorry Papa." Her father admonished her; "I think you need to direct your apology elsewhere." Meg turned to Jack and said; "I am deeply sorry," yet he could still detect an amused gleam in her eye. Jonathan told Meg to have tea brought in, she pulled a cord and Jack heard a bell ring somewhere in the house. An Indian woman wearing a sari appeared and Meg gave her instructions, as she left Jonathan noticed the look of amazement on Jack's face and said; "That's Bharti we brought her back from India with us." Jack admitted; "I aint never seen one afore, I 'erd zum of the blokes oo wuz over there wiv uver regiments talkin' about 'em, they calls 'em wogs." "That kind of ignorance is exactly what antagonizes so many of them;" Jonathan replied. Bharti returned with a tray on which were a silver teapot, milk jug, sugar bowl and three china cups and saucers. After placing the tray on the table in the center of the room, she fetched three small tables then placed one in front of each of them. Bharti then placed a cup and saucer on each of their tables, when she had left the room Meg got up and poured some tea into each of their cups. "Would you like sugar and cream in your tea Jack?" she asked. "Dunno Miss I aint never drunk tea afore." Jack replied. Meg exclaimed; "Goodness! What do you drink at the barracks?" Jack's reply was;"We gets water wiv brekfus un supper and small beer wiv dinner." Meg could hardly hide her disgust then said; "I think you'll like cream and sugar in your tea." She dropped in a lump of sugar and poured some cream into his cup then told Jack to taste his tea. After he had taken his first sip his face lit up as he exclaimed; "I aint never drunk nuffin as good as this in all me life!" Meg smiled and picked up a plate that Bharti had just brought in and held it towards him. "Here try one of these." Jack took a small triangular sandwich and swallowed it in one bite. Jonathan turned to Jack and asked him how old he was; Jack informed him that from what they had told him at the workhouse he was sixteen. "The workhouse you say, what workhouse?" Jack replied; "It's down the road zumwers, I runned away." Jonathan asked; "How did you come to be in the army?" Jack looked at Jonathan and had mixed feelings, if he told the truth he might never to be able to see Meg again, but he felt he couldn't lie to him. So with great misgivings he told him everything from the time he could remember up to the present. When he had finished his narrative he got up and said; "I s'pose ya wont want nuffin to do wiv me nah." Jonathan told him to sit back down and laughed; "So you were going to steal some of old Charley's bread, well God knows he could afford it, he's my brother in law you know." "Yes zur Miss Meg told me ee's 'er uncle." Jack answered. "How do you like the army Jack?" asked Jonathan. Jack replied; "I luvs it zur I gets fed good and I got a luverly "orse; "is name's Nipper." Jonathan smiled; "you named him after the little boy that died in the workhouse?" Jack replied;" Yes zur." Jack stood up again, I promised I'd jine the lads for a pint, I better be goin'." Jonathan and Meg walked Jack to the front door and as he was leaving Jonathan asked him when he would be free to visit them again. Jack surprised, told him if he didn't get guard or some other duty it could be next Saturday. As they walked back down the hallway after Jack had left Jonathan said to his daughter; "That's an interesting young man, I have to know more about him. And by the way, from your description of his uniform the blackguard that attacked you is in the 47th Foot, I know their colonel. I'll have a word with him." Meg protested; "Oh Papa please don't make any trouble!" Jonathan answered angrily; "Trouble you say? I hate to think of what might have happened had Jack not come along when he did, that colonel needs to get his men under control."

CHAPTER 5

THE IDYLL

AFTER LEAVING THE Langsbury residence Jack swaggered all the way back to the Crown, he didn't tell his mates about Meg, and when they asked him where he'd been he said he'd gone to have a look around town then got into a fight with a bloke from the 47th.. When he entered the Guardroom and gave his name to the Sergeant of the Guard sitting behind the desk. The Guard Sergeant made a tick mark by his name on the sheet asking. "Well Spratt did ya spend all yer pay?" Jack replied; "No Sar'nt only two bob." The sergeant smiled saying;" Well you don't look like youse bin drinkin' too much and I don't think yud get a whore for two bob." Jack smiled and said, "I jest spent the arternoon wiv zum nice people." The sergeant stated; "If I didn't know difrnt I'd swear you were in luv." Jack's smile got even wider as he wished the sergeant goodnight and made his way to his barrack block.

Sunday commenced as usual with church parade which was preceded by an incident which was to have some unfortunate consequences for Ginger who had obviously failed to heed Sergeant Deek's warning. When they fell in outside the barrack room for inspection Sergeant Hansen saw him stumble and noticed that his dress was not correct, when he got close he smelled drink on Ginger's breath. With a roar he ordered two corporals to fall out and double Ginger to the guardroom, "Tell Sergeant Deeks the charge is drunk on parade." Ginger was locked in a cell and told he would be on Commanding Officers orders Monday morning. Apparently he had smuggled a bottle of gin into barracks Saturday night and was drinking long after lights out.

Monday morning on first parade they were told they were going to witness punishment, when they arrived at the parade ground they were ordered into single file then turned inwards to face the center of the square. There they beheld Regimental Sergeant Major Royce and Provost Sgt.Deeks standing beside an X shaped frame with manacles at all four ends of the cross arms. After they were formed up they were stood at ease. The RSM then ordered the regiment to attention and saluted the commanding officer as he stepped onto the parade ground with the 2i/c and the Adjutant. Lt.Col. Butler returned his salute with the command; "Carry on Mr. Royce." The RSM then ordered; "Present the prisoner for punishment." At that point Ginger was marched onto the parade ground flanked by two corporals and brought up to face the RSM who addressed the prisoner; "Private Weston for being drunk on parade, drinking in barracks and conducting yourself in a manner unbecoming a 17th Lancer, your Commanding Officer Lieutenant Colonel Butler has ordered that you receive fifteen lashes, to be witnessed by all ranks of the regiment." The two corporals then removed Ginger's tunic and shirt and manacled him by his wrists and ankles; face forward to the frame. Even from where Jack was stood he could see the scars on Ginger's back, that he would proudly show off in the barracks; saying "Look this is wot they give me in Newgate." Ginger looked out of the corner of his eye at the cat o' nine tails Deeks was holding down to the side of his leg thinking; "no metal tips like the one in Newgate, shouldn't 'urt too much." He hadn't reckoned on the strength of Deeks arm. The RSM turned to

Deeks ordering; "Punishment will commence at the start of the count." On his count of one the first lash was delivered, Ginger thought; "Blimey this sod's really gonna 'urt me." The RSM continued the count while Ginger bit his lower lip determined not to cry out. However, when the count reached nine he let out a yelp, from that point to the finish he let out a howl with every stroke. After the fifteenth lash had been administered the RSM turned to the CO saluted, and stated; "Punishment carried out according to your orders sir." The CO returned his salute and ordered him to put the regiment at ease. After the order was given the RSM ordered the two corporals to release the prisoner and take him to the surgeon. They each draped one of his arms around their shoulders and carried him away groaning with the toes of his boots dragging the ground. The CO then proceeded to address the regiment; "Men of the Seventeenth Lancers you have just witnessed the punishment of Private Weston. Neither the Duke of Cambridge nor I will tolerate the kind of unsoldiery like behavior he indulged in, so it would be to your advantage to keep this lesson in mind." He then turned to the RSM and ordered him to dismiss the regiment. The RSM then ordered the regiment to attention saluted the CO and dismissed them. After he had marched them back to their barracks Hansen stood them at ease and proceeded to read off the squadrons to which they had been allocated. When Jack heard that he was going to 1st Troop 'A' Squadron he was delighted, that meant he'd be with Chalky, even hearing Ginger had the same allocation did nothing to deflate him. After the Troop Sergeant had read off their new assignments he gave them his final instructions; "Yew'll remove all yer kit and personal effects frum the training barracks and take it to yer new squadron. Report to the Squadron Orderly Sergeant wen yew gets there and he will tell where to find yer new troop. I won't be 'avin' nuffin to do wiv yer anymore so good luck, but if yew fucks up I'll know abaht it.

As Jack went through the week his thoughts were constantly on Meg, and he wondered if the Langsbury's would really welcome him if he visited them on Saturday. When Friday came he listened anxiously as the Troop Sergeant read the Saturday duty list and when his name was not called; he was elated knowing he would be able to go into town. Saturday, as soon as they were dismissed after dismounted regimental parade; Jack donned his patrols and was one of the first to arrive at the guardroom. He walked to town as fast as his feet would carry him, by the time he got to the Langsbury's door he was almost running. He pulled the bell chain and heard the bell ring inside the house then Bharti appeared at the door. "Beggin' yer pardon Miss: Mister Langsbury told me to cum 'ere today." In her singsong Indian accent she told him to wait while she ascertained if the Master was available. When she returned she conducted him to the room where he had met Jonathan Langsbury the previous Saturday. Langsbury who was already seated gestured to the chair Jack had sat in the previous Saturday saying; "Please sit down Jack." Jack thanked him and sank into the overstuffed chair. Jonathan asked him how his week had been, so Jack related all that had occurred since the previous Saturday. When he described Ginger's punishment Jonathan winced then said; "I've known Harry Butler since we were at school together and he's a damn fine fellow but he's always been a tough disciplinarian. D'ye think his punishment was fair Jack?" Jack's reply was heated; "Zur, I 'erd the Duke only gets paid five guineas from the guv'mint fer our 'orses an' ee buys 'em fer fifteen. We gets good vittles and he pays seamstresses to make our uniforms fit good. I think Ginger was a bloody fool! I'm sorry zur I dint mean to cuss, but he got wot wuz comin' to 'im." Jonathan observed; "I can understand your feelings Jack, and don't worry Meg's in the garden. Just be careful when she's around; but you know that already. I feel I should do something to reward you for protecting my Meg's honor last week, is there anything I can do to repay you?" Jack answered somewhat indignantly; "Zur, I dint 'elp 'er to get no reward, she was jest a young lady in trouble so I 'elped 'er." Jonathan adopted a soothing tone;"Let me put it another way, is there something you've always wanted?" Jack thought for a moment; "Well zur, I allus wished I cud read an' write." Jonathan exclaimed; "That's it; I have the perfect teacher for you!" Jack asked; "Oo mite that be zur?" Jonathan's reply startled Jack; "Why my Meg to be sure, she not only taught three of our Indian servant's children English, she also taught them to read and write in our language." Jack answered shakily; "Zur I don't wanta put you and Miss Meg to no bovver." Jonathan bristled; "Bother, bother you say! You have absolutely no idea what a valuable service you rendered Meg and me; do you? Tomorrow evening after church I'm having dinner with your Colonel, I'm going to request that you not be on Saturday duty rosters from now on so's Meg can tutor you every week." Still with a quavering voice Jack said; "Zur I don't want no speshul favors like that." Jonathan's tone showed his patience was wearing thin; "Dammit Jack! I'm going to do this for you even if I have to get Harry Butler to order you to comply," He was not aware that Meg was standing in the doorway until she cleared her throat, she addressed her father with a tone of rebuke in her voice; "I see your back to using colorful language Papa." Jack stood up when she entered the room. She bade him; "Please sit down Jack, I'm beginning to think Papa's trying to teach you bad habits." Turning to her father she enquired; "Just exactly what is it that you're going to have Colonel Butler order Jack to do?" Jonathan then told Meg his plans for Jack. Meg looked at her father with piercing green eyes tossed back her copper colored tresses and said; "And you decided on this without so much as asking me?" Looking rather crestfallen Jonathan said "I'm sorry Meg it was something that came to me on the spur of the moment." Meg laughed, and then replied; "Oh Papa I was only teasing you, I would love to be Jack's teacher." Never having experienced any kind of love, Jack thought of what this father and daughter shared and wondered whether he would ever know anything like the love they enjoyed. Bharti brought in tea and sandwiches and while they were enjoying the repast Meg started talking about her lesson plan; "The first thing I have to do is get you started on the alphabet, so I'm going to give you a book that you can take with you to see if you can identify some letters. Then when you come next week we can begin working on them." When Jack started to protest, Jonathan held up his hand; "the first thing you have to learn is when this young lady makes up her mind you'd do well to do as she says."

On his way back to barracks Jack went into the Crown and asked some lads from the regiment if they'd seen Ginger. One of the lads pointed to the back door and said; "ee went out back wiv a bint." The Crown's cobbled yard was flanked by stables where from one of the loose boxes Jack could hear mutters and giggles. When he found the source of the sounds and his eyes had become accustomed to the gloom, there was Ginger with Molly who was partly undressed up against the wall, Jack roared; "You stupid bugger ain't you learned nuffin since Monday?" Ginger turned from Molly and replied; "I ain't drunk and if yer don't mind I've got zum bizniss to take care of 'ere." Jack said; "Ginger, if yew gets the pox that'll be self inflicted injury, an' that'll get you a lot more than a floggin'." Molly shouted at him; "I ain't got no pox now get out of 'ere you jumped up prick." Jack bunched his fist and without warning hit Ginger on the point of the chin. Ginger's head snapped back and he sank to his knees; he then let out a groan and rolled on to his side. When Molly started screaming Jack glared at her shouting, "If yew doesn't stop that bloody noise you'll get the same as 'im!" His words had the desired effect, she obviously took him seriously. Jack dashed back into the Crown and asked two of the lads to come with him to help with Ginger. When they were inside the stable they looked down at Ginger and one of them muttered, "Blimey! Ee's out like a bloody light." Jack turned to them both; "elp me get im back to barracks 'ee don't need to get into any more trouble." Jack's intention had been to get Ginger back to barracks before he could get drunk and make sure he didn't smuggle drink in. He wondered how he could convince Ginger that he'd knocked him cold and dragged him away from Molly for his own good. They were almost to the main gate when Ginger came to and shook himself free from the two lads who were supporting him, telling them;" I don't need no 'elp from you buggers." He then glared at Jack. "Yew an' me aint finished yet Fishy, yew better watch out!" When he reported to the Guard Sergeant standing firmly at attention, the sergeant commented; "I see yer sober Weston, that floggin' must 'ave did yew zum good."

As they were falling in for church parade the following morning Ginger addressed Jack; "Me an' yew be'ind the stables after dinner." After the midday meal on Sunday those not on duty were able to enjoy an idle afternoon, but today would be different for 1st Troop "A" Squadron. Jack and Ginger made their ways to the stables separately and the other lads left the barrack room singly so as not to draw attention. When they arrived behind the stables Jack and Ginger stripped to the waist and faced each other inside a circle formed by their comrades. Chalky stepped between them and stated the rules; "No kickin' or eye gougin' an' wen one goes down the uvver steps back 'til ee's back on his feet. The fight ends when one of yer stays down past the count uv ten or gives up." He looked at both opponents then said; "Go to it." Just as they both moved toward each other ready to throw punches a voice bellowed; "Wot the bloody 'ell's goin' on 'ere?" It was Sergeant Woodford and his face was grim. "Give you buggers a couple 'ours off and yew gotta get inter mischief." He looked around and his glance fell on Chalky. "Wanna tell me wot's goin' on 'ere White?" Chalky came to attention answering; "Sojer's fight Sarge." Woodford then looked at the two would be pugilists. "An' wot 'ave yew two buggers got ter say fer yerselves?" They both answered together; "Nuffin Sarge." Woodford exploded; "Nuffin yew sez, nuffin? Well yew get yer arses back to the barrack room,

White I wants to see yew at my desk." After they had all got back to the barrack room Chalky went up to the door at the end of the room; and after knocking was told to enter. The room was hardly big enough to be called an office; it held a tall wooden locker and a table where the troop sergeant sat waiting, he asked; "Well White wot d'ye know about these two buggers and why wuz they gonna fight?" Chalky proceeded to tell him what he'd learned from the two lads that had helped Jack to get Ginger back to barracks. When his narrative was done the troop sergeant mused for a moment then exclaimed; "ee might 'ave saved Weston from another floggin' or worse. Go an' send those two young buggers in 'ere." After knocking they both entered and stood in front of Sergeant Woodford looking very sheepish. "D'ye know wot wud av 'appened if it 'ad bin an orficer an' not me that cawt yer? Yewd 'av both bin flogged! Now d'ye know wot yer gonna do? Yew'll both report to the cook'ouse kitchin tommorer and cook sergeant ull put yer to work, be there at four o'clock sharp. Now shake 'ands an' fergit about fightin'" Jack and Ginger looked at each other and both started to grin, Ginger said "Wot the "ell" and grabbed Jack's hand. After they had shaken hands Woodford told them that one of the relief guards would wake them at quarter to four in the morning.

When they reported to the mess hall the following morning a corporal led them to the back of the kitchen where they were confronted by a large heap of potatoes, two large cauldrons half full of water and an equally large empty bin. The corporal gave them each a knife with instructions to peel the potatoes then put them in the bowls and the peels in the bin telling them: "If yer don't finish by six yews'll be back 'ere tomorrer." They were done by half past five; the corporal inspected their work, and when he was satisfied he told them to get back to barracks.

After first parade Sergeant Woodford told Jack to report to the Regimental Sergeant Major's office right away. He smiled at the look of trepidation on Jack's face as he asked. "Wot's the

RSM want me fer Sarge?" Woodford replied; "I dunno yew'll 'ave to ask 'im." Jack doubled off to Regimental Headquarters and timidly knocked on the RSM's door. A voice from inside roared; "Come in." Jack entered and stood rigidly at attention in front of his desk saying; "Private Spratt reportin' as ordered zur." When the RSM said; "The Colonel wants to have a word with you." Jack was visibly trembling with fear. The RSM ordered him to about turn and marched him out of his office down the corridor to a door marked Lt. Col. H.M.Butler. The RSM knocked and they were ordered to enter, Jack was so scared he was afraid he was going to piss himself. The Colonel ordered him at ease saying; "Last night I had dinner with someone with whom it seems you are acquainted." Jack began to relax as the Colonel told him about Jonathan's surprising request. The Colonel went on; "So here's what I'm going to do Spratt, you're not going to be on the Saturday duty roster for the foreseeable future, and you will report to Mr. Langsbury's residence at 2 o'clock every Saturday afternoon. God help you if I should find out that you have failed to do so." He then turned to address the RSM and proceeded to tell him about Jonathans plan to have Meg tutor Jack, noting a look of disapproval he said; "Oh! He's not getting off scot free Mr. Royce; as long as he is being tutored you will see to it that Spratt pulls guard duty every Sunday. However, you may not disclose anything that has transpired here, I don't want any talk of favoritism. Spratt you're dismissed, Mr. Royce stand fast." After Jack had left he instructed the RSM to sit down and told him how Langsbury had come to make Jack's acquaintance, concluding with the statement; "I've known Jonathan Langsbury a long time and if he thinks this lad's got promise I have to believe him." Royce cleared his throat then asked for permission to speak. "After what Spratt did to their bloke are we likely to get trouble from the 47th?" The Colonel replied; "I've spoken to their Colonel and he assures me he will make sure his men understand that if they get into any brawls with ours they'll be flogged. You will make sure that our men get the same message."

Butler and Royce had a special relationship based on mutual respect. Butler's father was the youngest son of an Earl, which meant he had no title and his father had no personal fortune. Royce was the son of a village school master; which was why he was literate and explained his speech being more refined than most rankers. Butler's father had managed to scrape up enough money to purchase a cornet's commission for his son; purchasing any higher rank was out of the question for his limited means. Royce had joined the regiment as a boy trumpeter at the age of fourteen. His father was a bully and frequently gave his son severe beatings. Two days after his fourteenth birthday his father dissatisfied with the way he had performed a chore started to beat him with a large stick. Royce snatched the stick from him and proceeded to beat his father until he was unconscious. With his mother's help he then fled the village and on his way to the home of one of his mother's relatives he found himself outside the regimental barracks of the 17th Lancers and decided to become a soldier. The regiment was stationed in Ireland when Butler joined it as a young subaltern; Royce was now a Troop Sergeant. When Butler became Royce's troop officer Royce's reaction was typical of a seasoned NCO; "Another bloody jumped up snot nosed rich boy." When he found out how eager Butler was to become an effective troop officer showing willingness to learn and heed advice, his attitude towards him became one of respect. Butler in turn came to respect Royce for his patience as he explained and demonstrated the skills needed for commanding a troop of light cavalry. Lord Bingham soon noticed how well Butler handled his troop without leaving the onerous tasks to the sergeant; as did most other young troop officers. The eventual result was Butler's steady promotion, much to the disapproval of other officers who could afford to purchase the positions that he was appointed to on merit. Recognizing Royce's potential Butler recommended him for advancement whenever the appropriate occasion arose.

Jack made his way to the stables and upon arriving he was questioned by Sergeant Woodford as to the reason for the RSM wanting to see him. He answered Woodford's question with; "I'm sorry Sarge I bin ordered not to say anyfin, yew'll 'ave to ask 'im yerself." Woodford went directly to the Squadron Sergeant Major's office and told him about Jack's meeting with the RSM and his refusal to give an explanation. Sergeant Major Meade thought for a minute then called for the squadron clerk. When the clerk entered he ordered him to take his request for an interview with the RSM to regimental headquarters. Upon his return the clerk informed Meade that the RSM was free to see him, the Sergeant Major said to Woodford; "You might as well come along Frank, I'm sure he wont mind." When they arrived at RHQ they stated their business to a clerk who told them that the RSM was expecting them and to go on in. Royce told the clerk to close the door and said with a grin; "I'm not used to seeing you two buggers except when you're looking at me from over a tankard, so what can I do for you?" They explained their reason for wanting to see him and were surprised when they discovered that it was actually the Colonel who had asked to see Spratt. Royce stated; "All I can tell you is that he's going to be standing guard duty every Sunday until the colonel says otherwise." Woodford looked startled asking; "Blimey, wot ee do bugger one of the colonels dogs?" Royce and Meade both laughed and then in a more serious tone the RSM said; "I'm sorry boys; that's all I can tell you, and don't try getting anything out of Spratt unless you want to get on the wrong side of me and the Colonel!"

Harry Butler sat behind his desk in deep thought, what he and Jonathan Langsbury were about to set in motion was radical and went against the mores of both the military and civilian establishments. However, he had known Jonathan many years and he had a great deal of confidence in his judgment and moral

integrity. In Harry's estimation Jonathan was the most generous and kindly person on earth. However, most people of their
class did not approve of Langsbury's charitable attitude towards
the under privileged. People from both "John Company" and
the army had criticized Jonathan for his liberal attitude towards
the Indian natives. "He overpays his servants and he treats 'em
like white people!" He recalled what an officer just back from
India had told him about an incident when some drunken
sepoys started a mutiny. The commanding officer of their garrison had had his troops bring all the British civilians together
with the military families into the regimental compound. The
sepoys went on a rampage through the town looting and burning. Eventually when nearly all the mutineers were concentrated
in one part of the town the colonel sent out a mounted squadron
with a company of loyal native infantry who trapped most of
the mutineers while the cavalry rode down and killed those that
they were unable to arrest. The officer, whose troop was part of
the mounted squadron, overheard a sergeant who was reporting
to the Squadron Commander on the damage resulting from the
mutineer's rampage. "They burned three 'ouses to the ground in
Salisbury St., the rest of 'em wuz looted but they din't do nuffin to mista Langsb'ry's bungalow." An Indian halvidar who was
marching his infantry platoon alongside them exclaimed; Sahib
Langsbury and the Memsahib also, would have been safe to
stay." The squadron commander commented; "These bloody wogs
really love old Jonathan!" The officer said that it was on the tip
of his tongue to reply; "That's because he treats them like human
beings and doesn't call 'em wogs." Instead he said; "I decided to
be prudent and just answered with; "Yes Sir."

Jack's life settled down to the routine of a cavalry soldier in
barracks during peace time, the usual round of parades, inspections, stable chores and other mundane duties. The only difference in his case was that he was never on the duty roster on
Saturdays but stood guard duty every Sunday. Normally guard

duty came around about every fourth week; so it was inevitable that his comrades commented that he was standing guard every week and always on Sunday. When questioned about it Jack said; "I farted in church so they said I could praise the Lord doin' guard cuz I wuzn't fit ta be in God's 'ouse." When Sergeant Woodford heard how he was turning the questions aside he couldn't get to the Sergeant Majors office quickly enough. When he told Meade what Jack was saying they both went into gales of laughter, so much so that the squadron commander Major Sinclair-Johnson left his office to find out what was causing the commotion. They both came to attention trying to regain their composures when he came through the door enquiring; "What's going on Sergeant Major?" Mustering as much control as he was able Meade repeated what the troop sergeant had told him. Sinclair-Johnson was the only other member of the regiment, apart from Butler and Royce that knew the truth, he allowed himself a faint smile saying; "I suppose that explains everything. Now pull yourselves together you're setting a bad example to the men." That night after dinner in the officers mess Sinclair-Johnson asked the Colonel if he could speak to him in private. After Butler heard how Jack was dealing with being questioned they both broke into laughter, Butler exclaimed; "Damned if that lad's not a sharp one, looks like Jonathan's found himself a protégé!"

Jack would show himself at the Langsbury residence each Saturday afternoon at 2 o'clock, where Meg would tutor him until four at which time they would partake of afternoon tea. After tea they would continue his lessons until half past seven when Jack would leave before Jonathan and Meg got ready for dinner. Once, before the end of his third visit Jonathan invited Jack to stay for dinner. When he saw the look of fear on Jack's face along with his confused and stumbling declination he realized that he'd made a mistake he allayed Jack's anxiety with; "That's alright Jack I know you'd like to stop by the Crown and have a drink with the lads before you have to be back in barracks." Jack heaving an audible sigh of relief replied; "Thank ee zur I better be getting' off." After he'd left Jonathan turned to his daughter; "That was an awkward moment Meg, poor lad's afraid to eat with us." Meg replied; "I think he feels he might disgrace himself with his lack of etiquette, maybe that's something else I should teach him?" To which Jonathan replied; "Just be careful how you approach him on that, you wouldn't want to cause him further embarrassment."

Jack was a quick learner and an avidly attentive pupil. He was driven by an intense desire to be literate and he was also head over heels in love with Meg. He did everything he could to hide his feelings from both Meg and her father. For a long time Jonathan had no inkling, Meg had sensed it from their first meeting, but out of consideration for Jack's feelings gave no hint of knowing how he felt. The weeks went by with Jack making what Meg could only describe as astonishing progress.

No secrets last for very long in close knit communities such as regiment in barracks and soon the inevitable happened. One Monday evening Jack was sat on his bed polishing his saber scabbard when Chalky and Ginger came over and sat either side of him. Chalky opened with; "Reckon it's about time yew come clean Fishy." Jack looked at him with an assumed expression of bewilderment; "I don't know wot yer talking abaht." Then Ginger chimed in; C'mon yew goes over to this posh 'ouse ev'ry Satiday and then comes inta the Crown for a couple of pints afore gittin' back to barracks, so wot the bloody 'ell's goin' on?" Jack answered; "If yew two are reely me mates yer gonna 'ave ta trust me I can't tell nobody nuffin, if I duz I'll be done fer, and that's the Gawd's honest trewf." Chalky looked at Ginger and said; "Reckon we needs to leave 'im be, but we aint the only ones askin' questions."

The following morning while they were at the stables, Jack managed to get Sergeant Woodford to one side and asked him if he could get an interview with the RSM. The troop sergeant sensed it had some thing to do with Jack standing guard duty every Sunday but rather than ask for an explanation he told him he'd see what he could do. He marched into the squadron office and informed the clerk that he wished to see Squadron Sergeant Major Meade. After informing Meade of Woodford's request the clerk told the troop sergeant that the SSM would see him. When he entered the office Meade told him to sit down, "What can I do for you Frank?" Woodford answered; "Spratt's just asked ta see t' RSM, I think it's gotta do wiv the Sunday guard thing." Meade said; "Let's see what the RSM wants to do," Meade called for the clerk and told him to find out when the RSM could see them. When the clerk returned he informed them that the RSM would see them the following morning after first parade. Minutes after first parade was dismissed Meade and Woodford entered Royce's office as he looked up saying; "You two buggers again, now what are you up to?" Woodford informed the RSM of Jack's request and added that he thought it might have something to do with the Sunday guard duties. Meade added that the rumors that were circulating about Spratt needed to be put to rest. Royce answered; "Well boys I think I beat you to the punch, me and the Colonel discussed the problem yesterday and we think we have a solution." He then proceeded to reveal the conclusions that he and the Colonel had come to. "As you are probably aware Ned Perry's going to be time expired in two years and he's been pestering me for an assistant to train as his replacement. Well, as you know the Colonel would normally appoint a sergeant to the position however, Perry wants a private, a particular private." He paused for effect enjoying the looks on their faces. "Ned tells me the chap he wants is the best natural horseman he's trained in years. He's not only an expert rider but he's got a way with horses." Jack's horsemanship and his ability to handle difficult mounts was well known throughout the regiment, so when he saw their mouths drop open he laughed and exclaimed; "Yes, it's Spratt!" Woodford was so startled he forgot he was talking to the RSM and asked; "'ow the bloody 'ell is that gonna 'elp?" Royce ignored his outburst and told them what he and the Colonel were proposing.

Jack was to become assistant riding master and in recognition of the authority that position carried he would be promoted to the rank of corporal. The RSM was feeling somewhat guilty about the enjoyment he was getting from their reactions nevertheless he continued to lay out the rest of the plan. He then proceeded to tell them the truth about Jack's association with the Langsburys' and informed them that it need not be a secret once Spratt assumed his new duties and promotion. Royce knew that to make everything as acceptable as possible he needed to show respect for their areas of authority. He looked at them and stated; "Joe, Spratt's in your squadron and Frank, he's in your troop, I need to know that you find this acceptable." Woodford cleared his throat and asked; "Wot abaht the men givin' 'im trouble cuz of favoritism?" Royce told them; "He'll be a corporal so the privates daren't bother him, I'll let the NCOs know that if they pull anything they'll have me to contend with, and the Colonel will do the same with the officers. Meade looked at Woodford and said; "I reckon it's alright with me, what do you think Frank?" Woodford looked pensive saying; "I was guard sergeant the day the Beadle drug that young bugger in the gate an' I've been watchin' 'im ever since, ee's a good un an' I wishes 'im luck, ee's only seventeen; a bit young to be a corporal but I knows where ee come from and yew grows up quick in them places." Royce concluded the proceedings with; "The three of us have seen a lot of things and been to a lot of places over the years, but I don't think we could have ever dreamed of something like this." The clerk wondered at what they could be laughing about as they left.

The following morning Woodford informed Jack that he was to report to the SSM's office as soon as first parade was dismissed, as he was marching to squadron headquarters the troop sergeant fell in step with him Jack asked; "Yew comin' too Sarge?" Woodford grinned saying; "Spratt, I wouldn't miss this for the world." This set Jack to wondering what was going on; he was soon to find out. As they entered the office Woodford told the clerk they were reporting to the SSM, he told them to go on in. Meade ordered them at ease and proceeded to tell Jack about his new duties and his promotion. Observing Jack's reaction it was all the Sergeant Major could do to keep a straight face; "Well Spratt what've yer got to say?" Jack blurted a startled reply; "Zur I dunno wot ta say, d'ye reckon I'll be good enuf fer the job?" The SSM's reply was curt; "If we didn't think you were good enough you wouldn't be getting the bloody job." "Now you get your bleedin' arse over to the quartermasters and get chevrons for your uniforms. Then take your uniforms over to the tailor's shop and get 'em sewed on, after that report to Sergeant Woodford so's he can inspect 'em." As Jack came to attention he uttered a loud; "Yes Zur." The Sergeant Major ordered him to get on his way; "And wipe that stupid fuckin' grin off your face you're an NCO now!"

It was almost time for the for the evening meal and as Ginger came into the barrack room to get his mess utensils he passed Jack's bed space then turned around with an incredulous look on his face uttering aloud. "Wot the bloody 'ell?" The right sleeves of Jack's neatly folded uniforms each bore two chevrons. As Chalky entered Ginger gaspingly called him over; "Fishy's got stripes on 'is uniforms!" At that moment Jack came in and they saw the two chevrons on the arm of his stable dress blouse. "S'pose you blokes wants to know wot's goin'on?" "Yew bloody well got that right!" exclaimed Chalky. Jack replied; "I'll tell yew at supper." After they were seated at a table in the mess hall Jack proceeded to tell them everything from the time he met Meg to the present. They hung on to every word with expressions of astonishment on their faces. When he had finished relating his narrative there was a long silent pause, then in unison both Chalky and Ginger blurted out; "Well I'll be buggered!" Jack then made a statement that reflected the depth off the bond that existed between the three of them; "Yew'l 'ave to call me corporal on parade an' wen anybody's around but I wants us to stay mates." Ginger asked; "Er yew gonna stay in our barracks?" Jack replied apologetically;

"No Ginger, I gotta move inta RHQ barracks wiv the orficers mess orderlies an' the bloody clerks. But we'll still see each uver 'ere in the cook'ouse and we can ave a drink in the Crown." In a few years the strength of their bond was to prove itself under the direst circumstances.

CHAPTER 6

TO LONDON TOWN
AND BACK

A TROOP OF NEW recruits had just finished dismounted training and were assigned to the riding master for mounted instruction so Jack was kept busy working at the riding school and learning the skills of being an instructor. At the end of his first day when the trainees had been dismissed Perry took him aside to give him some advice. "When yew gives an order make it sound like an order, not a fuckin' request! D'ye remember 'ow I 'andled yew young buggers, did I ever sound like I was asking yew; or was it like I was tellin' yew?" Jack replied; "Yew was tellin' us zur." "Well that's the way yew gotta do it, yew gotta get that tone in yer voice that sez yew better do it and do it right else; I'll cut your balls off wiv a rusty saber! I seen the way you gentles an 'orse but that's not the way to 'andle them trainees, yew gotta kick their bleedin' arses." Jack answered "I'll try zur." To which the Riding Master responded; "No yew won't bloody well try- you'll bloody well do it!" Jack sat with Ginger and Chalky for the evening meal

and recounted Perry's instructions with a passable impersona-
tion of the Riding Master. They were all three laughing heartily when Sergeant Woodford who was orderly sergeant that day
overheard them while doing his rounds. He strode over to their
table to inform them: "Yew comes in 'ere to eat; not bugger about!
An' yew Corporal Spratt, remember you're an NCO now." When
Woodford was out of earshot Chalky commented: "I remembers
when I fust saw yew; now you're a bloody corporal, strewth, who'd
'ave known?"

The following morning Jack was instructing the trainees on
saddling techniques demonstrating on one of the wooden horses:
"Yew folds yer stirrups across the saddle so's they don't dangle,
swings it up from the left side, lets it down gently on 'is back
then brings the girth strap up through the buckle, tightens it
then knees the 'orse 'ard below his short rib. When he blows out
yew finishes tightenin' all the way. If yew doesn't do it right yer
saddle will slip round and yew'll fall off while you're ridin' 'im."
He pointed to three trainees and told them to saddle the wooden
horses as they had been instructed. When they had carried out
his orders his eye fell on one of the lads and he worked up a roar,
"I didn't see you knee 'im in the belly." The trainee replied; "But
I did Corp." Jack bristled visibly; "Yew call wot yew did kneein'
'im? Why d'ye think we pads them bloody 'orses? Its so pansies
like yew won't 'urt yer pretty girly knees, now yer goin' to do it
agin." He saw the other two grinning and roared again. "Yew
two buggers can do it agin fer laughing." Perry allowed himself a
smile making sure Jack couldn't see his approval, and thought to
himself; "The lad's gonna be alright."

Jack had to miss one of his lessons when the Langsbury's
went to London to spend Christmas with Jonathan's sister, (there
would be two more Christmas's at their present barracks). The
week before they were due to leave Meg asked her father what he
thought would be a suitable present for Jack. Her father thought
for a moment then said; "Don't get him anything expensive if

you do he'll be embarrassed." She asked: "Why Papa?" Jonathan explained; "Because he won't be able to afford an expensive present for you. I think you should just wish him a Merry Christmas, knowing his background I doubt he's ever had a Christmas present in his life." While they were gone Jack continued to study the lessons Meg had given him and also practiced correct speech habits. His noticeably more refined speech had brought comments from other rankers in the regiment such as Ginger; "Wot's next, yew gonna be a bloody officer?' He had finally given up trying to use correct speech only at the Langsbury's and put up with the good natured ribbing from his comrades. However, one incident caused some comment among the officers. A new subaltern had been sent over to the riding school by the Adjutant to have his mounted skills improved. Although the officers were usually skilled riders when they joined the regiment, there were many differences in riding to hounds and riding in the cavalry. The Adjutant had arranged a time with the Riding Master when there would be no rankers present, and the subaltern arrived at the riding school when ordered. When he entered the building leading his charger, he was obviously angry and feeling humiliated at having his horsemanship questioned and his glance fell on Jack. "Where's the Riding Master?" he grunted in a surly tone. Jack saluted and replied; "He had to go and see the Farrier Sergeant about a sick horse Sir." Ignoring Jack's salute and bristling visibly the subaltern asked in a vexed tone; "Then how am I supposed to get the stupid bloody riding lesson he's supposed to give me?" Jack's answer; "He ordered me to stand in for him." brought a screaming roar from the young officer; "It's bad enough being ordered to take lessons from a four bloody striper, but a fucking corporal? This is too much!" Harry Butler was riding by outside and hearing the furor decided to investigate, he dismounted and leading his charger entered the riding school. He addressed the young subaltern; "Mister Dalton-Jones would you like to tell me what all the noise is about?" Dalton-Jones replied; "Adjutant sent me here for riding lessons Colonel, and the Riding Master's not here." The Colonel then asked; "Did he not delegate a substitute?" The young officer's reply; "Yes he left me a bloody corporal!" brought a look of fury to the Colonels face and he turned to Jack saying; "Leave us Corporal." After Jack had left he turned to the young officer with a look of thunder saying; "You were sent here to start learning how to ride like a Seventeenth Lancer, you will find there are some distinct differences from what you and your steeple chasing friends regard as horsemanship. And by the way, that corporal is the finest horseman in the regiment and you'd do well to take his instructions seriously." Perry had instructed Jack on how to handle young officers; "Yew allus calls 'em zur or mister, and don't use cussin', other than that give 'em 'ell just like yew does the new lads." Jack took the Riding Master at his word and for two hours he worked the subaltern mercilessly finding fault with his posture, rein handling, over use of spurs and myriad other short comings. At the conclusion of the lesson Dalton-Jones dismounted led his charger out of the riding school and began to mount prior to riding back to the officers stables when the Colonel still on his charger reappeared. He rode up alongside the subaltern saying: "We might as well ride together." Dalton-Jones assented in a tone that came dangerously close to insolence. That evening in the Officers Mess, a group of subalterns were talking over drinks when the Adjutant passing by overheard Dalton-Jones saying; "It's not bad enough that he criticizes my riding ability, but he sends me to be taught by a bloody corporal. Not only that, this instructor, this damned ranker has airs and graces. He tries to act like someone above his station and talks like he's a fucking gentleman!" The Adjutant informed the Colonel of what he'd heard who decided to deal with the matter in the morning. The following morning after officer's call the Colonel dismissed the other officers but told the Adjutant and Dalton-Jones to remain. When his office door was closed the Colonel addressed the subaltern; "Peter, I think we need to get a few matters straightened out, what d'ye think?" Peter tried to look puzzled saying; "I don't think I know what you mean Sir." The Colonel thundered; "You know bloody well what I mean! Your belittling of one of my best NCO's last night was way out of line. The man you were putting down has worked damned hard to become an outstanding soldier and is also trying to improve his education and social graces. I doubt you have ever been as diligent at anything that worthwhile in your life." Dalton-Jones stung asked; "Who told you about this Sir?" Before the Colonel could reply the Adjutant stepped forward saying; "I did." Knowing it was a mistake almost as he said it Peter blurted out; "Just like some snotty nosed second former sneaking to the housemaster!" The Colonels eyes went hard and his voice was cold as he said; "You will apologize to Captain Barry immediately." Dalton-Jones then sealed his fate exclaiming; "I refuse to apologize and I wish I had never joined this regiment, you treat your officers like rankers not gentlemen!" The Colonel exhibited a grim smile then said coldly; "I will look for your resignation on my desk in the morning there is no reason why you can't be gone by first parade tomorrow, dismissed." Word spread quickly through the regiment that Dalton-Jones had resigned although the circumstances were not known outside the officer's mess until some weeks after the event. When Jack reported to the Riding School the following morning the Riding Master was waiting for him. Perry smilingly commented: "Yew must 'ave give that officer one 'ell uv a lesson Corporal." Jack smiled back saying: "If he buys himself another commission it better be in the infantry 'cos he'll never be a cavalryman!"

Jack continued to study during his free time and Meg always made sure he had a full lesson load before her and her father left for London. One evening just before the Langsbury's were due back from their third Christmas in London since Meg had been tutoring Jack; he was sat on his cot studying, when one of the RHQ clerks that shared his barrack room came in with some news; "The Regiment's going to Woolwich." Jack shot him a doubtful look; "Where d'ye get that bloody rumor?" "It's no rumor" the clerk replied; "I just seen the orders that come from 'orse Guards." Jack was stunned, his thoughts went to Meg and how much longer he would be able to see her, he questioned the clerk: "When we going?" The clerk answered; "Two months, third week of March." By morning the news had spread throughout the Regiment and the Cookhouse was all abuzz during break-fast. Jack was sat with Ginger and Chalky along with some other 1st Troop lads. When an Irish trooper by the name of O'Neill exclaimed; "Damn! I'd been hoping I might be going back to the Auld Sod so I was." Ginger looked up from his meal with a sly grin on his face; "So yew wanted to go back to see yer Pa?" The Irish lad jumped up loudly threatening; "I'll not be having you insulting me feyther you bloody spalpeen, let's go outside!" Ginger was now on his feet, then Jack stood up and moved between them saying; "They'll be none of that unless you want to be on orders tomorrow, now sit down both of you. Ginger mind that tongue of yours and Paddy get a bridle on that Irish temper." Ginger never one to hold a grudge looked at Paddy saying; "Sorry mate didn't mean to get yer Irish up." Paddy looked back at him the glare on his face softening to a wry smile; "That's alright, it's English you are and you can't be helping yourself." Ginger looked at Jack and said; "Wot the bloody 'ell does ee mean by that?" Jack's reply was; "I don't know I don't speak Irish." At that all four of them dissolved into laughter. From that moment their bond was extended to include a wild Irishman.

For Jack who was looking forward to seeing Meg again the days dragged by. By virtue of his position as Assistant Riding Master he was no longer required to stand guard as he was often required to give individual riding lessons outside of his normal working hours. One afternoon after they had finished instructing their current troop of trainees for the day Perry told him to return to the Riding School before supper. When he asked why the

Riding Master told him the Colonel was thinking about buying a horse for his wife and had asked him and the Farrier Sergeant to examine the animal, and he thought Jack might learn something worthwhile. When Jack arrived at the Riding School the first thing that caught his eye was a large man in tweeds holding the halter of a beautiful grey mare. Perry and Woden were coming out of the Riding School escorting a tall strikingly attractive lady, as Jack got up to them Perry turned to the lady saying" "This is my assistant Corporal Spratt, Ma'am." Then to Jack; "Corporal Spratt this is the Colonels lady." Jack came to attention, snapped a smart salute and said; "I'm honored to be your servant Ma'am." A slight smile crossed her aristocratic features as she commented; "Meg Langsbury has obviously been a good influence on you young man." Her smile became more obvious as she observed the blush that came to Jack's face. Perry then turned to the man in tweeds; "I got the Corporal 'ere so's ee could learn summat abaht wot yew needs know when yer buyin' a 'orse, I 'opes yew don't mind Squire." He and Woden then started to examine the mare. Woden turned to the Squire and asked; "You say she's four years old?" The Squire answered; "Yes we bred her for the first time last year, she threw a beautiful foal, a colt." Woden opened her mouth looking at her teeth intently. Meanwhile Perry ran his hand over her withers and checked her front hooves, fetlocks and pasterns. Both Perry and Woden explained to Jack what they were doing and why When they had both checked her hindquarters, legs and hooves the Farrier Sergeant took hold of her tail then looked at the Colonels wife saying; "Yew mayn't wanna watch this Ma'am." She snapped back furiously; "Dammit Sergeant Woden my father breeds horses; I grew up around 'em. And for your information I've already examined her myself. The only reason I agreed to let you look at her was to mollify the Colonel." Woden lifted the mare's tail and they concluded their inspection. Then Perry addressed Mrs. Butler: "I think yew 'ave a good 'orse 'ere Ma'am." The Colonels lady replied; "I know bloody well I have

Mr. Perry and thank you all for your time." With that she walked with the Squire to a waiting landau, the Squire then tied the mare's halter to the back of the vehicle after which he helped Mrs. Butler inside, he then he swung himself onto the driver's seat and took the reins. As the landau rolled away with the pretty grey mare trotting along behind, both Perry and Woden turned to look at a dumbstruck Jack and began to laugh uproariously. Woden stopped laughing long enough for a rhetorical question; "Aint yew ever 'eard a lady cuss before Corporal?" "Not a real lady, not like them bints in the Crown," Jack answered. Perry interjected; "She's a real lady alright, when me missus wuz took sick she looked in on 'er ev'ry day and brought soup and medsin." Then Woden rejoined; "And she's as tough as any trooper and she rides like one too." "Ow the 'ell did she know about me an' Meg?" said Jack lapsing back to his old manner of speech, which he was still inclined to do when angry or excited. Perry gave a short laugh; "Di'nt yew know the Butlers an' Langsburys 'ave bin tight as ticks' fer years?"

Finally Saturday arrived and found Jack pulling the Langsbury's bell chain. After he had been shown into the study Meg breezed in smiling her welcome with shining eyes; "Did you have a good Christmas Jack? Oh and please sit down." As he sank into the big chair his eyes glowing in admiration she seemed to have grown more beautiful than before. He told her as he had told her the two previous Christmas's about the officers serving dinner to the men (a regimental tradition) and how they had goose that day instead of the customary pork or mutton. Meg then turned to her father's desk, from which she took a book then gave it to Jack: "I picked this up in London; I think you're ready to read this now. Oh and by the way congratulations on your promotion." Jack stammered an awkward thank you then looked down at the front cover; the title was Oliver Twist by Charles Dickens. He then asked Meg about her Christmas. She described their stay at her aunt's but instinctively refrained from telling him about the parties and the ball which she had attended. Jonathan entered the room and Jack rose to his feet Jonathan gestured for him to sit back down; "Congratulations Jack, those stripes look good on you." Jack's answer; "Thank you sir but I don't know if I really deserve them." Brought a dark look to Jonathan's countenance; "Dammit!" Meg cleared her throat loudly. "What I mean is you've got to stop being so self deprecating." Jack looked to Meg, she explained; "What Papa means you have to stop trying to make your achievements look insignificant. We both know you're the best horseman in the regiment, we know how you try to keep your friends out of trouble. We also know what you told people who asked you why you were on guard every Sunday." The last said with a mischievous gleam in her eyes caused Jack to blush furiously. Jonathan chuckled; "She spends a lot of time with Cynthia Butler and Cynthia knows everything that goes on in the regiment, sometimes before old Harry does." Jack wondered to himself if Meg corrected the Colonel's wife for bad language. Jack wanted to change the subject so he quickly told them the news of the regiment's upcoming move to Woolwich. It was obvious by the looks on their faces that Meg had not seen Cynthia Butler since they had got back from London. Meg's face lost some color while Jack gazed at her like a sick puppy. That's when it hit Jonathan and he thought; "Oh my God they're in love!" Jonathan made an excuse to leave the room saying he had to see Bharti about some matter. In a hushed tone Meg asked; "Is there something you should be telling me, Jack?" He answered; "There is but I'm afraid to." She said; "I think I know what it is and there's no reason to be afraid." Then Jack stumblingly bared his soul; "Miss Meg, I've been in love with you since I first set eyes on you." She replied; "I've known from the start, and stop calling me Miss Meg it's Meg!" Jack was startled; "You've known all along, why you didn't say so?" Meg smiled archly; "Why didn't you?" He looked at her adoringly; "I was afraid you wouldn't see me again." She spoke chidingly; "Jack I would never send you away you see, I'm also in love with you." Jack was at a loss as he mumbled; "It can't be true." She looked at him with a soft light in her eyes; "It is true, now come over here and kiss me." Jack walked across the room bent down and kissed her shyly, just then Jonathan came back into the room. Jack startled and red faced pulled away from Meg blurting out; "We never did anything like this before." Jonathan started to laugh saying; "What are we going to do about this situation?" Jack had regained some of his composure and straightening up he said; "If I was making enough money to keep Meg properly I'd ask for her hand in marriage, but it wouldn't be possible on a corporals pay." Jack was startled by Jonathans reply; "Suppose I was to tell you not to worry about the money?" Jack then said; "What would people say, Meg a lady, marrying a ranker?" Jonathan looking somewhat impatient said: "Meg's mother was a baker's daughter and she knew how to put snobs in their place and I know Meg will do the same, she's a lot like her mother. I only have one reservation, you are both too young. I think Jack's going to Woolwich might be a good thing, you both need to be apart for a while." Meg remonstrated with her father; "But Papa I'm seventeen, lots of girls get married when they're only sixteen," Her father replied: "But Jack's only nineteen and most men don't get married until they are well in their twenties or later. If you still feel the same way about each other after you have both been apart for a year or so, I will happily give my consent and my blessing." Meg in a wheedling tone pleaded with her father: "Could I at least see Jack on Saturdays and Sundays until the Regiment leaves, now he doesn't have to stand guard any more?" Jonathan looked at her lovingly: "Of course you may, if Jack can get permission to bring Nipper you could go riding Saturday and Sunday afternoons."

The Monday morning after Jack's latest visit to the Langsbury's the Colonel instructed the RSM to tell the Riding Master to report to his office at two o'clock that afternoon. When Ned Perry arrived at RHQ he met Royce at the door he asked: "Wot's the

Colonel want wiv me?" The RSM replied: "Just knock on his door I'm sure you'll find out." He did not tell Perry that the Colonel had already discussed the matter with him. Ned knocked on the office door and Butler bade him enter. Upon entering he came to attention and saluted smartly. The Colonel addressed him while acknowledging his salute with a nod; "Close the door and sit down Riding Master." When he was seated the Colonel came right to the point: "I've made arrangements for you to stay here when we leave for Woolwich, you're time expired in six months and you can work at Garrison HQ. That way you can stay with your wife in that pretty little cottage you have on the outskirts of town. Ned protested: "Zur I'd reely like to stay wiv the regiment 'til me times up." The Colonel smiled: "Are you trying to tell me you love the regiment more than your wife? Nancy isn't it?" Perry started to splutter; "No sir, I means yes, I means, oh! I don't know wot I means! Well, I means I bin in the regiment longer than I bin wiv Nancy." The Colonel smiled again addressing the Riding Master informally: "Ned you and I and a few others that are left have been with the regiment a long time and we've all grown to love the old gal. If I recall correctly you were a corporal when I joined the regiment in Ireland, and you were a lot like that young assistant you have now. By the way, how's he coming along?" Ned replied; "Ees doin' reely good zur, but can yew let me serve me time out in the regiment?" The Colonel said; "I think I understand, But don't you let that wife of yours think it was my idea to drag you off to Woolwich." Perry replied; "She'll understand and thank you zur and please thank your lady agin fer bein' so kind wen 'er was sick." The Colonel laughed; "Mrs. Butler loves the regiment as much as we do Ned, and she's like a mother hen when it come to the soldier's families. Well that's settled, you'll be coming with us for your last few months." Ned stood to attention, saluted then thanked the Colonel again. After he had left the Colonel mused; "Ned Perry's a first rate soldier and an outstanding riding master, I wonder if young Spratt can fill his boots?"

The following morning the Colonel rode over to the riding school to tell the Riding Master he wished to borrow Jack for dispatch rider duty for two days. He instructed Perry to have Jack report to his office the following morning at nine o'clock dressed in patrols with riding boots and cartouche belt. Adding that he should carry his saber and have two loaded pistols in the saddle holsters, as an after thought he told Ned; "Oh and make sure he has his jacket." Referring to the three quarter length tarpaulin coat; worn by cavalry soldiers in inclement weather. Ned asked awkwardly: "Be it alright to ask wot 'eel be doing?" The Colonel answered: "He'll be carrying a letter to London for the Duke of Cambridge. Ned somewhat startled exclaimed; "London, 'ope ee don't need them pistols!" The Colonel agreed, but added: "I just think it's a wise precaution." The following morning Jack reported as ordered, leaving Nipper tied to the hitching rail outside RHQ. Handing Jack an envelope sealed with the regimental insignia the Colonel instructed him to give the letter to no one but the Duke himself; "I don't trust that bloody secretary of his." adding; "Stop by the mess hall before you leave, Sergeant Jackson has some food for you to take along, you'll need something to eat on a five hour ride. Oh I forgot your horse!" Jack replied; "I've got oats in the saddle bags for Nipper." The Colonel laughed; "I should have known you'd make sure you took care of that horse of yours." Butler then admonished him with; "Corporal, do not stop except refresh yourself and to feed and water your horse, and keep your wits about you at all times, there's still reports of high-waymen and footpads being active on that road and they might think you're carrying something more than a letter." Jack saluted and said; "With your permission I'll be on my way now sir." The Colonel nodded in acknowledgement to Jack's salute: "Have a good journey Corporal Spratt, tender my respects to the Duke and convey my request for overnight accommodation for both you and your mount."

As Jack rode Nipper along the High St. on his way through town at a walk, he heard hoof beats coming up behind him, it was Meg wearing a dark green riding habit; on her chestnut mare Sally. When she came up alongside him she also slowed to a walk asking; "And where do you think you're going Corporal Spratt?" Surprised and pleased at seeing her Jack's response was; "I'm going to London." Meg's eyebrows arched upwards in surprise: "Not Woolwich already?" Jack laughed; "No you silly goose, I'm taking a letter from Colonel Butler to the Duke of Cambridge." Just then; seeming to appear out of nowhere Cynthia Butler seated on her grey mare rode up to the other side of Jack, and after he had saluted her she commented: "Colonel told me he was sending you, damned good choice if you ask me." Jack looked at Meg whose eyebrows were arched this time in disapproval however; she did not reprimand the Colonels wife. When she saw the smile on Jack's face daggers shot from her green eyes as he tried to make it seem he was smiling in response to Cynthia's compliment saying; "Thank you Ma'am I feel privileged to have the Colonels trust." Mrs. Butler wheeled her horse, at the same time saying to Meg; "I've got things to do, be at my house for tea four o'clock sharp. As she started to ride in the other direction a cat ran out from a shop door causing the mare to shy, she let out a startled; "Bugger!" Then in loud tones to her horse; "The bloody cat's smaller than you, what d'ye jump at it for?" As Jack lay over Nipper's neck shaking and trying not to laugh too loudly. Meg slashed him across the shoulders with her riding crop; "What are you laughing at Jack Spratt?" With tears of merriment rolling down his cheeks he chokingly asked; "When were you going to tell her about her bad language Meg?" Meg tossed her copper tresses which cascaded out from under her pork pie riding hat; "How did I ever fall in love with you Jack Spratt?" Jack looking more serious replied: "I don't know Meg, but I thanks me lucky stars for it every day." Meg then asked; "When will you be back?" When Jack told her Friday she looked relieved saying; "Oh good! Then we can still go riding on the weekend." Jack looked at her adoringly; "I'm looking forward to it a lot." Meg pretended to glare saying; "Not as much as you're looking forward to telling Papa about Cynthia Butler's language." At this point they had reached the green in front of the Langsbury's residence. He was looking at her longingly when she said; "Aren't you going to kiss me goodbye?" Jack spluttered: "In the middle of the road, in broad daylight, what if someone sees us?" She moved her mare closer to Nipper then leaned towards Jack: "Kiss me now or I'll never speak to you again." After they had kissed she turned Sally towards the house and trotted away waving goodbye. Bharti looking out of a downstairs window clucked disapprovingly. Jack kicked Nipper into a trot as they left town and with his mind still very much on Meg he began to enjoy what was turning out to be mild early February day. The sun was shining and there were just a few wispy clouds in the sky, so Jack began to sing. Having no musical education his repertoire was limited to songs like "Pretty Polly Perkins of Paddington Green" and some bawdy barrack room ballads. After about three hours he rode into a village found a horse trough and dismounted while Nipper drank. He tied Nipper to a nearby hitching rail; then taking a feed bag out of one of his saddle bags he put some oats into it, then lifting the bag over Nipper's muzzle placed the strap behind his ears. While Nipper was noisily eating Jack examined the horse as the Farrier Sergeant had taught them, got water for himself and ate some bread and cold mutton from the rations the cook sergeant had given him. While he and Nipper were eating an old man walked over looked at Nippers shabraque (saddlecloth) then turned to Jack saying; "I joined 'em in Chichester in eighteen o'eight, we went to India, we wuz there fourteen year. I time expired in '37 at Northampton." "I was only a baby then!" Jack exclaimed. The old man shook his head sadly; "Doubt if any of 'em er left." Jack thought for a minute then said: "I think the RSM might have been in then." The old man brightened up: "Wot's 'is name?"

When Jack told him he asked; "Jeremy Royce wot talks like an orficer?" Upon Jack's affirmation he exclaimed; "Well I'll be buggered ee wur a private wen I left, wouldn't 'member 'im 'cept he talked posh fer a ranker. When yew gets back tell 'im Sergeant Major Capper sends 'is best." Jack introduced himself; "My name is Jack Spratt, I'm proud to know you sir." The old man looked at Jack; Yew be in the finest bloody regiment in the British army an' don't yew never fergit it." Jack stood up, shook the old man's hand saying; "I'll be sure to give your regards to the RSM, Sergeant Major." A smile came to the old soldier's face at being addressed by his former rank. Jack then began to take off the feed bag while telling Capper: "I'm going to let Nipper have one more drink then we have to be about the Colonel's business." The old soldier put his hand on Jack's arm: "'Ow is it yew talks like an orficer too?" Jack smiled: "That's a long story Sergeant Major, and you might not believe it anyway." Capper exclaimed; "An' that 'orse aint no nipper, ee be fifteen 'an 'alf 'ands!" Jack smiled again; "That's another story Sergeant Major." As the old man walked away his back ramrod straight Jack thought to himself; "I don't think I realized it till now, but I'm part of a family." Jack called out; "Is there anything you need Sergeant Major?" Capper replied; "Nothin', just tell the old gal I miss 'er." This caused Jack to ride off with a puzzled look on his face.

As he rode through the eastern outskirts of London the carriage, horse and foot traffic was beginning to get heavier. He drew up alongside a brewers dray to ask the drayman how to get to the address the Colonel had given him. The drayman gave him a quizzical look before giving him directions, after which he said; "That's where all them fancy lords 'an sich lives." Jack nodded and rode on finally reaching the Duke's home at half past two in the afternoon. When he reached the district of the Duke's London house he was awestruck by the opulence of the huge dwellings in the area, and mused on the contrast to the slums he had seen in other parts of the city. When he found the Duke's house he tied

Nipper to the hitching rail walked up marble steps and pulled the bell rope hanging down the side of the huge ornate doors. A servant in the duke's livery opened the door and asked what his business was. Jack came to attention pulled himself up to his full height and in a respectful but authoritative tone declared; "Corporal Spratt of the 17th Lancers with a letter from Colonel Butler for the Duke of Cambridge sir." The servant told him to wait and after a few minutes returned accompanied by a skinny, hump backed, sallow faced man with a big hooked nose and tiny coal black eyes. He was wearing a long black frock coat and he reminded Jack of the jackdaws that perched on the barrack buildings. He regarded Jack disdainfully and croaked; "You can give me the letter, I am the Duke's secretary." He was not happy with Jack's reply; "I'm sorry sir Colonels orders; I have to give it to the Duke himself." The "Jackdaw" went back into the house and eventually returned with another liveried servant. He croaked instructions to the servant; "Take this person to the library and make sure he doesn't touch anything." When they were out of earshot the servant laughed; "Don't mind ol' Grimes, we calls 'im the Raven." Jack's response brought another laugh: "I thought he looked like a jackdaw, but he does croak like a bloody raven." The servant knocked on an intrically carved oak door and a booming voice bade them enter. On entering Jack's escort bowed and addressed the Duke; "This is the soldier with the letter from Colonel Butler Your Grace." The Duke looked up from some papers on his huge mahogany desk saying; "You may leave us now Jenkins." He then turned his attention to Jack; "And who might you be young fella?" Emulating the servant Jack bowed from the waist, straightened to attention and announced; "Corporal Spratt with a letter from Colonel Butler for Your Grace, Sir." He had only seen the Duke once before at a distance, on parade, he now observed the florid complexion; the iron grey hair and mutton chop side-whiskers. The Duke leaned across the desk with an outstretched hand saying; "Where's this letter then?" Jack was struggling to slide his cartouche belt around his shoulder to get to the pouch holding the letter. He was having a problem trying to keep his pillbox hat under his left arm, which he had removed when he entered the mansion. The Duke made a loud Harrumph; "Put the bloody hat on the desk!" Jack startled at the Duke's language fumblingly removed the letter and placed it in the Duke's outstretched hand. After reading the letter the Duke looked up at Jack; "Did Colonel Butler tell you what was in this letter?" Jack replied; "No Sir he just told me to tender his respects." The Duke then enlightened him; "The regiment is going to have a farewell parade before it leaves for Woolwich. Your Colonel wants me to take the salute, and he needs to know what would be a convenient date for me to be present. There'll be a letter for you to take back in the morning; I have to find out when I'll be available. Have to see that doddering old fool of a secretary first." After sliding the cartouche belt back into position and retrieving his hat Jack was standing at attention again. The Duke picked up a small bell on his desk rang it once when Jenkins reappeared. The Duke instructed him to take Jack to the Butler and inform him that he was to make accommodation for him for the night, and arrange for him to have supper and breakfast with the staff in the kitchen. As they turned to leave the Duke enquired; "Where's your horse lad?" Jack replied; "He's tied up out front Your Grace." The Duke turned to Jenkins; "Have a groom take his horse around to the stables, tell him to feed and water him then bed him down for the night." Jack interjected quickly; "I'd rather take care of Nipper myself Your Grace." The Duke gave another Harrumph; "Nipper, what the hell did you ride here, a bloody Shetland pony?" Jack had to use all his powers of self control to stop from laughing; "I named him for someone I once knew Your Grace." The Duke bristled; "Stop calling me Your Grace I'm your Colonel in Chief, sir will suffice. Oh, and by the way I approve of the concern you show for your mount, Perry and Woden taught you well. One more thing how old are you?" When Jack told him nineteen the

Dukes eyebrows shot up: "A corporal at nineteen, well Harry Butler has to approve all promotions so I'm sure you earned the rank." After he and Jenkins had left the library Jack asked where the stables were the servant said; "I'll show you then we have to see the butler." When they arrived at the stables a groom was in the process of removing Nipper's saddle. Jack addressed the groom: "If you don't mind walking him for me I'll be back to take care of everything else." The groom replied with; "Alright Guvn'r, yew gonna be long?" Jenkins answered for him; "Be about ten minutes, we gotta see the butler." After the butler had shown Jack where he would be sleeping he told him to report back to him after he had finished at the stables and he would let him know when and where he would be eating supper. When Jack returned to the stables he found Nipper in a lose box wearing just his shabraque, Jack removed the saddle cloth and folding it placed it over a convenient rail. The groom appeared while Jack was pouring some oats into the feed trough, after checking that there was water in the other trough he started to curry comb Nipper. The groom showing obvious approval told Jack; "That be a damn fine looking gelding yew got there" Jack replied that's 'cos the Duke pays ten guineas more for our horses than the government gives him. Oh and where d'ye put the other kit that was on him?" The groom gestured to a door at the end of the two lines of loose boxes; "It's all back in that storage room and why ur them saddle bags so bloody 'eavy?" Jack laughed; "I've got oats in there for Nipper and the two loaded pistols might have something to do with it." The groom recoiled; "I'd a bin a lot more careful carryin' 'em if I'd knowed!" Jack laughed again; "It's alright mate the hammers are down and by the way what's your name?" The groom still looking somewhat apprehensive answered; "It be George." Jack held out his hand; "Mine's Jack, pleased to know you." After they'd shaken hands Jack told the groom he had to see the butler about supper. The groom told him not to bother the butler; "Yew'll be eating wiv us in the kitchin', no need to bovver "im I'll show yer were it's at." When they entered the kitchen Jack noted the long table with its scrubbed white top where some household staff was already seated. A woman in a white apron wearing a mob cap pointed to a place on the bench seat and told him to sit; "Butler said you'd be 'ere for supper, you'll have to wait till the others gets 'ere." Two more servants came into the kitchen, this seemed to be the signal for everyone to get up and move to the counter at the back of the kitchen on which was a stack of plates, a tower of nested bowls and a pile of spoons. Jack followed the lead of the servants as they each took a bowl and plate placing a spoon on the plate and moved along the counter. Further along the counter was a large trencher with loaves of bread, each one cut off a piece of bread with the knife that lay on the trencher and placed it on their plates. Then each went over to the stone fireplace where a scullery maid would ladle a savory smelling stew into their bowl. Jack sat beside Jenkins and found he was sat across from one of the housemaids; she immediately began flirting with him. She batted her eyelids, pursed her lips then asked him; "Er yew staying the night sojer boy? It's my night off and I can show yew the town." Jenkins laughed; "That aint all Maisie ull show yer." Maisie bristled; "Yew shut yer mouth Tom Jenkins yer just jealous 'cuz I won't let yew 'ave what yew wants." Jenkins laughed again; "The only thing yew got is the pox an' I don't want that!" Maisie started to open her mouth to reply when the cook walked over to the table; "That's enough from you two, shut up and eat!" Jack stopped laughing and began eating. He ate a spoonful of the savory meat and vegetable stew then took a bite of newly baked bread and washed it down with small beer; a tankard of which had been put at each place at the table. He started to make a comment on the food when Maisie hissed in a low menacing tone;" If yew goes round telling people I've got the pox; Tom Jenkins; I'm gonna cut yer balls off." Tom hissed back; "I reckon I wouldn't be the only poor bugger who lost is balls 'cuz of yew, and their peckers too I bet!" The cook was glaring at them across the kitchen. Tom decided to ignore Maisie and asked; "Wot were yer goin' to say mate?" Jack replied; "This stew is bloody delicious."Tom proceeded to enlighten him; "Wot yew be eatin' is venison stew from deer off the Duke's estate and them vegetables are from the estate farm, they brings 'em in fresh every day." Jack expressed his appreciation; "I thought the food was good back at the regiment but this is much better."Tom grunted; "'Ope they don't ever feed us no bloody army food." Jack who felt obliged to enlighten Tom explained; "We eat good cos we've got a good Colonel in Chief and a good Commanding Officer."Tom looked at Jack; "Ow does that give yer good food?" Jack went on to explain; "The government gives the regiment so much money to be spent on food, the Duke gives us extra out of his own pocket so Colonel Butler can buy us more and better food. And he sees to it that us rankers get our fair share. In some regiments the rankers eat slop and not too much of it. That's because their colonels' pockets some of the food money the government gives 'em." Tom gave Jack a questioning look; "Ow d'ye know all this?" Jack replied; "Because I sleep in HQ barracks where all the clerks are, they get the news from everywhere." Jack then asked Tom; "Is there a pub around here where we could have a drink before we turn in tonight?" Tom replied; "There's the Mermaid just down the road and round the corner, but I don't get off till eight." Jack shrugged; "I don't care to drink on my own so I might as well turn in early, got a long ride tomorrow."Tom said; "Sorry mate I'd 'ave liked to 'ave 'ad drink wiv yew."After he had finished his supper Jack went over to the stables where he found Nipper contentedly munching on some oats. He forked some fresh straw into the stall then spread it evenly over the floor. Putting his arm around the horse's neck he spoke to him gently; "We'll get an early start tomorrow and maybe we'll visit Meg on the way back to the barracks." Nipper answered with a soft whinny.

Jack walked to the back entrance of the mansion and climbed the three flights of stairs to the room the butler had shown him earlier in the day. He stripped down to his linen drawers, poured some water from a jug into the wash basin on the night stand and performed his ablutions. One of the many things Meg had taught him was to clean his teeth; now Jack worked away with the little wooden handled brush she had given him after sprinkling a generous amount of tooth powder on its bristles. He thought; "I wonder if she'd have ever let me kiss her if my teeth had still been yellow?" Having completed his ablutions he was about to put the lamp out before getting into bed when Maisie walked in through the door. She laughed at Jack who was covering himself with his hands even though he was wearing his drawers; "I jest come to tuck yew in dearie." Jack both embarrassed and angry lapsed into his former way of speaking; "Yew get yer bloody arse out of 'ere or I'll throw yew dahn the bleeding stairs." Maisie drew herself up and with a sly look in her eyes said; "If yew sends me away I'll tell 'ousekeeper yew tried to rape me." "No yew bloody well won't Maisie 'cos I'll tell'er the trufe!" Exclaimed Tom as he walked into the room. Tom looked at Jack; "I saw 'er comin' up 'ere thought 'er might be up no good." Tom turned to Maisie: "Now yew get yer 'oring arse back to yer own bed." Maisie left in a huff saying; "I aint done wiv yew Tom Jenkins." Jack addressed Tom; "Thanks mate she could have got me into a lot of trouble." Tom laughed: "She wouldn't 'ave if yew'd fucked 'er." Jack shook his head: "I've got a girl lives in the town where our barracks are." Tom regarded Jack with something like admiration; "'Er must be reel speshull." Jack's eyes shone with pride; "Meg's a lady and we're getting married one day." They said their goodnights and Tom left for his own quarters.

The following morning Jack sat with Tom at the table in the kitchen for breakfast where they enjoyed fried eggs on fried bread and bacon; which they washed down with milk, all from the Duke's estate according to Tom. Throughout the meal Maisie glared at them alternately, while Jack and Tom did their best to ignore her. When they had finished their meal Tom said; "I'll go tell the Duke you're ready to see him." As Tom left the cook came over to the table and gave Jack a linen bundle saying; "ere boy this'll keep yer belly full till yew gets back." Jack thanked her and then Tom reappeared informing Jack; "Duke ull see yew now." Jack followed Tom to the library after Tom had knocked on the door the Duke bade them enter. They both bowed then the Duke turned to Tom; "You can leave us now Jenkins." As Tom was leaving the Duke thrust an envelope at Jack, as he took it from the Duke's hand Jack noted the coat of arms stamped in the wax that sealed the flap. The Duke addressed Jack in his booming voice; "Well Corporal Spratt did my people look after you? I see by that bundle you have there that Cook took care of you." Jack gave the only reply he could: "Yes Sir." The Duke gave one of his harrumphs; "Make sure that letter gets into Colonel Butler's hands, and by the way you don't talk like a ranker; what's the story behind that?" Jack was flustered as he replied; "A young lady taught me to read and write and talk properly Sir." The Duke smiled at Jack's obvious discomfort; "Oh! And who might this young lady be?" Jack now even more embarrassed answered; "Miss Langsbury Sir." The Duke's eyebrows shot up; "Not Jonathan Langsbury's daughter, Meg isn't it?" Jack replied bashfully; "Yes Sir." The Duke laughed; "Letting that pretty young thing be around soldiers, Jonathan must be off his head!" Jack bristled defensively forgetting the Duke's position; "Your Grace, I wish you to know that I respect Miss Meg with every fiber of my being and I would defend her honor with my life." The Duke laughed again; "Struck a chord have we? Well I'll probably dine with Jonathan after the parade maybe he'll tell me the rest of the story. Now you be on your way and God speed Corporal Spratt." Tom was waiting outside the door as Jack left the library: "I'll walk to the stables wiv yer Jack." When they reached the stables George was stood outside, he greeted Jack with: "I fed and watered 'im fer yew." Jack went into Nipper's loose box and noted the water and oats in the trough: "Thanks George I'll take care of the rest." He turned to Tom: "It's been nice knowing you mate; maybe we'll meet again some day." As they shook hands Tom apologized; "Sorry abaht that bisniz wiv Maisie." Jack smiled; "Wasn't your fault, goodbye and good luck Tom." Jack went to the store room got his tack and kit then went back and proceeded to accouter, saddle and bridle Nipper. He took the pistols out of the saddle bags and checked them carefully before sliding them into the saddle holsters. George watched his preparations with interest; "Reckon you'll 'ave to use them pistols?" Jack laughed, "I hope not but if someone does give me trouble I'd prefer to use the saber on them."

Jack's return journey was without incident. He had hoped to see the Sergeant Major when he and Nipper stopped in the village for rest and refreshment, so he was disappointed when the old soldier failed to appear. He reached town about thirty minutes after noon and rode straight up to the Langsbury residence. Leaving Nipper at the hitching post by the gate he strode up to the front door and pulled the bell. Bharti opened the door eying him with disapproval, Jack asked if Meg were home and she went clucking back into the house to find her. A few minutes later Meg came flying to the door, threw her arms around him and kissed him passionately. Bharti, who was behind her, clucked loudly, Meg released Jack and turned to her saying; "I'm sure you have things to do, so please go and do them!" Jack grasped Meg's hands as he told her; "I couldn't wait to see you dearest, but I should have gone straight to the barracks. Meg kissed him again, and then asked; "But you will come tomorrow darling?" Jack replied; "Wild horses couldn't stop me." He kissed her saying; "I have to go now." As he left Meg ran back into the house shouting; "Papa, Papa Jack's back!"

With Nipper tied to the hitching rail Jack strode purposefully up the steps and entered Regimental Headquarters. A clerk came up to him and asked; "Wot yew want Corp?" Jack replied; "I've got a letter for the Colonel." The clerk offered to take it for him but Jack declined saying; "I have to give it to him myself." He walked down the corridor to the Colonel's office and knocked on the door. Colonel Butler called out; "Who's there?" Jack answered; "Corporal Spratt, Sir." The Colonel bade him enter. Jack saluted then took the letter from the pouch on his cartouche belt and handed it to Butler. After opening and reading the letter the Colonel looked up at Jack; "How went your journey Corporal?" Jack's reply; "Everything went as it should, Sir." Brought a roar from the Colonel; "No it did not Corporal, no it did not! Where were you just before you arrived back at the barracks? And don't lie to me if you value your life." Jack totally crestfallen mumbled; "I stopped by Mr.Langsbury's house, Sir." The Colonel then asked; "And what should you have done? And speak up dammit!" Jack in a louder voice answered; "Come straight here, Sir." Then in a somewhat softer but menacing tone the Colonel proceeded to castigate him; "I could have you flogged and broken back to private, then transfer you to the kitchen staff, well what d'ye say?" Jack's demeanor was now something like a frightened puppy but forcing himself to stand straight he answered: "If I've got it coming then I suppose I'll have to take my punishment, Sir." The Colonel in a calmer tone allayed his fears; "I'm going to let you off this time but God help you if ever you do something like that again." Jack started to thank him but the Colonel dismissed him brusquely; "Just get out of my sight." Jack saluted and left the office as quickly as he could. He was about to leave the building when he remembered that he had a message for the RSM. After knocking the door Jack was told to enter by Royce who with a half smile on his face said; "Well I guess you just had a right royal ballocking, so there's no point me going over the same ground, so what d'ye want?" Jack told him about his meeting with the old sergeant major and Royce now smiling faintly said; "Yes I remember Sergeant Major Capper. His time expired in Ipswich when I was still a wet behind the ears private." Jack thought it an opportune moment to ask the question that had been eating at him for two days: "He told me to tell the old gal that he missed her, what did he mean Sir?" the RSM laughed; "The Old Gal is the regiment Corporal, he misses the regiment." After leaving RHQ Jack rode to the riding school, as he was dismounting Perry came out of the door grinning: "I'm surprised to see yew still wiv them stripes on yer arm." Jack was startled: "You know about it too?" The Riding Master's grin got even wider; "The 'ol bloody regiment knows about it." Jack shook his head; "How could anyone have known? I was only at Meg's for a few minutes." Perry proceeded to enlighten him; "Missuses 'awkins wuz riding by on 'er way to the barracks and seen yew two a bussing. When 'er went in the Major's office 'er didn't close the door, the Colonel 'erd 'er tellin' 'im and so did a clerk, an' the clerk passed it on. It went round the regiment like bloody wildfire." Jack shook his head again: "Well I'll be buggered!" Perry laughed; "I thought the Colonel would've took care of that." Jack changed the subject and asked Perry if he could take Nipper to go riding with Meg. The Riding Master refused saying; "If I let's yew take yer 'orse out fer pleasure others might think they could too, and besides if I did the Colonel would cut me balls off." Jack realizing the wisdom of Perry's statement shrugged and said; "I think you're probably right Sir." He wasn't looking forward to telling Meg knowing that she would be disappointed. However, even if they couldn't go riding at least he would be seeing her again.

Saturday saw Jack striding through town on his way to the Langsbury residence. After he rang the bell Bharti opened the front door making no attempt to hide her usual disapproval. Meg dressed in her riding habit came flying up behind her, pushing past her and greeting Jack in much the same way as the previous day, while Bharti went clucking back into the house. Meg paused in her frenzied kissing of Jack long enough to look over his shoulder towards the hitching rail; "Where's Nipper?" Jack told her of Perry's decision as she pulled him into the house saying; "Let's see Papa." She ushered him into the study where Jonathan pointed to the overstuffed chair saying; "Sit down Jack, how've you been?" Jack replied; "I've been very well Sir, I hope you've been the same." Before he could reply Meg interrupted; "Oh Papa they won't let Jack bring Nipper to go riding with me." Jonathan annoyed at the interruption looked at his daughter scathingly; then his countenance softened; "He can ride Joe." Meg was both amazed and delighted; "But Papa you never let anyone ride Joe, not even the groom." Jonathan looked at Jack; "I've heard enough about this young man's way with horses from Colonel Butler; I'm sure he'll be good with Joe." Meg's profuse expressions of gratitude while she opened the French doors and dragged Jack through with her brought a doting smile to Jonathan's face he thought; "I could never have survived losing her mother had I not had Meg." Meg literally dragged Jack through the garden and across the cobbled yard and into the stable. Inside, after his eyes adjusted to the dimness Jack observed two of the loose boxes had names over their top doors. The first said Sally, Meg's mare, the other Joe. Jack went to Joe's box, looked over the bottom door and let out a gasp. Before he could catch himself he exclaimed loudly; "He's bloody beautiful!" Meg snorted; "What am I going to do with you and Papa? The Lord only knows how you express yourselves when I'm not around." Jack looked at her forcing an expression of contrition: "Meg I'm sorry but he's magnificent." He then turned his attention back to Joe and drank in the lines of the large, sleek dark chestnut stallion. Joe was at least a hand taller than Nipper and as he turned his head Jack saw the muscles in his neck ripple. He could hardly wait to mount this beautiful creature. He looked around and saw the saddle on its wooden block and the rest of the tack hanging from hooks. He took the bridle down and was approaching Joe's box when Meg cleared her throat loudly; "And am I to saddle Sally myself, are there no gentlemen here?" Jack turned to her: "I'm sorry; of course I'll take care of Sally first." He couldn't see the glint of amusement in Meg's eyes in the gloom of the stable.

When both horses were saddled they led them outside where Jack assisted Meg to mount Sally after which he swung himself up on Joe. As they proceeded at a walk towards the meadow that lay behind the stable Jack could not help commenting; "How is it that you and the officer's ladies ride sidesaddle and Mrs. Butler rides like a man?" Meg laughed: "Because Cynthia Butler likes to shock people and cause comment wherever she goes cursing and wearing Indian jodhpurs (a garment that would come into general fashion for riding much later in the century). By the way how did you manage to keep yourself from telling Papa about her language on the day you went to London?" Jack's reply; "I had forgotten, but if you'd like I'll tell him when we get back." Brought him a sharp cut across his back from Meg's riding crop. Jack cried out in make believe pain; "I'm not so sure that I should marry you, you have all the makings of a shrewish husband beater." Meg's green eyes shot the daggers which he had come to know so well as she exclaimed; "If you ever again call me a shrew I'll show you what a real beating is!" Pointing to a hay wain on the far side of the next field she challenged Jack to a race then she kicked Sally into a gallop. When she and Sally reached a five barred gate they seemed to float over landing without a stumble. Jack followed hard behind letting Joe have his head; they took the gate with ease. Joe was now fast gaining on Meg and Sally when Jack reined him in allowing Meg to arrive at the wagon first. She was dismounting when Jack pulled up alongside Sally. She glared at him accusingly; "You deliberately let me win." He was about to deny it and then realized that denial would put him on even more dangerous ground, instead he chose to compliment her; "Meg you ride beautifully, who taught you to ride?" She answered in mock anger; "All the flattery in the world will not cause me to forgive you." Jack dismounted and after he and Meg had tied their reins to the wheel of the wagon he took her in his arms and kissed her fervently. When they pulled apart she looked at him teasingly saying; "I suppose you think one kiss is all it takes to get back into my good graces?" Jack laughed: "Maybe not, but there's plenty more where that one came from." They kissed ardently for some minutes until Jack pulled away with a concerned look on his face. Meg looked at him questioningly; "Jack whatever is wrong?" He answered hesitantly; "Meg I'm getting feelings about you that seem wrong." She spoke to him soothingly; "I too get those feelings, but there'll be nothing more than kissing until we're married." Jack looked at her in wonderment; "Meg you are so wise." When they were sitting on the tailboard of the wagon with their arms about each other Meg upbraided him; "Jack you may be a year or two older than me but all your experience of life has been a workhouse and the barracks. I, on the other hand have been to school and traveled. One day you will probably be much wiser than me, and I demand that you stop behaving like you're my inferior. To answer your question about my riding ability; from the age of five until we left India when I was fourteen, I had an instructor who was a retired Rissaldar-Major of the Indian cavalry, and yes, I too can ride like Cynthia Butler. As to your concerns about our feelings (now she was laughing at him) do you think for one minute I would lose my honor to some blackguard in a pretty uniform?" Jack stammered: "I was, I was, oh! I don't know. Please don't think badly of me." It was time to smooth over his dignity; "Jack darling I could never think badly of you. Now kiss me." The afternoon was getting cold and daylight was fading when they started back to the stables. Meg demanded another race, Jack and Joe beat Meg and Sally handily, he decided not to tell her that he never let Joe have his head. He told Meg to go into the house and get warm while he took care of the horses. Half an hour later; removing his hat he entered through the French windows, Jonathan was sat behind his desk. Jack commented; "That's a magnificent stallion you have Sir." Jonathan looked up: "Yes we intend to put him to Sally eventually." Jack nodded approvingly; "I'm sure she'll have a beautiful foal." Meg entered the room; she had changed into a shimmering grey crinoline, Jacks eyes shone in unabashed admiration. Looking at her father for approval, she invited him to stay for dinner Jack accepted saying; "Thank you Sir, and you Miss Meg, I hope my mess hall table manners will not offend you." Meg exploded; "Jack Spratt, I have worked with you on your etiquette and I'm perfectly satisfied you'll not do anything to embarrass yourself. And as for Miss Meg, what did I tell you about that? If you make many more missteps I'll never marry you, even if Papa were to get on his knees and plead with me to do so!" With that she flounced out of the room. Jack stood with his mouth open. Jonathan smiling said;" That's one filly you'll never break Corporal Spratt." Jack still looking shaken replied; "I know one thing Sir, I'd never let her hear me describe her as a filly." This caused Jonathan to roar with laughter which brought Meg back into the room: "I've told Bharti there will be four for dinner and what are you two up to now?" They both looked sheepish as Meg left the room without waiting for an answer. Jonathan smiled at Jack again; "She has her mother's looks and her temperament." Jack's reply; "Mrs. Langsbury must have been a beautiful lady." brought a wistful look to Jonathans face; "She was Jack, she was, and let me tell you what you're in for. Meg is unpredictable; she'll constantly keep you off balance emotionally. But if you're like I was with her mother you'll love her in spite of it, or maybe because of it."

CHAPTER 7

FAREWELL

AFTER SPENDING TWO idyllic afternoons with Meg, Jack had to bring himself down to earth on Monday morning. On first parade when orders were read each squadron was informed of the upcoming farewell parade. The news that there would be four hours of mounted drill rehearsals every day for the next two weeks brought groans from the men and shouts of "silence on parade" from the sergeants-major.

The next two weeks consisted of rehearsal drills in the morning followed by fatigue details for the rest of the day. Every item in the barracks was either repaired or painted or both. Anything that was considered to be too badly deteriorated was replaced. Hitching posts, fire buckets feeding and water troughs, water pumps and almost every other stationery object sported a new coat of paint; all of course in the regimental colors of blue and white. Jack and Ned Perry had a five man detail repairing and painting the riding school inside and out. One afternoon when the work detail reported after the midday meal; Jack was delegating their tasks when Perry overheard one member of the work party complaining: "They'll be makin' us paint the bloody straw next!" Ned called Jack over; "Corporal, this lad just come up wiv a good idea." Jack looked at him quizzically; "What is it Sir?" The riding master had the gleam in his eye that Jack knew well; "'Ee thinks we awter paint the straw." The culprit started to protest; "I didn't mean nuffin' Zur." Perry keeping a straight face looked at Jack; "Now 'ee's bein' modest, take 'im out in the yard 'ee can start on that pile against the wall." Jack ordered the unfortunate soldier out to the yard where a large pile of soiled straw was waiting for one of the local farmers to take for use as fertilizer; "Get busy, paint one straw blue and the next one white until they're all properly regimental." The bemused lad looked at him pleadingly; "But this is the shitty straw Corp." Jack trying hard not to smile told him sternly: "We want everyone to know where it came from when they take it away, now get busy." When he got back into the riding school Jack found Perry in his office, he walked in; closed the door, and immediately burst into laughter. Ned who was also laughing gasped; "Well 'av yew put that young bugger to work?" Jack gasped back; "I think we'll both go to hell Sir." Perry gaining control said; "Maybe we can teach the Devil to ride?" Give that lad about ten minutes then we'll find 'im summat useful to do." At supper time when Jack regaled his three friends with the straw painting story their roars of laughter reached the ears of the erstwhile victim who asked the others at his table; "Wot the 'ell are they laughing at?"

At Cynthia Butler's suggestion the Colonel decided they'd make the day of the parade into a gala day. The parade was due to commence at eight o'clock Saturday morning Harry decided when the regiment was done on the parade ground the men and visitors should enjoy a festive afternoon. Discussing it with Royce he said; "I'll see if the Squire will let us use those two fallow fields behind the barracks, we'll set up some tents and see if we can get some of the town's shopkeepers to set up stalls with food and sweets." The RSM raised a question; "What about the cookhouse meals Sir?" Butler thought for a moment: "I think we can cancel dinner and supper that day, let the kitchen staff come out and have some fun." Royce posed another question; "Will the men have to pay for their food?" The Colonel smiled; "I think I can get the Duke to foot the bill." Royce grinned: "And what if he doesn't?" Butler grinned back; "Then I'll have to take it out of your pay Mr. Royce, but seriously have you any suggestions we can use?" Royce thought for a moment: "I think some competitive events would make it interesting, such as chota pegging and rings. If the Squire will give us permission we could set up a track for racing." The Colonel smiled approvingly; "Jeremy, now I know why I've kept you around for so long," The RSM laughed; "I was here before you Sir? The Colonel joined in with the laughter as the RSM got up and saluting said; I suppose I'd better get busy."

Cynthia had invited Jonathan and Meg for dinner that evening and after they had sat down to eat Butler proceeded to tell them what had been discussed that afternoon. They all nodded approvingly with Cynthia commenting; "That Royce has the finest mind in the whole bloody empire." Meg seeing the amused look on her father's face sent the daggers his way.

After much hard work by all regimental personnel the big day finally arrived. The parade went much the same as all full dress ceremonial's except there was no trainee troop so the Riding Master, Sergeant Hansen and Jack rode with RHQ. There were many more spectators due to some of the townspeople being invited. It being early March the spectators were dressed for winter weather the men in cloaks and greatcoats the ladies in furs. The visiting officers on the review stands wore cloaks over their uniforms but still looked grand nevertheless. Colonel Butler had discussed with his officers whether or not cloaks and jackets should be worn on parade, but they all decided against it. The Duke liked to see his uniforms uncovered and besides their tunics were well lined and there was also the warmth from the horses. Perry, Hansen and Jack brought up the rear of RHQ; and after they passed the reviewing stand they were still at eyes right as they came abreast of the spectators. Jack spied Meg waving frantically with one bare hand the other inside a fur muff. He had just caught a glimpse of her when the order came "eyes front," and the officers brought there sabers up from the salute to the carry. The rest of the parade went like clockwork. After each squadron rode off they proceeded to the stables where after dismounting they walked the horses for cool down. Before the men took care of the rest of their horse's needs each troop sergeant relayed the instructions which had been passed down from RHQ: "On the orders of Lieutenant Colonel Butler; those who are taking part in any of the competitive events will not feed their mounts and will allow them two measures of water only, the others will tend to their mounts as usual. Those who are taking part in competitive events will be dressed in patrols with gloves riding boots and spurs; carrying lances and sabers, others will be dressed in stable dress and work boots. Those taking part in competitive events, when dressed appropriately, will report to the stables where their Troop Sergeants will form them up as a mounted units, when they will proceed to the competitor's tent to register for their events. The others will report to their Troop Corporals who will march them to the gala area where they will be dismissed to enjoy the afternoon. The foods available at the vendors stalls will be free to rankers of the 17th Lancers by courtesy of His Grace the Duke of Cambridge. Beer will be served in the beer tent upon payment. Any man who becomes drunk will be subject to a flogging."

It was a chilly but bright early March day and a festive air prevailed among the colorful throng of fashionably dressed ladies and their escorts, the regiment's officers were still in their dress uniforms all intermingling with various colors of the visiting officer's uniforms. The townsfolk although dressed less ostentatiously were nevertheless enthusiastically enjoying the festivities; many purchasing food items from the various vendor's stalls. Jack together with Sergeant Hansen and the Riding Master on their mounts picked their ways carefully towards the registration, tent being especially careful of children who frequently ran out in front of them. Jack looked at Hansen and laughed; "It was a good idea riding with Mr. Perry; he being the senior rank has to salute all these bloody officers, his right arm is going to ache so much he should be easy to beat at the pegs and rings. Perry glared at them both; "I could beat both you buggers wiv me bloody arm tied be'ind me back." It was Hansen's turn to laugh; "I think you just missed an orficer Mr. Perry, Sir." The Riding Master regarded them both with a menacing scowl; "I'll deal wiv you two buggers all in good time." As they approached the registration tent Jack observed that four horses tied to one of the many temporary hitching rails: Joe, Sally, and Mrs. Butler's grey mare together with the Colonels charger. They dismounted at the tent, secured the reins and entered to find the owners of the four horses inside with the Duke. Perry saluted the Duke and the Colonel and his lady, after returning his salute the Colonel addressed Perry; "I think that will be your last salute today Riding Master, There's so many officers here today with all the saluting our lads wont be able to hold a lance tomorrow." He turned to the Duke who was standing with them; "I'm going to suspend saluting for the rest of the afternoon with your Grace's permission." The Duke gave one of his customary harrumphs; "Damn good idea Harry, your boys are beginning to look like a flock of one winged chickens saluting all those bloody officers." Jack could not resist a glance at Meg and Jonathan smiled as he saw her flush sending the daggers toward him. Meg and Cynthia Butler were both wearing jodhpurs, riding jackets and jockey caps but the similarity ended there. Cynthia Butler towered over Meg; she was almost as tall as her husband. Jack recalled that when he saw Sally she had the same kind of saddle as the other three horses not her usual sidesaddle. Meg's jodhpurs were of soft goatskin leather light tan in color; her riding jacket was dark green cut away to reveal a waistcoat of the same leather and color as her jodhpurs over a white silk shirt. At her neck was a dark green silk cravat. She wore a dark green jockey cap and her hair was tied back with a dark green satin ribbon.. Jack knew he was staring but he couldn't help himself he was so used to seeing her in crinolines or a riding habit. He looked into her eyes and could see that she was mocking him. He was brought back to earth by Cynthia Butler's voice; "Corporal Spratt are you deaf?" Jack looked startled: "No Ma'am." She addressed him with a tone of amusement in her voice; "I just asked you in what events you intend to compete." Looking flustered he answered; "I'm sorry, all of them Ma'am." She then turned to Perry and Hansen; "You too?" When they answered in the affirmative she commented; "I think we're in for one bloody exciting day." Jack deliberately avoided looking at Meg; he had no intention of being on receiving end of her wrath again. The Duke harrumphed once more; "If you boys are going to compete you'd better get your arses over to the table and sign in." Again Jack refrained from looking at Meg however; she did notice a slight twitching at the corner of his mouth. After they had signed in, and they started to leave the tent Meg demanded; "Corporal Spratt, I would have you show me around the grounds." Jack startled at her peremptory tone looked at Jonathan; "With your permission Sir." Jonathan nodded his head in assent. After they had left Cynthia turned to Jonathan; "That daughter of yours is a beautiful creature and I've come to love her as one of my own, but why is she such a bloody little prude?" Jonathan laughed; "When we were in India the only decent girl's school in my district was run by Wesleyans, two old spinsters and three younger women who were well on there way to being old spinsters. Elizabeth and I thought some prudery was a small price to pay to get her an education." The Duke harrumphed again; "Them bloody Methodists are a narrow minded lot. By the way I'm ready for another drink." An orderly with a decanter appeared from nowhere and proceeded to replenish their glasses.

As Jack with Meg's arm in his started towards the nearest vendors stall she said; "I saw you smirking at their coarse language, you should be ashamed Jack Spratt!" Jack made a half hearted attempt to apologize but he was too wrapped up in the elation he felt as he saw the envy in many of his comrade's eyes. As they were approaching Meg's uncle's stall, Ginger who had just got a free jam tart turned around and saw them; "Eh! Fishy wot you goin' in?" Jack answered; "All of them, I'd like you to meet Miss Margaret Langsbury; Meg this is Private Weston." Ginger try-ing to mind what little manners he had said; "Pleased to meet yew Miss." Meg with a twinkle in her eye asked: "Aren't you the one Jack's always getting out of trouble?" Ginger answered with a grin; "'Ee's a good mate Miss." When Ginger went to join his mates of first troop Meg asked Jack; "Why did he call you Fishy?" Jack was telling her about his first day with the regiment and how he came by his nickname when the RSM approached them: "Ah! This is the young lady who is able to divert Corporal Spratt away from his duties." Meg using all her considerable charm gave him a disarming smile and in a soft demure voice wheedled; "I'm so sorry Mr. Royce that was entirely my fault." Royce shook his head; "No you don't Miss Langsbury, it's very generous of you to try to protect this scoundrel, but that's water under the bridge." His eyes hardened momentarily as he looked at Jack; "The one thing that matters is that it won't happen again is that not cor-rect Corporal Spratt?" Jack's "Yes Sir." Caused Royce to smile, a smile he managed to conceal; until he had turned away from them. Meg exclaimed; "I think Colonel Butler was beastly to you about stopping to see me when you came back from London!" Jack came to Butler's defense; "He could have had me flogged and broken back to private and all he did was give me a right royal, (he caught himself before he said bollocking) telling off." A loud "Attention I have an announcement from Colonel Butler." Brought a hush to the crowd, Meg and Jack turned to see Colonel Butler and the RSM standing on a temporary rostrum erected in front of the registration tent. The Colonel nodded to Royce who proceeded to read from a sheet in his hand; "Firstly there will be no saluting until further orders." This brought wild cheers from the rankers until Royce's steely glare silenced them. Royce continued;" The first event will be chota pegs which will commence in fifteen minutes, the second will be the rings. Both these events will be run in heats; there will be an officers heat followed by the NCO's and then the privates. The winners of the three heats will compete against each other in the finals. The third and final events will be the on the course which the men of the regiment worked so hard to lay out. The first being the ladies race which will be followed by the officers, gentlemen's and men's races. I would like to call on Squire Granville who so generously gave us the use of his fields, would you please step up here Squire." As the Squire stepped up on the rostrum Royce exhorted the crowd; "Three cheers for the Squire!" The crowd duly gave three Hip Hip Hoorays. Then Royce called on the Duke: "If you would be so kind as to step up here your Grace." The Duke stepped up on the rostrum with his drink still in his hand; which brought some laughter from the crowd. Royce continued; "The free food for the men and the prizes for the events are all due to His Grace's generosity of which the regiment as so long been familiar, three cheers for His Royal Highness the Duke of Cambridge." After the cheers had subsided the Duke now somewhat in his cups addressed the throng: "I thank you all for your kind regards but what would you expect me to do for the finest bloody regiment in the world?" This brought a great cheer from the crowd especially the rankers. When Meg felt Jack drawing a breath to cheer she pinched the back of his hand viciously saying; "Don't encourage the old soak!" Before leaving the rostrum the RSM made one more announcement: "Registration will close in five minutes, all those wishing to compete and have not registered, please do so now." Realization now dawned on Jack and he turned to Meg saying; "That's why you're wearing jodhpurs, you're going to ride in the ladies race." Meg retorted; "Well! It took you long enough to come to that conclusion, and what's wrong with my jodhpurs? I wore jodhpurs in India for years." Jack once again on the defensive stammered; "No, nothing Meg, you look beautiful." Meg enjoying teasing him could not resist one more accusatory remark; "How many girls have you said that to Corporal Spratt?" Jack now realizing he was being teased said; "One day my girl I'm going to put you over my knee. In fact now might be a good time for a spanking, there won't be any flouncy crinoline to protect that pretty little backside of yours." As soon as he said it he blushed furiously and started stammering an apology then he saw Meg was laughing so hard that tears were running down her cheeks. When she was able to catch her breath she looked at him saying; "Oh! Jack, you do know how to compliment a girl." The Colonel and Mrs. Butler were standing close by with Jonathan, unseen by Jack and Meg and they had seen and heard the young couple's exchanges. Butler gave a chuckle; "Jonathan, she has him wrapped completely around her little finger." Jonathan shook his head; "I know, that's just how Elizabeth had me." Cynthia Butler interjected; "You still miss her don't you Jonathan?" He sighed; "Yes it's been seven years and I still miss her like the devil, if I didn't have Meg I don't know what I'd do."

Jack took his leave of Meg saying he wanted to give Nipper a good look over before the start of the chota peg contest. After thoroughly examining his mount he led him over to the area where the chota peg competition was to take place. The object of chota peg competitions was to lift tent pegs with a lance; the pegs were stuck in the ground in a straight line at regular intervals. This was done at the gallop but not only did the rider have to finish the course in good time but he needed to take the most pegs. Seconds were added to the rider's finishing time for every missed peg. The technique was to stick the peg with the lance then swing the peg on the lance point over the shoulder, discarding the peg and having the lance back at the ready for the next peg. The peg had to remain impaled on the lance head until it passed over the rider's shoulder or it was not considered a stick.

The officer's heat was won handily by Colonel Butler, and then it was the NCO's turn. Jack who had drawn last position, waited for the others to finish. The caller who called each rider up and then announced the results called for Jack; "Corporal Spratt to the start line please; " Then through his megaphone; " The leader still remains Riding Master Perry with a time of forty-three seconds and no pegs missed." Chalky who was nearby was waiting to enter the private's heat. Jack beckoned him over; "When I'm up go over to the Riding Master and keep him busy so that he doesn't see my run, and if you ever tell anyone I'll cut your balls off!" The caller announced; "The final entry for the NCO's heat will be Corporal Spratt." Jack urged Nipper up to the start line where a private who was the starter stood with a signaling flag held above his head told him; "When I drops this flag go." As the flag dropped Jack dug his heels into Nipper and they were off. Jack and Nipper were a team; the horse was at full gallop instantly and instinctively kept just far enough to the left of the pegs to give his rider the best possible aim. They thundered down the course Jack taking the pegs flawlessly. As he approached the last peg Jack glanced over his shoulder and saw that Chalky had the Riding Master's full attention, and at the last instant pulled his lance tip to the right missing the peg. After they had pulled up Jack walked Nipper back to the finish line as the caller announced; "Corporal Spratt had a time of forty-one seconds however, he missed one peg incurring a penalty of three seconds. Riding Master Perry is the winner of the NCO's heat by one second." The young subaltern who made the announcement had a puzzled look on his face when he saw Jack smile.

Jack was leading Nipper for his cool down before going back to the hitching rail when he passed Perry, a growl came from the Riding Master; "Come 'ere yew young bugger." Jack looked back; "Me Sir?" Perry growled again; "Yes, yew zur." Jack assumed an innocent look; "What can I do for you Riding Master?" Perry bristled;" Yew can bloody well tell me 'ow yew missed a peg."

Jack still trying to look innocent lied; "My hand shook Sir." Perry glared at him; "That damn fool White was asking me about a swollen fetlock an' I missed your run, but if I find out yew did it to let me win I'll 'ave yer arse!" Jack smiled; "I didn't know you were that way inclined Sir." Perry gave one more growl; "Be on yer way yew young bugger, afore I uses this lance on yew." Jack was unaware that Meg had been standing nearby and had heard everything. As he turned he was laughing, but when he saw her; his face went crimson. Meg scowled at them both; "Thank you for the colorful language Mr. Perry." Grasping Jack's free arm she said; "I think we need to talk." When they left the Riding Master his face was as red as Jack's. As he led Nipper with Meg holding his other arm she began to berate him; "Do I have to hear foul language whenever I'm around you?" Jack protested; "But I never used any curse words." She rounded on him; "No, but you encouraged him when he made that coarse reference to sodomy." Cynthia Butler was standing a few yards away with Jonathan and although they could not hear them it was obvious that Jack was getting a tongue lashing. Laughing, Cynthia turned to Jonathan; "I see that young man's getting a wigging from Meg." Jonathan with a wry smile on his face replied; "He might as well get used to it I'm sure this won't be the last time." Meg changed the subject abruptly her voice now had an accusatory tone; "Did you deliberately let Ned Perry win that heat? And don't lie to me Jack Spratt!" Jack hesitated then decided to come clean; "Meg darling, he's going to be time expired in a few months I'd help the old boy to win the final if I could." Taking him completely by surprise she stood on her tiptoes and kissed him saying; "You are one thoughtful old softy." Cynthia chuckled; "I see what you mean Jonathan, that poor boy is never going to know where he is with that little minx." After the final of the chota pegs was run the Riding Master had beaten Chalky who had won the privates heat and the last contestant to ride was Colonel Butler, he took all his pegs but his time was not as good.

When they came to the bakery stall Meg left Jack to talk to her uncle. He walked on to the hitching rail and while he was securing Nipper Chalky led his horse to the rail. While he was tying his horse's reins he said to Jack; "Perry won the final, he beat the Colonel's time by two seconds." Jack looking puzzled said; "But the Colonel's horse is faster than Perry's." Chalky with a knowing look on his face replied; "Yes he must 'ave throwed the race jus' like yew did Fishy." They both started laughing loudly then Jack looked around furtively making sure Meg wasn't within earshot; "D'ye reckon Perry gave the Colonel a bollocking like he gave me?" They were both laughing again when Meg arrived, she glared at them both; "And what have you two rogues found that's so amusing?" Chalky still laughing, in half choking voice blurted out; "Riding Master won the pegs final, Miss." Meg shook her head: "I can understand you feeling happy for him, but why such hilarity?" "We were sharing a soldier's joke" said Jack sheepishly. Meg glared at them both a second time: "I'm sure it wasn't a joke that could be told in mixed company." Just then Royce mounted the registration tent rostrum holding a megaphone in his hand. Lifting the megaphone to his mouth he proceeded to make an announcement; "Ladies and gentlemen it is now half past noon, there will be a one hour interval for refreshment. Officers their ladies and guests will be served refreshments in the officers tent. The men can take advantage of the selection at the vendor's stalls; and the beer tent. Men, once again I will remind you; anyone getting drunk will be subject to a flogging." Jack turned to Meg saying; "I'm going to get a meat pie then wash it down with a pint in the beer tent." Meg tried wheedling; "Jack darling can I come with you?" Jack standing firm for once said; "Absolutely not the beer tent is no place for a lady. Join your father in the officer's tent and I'll see you later." Meg turned and walked away pouting. Jack turned to Chalky: "Let's go and get something to eat and drink mate." After getting their free meat pies they walked into the beer tent and found Ginger drunk and rowdy. He was challenging anybody who felt they could take him on to fight. Ginger had not entered any of the events and it was obvious he had been drinking for some time. Sergeant Woodford walked in behind them and let out an exasperated; "Bloody 'ell!" Jack turned to Woodford; "If you stay in here Sarge you'll have to charge him and he'll be flogged, let me and White take care of this." Woodford answered; "If yew stays and don't charge 'im yew'll get charged." Jack said; "I know but you've got more to lose than me so please get out, just let me take care of it." Woodford left reluctantly as Jack turned to Chalky; "Find Paddy quick." Chalky pushed into the crowd of beer drinkers and a short while later came back with Paddy. Jack addressed the two of them: "Get Ginger knock him out if you have to, and then take him out to the back of the tent, I'll meet you there." They both looked at him with the same question on their faces. Jack now impatient: "There's no time for explanations, Go!" Ginger had now broken into song and was regaling his audience with a particularly bawdy barrack room ballad. Chalky and Paddy fought there way through the crowd, when they got to Ginger Chalky stepped behind him as Paddy swung an uppercut to his jaw. Chalky caught Ginger as he was going down, then they both got him under the arm pits and dragged him out through the tent's back flap. Jack was waiting for them with a vendor's hand cart: "Dump him on here and put this tarp over him." As they were wheeling the cart away the Provost Corporal approached with two of the day guard. He looked at the cart suspiciously and asked; "Wot yer got in there Fishy?" Jack feigned a concerned look; "I think you'd better get to the beer tent, sounded like there was a fight going on in there when we came past." The Provost Corporal and the day guard headed for the beer tent at the double. Paddy laughed and looked at Chalky: "I'll be telling you now; he's not only got the luck of the Irish, but he must have kissed the Blarney Stone an' all!" Jack grunted; "We aint there yet." Chalky asked; Where we takin' 'im Fishy?" "Back to his bed." Jack replied. The three of them managed to get to "A" Squadron's barracks without incident and as they laid him out on his bed. Paddy spoke up; "You two are both competing I'm not, so I'll stay here with this heathen spalpeen, for it's to be sure there's no knowing what he might be doing when he comes to." They both thanked Paddy and headed back for their meat pies and beer pushing the now empty vendor's cart. When they reached the beer tent Woodford was waiting for them: "Wot yew two buggers bin doin' wiv that cart and where's Weston?" Jack answered we took him back to barracks Sarge, and O'Neill's staying with him." Woodford realizing what the cart was for smiled grimly "After church parade tomorrer I'm going to take care of that young bugger, before I'm finished wiv 'im 'ee might think 'eed bin better off wiv a floggin'." Jack and Chalky dashed into the beer tent and were relieved to find their meat pies on the table where they had left them, they ordered pints and Jack paid for both. As Chalky was thanking him he looked up and saw Meg at the other end of the long table that served as a bar. He went to her with quick strides and a look of thunder on his face. He was so angry he completely forgot himself when he addressed her; "What the hell are you doing in here?" Meg put on her little girl I'm so sorry look; "Oh Jack! You were gone so long so I came looking for you." He was beginning to cool down when he realized that in his anger he had not noticed her fingers were wrapped around the handle of a half pint tankard. He exploded looking at the tankard he asked; "What the bloody hell have you got there?" Still appearing contrite, and glancing towards a private to her right she explained; "This young man was kind enough to buy me a beer." Jack was flabbergasted he started to stammer and wave his arms about and utter unintelligible noises. At this point Meg changed her tone and her mien; "Jack Spratt you had been gone long enough to eat a ton of meat pies and drink gallons of beer, so what was I expected to do?" Chalky brought Jack his meat pie and with it his tankard of beer; "Better get this dahn yer quick mate or yew'll be late fer the rings, I gotta go privates is first." Jack looked back to Meg; "We had to get Ginger out of here before he got into trouble, and I'm sorry I cursed at you but this place is not fit for a lady and I was worried." Meg drew herself up to her full height; "I think you should know Jack Spratt, since I entered this tent I had not heard one curse word; or seen any untoward behavior until you appeared. Now eat your pie you must be hungry." Jack dutifully munched on his now cold pie and washed it down with a drink from the tankard, calmer now he realized that the Provost Corporal's visit probably had something to do with restoring order in the beer tent. Meg was curious: "What kind of predicament did you get Ginger out of now?" Jack quickly finishing his pie and beer said: "May I tell you later? I've got to get over to the rings." As he left Jack could not help but notice that Meg was downing her beer while laughing with the private who had bought it for her. The rings competition required the contestants to pick brass rings off hooks with a lance at full gallop. The difficulty factor was that the rings were hung at staggered heights. This meant that while the rider had to have the lance head tilted upwards for one ring he would have to lower it for the next ring. It required great skill to take the lower ring quickly enough without losing any of the rings already on the lance. Jack won his heat, and in the final he bested Chalky by two seconds. As he was walking Nipper for cool down Meg rode up on Sally with her eyes sparkling, she gushed; "Jack darling you were magnificent, I have to report to the starter for the ladies race, wish me luck." As she rode toward the make shift race course she heard Jack call after her; "I've seen you ride Meg, you won't need luck to win."

Jack walked Nipper over to the course where the starter; a subaltern was walking his horse back and forth getting the contestants in line. When he was satisfied he turned and addressed them; 'Ladies, this race consists of three complete circuits of the course. Completion of the first lap will be indicated by a white flag, the second blue and the final lap by a red flag which will also be the finish flag. You may start at the sound of the pistol. He rode off far enough not startle their mounts, then with his pistol held high over his head called out; "Ladies ready." At the sound of the pistol they were off. Seven ladies had entered the race: Meg, Cynthia Butler, Majors Hawkins's and Sinclair-Johnson's wives and the wives of B, C and D squadron's commanders. When they came into the final turn Meg and Cynthia were neck and neck, leading the nearest of the others who were handicapped by riding sidesaddle and wearing riding habits by lengths. Jack who had tethered Nipper to watch the race was cheering Meg on frantically. When the red flag dropped as they crossed the finish line Sally and Cynthia's grey were together. As they were dismounting, a young subaltern doing duty as judge consulted with a sergeant who vigorously nodded in agreement, turned to Meg and Cynthia saying: "Congratulations Ladies that was a dead heat." Cynthia froze him with a withering glare; "Are you out of your mind young man? Miss Langsbury won by a nose." The young officer then made his big mistake; "But Ma'am the Sergeant and I both saw it as a dead heat." Cynthia exploded; "Then you and the Sergeant were both bloody well wrong!" The desperate subaltern pleadingly looked over to Butler who was stood with the Duke and Jonathan. Jonathan said; "Harry I think he's hoping you'll intervene." Harry made a snorting noise; "I may be in command of this regiment; but nobody's in command of Cynthia." The Duke harrumphed; "Henpecked are we Harry?" Butler laughed; "If I displease that lady it won't be a peck I'll get, it'll be more like a haymaker." The subaltern seeing there was no help to be had from his colonel decided that discretion was the better part of valor and declared that after review Miss Margaret Langsbury was the winner. Cynthia still feigning anger snorted; "After review? Jumped up puppy! Harry should put him on orderly officer duty for a year." Meg was about to say something in the young officers defense but on second thoughts decided that it would not be wise. Cynthia leading her mare marched over to Butler and addressed him belligerently; "Where d'ye get these young officers from Harry? Maybe I should check the applicant list from now on?" Cynthia had struck a sore spot, Harry's eyes went cold: "Enough Cynthia, everyone saw that as a dead heat, and who my officers are is my bloody business!" Everyone went silent while Cynthia stalked off leading her mare. When she was out of earshot the Duke harrumphed; "I suppose you'll catch hell tonight?" Harry smiled: "I doubt that Your Grace, I think I can look forward to a very romantic evening." The Duke laughed: "Damn me! Is that how it works?" Meg looked at her father saying; "I find it hard to imagine Cynthia being romantic." Jonathan looked at her dotingly; "You have a lot to learn about romance Meg. Now I have to get over to the start line for the race." Harry addressed Jonathan: "I'll have my orderly bring both our horses." Jonathan thanked him as they both walked over to the start line Jack approached them mounted on Nipper, the Colonel looked up at him: "Aren't you going in the wrong direction Corporal?" Jack's response: "Just going to congratulate Miss Meg, Sir." Caused Harry to turn to Jonathan: "Like he needs an excuse; eh?"

The field for the race which would be the final event of the day was considerably larger than the ladies. It included the Colonel; all six of the regiments Majors and riders of every rank, Jonathan and the Squire were the only two civilians. The track was barely wide enough to contain all the entries as Jack thought to himself; "I need to be out in front in the first furlong." After a furlong the track necked down to about half its width which would bunch up the field posing the potential for bumping and maybe riders being unsaddled. At the sound of the starter's pistol he had Nipper in full gallop almost instantly. When he eased his hands forward loosening the reins Nipper knew it was his signal to go full out. They reached the first turn in the lead with Jonathan on Joe coming up hard behind them. The turns on the makeshift course were tight and Jack reasoned that Joe being bigger horse and longer in the legs would have to take them wider than Nipper.

If he could pin Jonathan and Joe to the inside rail it would slow them down enough to give him the opportunity to take the lead at the last turn. As Jonathan and Joe caught up with them Jack moved Nipper over towards the center of the track allowing them to go to the inside. He had some help when two riderless horses that had unburdened themselves at the first turn when the field was bunched, came up between them effectively pinning Jonathan and Joe to the rail. Normally Joe would have pulled ahead of the other horses but they were not burdened by the weights of their riders. Meg was cheering alternately for her father and Jack until the final turn when out of confused frustration she decided to conserve her enthusiasm to congratulate whoever might be the winner. As they came into the final turn the riderless horses still had Joe pinned to the rail and despite Jonathan's urging he would not go all out; knowing instinctively that he could lose his footing. Jack sensing victory was in his grasp gave Nipper one final kick with his heels. As they approached the finishing line Nipper pulled away from the field and Jack distinctly heard Paddy's voice above the crowd; "There's a broth of a boy, now I know it's Irish he is!" Jack and Nipper crossed the finish line half a length ahead of Jonathan and Joe with the Colonel on Carrington coming in third. Jack hesitated a moment after crossing the line then headed to where he thought he had heard Paddy. When he found the jubilant Irishman he had a dark frown on his face; "Where the bloody hell is Ginger?" Paddy looked up at him smiling; "I tied him to his bed; so I did, I wasn't about to miss this event for all the saints in heaven." Jack smiled; "Better get back there before he gets loose." Jack rode back to where horses and riders were milling around at the finish line; as the subaltern announced the results; "The winner by a half a length was Corporal Spratt up on Nipper, second was Mr. Jonathan Langsbury on Joe and third Colonel Butler on Carrington. Meg hardly waiting for Jack to finish dismounting threw her arms around him kissing him profusely; much to the disapproval of many of the ladies present.

When she stood back from Jack and her father came over to congratulate him she looked at Jonathan; "Wasn't he magnificent Papa?" Then, seeing his look of chagrin; "And you rode magnificently also Papa." The subaltern announced that everyone was requested to be at the registration tent for the awards presentation at four o'clock. Jack started walking Nipper for cool down with Meg holding his free arm and Jonathan and the Colonel just behind them. Jonathan cleared his throat: "You know young man I saw something in you today, a killer instinct." Butler commented; "He might need it one day." Meg looked over her shoulder; "I pray he never will!" At the registrations tent the RSM had taken the rostrum with his megaphone and announced to the crowd that he was calling on the Duke of Cambridge to present the awards. The Duke stumbled up the steps and Royce gave the list with the names of the award winners. The RSM had wisely decided to let the Duke read out the names while he gave out the trophies. Before the presentation Royce informed the award winners that after the presentation the Adjutant would take charge of the trophies, which would be returned to them after they had been engraved. Jack and the Riding Master both got loud cheers when they went up for their trophies. Meg's trophy was a cut crystal bowl cradled in chased silver tripod. After she had received it she handed it back, and as she left the rostrum she went over to the Adjutant who was standing nearby. Turning on all her feminine charm she asked him; "Captain Barry, would you please have the trophy engraved "Presented to the 17th Lancers by Meg Langsbury" along with the date, and have it placed in the regimental trophy room." Barry who was well aware of the dead heat furor caused by Cynthia Butler smiled and said; "Certainly Ma'am if you so wish" Meg smiled back at the Adjutant; "Yes I do so wish, and thank you Captain Barry." After replying; "My pleasure Ma'am." He thought; "How did a ranker ever get a little beauty like that?" When she got back to where Jack was standing he had a quizzical look on his face; "What were you talking about with the Adjutant?" When she told him he looked at her with adoring eyes; "You always know the right thing to do." Meg laughed; "If you persist in looking at me with those puppy dog eyes people will start thinking you're in love with me." Jack retorted; "They would be right and I don't care!" Royce made one more announcement from the rostrum; "For the rest of the day all those not on special duty are free to enjoy their leisure. Sunday morning will be church parade as usual. After the midday meal all privates not on special duty will be marched to this location by their troop sergeants and form work details, and we will have this area back to the way it was when Squire Granville so generously permitted us to use it. Before you go about your leisure the Colonel wishes to address everyone." At this cue the Colonel mounted the rostrum; "I thank you all for attending both this event and this morning's parade. We leave this station with both painful regret and fond memories. The Seventeenth will always have fond remembrances of our time here. Farewell!" One of the locals in the crowd shouted;"Three cheers for the Seventeenth Lancers and Colonel Butler!"The cheers were loud and long. Jack turned to Meg saying; "I have to take Nipper back to stables and see to him, and then I'll be back." Joe and Sally had been taken to the officer's stables where the grooms saw to their needs. When he got back he found her talking to Cynthia near the officer's tent. When Cynthia left he said; "I have to get over to "A" Squadron to take care of a matter." Meg smiled archly; "Would that matter happen to be Ginger?" He felt somewhat uncomfortable under her gaze; "Meg dear, he's really a good man. You have to consider his background before condemning his behavior." She gave a little snort; "And you grew up in a grand house and attended an expensive school? Maybe what you told Papa and I about the workhouse was just a pack of lies." Jack wounded by her sarcasm replied sharply; "I think Newgate Prison was far more soul destroying than the workhouse. Furthermore, my life may depend on him someday, or on any of the other lads for that matter." Meg, now contrite spoke softly; "Jack I'm sorry, I shouldn't chastise you for being concerned about your comrades." Then laughing again: "Although I draw the line at adopting Ginger when we're married!" At this they grasped each others hands and began laughing aloud. While people around them were staring and wondering they walked arm in arm towards the officer's tent. Then Jack said; "If you'll join your father and the Colonel I'll find you when I get back." Meg in a wheedling tone pleaded; "Oh Jack! Can I not come with you?" He thought for a moment; "Alright but your not to come inside the barrack room." When they arrived at the barracks Jack admonished her; "Now you stand outside this door until I get back." After Jack had been inside for a short while she heard voices raised in anger. Her curiosity aroused she entered quietly and through an open door she heard Ginger shouting at Jack; "Ev'ry time yew saves me from meself Fishy, I ends up wiv a fuckin' achin' bloody jaw!" Before Jack could reply she entered the dormitory without Jack seeing her. She was standing behind Jack who was wondering why Ginger had suddenly gone quiet. She took in the scene, Ginger was tied spread eagled on his bed, both ankles and wrists secured with halter ropes. Another private with whom she was not familiar, sat on the edge of the bed looking past Jack at her with admiring eyes. Paddy then exclaimed; "I didn't think it was heaven I'd be going to today but I must be there, for by the holy St. Patrick it's an angel that I'm seeing to be sure." Jack looked at Paddy with a puzzled expression and then realized Paddy was looking past him. He looked over his shoulder and saw Meg standing there: "I thought I told you to stay outside?" Meg bristled; "First of all Jack Spratt, you do not tell me to do anything, you ask or request! Second, if I had not come inside I wouldn't have received that beautiful compliment, which was far more flattering than anything I've ever heard from you." Both the privates were grinning, Jack red faced and flustered instructed Paddy to untie Ginger; "Private Weston you're confined to your quarters until reveille tomorrow morning, that is an order! After that you'll be Sergeant Woodford's problem and God only knows what he has in store for you." He looked at Paddy; "Thanks for taking care of him you might as well get back to the beer tent, in fact I'll buy you a beer." Meg batted her eyelids at Jack; "Would you buy me a beer Corporal Spratt?" Jack trying to look stern replied; "I might as well now you've got a taste for it." Paddy looking at Jack laughed inwardly thinking; "She's got him broken, trained and fully in hand, let's hope she never decides to geld him!" Then looking at Jack he said; "Are ye not going to introduce me to this vision from paradise?" Jack apologized; "Meg, this is Private O'Neill. Paddy, this is Miss Meg Langsbury." Paddy turning on his charm asked; "Would Meg be for Margaret?" When Meg answered in the affirmative Paddy gave her a disarming smile; "Well by all the saints in heaven if that's not me own aunt's name, me sainted mother's sister that is." Jack was smiling: "Meg, this rascal is using his blarney on you; but we've got another name for it in the regiment." Meg glared at him; "I think I'd sooner not hear what that is." All the way back to the beer tent, Paddy regaled Meg with his Irish brogue, as she laughed merrily Jack seethed silently. In the beer tent Jack ordered pints for Paddy and himself and a half for Meg. When she protested because he did not order a pint for her Jack became exasperated: "Next thing I'll be finding you in the Crown on payday." Meg, back to teasing looked at Jack with mischief in her eyes; "I thought the girls in the Crown drank gin." She smiled impishly at his response; "It's not too late for that spanking, young lady!" After Jack and Meg finished their beers they took their leave of Paddy and went to look for Jonathan. Just outside the registration tent they ran into Cynthia who informed them that Jonathan was in the officer's tent with the Colonel and the Duke. Cynthia laughed: "The drunken old bugger's passed out, the Duke I mean not your father." Jack turned to Meg: "I can't go in the officer's tent so I'll have to leave you there." Meg's response was defiant; "I'll go in and tell Papa where we'll be, then we'll go back to the beer tent." Before Jack could protest she was gone. When she entered the officer's tent, she saw a group of tittering young officers looking over towards a corner of the tent where the overhead lamps hardly cast any light. When she got closer she saw what they found so amusing, it was the Duke who lay snoring on an officers campaign bed. She found Jonathan with the Colonel and told him that she would be in the beer tent with Jack. The subaltern who had officiated at the finish line walked over and asked if he could get her something. Meg told him yes, if he would like to come back to the beer tent with her. Harry smiled when he slunk off with his tail between his legs. Meg looked at her father: "How long has the Duke been like that?" Jonathan said; "I think about an hour." Butler looking concerned addressed Jonathan; "There'll be hell to pay if this gets back to the Queen!" Meg took her leave and went back to where she had left Jack: "Come on darling let's go back and enjoy your friends." Jack still with some reservations allowed her to lead him back to the beer tent. Once inside they rejoined Paddy who was drinking with some other first troop lads. Jack confided in Paddy; "I don't think it's a good idea to bring her in here." Meg, who had overheard; cast a withering glance at Jack,. Paddy gripped Jack's arm; "Look around, no ones cursing out of respect for the lady." Looking at Meg he said; "And I'll be telling you Miss this laddie of yours may not be the biggest boyo in the regiment but they all have respect for his fists an all!" As the late afternoon turned into an early winter evening Meg drank and laughed with the rankers and without knowing it became a daughter of the regiment. At eight o'clock the RSM came into the tent and called time. Jack walked Meg to the officer's tent and asked if he should get Joe and Sally from the officer's stables where they had been taken after the days events. Meg said that it would not be necessary but that Jack could walk her to the stables. She went into the officer's tent to inform her father that she would wait for him at the stables. As they walked arm in arm toward the stables Meg looked up at Jack: "Thank you for a lovely day darling." He squeezed her arm saying you should thank the Colonel and the Duke." "No" she replied, "Without you it would have meant nothing." Jack took her in his arms and kissed her hungrily. Startled by a loud cough from behind they pulled apart guiltily, when they looked behind they saw Jonathan's silhouette. As he came up to them although they could not make out his features in the darkness they sensed he was smiling; "Anymore of these unseemly public displays and I might question your intentions Corporal Spratt." Jack spluttered; "My intentions toward Meg are only the best Sir, I assure you." Jonathan chuckled; "No wonder it's so easy for Meg to get a rise out of you!" When the grooms brought the horses out Jack helped Meg to mount even though she had no need of his assistance. She leaned down and kissed him; "I'll see you tomorrow afternoon, goodnight my darling."

Sunday morning after church parade before First Troop was dismissed Sergeant Woodford looked straight at Ginger and barked out; "After dinner Private Weston will report to me, First Troop fall out." After the midday meal Ginger duly presented himself before the Sergeant's desk. Woodford looked up at him: "Weston you're a fuckin' disgrace and one of these days Corporal Spratt won't be 'round to pull yer irons outta the fire. Yesterday ee coulda got 'isself into a lotta trouble becos of yew." Ginger looked down and shuffled his feet. Furious, Woodford raised his voice and his words penetrated the door: "Stan' to attention when I'm talkin' to yew, well wot 'ave yew gotta say fer yerself? Ginger totally cowed protested; "I didn't know Fishy…" before he could finish the sergeant roared; "Fishy wot the bloody 'ell d'ye mean Fishy?" Ginger amended his explanation; "I didn't know Corporal Spratt ud do wot ee did." Woodford, still irate was trembling: "Since yew got yer floggin' ee's watched over yew like a muvver 'en. I don't know why cuz yew aint werf a shit! So let me tell yew wot I'm goin' to do wiv yew. To start wiv when we goes over to the Squires land to clean up I'm telling the other sergeants that yew'll be picking up all the 'orse shit on yer own fer ev'ryone. Yew'll pull the cart an' yew'll shovel the shit all by yerself, an' if I finds one turd when we're finished yew'll spend the night in the guard'ouse. After that you'll take the buckets from the temp'ry latrines to the cess pit. Empty 'em, wash 'em out and return 'em to Quarter Masters." Ginger in a contrite tone muttered a muted yes Sarge and turned to leave. Woodford let out a bellow; "Did I say yew wuz dismissed?" Ginger stood fast and said; "Sorry Sarge." Woodford could hardly contain himself, his face was deep crimson as he exclaimed; "I aint finished yet. So's yew don't put Corporal Spratt on the spot any more I'm tellin' the troop that if yew gets in any more trouble they'll all be punished." Ginger protested; "But that's not fair, the lads' ull 'ate me!" The Sergeant still red and trembling visibly roared again: "Fair yew says, fair! Would it be fair if Corporal Spratt 'ad lost 'is stripes for savin' yer rotten arse, 'stead a charging yew like ee should? One more thing before I dismisses yew, yer confined to barracks till we leaves fer Woolwich. They'll be no more drinking yerself silly and fuckin' those poxed up bints in the Crown Saturdays. Now yer dismissed." Ginger turned and as he walked out into the barrack room he could feel the anger of the lads who had heard every word. Chalky stepped up to him; "Ginger, yew fucks up jes once more an' we'll all kick the shit outta yew. Yew'll be dead or as good as, when we've finished wiv yer!" Ginger, who had heard stories about "barrack room courts martial", shuddered visibly.

Monday morning after first parade Perry informed Jack that they were to report to the Colonels office at 10 o'clock. When they arrived at RHQ they found Sergeant Jackson the cook sergeant and Sergeant Griffiths of the officer's mess with the RSM. Royce greeted them; "Adjutant's in there with the Colonel, they'll be calling you in soon." Almost as soon as he had said it the Adjutant opened the Colonel's office door; "The Colonel will see you now. They filed in the RSM bringing up the rear. When they were all stood to attention in front of the Colonel the RSM having the senior rank saluted the Colonel. Butler acknowledged his salute with a nod the RSM then left for his own office. The Colonel addressed them: "I'm sure you're all wondering what this all is about, Captain Barry has already been briefed so now I'll let you in on what's going on; "Those of you present are going to Woolwich as a reconnaissance party; under the command of Captain Barry.. Along with a clerk and Captain Barry's orderly you will leave tomorrow morning at 6 'o clock sharp, Captain Barry will tell you where to assemble. The clerk and the orderly will report to the Quartermaster who will issue them a pack animal equipped with panniers to carry the rations you'll need for the journey. They will report to the men's mess at half past five and draw rations." Looking at Sergeant Jackson and smiling he continued; "I'm sure the Sergeant will see you have adequate food for your needs." The commanding officer of the regiment has been informed of your impending visit and on arrival you will find the captain in charge of their rear party is expecting you. While there you will inspect the barracks and prepare a detailed written report for my edification. Captain Barry take over!" Barry stood up; "Follow me to my office where I will instruct you on your duties." He saluted the Colonel; "Thank you Sir." He then preceded them to his office where he gave them detailed instructions on the duties they were to carry out. When they were leaving RHQ Jack turned to Perry: "So we've to check the stables and report on the conditions and any improvements that may be needed?" Perry grunted; "Yeah, I reckon the Colonel sent both uv us cuz we aint got a trainee troop."

Tuesday morning they rode out, with the Adjutant in the lead followed by the two sergeants, and then came the orderly and the clerk, the orderly leading a pack horse with loaded panniers. Bringing up the rear were Jack and the riding master. As they were walking their mounts along the High St. Meg on Sally rode up to the side of Jack and Nipper. Jack startled asked; "What are you doing about so early?" Meg smiled; "Cynthia told me about your going to Woolwich so I came to see you off." Jack became agitated; "Meg darling, I can't stop!" Just then Barry rode back and seeing Jack's predicament said; "You have five minutes Corporal, then catch up." Jack saluted but before he could thank the Captain Meg spoke up; "Thank you Captain Barry, you are an absolute darling." This brought smiles to the faces of the others. As the entourage moved on Meg looked at Jack; "Get off that horse so that you can kiss me goodbye properly." They dismounted and were kissing hungrily when Cynthia rode up exclaiming; "Right in the middle of the bloody High St. at ten past six in the morning, damned if I won't have to throw a bucket of water over you two if this behavior continues!" Jack broke loose to salute the Colonels wife but Meg with her hands on either side of his face pulled him back to her lips; "There's no time for that we've only got two more minutes." Cynthia rode away after uttering a loud; "Well I'll be buggered!" Finally, Jack broke away from Meg and mounted Nipper: "I've got to catch up with the rest." As he urged Nipper into a canter Meg caught up with him and rode by his side until they reached the green in front of her house. She leaned toward him; "Kiss me one more time dearest." After they had kissed she turned toward the house, Jack kicked Nipper into a gallop and through the window Bharti clucked.

They stopped at the same village where Jack had stopped on his way to the Duke's and were watering the horses when Sergeant Major Capper appeared; he spied Jack and walked over to him; "Well 'ere yew are agin young fella! Wur yew goin' this time?" Before Jack could reply Ned Perry came over; "And 'oos this gen'leman Corporal Spratt?" Jack's answer; "This is Sergeant Major Capper, Sir." Brought a gasp from the Riding Master; "Bloody 'ell! I aint seen yew since thirty-six, I wuz a corporal in your squadron." Capper studied his face for a moment; "Yew be Perry of Third Troop, yew've got four stripes now." Perry smiled; "I bin riding master since thirty-nine." The old Sergeant Major grunted his approval; "As I remembers you were bloody good wiv 'orses." Captain Barry who'd overheard their conversation introduced himself; "Sergeant Major I'm pleased to meet you, I'm Captain Barry the Regimental Adjutant." Capper came to attention out of habit: "It's an honor, Zur, wuz yer daddy the Major Barry that commanded "B" Squadron in India?" Barry nodded; "The very same." Capper grinned; "Ee wur my squadron commander an' a good un too, sat an 'orse better than any other orficer in the regiment." The Captain addressed both men; "We're going to be here half an hour. If you two would like to go over to that tavern and talk about old times, Riding Master Perry has my permission." They both came to attention; Perry saluting said; "Yes, Sir Thank you Sir." Barry admonished them; "And don't get drunk!" Capper laughed and turned to Perry; "Wish I knowed 'ow to get drunk in 'alf an hour." Jack fed Perry's horse while tending to Nipper, so that when the Riding Master came back from the tavern they'd be ready to continue their journey. When Perry and Capper reappeared they had their arms about each others shoulders; while they shook hands Jack thought he saw tears in their eyes. He thought; "If some of the poor bastards he's had in his training troops could only see him."

They continued on to London turning to a southerly direction when they reached the eastern outskirts. It was just gone half past twelve when they came to the main gate of the barracks they were seeking. The main gate sentry came to attention and brought his saber up to the present and gave the challenge; "Who goes there?" Barry replied; "Captain Barry with an appraisal party from the Seventeenth Lancers, I was told to report to Captain Lawler upon arrival." The sentry brought his saber back to the carry, and then pointed to the guardroom; "If yew lets the Guard Sergeant know ee can send fer the Captain." After Barry ordered the detail to dismount; they led their horses to the guardroom and waited for the private the Guard Sergeant had sent to return with Captain Lawler. They had just secured their mounts to the hitching rail when the private returned with a captain. The two captains exchanged salutes and introduced themselves Lawler turned to the private; "Show Captain Barry and his party their accommodations then take them to the cookhouse." He then turned to Barry; "I'm sorry Captain Barry, but we're only a small rear party so everyone eats in the men's mess." Barry nodded: "I can see it would be impracticable to keep the officer's mess open." They ate their midday meal in the cookhouse, Lawler and Barry sitting apart from the rankers at another table. When they had finished eating Barry came over to give them instructions; "We might as well get busy right away. Riding Master you and Corporal Spratt will inspect the squadron's and officer's stables and the farrier's shop. Corporal; you will take notes from which you will compile a written report at the completion of our inspection. Sergeant Griffiths you will inspect the officer's mess and single officer's quarters, also taking notes which you will hand over to (indicating the clerk) Private Hughes to compile a report. Sergeant Jackson you will take care of the cookhouse inspection and also take notes which you will then hand over to Hughes." Glancing toward his orderly he concluded: "Webb and I will inspect the barrack rooms and the offices. The reason we are starting right away is that I intend to complete our business by Thursday evening so as to get an early start Friday morning."

They finished before noon Thursday and after they had eaten their midday meal Barry came over to their table in the cook-house; "Lads you did really well to finish this soon. You can all take the rest of today off and you may leave the barracks if you wish. However, you will be clean and properly dressed and you will be back in barracks by ten." Then, looking at Perry; "Riding Master as senior NCO I will expect you to see that my orders are complied with, I will be going into the city with Captain Lawler as a guest at his club." Perry stood up; "Zur, I wants to thank yew fer me an' the lads, I'll make sure they all be'aves 'emselves."

On their way out past the main gate Perry stopped to ask the private who had fetched Lawler when they first arrived; where they could find a public house. The private gave them directions to the Gunner's Arms. When they entered the barroom it became obvious that this was a favorite drinking place for military personnel, most of them appeared to be soldiers of the Royal Artillery. Perry said; "I'll get the first round, you blokes go find a table." In the back of the room they found a long table with six places where Perry joined them. Shortly after the Riding Master sat down, a barmaid wearing a low cut blouse leaned low over the table where she laid down a tray containing six tankards. Webb let out a gasp; "Bugger, I'd like to get me 'ands on them two beauties!" Griffiths gave him a warning glance: "If you messes around wiv the girls in 'ere some of the reg'lers ull beat the shit outta yew! Remember this is a garrison pub." Perry smacking his lips after savoring his first gulp of porter cautioned them all; "If anyone of yew does anything to cawse trouble, I'll make it me business to see yer on orders when we gets back, 'an that'll mean a floggin'!" A piano struck up and everyone joined in enthusiastically with the spontaneous singing of a medley of barrack room ballads and music hall songs. The barmaid appeared with their second round of drinks and Webb fixated on her exposed breasts again. Sergeant Jackson jabbed Griffiths in the ribs with his elbow; "Look at that young bugger, 'is fuckin' eyeballs er stickin' out like chapel 'at pegs!" They left the Gunners Arms at half past eight all six of them in a happy go lucky mood, but not drunk. Perry had made sure that no one drank more than six pints. As they approached the main gate Perry admonished them; "Yew buggers get straight to bed we gotta be up early tomorrer." Griffiths laughed; "After starin' at that barmaids tits all evenin', we knows wot that young bugger Webb's gonna do afore ee goes to sleep." They were all laughing at the discomfited Webb as they walked into the barracks. The main gate guard commented; "Reckon yew lot 'ad a goodtime tonight."

The following morning as they were leaving Captain Lawler was at the main gate to see them off, after he and Captain Barry

had exchanged salutes. Barry thanked him for the hospitality then added; "I'll see if I can't be with our advance party, I
really enjoyed your club." Lawler laughed; "Maybe we won't have
to get up so early next morning then? " The journey to the half
way point at Sergeant Major Capper's village was without incident except for some intermittent cold rain showers. When they
reached the village Capper appeared as they were attending to
the horses; Captain Barry asked Capper if the landlord of the
pub would let them eat their food inside out of the rain. Capper
laughed; "Bless yew zur, as long as yew buys summat t'drink
old Teddy won't care." Barry turned to Jack; "Corporal Spratt
enquire of the landlord if we can shelter our horses in his stables; while we enjoy his hospitality." Jack came back to say; that
the landlord would be happy to let them use his stables. Barry
addressed Perry; "Forget about the rations Riding Master, I'll buy
breakfast." Perry's eyes lit up; "Thank'ee zur the lads ull 'preciate
that." When they were seated at one of the pub's long tables the
landlord came to greet them; "What be yew boys drinking?" The
Captain smiled; "We're not only drinking but we'd like some vittles landlord." It was the landlord's turn to smile; "Jes 'ave these
lads tell me wot they wants; an' I'll 'ave Polly git it fer 'em, yew
can call me Teddy." When they had each given their orders to the
landlord, Barry looked over to Capper; who was standing at the
bar; "Come over and sit down Sergeant Major you're included
in this breakfast." Capper sat down next to Perry winking at The
Riding Master he said; "That's a bloody fine orficer yew got there
Ned." Perry replied; "If they aint no good our colonel makes sure
they don't stay around very long." Then he proceeded to tell him
about Dalton-Jones. He'd just finished his narrative when the
landlord returned to their table with a tray full of tankards followed by a serving wench with some of their food orders. Teddy
informed them; "We'll go back and get the rest of yer vittles then
yew should be alright fer a bit." As the girl leaned over to lay
the food tray on the table her breasts were almost completely

exposed, Ned jabbed Capper with his elbow, nodding toward Webb he laughed; "Watch that young bugger's face!" The old sergeant major observed the look of transfixed fascination and naked desire on Webb's face; "I reckon that young bugger ull 'ave an 'ard time mountin' when yew boys leaves." Ned with a grin on his face concurred; "Jake, wot I'm worried about is wot way ee might be mountin' 'is 'orse!" Clapping each other on the back they both exploded into laughter, causing everyone at the table to stop eating or drinking to stare at them. Captain Barry enquired; "Is this a joke we can all share Riding Master?" Perry recovered enough to answer; "Old sojers joke Zur." When Teddy came back with rest of the food, Jake Capper said; "Captain, Teddy 'ere is an old 'orse sojer too." Barry looked up from his platter; "What regiment landlord?" Teddy took a gulp of porter; "11th Hussars Zur, I time expired six months ago. Now I 'elps me missus run this place, its bin in 'er family fer years." The Captain nodded approvingly; "That's a fine regiment landlord." Teddy shook his head in denial; "It wor 'til that bastard Cardigan got a 'old uv us!" Barry cleared his throat; "I really shouldn't be listening to criticism of a fellow officer." Teddy's reply took them all by surprise; "Beggin' yer pardon Zur but now I got started I'll get the rest off me chest, an' then 'old me peace. Arter ee took over; us we 'ad more floggin's in a month than we ever 'ad afore in a year an' now I can say it wiv out getting' flogged, ee's a bloody tyrant!" Barry shook his head, Lord Cardigans's reputation was well known throughout the cavalry corps, but as a serving officer he could not be in open agreement with Teddy. The Riding Master saw a chance to change the subject and kill an awkward moment; "Teddy get that wench over 'ere agin so's we can watch Webb's eyeballs rollin' all over 'er titties." This caused everyone except the discomfited Webb to break out into ribald laughter. After they had finished breakfast Barry ordered them to get their mounts and be ready to leave. When they were mounted up the Captain turned to Jake and Teddy who'd come out to see them off; "D'ye know of a needy family that could use some vittles?" Capper looked up at Barry; "There's a family staying wiv me sister 'an 'er 'usband. The father lost 'is job on the estate an' them 'ad to get out of their tied cottage." Barry looked at Webb indicating the rations they had replenished before leaving Woolwich; "Get those rations out of the saddle bags and give them to the Sergeant Major." Addressing Capper; "Tell 'em the food is compliments of the 17th Lancers." Both Capper and Teddy chorused in unison; "God bless you Captain." Then Capper added; "And the regiment." As they rode out of the village Perry turned to Barry; "When I gets 'ome I'm gonna see if Nancy ud go fer selling the cottage and movin' 'ere, I got me a good mate wiv old Jake Capper, an' I'd like ta see more uv 'im wen I gets out." The Captain laughed; "I'm betting it wouldn't be long before your wife realizes that you'd be spending a lot of time at the tavern with the Sergeant Major and Teddy if you moved here."

It was about one o'clock when they rode into the High St. and sure enough Meg mounted on Sally was waiting there; wearing the dark green riding habit which she knew was Jack's favorite. Captain Barry called back: "No tarrying this time Corporal we need to get back and report to the Colonel." As Jack drew abreast of Meg he whispered; "You heard the Captain, I can't stop now." Meg's eyes took on a look of mischief; "I think I'm going to kiss you right here and now, Corporal Spratt." Jack's face took on a look of alarm, and then Meg curveted Sally and rode away laughing impishly. The Riding Master smiled at Jack: "You'd better get that young filly broke afore she breaks you, young un." Jack smiled back; "Like I told Mr. Langsbury, I'd never let her hear me call her a filly." When they reached RHQ Barry ordered them to take care of their horses and with the exception of his orderly Webb, to report back to RHQ at 3 o'clock. When they were assembled in front of the Colonels office Royce came out to inform them that the Colonel was ready to see them. Butler ordered them at ease and began by commending Hughes; "Private Hughes this report that you put together from the party's notes is extremely well written. Thank you, you are dismissed." Hughes came to attention and saluted, stammering a barely audible thank you Sir as he left. After Hughes departure the colonel addressed the group; "You all seem to have done a very thorough job, Captain Barry tells me you worked hard to complete the task in a very timely manner. From the contents of this report it seems that our new home leaves a lot to be desired. Captain Barry and I now have to assess the requirements of the advance party which will be leaving next Wednesday."

Saturday saw Jack at the Langsbury residence once again; it was a typical south of England March day of grey skies and cold rain. Jack stood at the front door with rain running off his pillbox hat and down his tarpaulin jacket. Bharti opened the door and as he stepped onto the mat inside the threshold she instructed him to remove his boots and pointed to a pair of slippers. He had already left his jacket and hat under the porch. Meg come flying along the hall threw her arms around him and kissed him boisterously, Bharti clucked. Meg turned to her; "Please see that Corporal Spratt's hat and jacket are dry and his boots cleaned before he leaves. Hardly giving him chance to pull on the slippers she started dragging him to the study where Jonathan was seated behind his desk. He pointed to the overstuffed chair and told Jack to sit down; "Well I suppose you two won't be going riding today." Jack grimaced; "No Sir, I don't think it would be a good idea." Jonathan laughed; "It's just as well because I think we have something to talk about." Jack looked perturbed; "What would that be Sir?" Jonathan looked at Meg; "Well, don't you have something to say young lady?" For once Meg seemed to be at a disadvantage; "I have asked Papa if I can attend a ladies finishing school." Her father said;"Continue Meg." Shuffling her feet she added; "The school is close by my Aunt Letty's Surrey house and if I stay with her I can be a day student." Jonathan was smiling; "And tell us where else it's close to." Meg was blushing; "Oh Papa please stop teasing me." And then defiantly; "It's near Woolwich!" With that she flounced out of the room. Jonathan smiled; "My sister Leticia has a house in London but she prefers to stay at the Surrey house except during the social season." Seeing Jack's puzzled expression he explained; "The social season is when the wealthy and idle element of society have their rounds of balls and parties. Well what d'ye think, Jack?" Jack asked a question to which he already had the answer; "Could her request have anything to do with the regiment's moving to Woolwich?" Jonathan laughed so loudly it brought Meg back into the room; "Come now Jack don't be getting disingenuous with me, you know full well she wants to be near you." Meg who had regained her composure scowled at her father; "You make me seem like some wanton hussy Papa, a camp follower maybe." Jack jumped up his agitation causing him to lapse into his old argot; "You aint no 'ussy or camp follower yer a lady!" This caused both Meg and her father to erupt into laughter, and then Meg turned to Jonathan; "It's a good thing I have Jack to defend my honor when my own father makes me out to be a strumpet." This brought laughter from all three of them as Meg sat on the arm of Jack's chair and gave him a peck on the cheek; "Thank you darling, that was very gallant of you." Jonathan got serious: "Now that everyone knows your eventual intentions I think it might be time for a formal betrothal." This brought gasps from both of them. Meg got up from the arm of Jack's chair and ran over to her father kissing him on the cheek and forehead; "You're a darling Papa, and I forgive you." Jack remained seated wearing a stunned look his mouth open. Meg looked over at Jack; "Well say something, or am I to become engaged to someone that looks like a codfish on the fishmonger's slab?" Jack regained his composure; "Sir I don't know how to thank you." Jonathan now spoke seriously; "You can thank me by cherishing my daughter for the rest of your lives, and giving me some grandchildren." Meg blushed furiously; "Papa it's much too early to think about that!" Jonathan laughed; "I would hope so. Now Meg; why don't you go and help Bharti with dinner, I have something I wish to discuss with Jack." When Meg had left the room he addressed Jack; I don't want to embarrass you but could I lend you some money to buy Meg's engagement ring?" Jack's answer took him by surprise; "Thank you Sir, but I can take care of that matter myself." Jonathan gave Jack a quizzical look asking: "On a corporal's pay?" Jack then went on to explain how Meg had persuaded him to open a bank account. Upon the third time he had visited her she had asked him what he did with his pay. Jack had told her he kept it safe under the trough in Nipper's stall. She had expressed alarm and asked; "What if somebody finds it and steals it?" When Jack's only answer was a shrug she told him; "You are going to open a bank account, bring your money with you next week." The following Saturday she had taken him to the bank in the High St. where she helped him open a bank account. The bank clerk had exclaimed; "This seems a lot of money for a soldier!" Jack explained that it was four weeks pay. Jack then went on to explain to Jonathan; "Now when I come into town I deposit my pay in the bank, I just keep enough for a pint or two in the Crown on the way back to barracks." Jonathan had a pleased look on his face; "It's been nearly two years now, you must have quite a bit." Jack Shrugged; "I don't know for sure I give the receipts to Meg for safe keeping." Jack's face took on a look of embarrassment; "I have a very delicate question I'd like to put to you." Jonathan somewhat warily said; "Ask away." Jack preceded his question by describing the diatribe with the Riding Master after the chota peg competition, and Meg's remarks having overheard the two of them which brought a smile to Jonathan's face. Jack then asked; "How does she know about sodomy?" Jonathan still smiling said; "She went to a girl's school, and from what Cynthia Butler has told me they learn a lot more in those places from other girls than you'll find in the curriculum." Just then Meg came into the room; "If you two rogues are finished with the mischief you're cooking up; dinner's ready." On his way back to the barracks Jack went into the Crown for his usual pint, the girls who had long ago realized they were wasting their time on him reserved their charms for the other lads. Jack saw Chalky and sat down by him; "It's quiet in here tonight." Chalky laughed halfheartedly; "Ginger aint 'ere." Jack nodded; "Better than him getting flogged." Chalky agreed; "Reckon' yer right Fishy." On their walk back to the barracks Chalky asked; "Why d'ye bovver wiv 'im?" Jack turned to Chalky in the darkness; "Ever since I first saw those scars he got in Newgate I've felt that he's someone that needs to be looked after." Chalky chuckled; "Why, yer a big old softy." Jack laughed into the night; "Someone else told me the same thing but she was a bloody sight better looking than you, you ugly bugger!" Chalky could not resist another comment: "'Ope she wuz talkin' about yer good nature and not summat else." As they were entering the main gate Jack cuffed him playfully, Paddy who was on guard exclaimed; "Here I am keeping the regiment safe while you spalpeens are out on the town having a good time." They both laughed and bade him goodnight as they entered the guardroom to sign in.

The following week was filled with preparations for the move, the advance party who were leaving Wednesday got busy immediately after Sunday's midday meal. Amongst the advance party's personnel the Colonel had ordered that a blacksmith and a carpenter be included. This was based on requirements indicated in Captain Barry's report. The rest of the party included two privates from each squadron, a corporal and a private from the cookhouse and a corporal from the officer's mess, and Captain Barry who had managed to persuade the Colonel to place him in charge of the detail. They rode out Wednesday morning with four supply wagons with two of the privates from the squadrons in each wagon with their horses tethered to the tailboards. They left amid a chorus of cheers mixed with some ribald remarks, Ginger shouting out; "Don't fuck all the bints in Woolwich, leave zum fer us." Jack who was stood behind him exclaimed; "Sometimes

I think you just want to get flogged!" With the advance party on its way preparations continued for the main party's departure the following Wednesday; a much larger undertaking. With so much work to be done the week flew by.

Saturday was a bright cold day when Jack strode along the High Street to the bank. When he found the clerk who had helped him open his account he informed him that he wished to withdraw five pounds. The clerk seemed taken aback; "That is rather a large sum Sir!" Jack replied: "I know, it's for something very special." After drawing the cash Jack addressed the clerk; "I will be closing my account next Saturday, we will be leaving for Woolwich the following Wednesday." The clerk looked up: "We have a branch in Woolwich Sir." Jack was pleased; "Then in that case please transfer my account there." From the bank he went to the jewelers and pointing through the plate glass counter top he told the jeweler: "I want that ring." The jeweler looking skeptical said; 'It's four guineas Sir." Jack laid five sovereigns on the counter; "Good, do you have it in this size?" Jack gave the jeweler one of Meg's rings that Jonathan had given him. The jeweler went to the back of the store then came back with the ring Jack had selected; "This is the size you require sir, may I ask what the occasion is?" Jack smiled; "I'm going to marry the most beautiful girl in the world!" As he picked up the leather ring box and his sixteen shillings change and walked out into the High St. he was unaware that the news would be all over town in less than an hour. When he arrived at the Langsbury residence Meg met him with an accusatory glare asking; "Where have you been Corporal Spratt?" He tried to look contrite; "I had some business to take care of." Meg's eyes flashed as she tossed her copper tresses; "And pray what business out there is more important to you than I?" Jack was flustered; "May we go to your father?" Meg stamped down the hall to the study, Jack followed sheepishly. When they reached the study Meg announced; "This miscreant was loitering outside, he insists on seeing you." Jonathan looked up, an amused smile on his face; "What is your business with me, miscreant?" Jack turned to Meg and in one motion took the ring from his pocket and slid it on the third finger of her left hand; "Will you marry me Meg?" Meg was taken aback causing her father to laugh; "Well for once young lady you're speechless." Meg recovering looked at Jack adoringly; "Oh Jack and I was so beastly to you. There is nothing I want more than to be your wife. And this is such a beautiful ring." She called for Bharti; "You must see my ring!" Bharti examined the ring and for the first time looked at Jack with what appeared to be approval; "It is a very beautiful ring Memsahib and the emerald is like your eyes." Meg looked down at the emerald flanked by two smaller diamonds; "Jack you picked this ring out to match my eyes." Jack feigned a look of surprise; "Oh I just went into the shop and asked if they had any cheap engagement rings." Meg gave out an exasperated huff; "Jack Spratt I will not stand for you teasing me this way." Jonathan laughed; "Isn't this where I come in with something about pots and kettles?" They all three dissolved into laughter. Jonathan said; "I think this definitely calls for a celebration, Bharti please bring the sherry." Bharti left the room then shortly reappeared with a tray on which there was a decanter and wine glasses. Jonathan poured sherry into three glasses handed one each to Jack and Meg then took one for himself. Hoping to stay in her good graces Jack asked; "Shouldn't we have Bharti celebrate with us?" Jonathan smiled; "I'm sure Bharti wishes you both well but she's Hindu, her religion doesn't permit her to drink alcohol." They raised their glasses and clinked them together Jonathan saying; "To the happy couple, may they always be that way." After they had drank their toast Jonathan said; "Now you two get off to your ride, I'll have some things to discuss when you get back." While they were riding across the fields at the back of the house Meg spotted Cynthia in the distance, she turned to Jack; "I just have to show Cynthia my ring!" She took off at a full gallop waving and shouting. Cynthia saw her and turned towards them, as Cynthia and Meg reined in their horses, Jack rode up on Joe saluted and greeted Cynthia with; "Good day to you Ma'am." She smiled; "And a good day to you Corporal Spratt. Meg started to gush; "I have something I simply have to show you!" The Colonels wife smiled indulgently; "What are you so excited about child?" Meg carefully pulled off her left riding glove: "Look what Jack just gave me." Cynthia's features took on a roguish look; "So he's going to make you an honest woman eh?" Meg glanced quickly at Jack; "She's only joking." Cynthia asked; "What d'ye have to tell him that for?" Meg replied; "He's sometimes too quick to defend my honor." Cynthia laughed heartily; "Well at least you've still got your honor and you've also got someone to defend it." Meg blushed; "You're incorrigible Cynthia!" Mrs. Butler laughed again; "Congratulations to both of you, Meg you've got a beautiful ring and the best bloody horseman in the Seventeenth Lancers, how many gals can say that eh?" She then wheeled her horse and rode off laughing. Meg looked at Jack; "Why aren't you smirking at her language?" Jack struggled to keep a straight face; "I think I've become used to it." Later when they dismounted at the stables Meg rounded on Jack; "You blackguard, you haven't kissed me today." Jack grinned:" I've heard old married couples get past that kind of thing after a while." Meg glared; "Well, we're not married yet and you'd do well to never get past it!" They kissed hungrily until Jack said; "You had better go into the house while I take care of the horses." When Jack entered the study Jonathan indicated for him to sit down: "Let's wait till Meg gets here, would you like another sherry?" Jack declined: 'I don't think I should have another on an empty stomach." At that point Meg came through the door, the crinoline she was wearing was the same color as her riding habit, contrasting with her hair and matching her eyes. She saw the look in Jack's eyes; "I just had to wear this gown to go with my ring." Jonathan addressed them both; "Let's talk about this party." They both looked at him in surprise; "Party?" Jonathan smiled; "Yes, an engagement party." Jack said hesitatingly; "But we leave for Woolwich a week from Wednesday. The main party's going this coming Wednesday." Jonathan nodded; "That's why we must have the party next Saturday." Meg having got over her surprise was delighted; "Oh Pappa, where are we going to have the party?" Jonathan answered; "The large reception room at the Sheridan Arms Hotel has been reserved for the event." Meg looked accusingly at her father; "You knew Jack was going to give me my ring today and you arranged a party without telling me, you old ogre." Jonathan laughed; "Well it's not completely arranged, we still have to invite guests, so who would you like to invite Meg?" She thought for a moment; "I'd like to invite Cynthia and the Colonel and that nice Captain Barry, but they'll be in Woolwich, and Aunt Letty and Cousin Jane too. But they're all so far away." Jonathan smiled; "The Butlers have already accepted as have Letty and Jane, and I'm sure Captain Barry will accept when Harry hands him the invitation on Wednesday." Meg was flabbergasted; "You have already invited the people I would want at my party? Papa, you really are an ogre, a wicked old mind reading ogre!" Jonathan's smile got wider; "Well, I didn't think of Captain Barry, and if you keep calling me names young lady, I'll invite Jack to give you that spanking he promised you last Saturday." At this they both looked at each other visibly startled. Jonathan laughed; "You two should really be more careful about what you say and do at public events." He turned to Jack; "How about you Jack, have you got some friends you'd like to invite?" Jack looked decidedly uncomfortable; "I don't know if my friends would know what to do in such fine company." Jonathan dropped his bombshell; "Chalky, Ginger and Paddy have already assured the Colonel that they will be on their best behavior and I know they will out of respect for you and Meg, who by the way; is now considered to be a daughter of the regiment." Both their jaws dropped, Meg was the first to recover; "Papa you really are an ogre, a beautiful and wonderful old ogre and I love you so much." She kissed him on the cheek; "Thank you." Jack visibly flustered stammered a shaky thank you. Then Jonathan asked him; "Is there anyone else I didn't think of that you might wish to invite?" Jack had now recovered; "Yes Sir, I'd like to invite the Riding Master and Sergeant Woodford." Jonathan thought for a moment; "Ned Perry and you are in the rear party, and the Colonel has already arranged for the lads from first troop to be with you. I'm sure he can arrange something so that we can include Sergeant Woodford." Jonathan looked enquiringly at Jack; "Is there any particular reason for inviting Perry and Woodford?" Jack looking very serious said: "Until I was sixteen I had no father, now I have three: the Riding Master, Sergeant Woodford and yourself." Jonathan beamed; "Why thank you Jack I'm flattered, have you added anyone else to your extended family?" A mischievous twinkle appeared in Jack's eyes; "Yes Sir, I also have two sweethearts." Meg's eyes flashed dangerously; "And who pray might they be Corporal Spratt?" It was now very obvious that Jack was mocking her as he answered; "Well one is the Seventeenth Lancers but I can't seem to remember who the other could be." Meg flew across the room and started beating on his chest with both fists; "Why did I leave my riding crop in the stables? Jack Spratt you are a beast!" Jack grasped both her wrists and looking into her eyes said; "And you Meg Langsbury are the best thing that ever happened to me." Jonathan discreetly left the room as they kissed.

Monday morning Harry Butler called a clerk into his office and gave him a list of names; Find these people and tell them to report to my office at 2 o'clock. Five people stood outside his door at the specified time when the RSM came out of his office. He knocked on the Colonels door, at Harry's bidding he marched them inside. After Royce had saluted Butler dismissed him and ordered the five to stand at ease; "I suppose you're wondering why you're here. Riding Master, Sergeant Woodford; Corporal Spratt has invited you to his engagement party, this event will take place at the Sheridan Arms at 6 o'clock Saturday. White, Weston, and

O'Neill you already know about your invitations and I will repeat my warning, you will comport yourselves in the manner expected of men of this regiment!" His eyes fell on Ginger: "I do not want any kind of behavior to occur that will result in a flogging. There's one more thing I am permitting all of you to ride your horses to the party. The Sheridan has an excellent ostlery, there's no reason why they can't let you stable your mounts there for a few hours." Fastening his gaze on Ginger once again he addressed the Riding Master; "Mr. Perry you will be responsible for assembling this group at half past 5 o'clock and making sure they proceed in an orderly manner. The privates will not leave barracks beforehand." He then dismissed the privates telling Perry and Woodford to stand fast; "You are two of my most trusted NCO's and I know you'll see that things go smoothly, it's going to be a most unusual evening." Woodford asked for permission to speak: "When the Beadle brought 'im inta the guardroom straight from the work'us I'd never 'ave guessed 'eed be gettin' married to a beauty like Miss Langsbury. But I knows one thing, I wishes 'im an' 'er all the best." Then as an after thought; "I come from a work'us to the regimint jes like 'im." The Colonel dismissed them with his thanks.

The banquet room where the party was to take place had a large table at one end, on which was cradled a barrel of beer. Set strategically underneath its brass spigot was a cluster of pint tankards also; there were plates and eating utensils. The rankers were the first to arrive dressed immaculately in their patrols; Perry and Woodford had made sure that they were looking their absolute best for this special evening. They had removed their hats, jackets and spurs in the hotel lobby giving them to a flunkey who couldn't comprehend why common soldiers were attending such a grand affair. They had just entered the banquet room when Jonathan appeared. He was dressed in a dark grey cut away coat with matching stirrup trousers and shiny black half boots, a crimson waistcoat and a white silk shirt with a ruffled crimson lace cravat at his throat. He strode over to the group shook hands with each one and said; "Help yourselves to the beer boys, the food will be in shortly." He then left the room to reappear with Leticia on his arm, followed by the Colonel and Cynthia after which came Meg and Jack, then Captain Barry with Jane on his arm. Jonathan walked to the center of the room to make an announcement; "It gives me great pleasure to welcome you all to this celebration of my daughter Meg's betrothal to Corporal Spratt, please charge your glasses." Perry nodded to the lads to fill their tankards while Jonathan waited until flunkeys had made sure the other guests had full glasses in their hands. Jonathan raised his glass; "Here's to Meg and Jack may they share a blissful and loving life and give me beautiful grandchildren." Then everyone echoed; "To Meg and Jack!" Meg blushed furiously; "He does things like that just to embarrass me; the old ogre!" Jonathan addressed the guests once more; "Now we have disposed of the formalities please feel free to enjoy yourselves, the hotel staff will be bringing in refreshments and they will be on hand to replenish your drinks as necessary." Colonel Butler had furnished a chamber orchestra comprised of musicians from the regiment's band to provide music for the evening. In addition to the table with the beer there was also another large table which also had plates and cutlery and a punchbowl filled with an amber liquid festooned with cups hanging from its rim. A parade of flunkeys loaded the tables with roast beef and pork, fresh baked bread, farmhouse butter and cheese. There was a great variety of pickles and chutneys, sausages and canapés. Alongside one wall were a number of small tables each with four chairs. The guests started to fill their plates from the large platters on the tables then sat at the small tables to eat. During the general movement towards the tables for refreshments Jack began observing the guests. The Colonel and Captain Barry were dressed in the height of male fashion; they had not worn uniforms as the party wasn't a military function. However, the ladies had out done themselves to look as attractive as possible. Meg was wearing her dark green silk dress with a choker and a hair ribbon of the same color. The choker had a cameo locket which Jack found out later had belonged to her mother. Her hair fastened by the ribbon cascaded down her back like sunset on a waterfall. The other ladies were also dressed to catch the eyes of the men and hopefully the envy of the other women. However, Cynthia Butler seemed to attract more attention than the others especially from the men. She wore a saffron silk crinoline with a daringly low neckline which was set off by a gold locket and chain. Her hair was piled atop her head in curls making her appear even taller than usual and her figure gave no indication that she was a mother of grown children and in her forties. While the other men in the room stole surreptitious glances; Jack stood and openly stared. He started when he heard a loud cough behind him, he turned to see Meg's eyes flashing fire; "So Corporal Spratt, you're planning to be unfaithful to me already?" Jack spluttered; "No Meg, I've never seen Mrs. Butler dressed before, damn, I mean in ladies clothes. She's always in riding togs." Meg laughed; "C'mon Jack let's go mingle with the guests. They moved over to where her father was talking to Captain Barry, Jane and Leticia. As they joined the group Jonathan asked if they were enjoying the evening. Meg replied; "This blackguard appears to have designs on Cynthia Butler." Cynthia was walking behind them on her way back to join the Colonel and overhearing laughed loudly: "Dammit if I was twenty years younger I'd tumble the young bugger. Who wouldn't like a romp in the hay with the best bloody horseman in the regiment?" Jonathan and Barry laughed raucously, Jane's face turned a deep crimson, and while Jack tried to hide his embarrassment, Meg stamped her foot in fury. Jonathan looked at Meg; "You know Cynthia is an extremely striking woman, and I'm sure Jack was only staring out of admiration." Meg drew her lips into a pout; "It's our engagement party and I'm the only woman he should be staring at!" Jack started to stammer an apology but Jonathan interrupted; "Meg, I know I've spoilt you since your mother died, but it's high time you grew out of these tantrums. And as for you Jack, you'd better take her in hand before things go too far. This is the last time I'll interfere between you two, now go out on the balcony and make up." When they were on the balcony Jack started to apologize but Meg stopped him; "Jack, I know I've been beastly to you but I love you so much I can't help myself!" Jack remembering Jonathan's admonition became more assertive; "Meg I've never been unfaithful to you and I never will, but if I can't admire an attractive woman without you throwing a fit I don't know what to do. The fact that I can appreciate another woman's good looks yet still stay faithful to you should tell you how deeply I love you." Meg now became contrite: "Jack I'm sorry, it won't happen again." Even though he knew it probably would happen again, Jack accepted her apology saying: "Lets get back to our guests; they'll wonder where we are." When they re-entered the banquet room Jack steered Meg towards the group of rankers; "Let's go and talk to the lads for a while." Meg nodded her assent and smiled as they passed Captain Barry openly flirting with her cousin. Jane was wearing a shimmering sea green dress demurely fastened at the neck with a lace collar. In contrast to her mother who was almost as striking as Cynthia in a pale mauve crinoline that exposed a considerable portion of her bosom. Letty was in deep conversation with Jonathan. Just before they reached the lads Jack asked: "Seeing as your uncle's been dead over four years, why hasn't your aunt married again?" Meg laughed; "She's convinced every suitor is after her money, of which she has great deal." When they joined the rankers Jack asked them if they were enjoying the party, as they expressed their appreciation Ginger piped up; "Fishy, this do's fit fer a king." Then Paddy chimed in; "'Tis as fine a hooley as there ever was, but nothing could be as fine as that angel you have on your arm." Meg smiled; "Well it's certain you haven't become tongue tied since last I was in your company. But as I recall Private Weston was tied back then, though not by his tongue." They all laughed except for Perry who looked puzzled so Woodford proceeded to enlighten him. They had all failed to observe the approach of the Colonel and Cynthia Butler when suddenly Perry came to attention. Looking at Jack; Colonel Butler feigned a scowl; "So you're the rascal that denied me the pleasure of having Private Weston flogged again?" Before Jack could reply, Ginger jumped in; "Zur, ee wuz only lookin' out fer a mate." Cynthia laughed, looking at Meg she commented; "If he looks after you as well as he does his horse and his mates you'll never have anything to complain about." The Colonel in a serious tone declared; "The most distasteful task my office ever requires of me is to order a flogging, and I sincerely hope I may never be required to do so again." Ginger felt the need to make a request; "Zur, I 'ad it coming but if I 'as to get annuver one, can yew get somebody that aint as strong in the arm as Sergeant Deeks to do it?" This caused them all to dissolve into laughter. As the Colonel and Cynthia moved away Ginger said in a low voice; "I don't care if ee did 'ave me flogged, the Colonel's a toff!" Meg and Jack started towards her father and Aunt Letty when Meg took Jack by surprise; "As the Colonel was so kind as to provide the musicians, I think it's only proper that we should dance!" Jack completely taken aback replied; "There are two reasons why I think that's a bad idea, one: I'm wearing riding boots, and two: I can't dance." Meg laughed; "I'll get them to play a polka, anyone can dance a polka even in riding boots." She went over to the orchestra and spoke to the bandmaster who was leading them. As she walked back they struck up a lively polka upon which she grabbed Jack's hand and swung him out onto the floor. In a few moments the Colonel and Cynthia, Jonathan and Letty and Barry and Jane were out on the floor also. After a few whirls Jack found himself getting confident with the steps and started taking the lead. The lads had put down their tankards and were clapping heartily to the music. When the polka ended everyone applauded and the dancers went over to refresh themselves at the punch bowl, while the lads upended their tankards. Although Jack's dancing skills left something to be desired Meg managed to get him on the floor for two more dances then suggested he ask Cynthia Butler to dance with him. Jack looked at her in astonishment; "There's two reasons why I won't do that; firstly she's the Colonel's wife and secondly she's four inches taller than me." Meg corrected him; "Four inches taller than I." Jack glared; "Yes teacher! And I know why you suggested I dance with her; you're trying to prove that you can trust me. Well you don't need any proof so let's drop the subject." Just then the orchestra struck up a Viennese Waltz,. Meg laughing whisked him out onto the dance floor. When the waltz was over, the ladies sat down at the tables; while the men brought drinks and refreshments to them. Satisfied that the lads had finished their sixth and final pint; the Riding Master went over to where the Colonel and Cynthia were sat; "Beggin' yer pardon Zur, me an' the boys should be getting' back to barracks." The Colonel pulled a watch from his fob pocket; "Why? It's only nine o'clock!" Perry explained; "They've 'ad six pints apiece 'an they gotta take care of the 'orses when they gets back." The Colonel returned the watch to its pocket; "I had forgotten about the horses, you have my permission, but take your leave from Mr. Langsbury and Meg before you go." Perry ushered them over to where Jonathan and Letty sat with Meg and Jack. He addressed Jonathan; "Thank yew Zur, fer 'avin me an' the lads fer the party we 'ad a real good time." Jonathan smiled in response; "Thank you for attending I'm sure your presence livened up the proceedings a little, and I know Jack appreciated your company." The Riding Master looked at Meg and Jack; "I knows I speaks for all of us when I says I 'opes yew 'as a long 'an 'appy life together. Goodnight Ma'am, Zur and Miss Meg. Corporal, I'll see yew back at the barracks." As they were leaving Jack turned to Meg; "I'll have to go soon, I'd like to be in barracks by quarter past ten." Meg looked disappointed; "Why so early darling?" Cynthia who always seemed to come within earshot at inopportune moments chimed in; "He has to

See that Nipper's safely tucked in before lights out." The Colonel who had got up with Cynthia to ask the orchestra to play a waltz laughed; "I think you have a rival there Meg." Although embarrassed Jack laughed with them; "Well he did beat Joe and Carrington last Saturday." This brought a laugh from Cynthia; "Bloody well had you there, didn't he Harry?" Jonathan felt obliged to comment; "Nipper had a damn good jockey up!" Jack noticed that Meg seemed to getting more tolerant of colorful language and wondered if the punch had anything to do with it.

After staying the night at the hotel the Colonel and Captain Barry headed back to Woolwich with Letty and Jane in Letty's carriage. The two officers took their leave from the ladies upon arriving at the barracks in Woolwich, after Barry had gained Letty's permission to call on Jane. Letty and Jane then continued on to Letty's Surrey house out on the Hemel Hempstead road Cynthia had remained at their house near the old barracks, where she was staying until they could find a suitable house in the Woolwich area.

Wednesday saw the rear party moving out, the entourage was led by Captain Metford the second in command of "A" Squadron who was flanked by the Riding Master and Sergeant Woodford. After them followed six heavily laden four in hand supply wagons. Behind the wagons came twenty-one troopers, riding in columns of three. Bringing up the rear were Jack, Chalky, Ginger and Paddy each leading a spare remount. As they rode up the High St. they were cheered by local residents lining the road. Jonathan on Joe, Meg on Sally and Cynthia on her grey mare sat watching their progress from the forecourt of the Crown; Jack noted that Meg was wearing his favorite riding habit. When the last of the entourage was passing them Meg was waving with tears coursing down her cheeks. Cynthia turned to her; "Tush girl! You'll be going to Letty's in a couple of weeks, and I'm sure he'll be calling on you every chance he gets. And let me tell you this my girl, if you're going to marry a soldier you'd better get

154

used to goodbyes." Meg looking at Jack's back sobbed; "But I'll miss him so!"

When the rear party arrived at the Woolwich barracks the Colonel was sat waiting on Carrington after returning Metford's salute he asked; "Did everything go as planned Johnny?" Metford replied; "Yes Colonel, we handed over after their advance party's inspection yesterday and left at six this morning." The Colonel nodded his approval; "So the Dragoons were happy, well done, see that the men get to eat as soon as they've taken care of the horses." Turning to the RSM who was stood nearby he ordered; "Mr. Royce, get a work detail to unload the wagons, the drivers and their mates will be going to eat after they've attended to the horses." Royce saluted; "I'll take care of that right away Sir." The Colonel returned his salute and rode off toward the new RHQ building. Now the complete regiment was in its new home where they would reside until becoming part of one of the greatest travesties in Great Britain's military history.

CHAPTER 8

WOOLWICH

THE REGIMENT'S NEW home was somewhat similar to the previous barracks except that they were red brick rather than grey limestone; the one big difference was that they were now part of a much larger garrison. The advance party had done a great deal toward having the barracks up to the standard that Butler and Royce demanded. Harry secretly congratulated himself on having the foresight to send the reconnaissance party. Their report ensured that the advance party were prepared and equipped to start getting things in order as soon as they arrived two weeks ago. Those tasks which required additional manpower were accomplished by the main party under the watchful eye of the RSM. When the rear party arrived almost everything was in place and in Royce's words; "The 17th Lancers were operating like a well oiled machine."

Immediately after Jack had finished his meal a clerk appeared to inform him that he was to report to the Colonel's office immediately after first parade the following morning. In the morning he reported to the Colonel's office as ordered and was given a letter which he was to deliver to the Duke. On handing him the letter Butler remarked; "It's not as far this time, you should be back before the midday meal. With a slight smile on his face he added, that is if you don't decide to ride to the Langsbury residence on the way back, then you would be posted as a deserter." Jack looked down and shuffled his feet. The Colonel chuckled; "Be on your way Corporal, report to me when you get back." Orders were posted and the squadrons informed on Friday morning's first parade that a week from Saturday there would be a full dress review with the garrison's commander Major General Sir William Anderson taking the salute. Ginger remarked at the midday meal; "S'pose that's to let the bloody garrison know we're 'ere. And that's gonna mean a week of fuckin' drills!" Paddy laughed; "And exactly what else did you have planned boyo?"

The parade was a resounding success with a huge turnout of civilian spectators. The General caparisoned in a red tunic with the Order of the Bath sash and star and his black fore and aft hat with a white ostrich plume was flanked by the Duke and Lt.Col. Butler in their blue and white 17th Lancer ceremonial uniforms. They inspected the troops amid loud applause from the spectators. Applause got even louder when the regiment passed in review almost drowning out the band. Jack was surprised and delighted to see Meg, Jonathan, Letty and Jane among the spectators. Before the regiment was marched off the RSM ordered them to stand fast, and asked the spectators to be silent for an announcement by Sir William. The General cleared his throat; "Your Grace, Lords, Ladies, Gentlemen and officers and men of the 17th Lancers. I thought that on this occasion it would be most appropriate to announce the promotion of Lieutenant Colonel Butler to that of Colonel." The spectators erupted in a thunderous clamor of cheering. The RSM waved his arms back and forth to silence them and finally had to resort to his parade ground bellow; "Quiet please while Sir William completes his announcement!" After they had quieted sufficiently the General continued: "Colonel Butler's title will be Commandant of the

Garrison Cavalry Training School where he will be responsible for the instruction of newly commissioned officers. He will report to me directly in all things and will be replaced by Major Hawkins the present 2/IC as interim commanding officer of the 17th Lancers." A roar of approval went up from the spectators; when the noise subsided the RSM of his own volition shouted three cheers for Colonel Butler which was taken up by everyone, the most enthusiastic being the officers and men of the regiment. As they marched off Jack caught a glimpse of Cynthia Butler and thought he saw tears running down her face, but dismissed the thought telling himself he had to be seeing things.

Jack was inside the riding school walking Nipper for his cool down when he heard Perry call attention in a loud roar, before he could look outside to see what was happening, the cause of Perry's order entered the riding school. Jack found himself confronted by the General, the Duke and Colonel Butler. He called the men inside the riding school to attention and saluted; the General returned his salute then ordered them at ease, Sir William addressed Jack; "The Colonel tells me you're Corporal Spratt and something of a legend when it comes to horsemanship." Jack came back to attention: "Permission to speak Sir?" The General granted permission: "Everything I know about horsemanship I learned from Riding Master Perry." The Duke chimed in: "There's only so much one can be taught about horsemanship the rest comes from instinct. I've seen this young bugger ride. He has that instinct; he even had to cheat to lose at chota pegs." Jack now realized that the Generals party consisted of more people than he had first observed. Behind the officers were Meg, Jonathan, Letty, Jane and Cynthia Butler, he noticed that Cynthia's eyes were red. Ned Perry was at the back of the party and Jack saw the look in his eyes when the Duke mentioned the chota peg event. The General looked around then said to the Colonel; "C'mon Harry let's see the rest of your dog and pony show." Jack called for attention and saluted as the party left, Meg stayed behind. She looked at him adoringly; "So Corporal Spratt, complimented by a Duke and a General, maybe I should kiss you to celebrate." Noticing Jack look around nervously at the privates still in the riding school she gave one of her impish laughs; "I'm not going to embarrass you, I'll see you at RHQ in half an hour, now I have to catch up." Jack looked around to see a bunch of smirking privates; "That's enough cool down, now get them fucking horses in their stalls, feed and water 'em and get busy with the curry combs. He took Nipper in to his stall and took care of his needs after which he patted his withers and wished him good afternoon. After he had left one of the privates laughed; "Talks to that bloody 'orse like its 'uman." Another private spoke up; "'Ave yew seen 'ow Nipper works wiv 'im? I think ee is part 'uman!"

When Jack reached RHQ Meg was standing outside the main entrance talking to Cynthia, before Jack arrived Cynthia went inside. When he reached Meg he asked; "Was she crying after the Generals announcement?" Meg smiled; "Yes darling that was a very emotional moment for her!" Seeing a look of puzzlement on his face she continued; "The only commission Harry Butler ever purchased was when he entered the regiment as a cornet, since then each one of his promotions has been on merit." She observed the look of respect on Jack's face as he replied; "I've always liked and respected the Colonel, there's something about him that makes you feel like you could follow him into hell if he ordered it." Meg smiled again; "Harry Butler is a wonderful darling of a man; remember the moment when you saw Cynthia crying, I don't think that happens very often." Jack voiced a thought that was in the minds of most of the members of the regiment after their elation at the Colonels promotion; "I hope Major Hawkins can purchase command of the regiment, we don't need some bloody jumped up popinjay like Cardigan taking over!" Meg's eyebrows shot up; "There you go with the cursing again; but I must agree with you." Jack was apologetic; "I'm sorry darling but the thought of having someone like Brudenell take over the regiment makes me furious." Then Meg changed the subject; "I'm hungry, is there somewhere we can go to eat?" Jack somewhat cautiously suggested The Duke of York's Arms. Meg looked at him; "Why so hesitant darling?" Jack explained; "The lads will probably be there but there's a back room where we can eat and I recommend their pork pies." Meg laughed; "I'm a daughter of the regiment, now I'm one of the lads." Jack smiled; "You don't look much like one of the lads to me."

Meanwhile a heated conversation was taking place at the barracks in the officer's mess, the Duke who was well in his cups was giving forth with a vengeance; "Unfortunately I may not have any control over who takes command of the regiment. I've used my influence as much as possible to make sure the regiment had efficient officers, but I have to battle with Horse Guards, and it's like Wellington still has the Queen's ear even 'though the old bugger's dead. If it hadn't been for the Brudenells having so much influence with the Queen; Cardigan would never have got the 11th Hussars. And then there's the bloody government." Sir William was looking decidedly uncomfortable as though he wished he were somewhere else when Cynthia felt the need to ask a question; "Why was the Duke of Wellington so much in favor of purchasing commissions?" Cambridge harrumphed; "God knows! Napoleon didn't have any officers who bought their commissions." The General felt he should contribute to the discussion; "But Wellington defeated Napoleon at Waterloo." The Duke gave an even louder harrumph; "He did well enough in Portugal and Spain but he never faced old Boney in the field directly until Waterloo and then it took a bloody Prussian to pull his irons out of the fire." Sir William felt the need contradict the Duke; "I think Wellington would have prevailed without the Prussians anyway." This time the Duke didn't even bother to harrumph; "Bullshit! If it hadn't been for Blucher and his artillery we'd all be eating frog's legs and snails." Colonel Butler thought that it was time to steer the conversation in another direction;

"Your Grace, Sir William, with all due respect I think it's time to agree to disagree." The Duke snorted I suppose you're right Harry. Sorry Billy, I shouldn't have got so hot under the collar." Then he turned to Colonel Butler laughing; "Can't wait till you're a general eh Harry? Becoming a bloody politician already." This caused them all to dissolve into laughter and relieved the tension considerably. The General was to confide in Harry later; "The way he expresses his views about the government and the court; I think he'd be in the tower if he weren't the Queens uncle."

When Meg and Jack were seated at their table in the back room of The Duke of York's Arms a serving girl brought in a trencher loaded with pork pies, new baked bread, farmhouse butter and cheese, pealed raw onions and pickled onions. Jack ordered a pint of beer for himself and a half pint for Meg, after the girl had left Meg asked: "How are we going to eat all this?" Jack replied; "I'll send what's left into the lads." Hearing the increasing noise from the public bar, Jack smiled and looked at Meg; "Sounds like the lads are already getting started on the evening." Meg looked at him archly; "Maybe you'd like to be back there with them? I can hear some girls." Jack's eyes grew cold; "I'll say this to you just one more time, I love you and there's no one else, nor will there ever be. If you persist in making such inferences I might wonder if you can be trusted!" Meg looked contrite; "Once again I'm sorry darling; it's just that there's some demon in me that likes to tease you." Jack's countenance lightened; "Maybe that spanking I promised you might exorcise that demon?" Meg laughed; "When you decide to carry out your threat pray that my riding crop's not within my reach." Just then the door opened and Chalky's head appeared; "Thought you might be here mate, hello Miss nice to see yew ag'in." Meg smiled at him and said; "When we've finished eating we'd like to come and join you." Chalky smiled back; "We'd luv to 'ave yew Miss Meg, but I don't know if a lady should be mixing wiv us lot." Meg decided to give them both something to think about; "If I'm to be a daughter of the regiment I'll bloody well drink with my regiment!" The looks on both their faces especially Jacks caused her to go into peals of laughter. When he was finally able to speak Jack stammered; "I never heard you cuss before, I thought you didn't like cursing." Meg was still laughing as she said; "I don't but I thought it might get your attention and make you realize that I mean what I say." After they were done with their meal Meg insisted they join the lads in the public bar. When Paddy saw them come through the door he exclaimed; "There's me darling angel so it is, where's the other saints? For this has to be heaven I'm in!" Ginger grinned; "There ee goes with the bull…. blarney agin." They spent about an hour with the lads who stayed on their best behavior in deference to Meg who was now drinking beer out of a pint mug much to Jack's chagrin. When Jack suggested they leave Meg was reluctant; "Darling I'm having such a good time with the lads, can't we stay?" Jack drew her attention to a group of local girls who'd stayed across the other side of the room while Meg and Jack had been drinking with the lads; "If the boys don't get back to those girls soon, they'll be leaving for the Gunners Arms where the Artillery will take care of them." Realization came to Meg; "Oh, we've been getting in the way." Jack explained; "There are two things a soldier thinks about when he's got money in his pocket, drinking and whoring and those lads were paid today." Meg's demon took over as with an impish smile she said; "And didn't you get paid today Corporal Spratt?" Jack was angry; "You're the only woman I want!" Meg feigned anger; "So I'm to be your whore now?" Jack pushed her through the door waving goodbye to the lads as they left. Once outside Jack turned on her in a fury; "I have never had a woman in my life. The first time I had the opportunity I was so scared of getting the French pox I ran away. Then I met you and since then you are the only woman in my life. I have been tempted from time to time and have not always found it easy to resist, but you are so dear to me I could never give into my desires." Meg was genuinely contrite, with tears running down her cheeks she made her apology; "Jack darling I will never say anything like that again, please forgive me." Jack took her into his arms;"Meg darling when I get angry with you I think it hurts me as much as it must hurt you; let's try not to hurt each other from now on."

As Jack and Meg left the girls rejoined the lads one who's name was Daisy asked Ginger; "Wuz that corp'rl one of them gentlemen rankers?" Gingers reply surprised her; "Nah, ee wuz born in a work'us an' run away w'en ee wuz sixteen." Daisy had another question; "Wot abaht 'er?" Ginger answered; "She's a real lady, it's 'er that learned 'im to talk proper." Daisy's comment of; "I'll be buggered!" Brought a laugh from Ginger; "Maybe I can 'elp yew wiv that?" Daisy's reply brought laughter from everyone within earshot; "Yew bloody donkey wallopers spends so much time lookin' at the back end of the 'orse in front of yer, all yew can think of is arse!"

As Jack and Meg walked back toward the barracks hand in hand she caused him to pause in his stride; "Jack I want us to get married soon." Jack turned to look at her under a gaslight; "So do I, but your father said we have to wait, and where would we live?" As they started walking again Meg said; "Well I've got all day tomorrow to try to talk Papa around oh, and by the way you're invited to Aunt Letty's for dinner tomorrow night." Jack stopped again; "Meg I have no way of getting there." Meg smiled; "She's sending her carriage for you." Jack looked alarmed; "I can't be seen getting into a carriage in front of the barracks!" Meg was still smiling; "I thought of that, just walk down the road and around the corner. It'll be waiting there at 5 o'clock." They had continued walking again when Jack asked; "When will I see you again?" Meg replied; "Oh, sometime next week I expect." Jack was surprised; "But aren't you going back with your father?" Meg shook her head; "No I'm enrolling at the finishing school on Tuesday, Papa will be going back Monday morning but I'll be staying with Aunt Letty." Jack could not resist teasing her; "Isn't that were they'll teach you to be a proper lady?" She turned on him; "Are you inferring that I'm not a proper lady Corporal Spratt?" He grinned; "Anyone who'd seen you drinking beer out of a pint mug could have been forgiven for having their doubts." At this they both burst into laughter, and they were both still laughing when they entered the main gate of the barracks. As they reached the guardroom Jack went inside and found Woodford sitting behind the desk: "Hello Sarge, d'ye know where the Duke's party is?" "Woodford tried to look grim; "So yew bin out gallivatin' while I'm stuck 'ere doin' guard sergeant duty, and now yer gonna jine the toffs! Well they're all in the officer's mess." Jack smiled; "You know I can't go in the mess, I just want to get Miss Meg back to her father, but if you'd like to talk to the Duke maybe he'll make me an officer so that I can go in with her?" Sergeant Woodford growled; "Get on yer way yew cheeky young bugger afore I 'as yew locked in a cell."

The Duke had declared that it was to be ladies night so they all ate dinner in the mess while discussing the day's events. The General made many favorable comments about the regiments appearance and drill as well as complimenting Colonel Butler on the improvements that had been made to the barracks. The Duke with his customary lack of tact commented;"Billy, if you'd spent enough time with the regiment you'd see the way things should be done! Harry here maintains the highest degree of discipline with the least amount of corporal punishment. His officers and rankers would follow him through the gates of hell and still look smartly dressed when they vanquished the devil and his minions!" The General then observed that he had detected a definite atmosphere of "esprit de corps" among the troops. The Duke reluctant to drop the subject added; "That's where you see the difference, there's not one man in the 11th Hussars that wouldn't stick his saber clean up Cardigan's arse if he thought he could get away with it." Sir William anxious to change the subject turned to Colonel Butler; "I meant to ask you about this during the inspection tour; you have a number of hip baths installed in every squadron's wash house." Harry pleased to enlarge on one of his pet projects replied; "Yes Sir William, there's a great deal of empirical evidence indicating that personal cleanliness reduces the likelihood of vermin and disease. The men are required to bathe at least once a week and to keep their hair cut short. But I won't be satisfied till I can get the rankers to brush their teeth every day." Cynthia couldn't resist a comment; "Jonathan's daughter got Spratt to brush his teeth, I heard he does 'em twice a day." The Duke laughed; "There you are Harry, recruit Meg Langsbury and appoint her hygiene officer. But seriously it wasn't until Harry showed me some of the scientific evidence from the Royal Society that I became convinced. Until then I thought the only reason for bathing and brushing your teeth was to smell good and look nice." It was Jonathan's turn to laugh; "I think if you made Meg an officer in the Seventeenth you'd have a mutiny on your hands within a week, have you seen how she treats Corporal Spratt?" Cynthia could hardly wait to comment; "Just goes to show how much you know Jonathan! She is adored by every man jack of the rankers, that's why they adopted her."

When they arrived at the officer's mess they found Letty's carriage in front together with the footman and driver who were both leaning on the boot smoking pungent smelling churchwarden pipes. They both doffed their hats to Meg and good evenings were exchanged. When they reached the door Meg kissed him, when Jack wished her goodnight and turned to leave Meg pulled him back saying; "D'ye really think you're going to leave after just one kiss?" They were still kissing when Cynthia Butler appeared; "You'd better get inside young lady they require your company. Damn! there's never a bucket of water handy when I need one." As she turned to go back inside Meg kissed Jack hastily; "I'll see you tomorrow darling." She then hurried after Cynthia. When she entered the dining room the men stood while Captain Barry pulled a chair out for her. When they were all seated Jonathan looked over at Meg; "Have you eaten Meg dear?" She replied; "Yes Papa we had a wonderful meal at The Duke of York's Arms." Jonathan asked is that a hotel?" The General laughed; "It's a tavern the other side of town from The Gunners Arms." Jane looked alarmed; "You mean a public house, whatever kind of food do they serve in such a place?" Meg laughed merrily and proceeded to describe the fare of which their repast had consisted. As Jane's nose wrinkled Cynthia exclaimed; "From what I saw outside a couple of minutes ago I hope you both ate the onions." The General cleared his throat; "I eat there quite frequently the landlord's wife bakes the most delicious pork pies I've ever tasted. And by the way the landlord Gus Davidson is an old cavalryman, 3rd Dragoon Guards I think." The Duke harrumphed; "Damn Billy, why didn't you tell me about this place before, you have to take me there sometime." Sir William smiled; "I've eaten at your house Your Grace, I didn't think you'd be interested in something as humble as a tavern pork pie." The Duke harrumphed again; "Good food is good food no matter where it's served." The General addressed the table; "Next time any one of you are in this part of town I will be happy to take you there for a meal." Meg looked at Cynthia; "We sent a lot of our food into the public bar for the lads. Poor Jack, he was dying to eat a pickled onion but he was waiting to for me to eat one first; I kept him waiting forever, but I finally gave in." Jane giggled; "Oh Meg, you are incorrigible!" Cynthia remarked; "That's what she says about me."

When Jack signed out at the guardroom at quarter to five Sunday afternoon the guard sergeant; Sergeant Wilkins of "B" Squadron commented; "Yew're spiffed up good enuff fer a gen'ral's inspection." Jack laughed shakily; "I think this evening is going to be a sight more nerve wracking Sarge." He strode briskly down the road and around the corner where he found Letty's carriage waiting. The footman put two fingers up to his forehead then opened the door and pulled down the steps. Jack stepped up into the carriage and sat back into the plush velvet seat. As the driver urged the four in hand down the Hemel Hempstead road he thought to himself; "Who'd have thought three years ago I'd be sitting in a fancy carriage on my way to dinner at a fine country house? Not that bloody workhouse master that's for certain!" After about a half hour they turned off the road, through a pair of open wrought iron gates and followed a graveled driveway lined by Lombardy poplars to the house. The carriage came to a halt in front of a three story Tudor style mansion. When the footman opened the door and drew down the steps Jack stepped down from the carriage then stood and stared in awe. Although he had seen many large houses since coming to London including the Duke's mansion, he'd never seen one surrounded by gardens, lawns and trees. He was standing and staring in awe when Meg came flying out through the huge doors and down the steps, and with total disregard of the on looking footman and driver threw herself in his arms. Jack let out a loud oof; "Steady Meg, you knocked the wind out of me." Before he could say anymore she was kissing him, then she grabbed his arm and began to pull him up the steps. She led him through a palatial reception area then through a door into a large library. In the library were seated Letty, Jonathan and another very attractive woman. Jack hastily took off his hat which he had failed to remove before; due to Meg's hurried behavior. Letty greeted him; "Good evening Corporal Spratt you and I were introduced at your engagement party so you know I am Meg's Aunt Leticia. My dear brother Jonathan has told me many good things about you." Indicating the woman seated at Jonathan's side she continued; "May I intro- duce Lady Hermione Willoughby, Lady Willoughby please meet Corporal Spratt." Jack gave a slight bow; "It's a pleasure to meet you; Your Ladyship." Hermione replied; "From what I've heard the pleasure should be all mine. Cynthia Butler absolutely raves about you!" Jonathan laughed; "Now, now Hermione you'll make Meg jealous." Meg seized the opportunity to turn attention away from herself; "Papa has been discretely seeing Lady Hermione for some time now, and he thought he'd surprise me by introducing us today. What he didn't know is I have known for quite a while, and Hermione and I have become good friends." Letty suddenly aware that Jack was still stood stiffly to attention said; "I'm sorry young man please sit down." She indicated a chair that was much like those in Jonathans study. After he was seated she suggested; "How about a drop of sherry while we wait for dinner? Jane went into the city with Captain Barry and they will join us after dinner" A servant appeared as if by magic carrying a tray on which was a decanter of sherry and glasses. When they had all been served Hermione addressed Jack; "So young man, from what Meg tells me you have a very interesting history." Jack visibly uncomfortable replied hesitantly; "Well Ma'am, I don't know if you would call it interesting but it was never dull." Hermione laughed; "From what Jonathan has told me it was far from dull." The next half hour was taken up with small talk until just before the dinner gong sounded when Hermione asked Jack what he thought about the Colonels promotion. Jack's reply was guarded; "I think no one deserves it more than Colonel Butler, but the regiment will miss him. We're all hoping Major Hawkins will be our next Commanding Officer." Just then the dinner gong sounded and Letty's butler appeared to usher them into the dining room where Jack was greeted with the dazzling sight of Letty's table. There were place settings for each guest at which was an array of eating utensils, a knapkin and glass of water and a glass of wine. Letty went to the head of the table where the butler pulled out her chair; servants did the same for Meg and Hermione. Before the men could be seated Letty raised her glass; "Gentlemen please remain upstanding, I have a toast. To Her Majesty the Queen, God bless her!" They all raised their glasses and echoed; "God bless her!" When the men were seated the servants brought round the first course. Although Meg had worked diligently on Jack's etiquette she whispered to him; "Remember work from the outside in, just follow my lead." After the third course Letty tapped her wine glass with a spoon; "Honored guests, before dessert is served my brother wishes to make an announcement." Jonathan stood up and looked around the table; "I have in fact two announcements if you would please bear with me. First, I have asked Hermione to marry me; she graciously accepted and we plan to celebrate our nuptials in June." Jonathan looked over at Meg and smiled at her look of astonishment; "You didn't know about that, did you daughter?" Meg jumped out of her chair; hugged Lady Hermione then kissed her father's cheek; "I am so very, very happy for both of you." While she was returning to her seat Letty and the guests were expressing their congratulations. Jonathan remained standing and with a look on his face that could only be described as that on the face of the cat that ate the canary continued; "Last but definitely not least, after much consideration I have decided to give my full blessing to Meg and Jack and grant permission for them to marry at their convenience." He looked at Meg and smiled at the look of astonishment on her face, then looked startled as Jack stood up and in a choking voice begged Letty's permission to leave the table. He ran out of the dining room, Meg looking alarmed ran after him. When she caught up with him he was looking out of a window his shoulders heaving while sobbing softly. Meg pulled on his arm and when he turned to face her there were tears coursing down his cheeks she asked: "Jack darling whatever is wrong?" Jack got himself partly under control; "On the way here today I was thinking about the workhouse and the blokes I knew back there, things like how Nipper died without ever really having a life. When your father gave his permission for us to marry just now, I thought why have I been blest with all this happiness when the people I left behind are doomed to a life of hell?" Meg wrapped her arms around him; "That one person, like yourself, was able to leave that life behind is a small triumph. You should not feel guilty for your good fortune, I know if you could help any of those poor unfortunates you would." Jack drew his shoulders back; I'm sorry I made such a damn fool of myself. I hope I didn't cause your aunt and her guests too much embarrassment." Meg gripped his arm: "Let's rejoin the guests and let me do the talking." As they walked back into the dining room Meg addressed Letty and her guests; "Jack begs your forgiveness, he was overcome with Papa's announcement and felt that the company might be embarrassed by seeing him show emotion." Letty smiled; "I think I speak for everyone present when I say there's nothing to forgive." Jack replied shakily; "You're too kind Ma'am, you are all too kind and I'll endeavor to keep my feelings under control from now on." Meg looked at her father; "Oh! Papa I didn't thank you." She came up behind Jonathans chair and threw her arms around his neck kissing him on the back of the head; "You are the nicest, kindest old ogre there ever was." Now they were all seated and Letty said; "While we are enjoying dessert you young people can start thinking about a wedding date." After dessert Letty suggested the men repair to the drawing room while the ladies retire to the library. She informed Jonathan and Jack; "There's port wine and cheese and also a humidor of cigars. We ladies have wedding plans to discuss." When Jack and his father in law to be were comfortably settled in overstuffed leather chairs with their glasses of port, Jonathan smoking a cigar while Jack munched on cheese; Jonathan apologized for causing Jack discomfort with his announcement. Jack responded; "Sir you shouldn't blame yourself I think it was something that's been building up in me for a long time. If you think about where I was three years ago and what's happened to me since then, how many people have ever been so lucky? I got away from the workhouse, the magistrate sent me to the regiment instead of prison, I got promoted so's I could do the job I love most and, well you know Meg and all. Everything has been so far beyond anything I ever imagined. And I'm afraid, afraid something may happen to take it all away. If I lost Meg I wouldn't want to live!" Jonathan sighed; "I thought my life was ended when Meg's mother died, it was only the realization that I had a child who needed me that prevented me from giving up on life. The irony of it is that I came to find that I needed Meg more than she needed me. One thing I want you to promise me Jack, you'll never give up on yourself whatever happens; for Meg's sake as well as your own. Jack solemnly assured him; "You have my promise Sir, and I'll do everything I can to make Meg happy." Before Jonathan could reply Captain Barry came into the room. Jack came up out of his chair to attention. Barry waved him down; "Don't let's stand on ceremony this evening Corporal." Turning to Jonathan he said; "I rented a landau and took Jane into the city. Damned if I didn't propose to her on the way back. When I took her in to join the ladies I found out what you two had been up to, looks like we've got an epidemic on our hands." Jonathan laughed: "Did you get Letty's blessing?" The Captain looked bemused; "Yes and I was surprised how happy she was to grant it." Jonathan laughed again; "Even though she's known your family for years she's been making enquiries since Meg's engagement party, you must have passed muster. Pour yourself some port and join us." After a while they rejoined the ladies and Jack thanked Letty for her hospitality and suggested that he should be leaving soon. Meg protested; "Jack, the evenings still young; surely you can stay a while longer." Jack answered regretfully; "It's a half hour to the barracks and half hour back, I'm sure the driver and the footman would like to get back and have some time to themselves." Then Jane spoke up; "They'll just go down to the village pub, that's what those kinds of people do." Jack's voice was cold; "Begging your pardon Miss Jane, but I'm those kinds of people." Then he softened his tone;"I'm sorry I didn't mean to offend but that's where my origins are." Jane was looking contrite but before she could say anything further Letty spoke up; "You're quite right young man, since going to that fancy boarding school Jane sometimes tends to forget her origins. Her father's family were watermen; they plied the Thames for fares. It was her great grandfather that started our merchant fleet with a decommissioned old sloop he bought from the navy." Jane was contrite; "I'm sorry Jack, I was getting above myself." Jack smiled I'm sure it was just a slip of the tongue Miss Jane, I think we should forget all about it." Jane smiled; "I'd like that, I would also like if you were to cease from calling me Miss Jane. If we are to be related I think Jane will suffice." Jack said his goodbyes and turned to the door when Meg spoke up; "Where are you going Jack, do you not want me to see you to your carriage?" Jack laughed; "It's not my carriage, and yes you do have my permission to see me to the carriage." Meg bristled; "Permission, permission you say! Now who's getting above themselves?" The whole company was laughing as they exited the library. When they got to the carriage Meg asked Jack when they should get married. When Jack said he'd leave it up to her she got impatient; "Jack Spratt, do I have to make all the decisions? This is something we should decide together." Jack's answer did nothing to improve her demeanor; "I'd marry you tonight if I could." Meg was exasperated; "You know that's not possible. On Saturday we must sit down and decide on a date." Jack thought for a moment; "I have to find a way to get here." Meg smiled; "I'll come to you." Seeing the puzzled look on his face; she continued Papa's coming back on Friday, I've given him a list of things I need for Bharti to pack and he's bringing Sally." Jack kissed her then got into the carriage. Before the footman closed the door he said; "Tell the driver to stop after he turns onto the road." When they reached the road the driver halted his team and Jack shouted for the footman to come down off the back. When he appeared Jack said; "Get inside I could use some company." The footman started to protest; "We aint allowed inside Guvn'r." Jack grinned; "You are today and if they find out I'll take the blame." The footman climbed in somewhat hesitantly saying; "I 'opes she don't find out, Miz Jane's real strict about usn's knowing our place." On the ride back to Woolwich Jack plied the footman with myriad questions about Aunt Letty and her family. She had been married to Jasper Harvey who had inherited the family shipping business which was founded by his grandfather the son of a Thames waterman. He had started the enterprise with an old decommissioned Royal Navy sloop. Jasper had taken passage on one of his ships to negotiate some business in India. The ship went down with all hands except one survivor when they ran into a storm in the Bay of Biscay. The lone survivor claimed that Jasper (an accomplished seaman) had taken the ship's wheel but too late. She had already sprung her seams on the windward beam and taken on too much water. The weight of the water on one side of the ship capsized her in minutes.

Around the corner from the barracks Jack got down from the carriage and walked to the main gate. When he entered the guardroom to sign in, Sergeant Wilkins looked up from the desk to see the radiant expression on Jack's face; "Blimey Corporal, yew looks like the Queen made yew a bloody lord!" Jack smiled; "I was made a king and I'll soon have a queen of my own." Wilkins shook his head and turned to the Corporal of the Guard; "That poor young bugger's in love." Jack was on his way to RHQ barracks when he ran into a distraught Ginger; "Fishy yew gotta 'elp me!" The smile on Jack's face turned in to a look of impatience; "What have you done now Ginger?" Ginger started mumbling something about girls and babies. Jack snapped at him; "Speak up and control yourself!" Then Ginger told his story; "We wuz in the Duke of York's an' one of the girls sez; "Your names Ginger aint it?" Wen I told 'er it wuz she said I got 'er cousin in the family way." Jack shook his head; "I thought you'd used up all the different ways to get in trouble; but you had to go and find one more." Ginger said; "I'm sorry mate, but she's got two big bruvvers and 'er pop's a blacksmith." Jack asked and what's this girl's name?" Ginger looked sheepish; "It's Molly from the Crown back by our old barracks." Jack gave an exasperated sigh; "Why did I ever bother with you, does she know you're here?" Ginger was looking down at his boots; "The girl in the Duke's old man is a carter ee goes dahn there twice a week." Jack exclaimed; "There's only one thing to be done, Ginger, you have to marry her." Ginger looked terrified; "On a privates pay?" Jack replied; "Give the baby a name and hope her family will take care of her. You can send her half your pay every week." Ginger started whining; "But I don't wanna marry 'er, Fishy." Jack was angry; "If she was good enough for you to fuck, she's good enough for you to marry! I'll talk to Woodford and see if he can get you some leave, then you can go back there with the carter and take care of things." Ginger was still whining; "Alf me bloody pay, I aint marrying no bint an' givin' away 'alf me fuckin' pay." Jack was furious; "If you don't marry that girl and help support her and the baby, just what d'ye think's going to happen?" Ginger shook his head; "I don't know, maybe someone else is its favver." Jack exploded; "With all the blokes she's been with I'm sure at least one makes more money than a bloody cavalry private. She has no reason to lie, and let me tell you what's most likely to happen to her if you don't do the right thing, her family will throw her out in the street. She'll probably end up in a workhouse where the baby will be born, and neither of them will ever have a decent life. Before I let that happen I'll stick a lance so far up your arse the point will be picking your fucking nose!" Ginger became defensive; "Yew came from a work'us an' yew done alright." Jack was at the end of his tether; "And you came from Newgate Prison and we've both been fucking lucky. You'll do what's right, or after I've beaten the shit out of you I'll never have anything to do with you again!" The following morning after church parade Jack went over to 'A' Squadron and told Woodford about Ginger's predicament. Woodford smiled at first then became more serious; "Yew know wot usually 'appens. If they comes lookin' fer 'em we 'ides 'em an' sez they bin posted somewheres else." Jack showed his concern; I'm afraid the girl and her baby will end up in a workhouse, I've been there and if we can stop that happening I think we should." Woodford smiled again; "Corpr'l Spratt, yer a connivin' young bastard! yew knew I come from a work'us; an'like yew don't wanna see any uvver poor bugger 'av to go there."

Monday morning as first parade was dismissed, Perry told Jack to report to the Colonels office. After he presented himself Butler ordered him at ease: "Well Corporal Spratt, I've heard there's going to be a wedding soon." Jack looked puzzled; "How did you know Sir?" The Colonel smiled; "Captain Barry spilled the beans." Jack tried to be evasive; "You'll have to ask Captain Barry and Miss Jane or Mr. Langsbury and Lady Hermione." The Colonel was still smiling; "Don't be coy with me Corporal; I'm talking about you and Meg." Jack's face reddened; "When I asked Meg to decide on a date she said we should make the decision together." The Colonel laughed out loud; "That sounds like Meg, but you know it'll be her decision in the end." This caused Jack to smile; "I knew from the beginning it would be, but I thought it better to play along." The Colonel laughed again; "I'm going to miss you Corporal but when I go up to Brigade I'll know I left a good man behind." Jack came to attention expecting to be dismissed when Butler waved his hand; "At ease man I've not done with you, I understand that you've arranged for Private Weston to share the same grim fate as yours." Jack grinned; "He's a good bloke really Sir, he just needs someone to keep him on the right track." The Colonels response startled Jack; "He needs to learn to think with his head like you, instead of his pecker." Are you going to his wedding?" Jack grinned again; "He's asked me to be best man." Butler nodded; "Just let The Riding Master know when, I'm sure he'll give you leave. You're dismissed Corporal." Jack came to attention and saluted; "Thank you Sir."

Saturday noon Jack was just leaving the stables after attending to Nipper's needs when a clerk from RHQ approached him; "Corp; "Guard Sergeant said there's two civvy's to see you, ee sent 'em to HQ block." When Jack arrived he was greeted by the sight of Meg wearing his favorite riding habit securing Sally to the hitching rail. She had her back to him as he came up behind her

stealthily and grasped her around the waist. She swung around
with her riding crop held high and then she gasped; "Jack Spratt,
I should go ahead and whip you; you scared me half to death!"
Jack laughed, and then a thought came to him; "Did you ride
here from your aunt's on your own?" Meg's eyes took on an impish sparkle; "Oh yes, it was such a pretty April day I really enjoyed
the ride." Jack was angry; "Don't ever do that again, you don't
know who you might meet up with on the road!" She laughed;
"No silly, Aunt Letty made me bring along a groom, he's stopped
to talk to a lancer he knew from their home village." Jack smarting
from being teased said; "It's not too late for that spanking!" Meg
laughed again her eyes turning to her riding crop; "Try it now
Corporal Spratt and I'll give you a good horse whipping." They
smiled at each other then Jack took her into his arms. He was
just about to kiss her when the sound of someone clearing their
throat came from the main door of RHQ. Jack looked up to see
the RSM on the top step looking down at them: "Corporal Spratt
come with me to my office, looking at Meg he said we won't be
long Miss." Inside his office he looked Jack up and down; "What
the bloody hell d'ye think you were doing out there?" Jack tried to
justify his behavior but everything came out in a jumble of words;
fiancée, not seen in a week, love and various other garbled mut-
terings. Royce continued; "You don't stand outside RHQ behaving like the regimental barracks is a fucking knocking shop!" Jack
already at attention apologized; "I'm sorry Sir, it won't happen
again." Royce growled; "Bloody right it won't happen again, now
get out of my sight and take that young lady somewhere nice for
the rest of the day." When Jack got outside he noticed that the
groom had arrived mounted on a dapple grey hunter, then he
saw Ginger; "Hey Ginger come over here." When Ginger got
to them he was given instructions; "Take these two horses, then
he looked at the groom, Meg interjected; "His name is Albert."
and Albert and you can feed and water 'em. Take off their saddles and tack and curry them if needs be." Meg protested; "But

Jack, Ginger probably wants to go out with the lads." He looked at her with a grim smile; 'Ginger's confined to barracks. Sergeant Woodford said it's wrong for a man who's about to get married to go whoring in public houses." Meg looked startled; "When, how, where?" Jack smiled; "I'll tell you all about it later. Right now I have to get bathed and change into my patrols before I take you anywhere." Meg put on her impish smile once more; "Would you like me to help you darling?" Jack sighed; "That spanking is getting closer all the time." Meg laughed; "I still have my riding crop. Oh, and I need to have somewhere to wait for you. Papa said to give his regards to Colonel Butler, would it be proper if I went in to see him?" Jack replied; "Let me ask the RSM first." He went into RHQ, knocked on Royce's door and acquainted him with Meg's request. After relaying her request to the Colonel, the RSM returned to tell Jack that the Colonel would be happy to receive her. He walked to the main door with Jack then said; "Go on about your business, I'll see the young lady to the Colonels office." After knocking on the door Royce entered with Meg saying; "Miss Langsbury to see you Sir." Harry stood up and smiled; "Thank you Mr. Royce, please be seated Meg. To what do I owe this pleasure?" Meg turned on a winsome smile; "Well Colonel I rode in to see Jack oh, and Papa sends his regards." A look of concern came to Butler's face; "Did you make that ride alone?" Meg still smiling said; "No Colonel, Aunt Letty made me bring a groom along, coincidentally Jack asked me the same question." Harry smiled; "I wouldn't expect anything less from him, that young man adores you. And what are your plans for this afternoon?" Meg put on a conspiratorial smile; "After a nice walk we'll go to the Duke of York's and enjoy some delicious pork pies." The Colonel nodded; "It appears that Corporal Spratt has a pleasant afternoon planned for you both." Meg laughed; "He doesn't know yet." It was the Colonels turn to laugh; "I have mixed feelings about the two of you. On the one hand I'm happy for you both, and on the other I feel sorry for that young man, where you're

concerned he doesn't know whether he's on his head or his heels."
Meg still smiling regarded the Colonel intently; "I know I can
trust you never to tell him, but Jack knows exactly what I'm doing
and when I go too far I'm sure he'll put his foot down." Harry
shook his head; "If you can read men that well at your age I dread
to be around when you're as old as Cynthia, please don't tell her
I ever made any reference to her age." Meg gave a tinkling laugh;
"Why Colonel, it seems you've given me something to hold over
your head." Butler shook his head; "It's not hard to see why you
have poor Corporal Spratt all at sixes and sevens." They continued
with small talk for a few minutes when the Colonel hesitantly
brought up the topic of Jonathans impending marriage; "Please
convey my congratulations to your father on his upcoming nuptials." He looked intently into her eyes for a reaction. Meg's laugh
filled his office; "Why bless you Colonel, you want to know if I
approve." The Colonel thought to himself;" good God this girl
can read minds!" Then to Meg; "It's just that you and your father
have been together for so long I thought you…" His voice trailed
off. Then Meg interjected; "That I might be jealous?" The Colonel
continued; "It's just been you and your father for seven years, I
thought you might feel some resentment." Meg smiled; "Colonel
Butler you're an old darling to be so concerned. But I'm really very
happy for him, for them both. And Hermione is an absolutely
wonderful companion for him." Harry smiled a smile of relief;
"I think that young man should be back by now, and Meg, my
heartiest congratulation to both of you." With that the Colonel
turned around in his chair and looked out of the window; "There
he is all bright and shiny like a new button. I'll tell you something
Meg; I think he would have made a good soldier anyway, but
you've helped him to become a fine young man." Meg blushed;
"You give me far too much credit Colonel." Meg stood up; "With
your permission I would like to join him." Laughing as he came
to his feet Harry could not resist saying; "My dear Meg you don't
need my permission but I'm very flattered, I doubt if few men or

any man have had you ask their permission." Meg hurried to join Jack; her tinkling laughter echoing through the corridor.

Jack entered the guardroom and signed out. Sergeant Braithwaite of 'C' Squadron was Guard Commander; "Where you off to Corporal?" Jack smiled; "I'm going walking with the most beautiful girl in the world!" As he left the guardroom Meg came up beside him and put her arm through his, she asked; "Where are we going darling?" Jack thought for a minute; "We haven't seen much of Woolwich yet; why don't we both do some exploring?" They strolled around the garrison town for close to an hour. When they passed the Gunners Arms Meg said; "It sounds like the lads are having a good time." Jack shook his head; "Not our lads, that's the Artillery boys. Our lads will be at the Duke." Meg was curious; "Why not our boys?" Jack's answer took her by surprise; "The Colonel ordered that any lancer caught fighting in public is to be flogged. By staying away from The Gunners Arms they make it less likely for them to have a problem with the Artillery." Meg was incensed; "That hardly seems fair! Why should our boys not be able to drink in the Gunners?" Jack replied; "The Artillery's been here a lot longer than us, and they've been using that pub for a long time. They consider it their territory and if any of our lads were in there it would be just a matter of time before there was a fight." Meg, her indignation somewhat diffused demurred; "Yes, I suppose that makes sense." Jack felt compelled to say something more; "Some of the lads know what a flogging feels like and we all saw Ginger get his back at the old barracks, and I think we should change the subject to something more suitable for a beautiful lady's ears."

They were seated in the back room of The Duke of York's Arms waiting for their food to be served when Chalky came through the door; "Guess what Fishy. Oh! 'ello Miss." Jack glared at him; "What?" Chalky grinned; "We're 'avin Lewis's farewell bash." Jack softened his expression; "Corporal Lewis? I didn't know he was time expired." Chalky's face was one big grin; "Yeah and their promotin' me to Troop Copr'." The announcement brought a smile to Jack's face; "Congratulations Chalky you deserve it. When we've eaten we'll come in and have a drink with the boys." As he was leaving Meg called out; "Congratulations Chalky." She barely heard his "thank yew Miss" over the noise from the Public Bar. Their appetites sharpened by the long walk and the fresh air; they did full justice to their meal. While they were enjoying their repast Jack brought up the subject of their marriage date. Meg asked; "What date would you suggest darling?" Jack feigned thoughtful concentration for a while then suggested a date in May. Meg looked surprised; "But isn't that rather soon?" Jack replied; "I know but it's a Saturday and it's also your birthday." Meg nodded her assent; "I'll tell Papa as soon as I get back to Aunt Letty's tonight." As they were finishing their drinks Meg laughed; "Poor Sally she'll hardly be able to carry me home with all this pork pie I've eaten." Jack said; "Let's have a quick one with the boys then get you back to the barracks. I want you back at your aunt's before dark." They joined the lads in the public bar where they raised their glasses to Chalky's.promotion and Lewis's retirement. Jack had acquainted Meg with the circumstances of Ginger's upcoming marriage during their walk. Her eyes surveyed the room; "Which girl is the cousin of Ginger's bride to be?" Chalky pointed to Molly's cousin; "'Er names Binnie." Meg walked over to her; "Please give my best wishes to your cousin on her pending marriage." Binnie grinned: "If it 'adn't bin fer yer bloke she wouldn't a bin getting' wed." Meg walked back to Jack and Chalky with a puzzled look on her face. Jack asked; "Is something bothering you darling?" When she recounted Binnie's words Chalky started to laugh; "I told 'er Fishy was gonna beat the 'ell out uv Ginger if ee didn't do the right thing." It was Meg's turn to laugh; "As I said before you really are an old softy darling." Jack glared at a grinning Chalky; "One word from you and you'll get what I promised Ginger!" They took their leave from the lads of First Troop and walked out into the street. As they were walking back to the barracks Meg asked; "Why did you threaten Chalky just before we left?" Jack attempted to be evasive; "Oh, it was nothing really." Meg persisted; "Either you tell me, or next the time I get Chalky on his own I'll get it out of him." Jack reluctantly recounted Chalky's comments about him being an old softy. To his surprise Meg was not offended, in fact she began to laugh; "Darling, I've every confidence that you'll come up to my full expectations." Jack was aghast; "You're not supposed to know about things like that!" She smiled enigmatically; "You'd be surprised what I know."

After Jack had signed in at the guardroom they went to look for Ginger and Albert, who they eventually found in the stables. They were both sat on a bench laughing uproariously. Jack glared; "What's the joke?" Ginger looked up; "Not one we can tell in front of the lady." Jack was impatient; "What have you been doing since we left?" Albert spoke up; "'is sergeant got permission fer me to eat in the cookhouse, and then Ginger showed me round the barracks." Ginger piped up; Yeah I asked Sarge if ee could eat in the cook'ouse uvverwise poor bugger ud've starved." Jack addressed Ginger; "Did you take care of the horses first?" Ginger answered: "Jest like you said." Jack gave an order; "Get the horses ready to leave; Albert can lead Sally, we'll meet him at the main gate. And Ginger thanks." They walked back to the main gate where Jack led Meg around the back of the guardroom out of sight. They were kissing when they heard Albert coming. When they stepped out from hiding Jack walked Meg over to Sally and assisted her to mount. She looked down at him smiling; "Darling you know I don't need help to mount." Jack smiled back; "I just love to do things for you." Meg leaned down and they kissed once more, she laughed; "I hope Mr. Royce didn't see us." Jack looked at Albert; "You take good care of her!" He then stood outside the main gate and watched until they were out of sight.

Daylight was fading when Meg and Albert arrived at Letty's house she jumped off Sally throwing the reins to the groom, and ran up the steps so fast that the footman who was waiting ready had barely opened the door before she was through it. She burst into the library where Letty and Jonathan were sitting and breathlessly announced; "We're going to be married on my birthday!" Both Jonathan and his sister looked up in surprise, Jonathan exclaimed; "That's just a few weeks from now." Then Letty added; "And just a few weeks before yours and Hermione's wedding." Meg looked concerned; "I hadn't thought about that and I knew Jack would suggest my birthday, although he thinks it was his idea. What about Jane and Captain Barry?" Letty answered; "They're getting married on what would have been mine and Jasper's twenty third wedding anniversary, that's in October." Jonathan looked somewhat relieved; "Well at least theirs is not too close!" Letty observed; "We're going to have to get busy." Meg was bubbling; "I have to get bridesmaids and I'd like Cynthia to be my matron of honor and Jane to be maid of honor." Jonathan held up his hand; "Cynthia's not a good idea, although I'm sure she would accept; she thinks the world of you. But she is the Colonels wife and Jack is a ranker and she's also taller than both of you. Why don't you settle for just a maid of honor I'm sure Jane will be flattered. Royce, Woodford and Perry all have daughters who I'm sure would be delighted, or maybe some girls from that school you've just started attending." Meg's mouth registered disapproval; "Oh pooh on the school Papa! I'll ask Mr. Royce and Mr. Perry and Sergeant Woodford their daughters are all around my age, I'd much rather have girls from the regiment." Looking at Letty, Jonathan laughed; "She takes this business of being a daughter of the regiment seriously."

Sunday morning after church parade Perry approached Jack; "RSM's orfice right after fust parade tomorrer. Jack enquired; "What dress Sir?" Perry shrugged; "Yew'll be in stable dress, that'll do. Monday morning Jack marched into RHQ and found the Riding Master waiting outside the RSM's office. The door was open and the RSM called them in. When they were stood in front of his desk he ordered them at ease; "Well Corporal Spratt you're about to become a sergeant." Jack was taken by surprise; "But Sir I don't understand!" Royce barked; "What don't you understand Corporal?" Jack was at a loss; "Two years ago you made me a corporal even though there were many privates with much longer service with the regiment, and now this." Royce softened his tone; "And why did we make you a corporal?" Jack answered; "I suppose it was because I could ride fairly good." The bark came back in the RSM's voice; "Ride fairly good! I've got a regiment of men who ride damned good, why would you get promoted for riding fairly good?" Jack shook his head; "I don't know Sir." Royce's voice went up half an octave; "Because you don't ride fairly good you ride like a fucking Valkyrie! Now let me tell you why you're being promoted to sergeant. As you know Mr. Perry becomes time expired in a few months and the Colonel has granted him two weeks leave starting next Monday to take care of some personal matters. Moving to Jake Capper's village is one of them and who knows what mischief the two of them will get into?" Perry shook his head; "I reckon Nancy 'ull be watching me like a bloody 'awk." Royce smiled; "We have a new troop of recruits coming up for mounted training and you're going to be in sole charge while the Riding Master's on leave. Also, after Mr. Perry's gone you'll be carrying out the duties of riding master for the foreseeable future. Now get your chevrons from the quarter-masters, and have the seamstresses sew them on, after which Mr. Perry will inspect them." Jack stood staring at the RSM looking totally nonplussed. Royce addressed him in an exasperated tone; "Sergeant Spratt get your arse out of here and go do what I ordered before I change my mind and make you a bloody private!" After Jack's departure Perry informed Royce that he had granted Jack two days leave to attend Ginger's wedding; "I 'ope yew don't mind Jeremy but ee's best man." The RSM smiled; "Yes that's alright Ned, Weston's been granted a week, the others Saturday and Sunday." Ned was curious; "Others?" Royce informed him;

"'A' Squadron's letting some 1ˢᵗ Troop lads off to attend the wedding; Corporal White and Private O'Neill." Perry had another question; "Ow they all gettin' there?" Royce grinned; "Simpkins the carter is the bride to be's uncle so they'll be riding on the van with him and his wife. My guess is Spratt's planning to be with them." Ned had yet one more question; "'Ow they getting' back?" The RSM enlightened him; "The Colonel contacted Mr. Langsbury and he's putting them up in a room over his stables, they'll be coming back with Simpkins on Sunday." Perry shook his head; "We're gonna miss the Colonel, he reely knows 'ow to take care of the men." Royce smiled; "Things may not change that much." Seeing the puzzled look on The Riding Masters face he went on; "This is not official yet so keep it to yourself, the Duke persuaded the Queen to let him promote Major Hawkins." Perry beamed; "The owd Duke's a good un!" Royce still smiling added; "And I understand we'll be attending a wedding soon, the 1ˢᵗ Troop lads have asked permission to form a guard of honor for Spratt and his bride."

Five o'clock Saturday morning saw Jack, Chalky, Paddy, Binnie and the bridegroom Ginger in the back of Simpkin's covered van on the way to the wedding. They stopped in Jake Capper's village at the tavern for breakfast which Jack and Chalky paid for to celebrate their promotions. While they were eating Jake Capper came through the door, when he saw the four lancers dressed in their patrols he called the landlord over; "Eh Teddy er these blokes goin' back to their owd barracks?" Teddy enlightened him; "Na Jake their goin to a wedding." Simpkins looked up from his gammon rasher and eggs and pointed at Ginger; "That young bugger there got me niece in the family way." Jake laughed; "Good to see the owd seventeenth are still keeping their lances up!" He then observed that Jack now had three stripes on his arm; "Bugger me! I thought yew wuz young fer a corpr'l now yer a bloody sargn't." Ginger spoke up; "Yeah ev'ry bugger's getting stripes 'cept me." Paddy laughed; "You've got more stripes on your back than there's saints in heaven." After a hearty breakfast they continued their journey until they halted the van at the door of Molly's cottage. Mrs. Simpkin's warned Ginger; "Don't yew go inside, it's bad luck fer yew to see the bride before the wedding. Yew all best go to the chapel and wait there." As the van was doubling for a bridal carriage the four lancers headed for the chapel on foot. As they were marching along the street to the small Methodist chapel where the nuptials would be taking place Chalky started to laugh: "Bad luck fer yew to see the bride, aint yew seen all there is to be seen already Ginger?" Ginger snarled; "Fuck yew Chalky!" They all started laughing when Paddy chimed in; "Better watch out laddie or he'll be getting you in the family way." Some people were already inside when they arrived. Chalky found a pew in the back row while Paddy remained outside. Jack and Ginger walked up to the front of the chapel and the preacher told them where to stand and wait for the bridal party to arrive. After ten minutes the sound of hooves could be heard on the cobbles and the bridal party entered the chapel. As they proceeded up the aisle to the squeaking of a wheezy harmonium playing something that resembled the wedding march, Jack saw that Molly's maid of honor was one of the girls that frequented The Crown, he smiled to himself; "Some bloody maid she's got there!" Then he came up with a start, after the wedding party Meg and her father entered and sat down in the back pews. He just had time to see her smile at him before he had to turn his attention to Ginger and Molly. After the ceremony they all gathered outside for the rice throwing and to see Ginger and Molly off in the van. Jack walked over to Meg and her father. Before he could ask the question on his mind Molly's father the blacksmith came over and addressed Jonathan; "Zur, seein' as yew wuz kind enuff to jine us fer the wedding, would yew an' Miss Meg like to come to The Crown fer the weddin' feast?" Looking at Meg Jonathan answered in his usual gracious manner; "Thank you Mr. Fletcher, I think I can speak for both of us when I say we'll be delighted." Jack was on tenterhooks; "Meg what are you doing here? I thought you were at your aunt's." Meg smiled; "Aunt Letty wanted to see Papa about our wedding arrangements so I came down with her." A look of concern came over Jack's face; "You ladies didn't come down alone?" Meg could not help laughing; "No silly, we came in the carriage. Jane was with us and Captain Barry, what with the driver and the footman we were perfectly safe. Jack turned to Jonathan; "Sir, please excuse my rudeness I didn't mean to ignore you but…" his voice trailed off. Jonathan smiled; "I know you were concerned for the ladies and that does you credit. If you two would like to set off for The Crown I'll follow along with your comrades.

Tables had been set up on the Crown's second floor for the wedding guests with a large tapped barrel of beer set up on its own table and tankards lined up along the guest's tables. Ginger and Molly sat at the head table and waited for the guests to be seated. Jack reluctantly left Meg with her father to sit with the wedding party. He was seated on Ginger's left with one of Molly's brothers beside him. On Molly's right was her father and mother and her other brother who happened to be Jonathan's groom. Looking at the three men he thought; "They're some big buggers, bloody good job Ginger did marry her!" The serving girls began to bring the food in first there were two large roasted geese then a huge beef roast this was all served up with a large selection of vegetables. Jonathan thought; "It's April, so someone had to really empty out the root cellars." Many of the guests had started to up end their tankards when Molly's father stood up and with a loud bellow got their attention: "Quiet please while we 'as the toast to the bride and groom." This was Jack's cue to stand up and lift his tankard: "To Molly and Ginger, and let's hope she can keep a tight rein on him." the rest of the guests stood and raised their tankards or glasses saying; "To Molly and Ginger!" Just at that moment Squire Granville entered the room and breathlessly strode up to Molly's father. "I'm sorry Bob I wanted to be at the church but we had a cow go down having her calf, I had to go help the boy's get her up." The blacksmith looked up; "That be alright Squire, 'ope the calf wuz 'ealthy." The Squire smiled; "A fine bull calf, one of my prize herd, he'll fetch a good price." He dug down into his pocket and brought out five sovereigns and gave them to Molly; "This'll help you two young'ns to get started." Molly and Ginger got to their feet to thank him; Molly curtsied as Ginger stammered out a thank you. As they sat back down Ginger turned to Molly; "I aint never seen that much money in me ol bloody life!" Molly handed the sovereigns to her father; "'Ere Pa yew keep these fer us." Ginger looked on in dismay as Fletcher pocketed the coins; "Wot's yer owd man gonna do wiv our money?" Molly hissed at him; "ee'll see it gets to 'elp me an' the baby so's yew can't go pissing it away on beer an' 'ores." Ginger bridled; "Yer a good un to be talking abaht 'ores." Molly rounded on him; "I'm done wiv all that, I'm goin' to be a 'spectable married lady." Jack could contain himself no longer; "What are you two doing fighting on your wedding day? Now kiss and make up." Ginger smiled then grabbed Molly and gave her a long kiss which brought loud cheers from the guests.

After the dinner; the tables with the exception of the head table were moved back to the walls. Then three of the guests produced musical instruments as they stuck up a reel Molly's mother urged the bride and groom onto the floor. They moved to the music awkwardly at first, then as the guests applauded their movements started to coordinate while some of the guests also joined in dancing to a wheezy concertina, a squeaky fiddle and a reedy flute. Jack took the opportunity to go over to where Meg and her father were standing; "Sir I wish to thank you for providing the lads and me accommodation for the night." Jonathan replied; "That room over the stables is hardly ever used, but Bharti made sure it was all ship shape and Bristol fashion." Meg laughed; "Now Bharti approves of you she can't do enough for Mister Jack. Jack smiled; "I must make a point of thanking her." Meg laughed again; "Just seeing you with those three stripes on your arm will be thanks enough for her." Jonathan addressed them both; "If you two will excuse me I wish to have a word with the landlord." With that he crossed the room to speak to a slightly built man with a weather beaten face, a wooden leg and a gold earring in his left ear; "Mr. Wilson how much are you planning to charge Bob Fletcher for this reception?" Wilson answered; "Seein' 'as 'im an' 'is boys is sich good customers I thought fower pahnds ten wuz enuff." Jonathan handed him five sovereigns; "I'll take care of it." When Wilson dug into his pocket for change Jonathan waved his hand; "No keep the ten shillings, use it to buy something nice for that niece of yours." Wilson's gratitude showed in his eyes; "Why God bless you Zur, I'll see she knows where it come from." When he returned Meg had questions; "Why were you giving Mr. Wilson money and why do they call him Gunner Wilson?" Jonathan smiled; "You always were an inquisitive little minx. As to your first question: I paid for the reception, Bob's done some good work for me and his son Will is an excellent employee. As to the second: Wilson was a Gunner's Mate in The Royal Navy. He lost his leg the last time he was in action and came home with some prize money; with which he bought this establishment. To answer the question you didn't ask: The woman who lives here is his widowed sister and the little girl is her daughter. Meg smiled up at her father; "And did you give him money for the little girl?" When her father nodded yes a tear came to Meg's eye; "Papa you're such a wonderful, generous old ogre I love you so much." Jonathan smiled; "I know one thing young lady if you persist in calling me an ogre I'll have to administer that spanking that Jack once threatened you with." Jack laughed; "Just make sure her riding crops not within her reach, she's promised me a horse whipping more than once." Just then Bob Fletcher came up to them; "Wot yew wanta go do that fer Mr. Langsbury?" Jonathan feigned bewilderment; "Do what Bob?" Bob looked exasperated; "Why, pay fer the reception that's wot." Jonathan shrugged; "Consider it payment for the last time Joe bit you." Bob laughed; "That stallion be a "igh spirited bugger alright. Thankee Zur, me an' the missus an' Molly is in yer debt."

The following morning Simpkins halted the van at Teddy's tavern and they enjoyed another good breakfast, Jack enquired about Jake Capper's whereabouts. Teddy informed him that he was helping to get Ned Perry's cottage ready. Jack recalled that Perry was having the next two weeks to move. Teddy explained; "'is missus is moving in next week, they sold their old place already." When they arrived at the barracks the RSM was just coming out of the guard room and saw the van stopped outside the main gate. He walked over as the three of them were dismounting, he addressed Simpkins; "Mr. Simpkins, the Adjutant instructed me to thank you for transporting our lads, and to tell you that if the regiment requires cartage services you will be our first consideration." Simpkins replied; "It wur no trouble, I wuz goin' there anyways." With that he shouted; "Gee Up!" And the horses clattered off down the cobbled road. After they had signed in at the guard room Jack turned to read regimental orders posted on the inside of the door. He turned to Chalky and Paddy; "There's going to be a farewell parade for Colonel Butler next Saturday." Paddy laughed; "And Ginger's not here to complain about having to drill for a week."

Late the following Friday afternoon the guard sergeant, Sergeant Matthews of 'D' Squadron was surprised to see Ginger enter the guard room to sign in; "Wot yew doin' 'ere Weston, aint yew got annuver days leave yet?" Ginger grinned; "I 'erd they was 'avin a send off fer the Colonel, I weren't gonna miss that." Matthews shook his head; "Yer the last bugger ee ever 'ad flogged an' yer givin' up a days leave to see 'im off!" The following morning after breakfast Woodford entered 1st Troop's barrack room and walked over to Ginger; "Sergeant Matthews told me yew wuz back." Ginger looked up from polishing his saber scabbard; "Yeah Sarge thought I'd 'elp yew see The Colonel off."

Woodford grunted; "Yew got five minutes to get into stable dress and fall in outside, we got stables to clean an' 'orses to get ready fer the parade."

The reviewing stand was a riot of color from the different uniforms of the variety of regiments that were represented. Seated in front were Colonel Butler with Cynthia flanked by the Duke of Cambridge and Major General Anderson, the now Lt/Colonel Hawkins sat on the Duke's right. When the regiment passed in review order everyone came to their feet as Colonel Butler took the salute looking splendid in his staff officers red tunic, complete with full colonel's gold epaulettes on the shoulders. On his head was a black fore and aft hat with a white egret's plume. The ensemble was completed by black breeches with a red stripe over which he wore black riding boots. As they passed the spectators Jack managed to glimpse Meg and her father with Hermione, Letty and Jane applauding furiously with the rest of the spectators.

After the parade Jack was in the riding school walking Nipper when the VIP entourage accompanied by the ladies entered. Completely taken by surprise he came to attention and saluted. Colonel Butler feigned a glare; "Sergeant Spratt, who's the other soldier with you?" Jack responded with; "Why, it's Riding Master Perry Sir." The Colonel turned his glare on Perry; "Yes I saw you in the parade, aren't you supposed to be on leave getting your new home ready?" Without waiting for an answer the Colonel turned to Jack; "Where's Private Weston, I saw him in the parade also?" Jack was alarmed; "He's probably over at 'A' Squadron's stables taking care of his horse Sir." The Colonel barked; "I want him here at the double!" Jack spotted a private at the back of the riding school paralyzed at attention and ordered; "Watkins get over to A's stables and bring Weston at the double!" Watkins seemed frozen with fear. Jack roared; "Go, did you not hear The Colonel?" Watkins fled and within a few minutes was back with Ginger. As they both came to attention Butler called Ginger forward. When he had Ginger and Perry standing side by side he looked from one to the other; "So, the Regiment had the goodness of heart to grant you two leave, and you show your gratitude in wasting a day of that leave by attending a bloody parade." By now there was a smile appearing on The Colonel's face; "And I want you both to know I will always remember this token of personal loyalty." Perry requested permission to speak which was granted; "Zur, yew'll be missed a lot, but I knows I speaks fer all the lads wen I sez we wishes yew all the best in yer new job." Perry punctuated his statement with a snappy salute which The Colonel returned. As the VIP party left the riding school building Ginger spoke up; "I've zed it before and I'll say it agin; The Colonels a bloody toff!" As they were making their way towards the officer's mess the ladies were all visibly crying with emotion, even Cynthia Butler finally broke down. Then she got herself under control; "What am I doing blubbering like a silly bloody schoolgirl?" Meg smiled through her tears; "You're just proud and happy for the man you love." Cynthia turned and smiled at her; "Yes you're right Meg, he not only earned his rank he earned the loyalty of his men." Meg still smiling added; "He earned more than their loyalty, he also earned their love."

The Duke had declared it ladies day in the officer's mess and Meg asked if she could be excused for the afternoon.. The Duke granted his permission but stated his wish that she make sure she be in attendance for dinner, then he turned to The Colonel; "Harry it's my experience you can't have enough beautiful women around you in life. When I'm dead; where I'll be going there may not be any." Harry laughed; "If you're going to hell Your Grace; then you can rest assured many lancers, me included will be in your good company." The Duke harrumphed; "I suppose she'll be gallivanting around town with that new made sergeant of yours." Harry laughed again; "I think we can safely make that assumption." As they made their way to the officers mess Meg headed towards RHQ to meet Jack. When she was out of earshot the

Duke turned to Meg's father; "Jonathan, I swear that gal of yours gets prettier every time I see her. If I wasn't married and ten years younger I'd be after her meself!" Jonathan smiled wistfully; "She looks like her mother when she was that age." It was the Duke's turn to laugh; "Wish I'd known her, you would have had some serious competition."

When Meg arrived at RHQ Jack was waiting outside dressed in patrols. As he grasped her hands she sighed regretfully; "Jack darling I'm so sorry I can only be with you for the afternoon, I have to be back at the officer's mess for Colonel Butler's farewell dinner." Jack smiled ruefully; "He's probably the only man in the world for which I would be happy to sacrifice time with you." Meg rounded on him; "You mean to tell me that you're happy about not spending this evening with me?" Jack realized that he made an unfortunate choice in words; "Sorry Meg, I should have said willing." Her laughter caused him to comment. "Careful my girl you don't have your riding crop" This only succeeded in making Meg laugh louder. After she'd regained her composure she asked Jack; "What do you want to do this afternoon?" He replied; "I haven't got Ginger and Molly a wedding present yet." Meg's eyes lit up; "Oh Jack, let's get one from both of us." They walked around the garrison town for more than an hour discussing what might be a suitable present, when they stopped in front of large shop advertising furniture and household fixtures. Meg pointed at an item in the window; "Darling, that's it!" Jack looked where she was pointing; "The bassinet?" Meg was getting exited; "Molly's having her baby in seven months and I'll wager no one else thought of it. They walked into the shop and Jack asked an assistant the bassinet's price. The assistant stole a covert glance at Meg's belly, but Jack saw him and in a low menacing tone he said; "It's a gift for friends!" The assistant scurried to get the bassinet from the window. It was mounted on crosswise rockers and made of polished cherry wood with mother of pearl inlaid patterns on the head and foot and both sides. Jack asked the assistant; "How much?" Upon his reply of nineteen and six Jack produced a sovereign. After the assistant had given Jack his sixpence change and receipt Jack instructed him; "Hold onto the bassinet until someone comes in for it with this receipt." As they left the store Meg asked; "How are you going to get it to Molly?" Jack said; "I'll have Simpkins pick it up and he can take it next time he goes down." Then Meg started to laugh. Jack looked at her; "What's so funny?" Meg managed through her laughter to stammer out; "That assistant thought the bassinet was for us." Jacks reply brought a pause in her laughter; "This time next year or maybe sooner that might be the case." She grasped his arm tightly; "Oh Jack, I do hope so." They kissed then started to walk in the direction of The Duke of York's Arms, when they entered the public bar Chalky came up to them; "Yew not going back to the private to eat?" Jack explained that Meg was dining in the officers mess but that he'd be back to join them; "But let's have one on The Colonel before we go." Chalky brought two tankards of beer and while they were toasting the Colonel; Jack wondered if he would ever get used to seeing Meg drinking beer from a pint mug.

When they arrived at the officer's mess Letty's carriage was waiting at the entrance with the driver and the footman smoking their churchwarden pipes as if they had not moved in two weeks. This time in order to say goodbye; Meg and Jack went to the side of the carriage where they were out of sight from both Letty's servants and the officer's mess. After they had kissed fervently for some minutes Meg pulled away; "Darling I mustn't be late, I'll see you tomorrow." She then ran through the doors and attempted to make a dignified entrance into the dining room. Cynthia noting her flushed appearance commented mischievously; "Is it cold outside Meg dear? Your cheeks are very red." Meg flashed her daggers at The Colonel's wife and hissed through clenched teeth; "I was running so as not to be late!" An orderly pulled out a chair next to her father and Meg sat down with an exasperated sigh. After they had left the riding school the entourage had walked to the officer's mess for a light luncheon. Following lunch they had remained talking until it was time for the officers to retire and change into mess dress, and the ladies to change into the evening gowns they had brought for the dinner. Meg who was still dressed in street clothes gasped; "Papa, I have to change into my evening gown!" Colonel Butler beckoned the orderly; "Show Miss Langsbury to the room we allocated for the ladies." When Meg had left Cynthia stood up; "I'll go and see if she needs any help." Meg was in her chemise taking her green gown from the large closet which now held the other ladies day clothes when there was a knock at the door. Cynthia identified herself; "Meg, it's Cynthia, may I come in?" Meg answered petulantly; "If you must." Cynthia entered warily; "I thought you might need some help with your gown." Meg still inwardly fuming answered; "I have always managed on my own until now." Cynthia moved swiftly across the room and swept Meg into her arms; "Meg darling I love you like my own daughter and if I've said anything to offend you I'm deeply sorry." Meg with her face buried in Cynthia's ample bosom had to push herself away before answering, she looked up at the older woman; "Maybe I should not be so sensitive, when I enjoy teasing others so much, but I am so much on edge with the wedding day getting closer." Cynthia smothered her again; "My darling little child of course you're nervous and I should not have been so insensitive." After Cynthia had helped her dress they returned to the dining room. A few minutes after they were seated the wine was poured and the first course served. There was a deal of small talk around the table and the General commented on the regiment's turnout and how much he was impressed with the show of loyalty by The Riding Master and Ginger. The Duke who had been drinking steadily since luncheon harrumphed; "Should have had that bastard Cardigan here to see how a regiment can work without stripping the bloody flesh off the men's backs!" As the General began to look decidedly uncomfortable the Duke fell forward his face joining the fish on his plate. Colonel Hawkins acted swiftly beckoning to a waiter he ordered; "Get two more men and take the Duke up to my quarters put him to bed and all three of you report back to me immediately!" When they returned he asked; "Is the Duke alright?" The waiter answered with a slight smile on his face; "Sleeping like a baby Sir." Hawkins continued; "Did anyone see you?" The waiter replied; "Just one of the officer's orderlies." Hawkins barked an order; "Go and get him immediately!" when the waiter returned with the confused looking orderly Colonel Hawkins addressed the four of them; "You did not see what you saw tonight, if one word of this gets out I can promise the four of you will rue the day! Do you all understand me?" After a chorus of "yes sir" he dismissed them. Then looking around the table; "I know I can rely on everyone's discretion." Harry was smiling as he said; "Well handled Reggie, and the Duke accused me of being a politician." Colonel Hawkins had not been present on the occasion when the Duke had made his statement. After Butler recounted the incident they all joined in the laughter.

When Jack got back to the Duke of York's he sat at a table in the public bar and ordered a pork pie. While he was eating Chalky and Ginger joined him. Jack looked up; "Where's Paddy?" Ginger grinned; "ees in love." Jack looked at Chalky; "What's going on?" It was Chalky's turn to grin; "'Ees out walking wiv Binnie Simpkins." Jack looked concerned; "Does she know Paddy's a Catholic?" Chalky laughed; "The Simpkins's is Catholics." Jack's face showed surprise. Chalky continued; "Dint yew notice that Simpkins and 'is missus dint go in the church fer the weddin'?" Jack's expression showed recollection; "That's why Binnie wasn't a bridesmaid." Ginger with his usual lack of subtlety spoke up; "Yeah them bloody Papists wud never set foot in a Methodis' chapel." Chalky changed the subject; "'Ow's it goin' wiv yer wedding 'rangements?" Jack paused from chasing a pickled onion around his plate; "Meg's aunt and the other ladies are taking care of most of the arrangements. I'll find out more when I see Meg tomorrow afternoon."

The days flew by and on the Saturday two weeks before their wedding Meg told Jack that Letty would be sending the carriage for him Sunday afternoon. Jack's quizzical expression prompted her to explain; "She wants us to have dinner with her and I think she and Papa have something up their sleeves." They were in the private bar partaking of their usual Saturday repast while the lads were reveling in the public bar. On one occasion Meg had suggested they have their meal in the public bar. But Jack had demurred saying it was better they be alone together. However, they still went back and joined the lads for a drink before they left.

After dinner on Sunday Letty asked everyone to remain seated as Jonathan and she wished to address them. She looked at Jonathan indicating that he was to be the first to speak. Jonathan cleared his throat; "When Meg's mother and I got married Letty and Jasper gave us a very generous wedding gift. When you approach this house from the direction of Woolwich you will see a beautiful little cottage set back from the road. We only lived there for a few months before we left for India. Letty has taken care of it since and currently her gardener and his wife are living there. However, they are retiring next week and moving to the Isle of Wight to take care of the gardener's invalid mother. Letty and I have decided that we both wish you to have this cottage as a wedding gift." Jack and Meg who had both admired the cottage sat speechless. Letty rose up in her chair; "Well what d'ye have to say?" Meg looked at Jack; "Say something!" Jack stood up; "Ma'am, Sir, I don't know how to thank you, this is too generous. I only hope I can get The Colonels permission to live outside the barracks." Jonathan commented with a knowing smile; "I don't foresee any problem there." Meg was less formal in showing her gratitude; she jumped out of her chair and ran round the table to Letty. She hugged her aunt's neck smothering her with kisses while repeating over an over; "You're the most darling aunt who ever lived." Then she turned her attention to her father, she hugged him as she had Letty; "You deceitful old ogre why didn't you give me some warning?" Jonathan smiled; "We wanted it to be a surprise for both of you. And woe betide you if you teach my grandchildren to call me an ogre." While they were all laughing Letty told Meg to sit down; "There's more. A retired general who breeds horses was a good friend of my late husband Jasper. He owned a stallion which my husband admired greatly and the general promised my husband first bid on the first colt he sired. My husband was lost at sea long before the colt was born so I bought him in memory of Jasper; he's now two years old, only half broken and untrained. Jack he's yours." Jack's face was comical to behold: mouth agape, eyes wide and unintelligible noises bubbling up from his throat. He finally regained enough composure; "Ma'am I don't know how to respond to so much generosity." Letty replied with; "Tush boy! No one can ride him Albert has to exercise him by leading him when he rides one of the others. Bloody creature bites him at least twice a week." Jack came down from his elation with a sobering realization; "Ma'am, I would hate to seem ungrateful but I've no way of taking care of him." Letty's answer was obviously rehearsed; "He will remain in our stables until you move into the cottage. There's a small stable out back where we've been keeping Sally. You can put the stallion in the cottage stable and Sally can move into our stables, we have all geldings." Jack was still concerned; "What about tack, feed and…" Letty interrupted; "Stop right now! We have plenty of tack, two spare saddles and I can sell you straw, hay and oats at a good price seeing as we grow our own. Now let's all go down to the stables and take a look at your wedding gift." With that they all rose and headed out through the French doors toward the stables.

When they entered the stables Letty pointed to the third loose box from the door; "He's in there." Jack gasped, and forgetting the company blurted out; "He's bloody magnificent!" This brought a censure from Meg to which Jack replied; "Come here and look at this beautiful creature." They both stood transfixed gazing at a large stallion with a gleaming solid black coat. Jack spoke in an awed whisper; "He's bigger than Joe." Jonathan laughed; "And a damn sight meaner!" The stallion was beginning to stamp a forefoot impatiently, he was not happy with all these people staring at him over the half door of his loose box. With his ears back and neck stretched he gave out a challenging neigh. Jack opened the door and entered the loose box. Meg gasped; "Be careful darling!" He approached the stallion making almost inaudible murmuring sounds. At first the black horse rolled back his eyes showing the whites. Laid back his ears even flatter and stretched his neck with lips rolled back. He stamped even harder, and then just as everyone thought he was about to rear he suddenly became calm. His ears pricked forward then he raised his head and nickered. Jack draped his arm over the stallion's back and laid his head against his withers saying; "There, there boy, I think we're going to be great friends." Captain Barry who was standing at Jane's side uttered an exclamation of amazement; "Egad! I've never seen anything like that in all my life." Letty broke the spell with; "He hasn't been named yet." This was Meg's cue unable to hide her excitement she urged; "Name him Jack, name him now please." Jack looked at Letty; "There's only one name I can think of. With your permission Ma'am I would like to call him Jasper." A tear rolled down her cheek, chokingly she replied; "Thank you Jack he would have liked that. Now I have to let General Willingham know he has a new owner. He was trying to persuade me to have him gelded." Jack gasped; "That would be a sin! He should sire some fine foals." Then Meg exclaimed; "General Willingham, General Sir Martin Willingham. That's Cynthia Butler's father. I'll be surprised if she didn't have a hand in this." Letty smiled archly; "D'ye really think so?" Before Meg could make reply she turned to Jack; "No more Ma'am, its Aunt Letty from now on." Jack answered; "Yes Ma...Aunt Letty." Letty wished to know how Jack would handle Jasper; "How're you going to get him to behave?" Jack laid out his method; "First I'll spend as much time with him as possible, just grooming and talking to him. When I've got his trust I'll work him on the long rein unsaddled, and later with a saddle. When he's used to the saddle I'll put the dead man (full sized stuffed replica of a rider) on him. Once he's accepted the dead man it'll be my turn." Jane seemed concerned; "What if he doesn't accept you and throws you off?" Jack replied then I'll go back to where he was easy to handle and we'll work our way forward again." Captain Barry asked; "Would you consider breaking him like they do it in Australia and America, isn't it quicker?" Jack was emphatic; "No Sir, that way the horse will either never be manageable or his spirit will be broken. I want him to be a friend not an enemy or a slave. And from what I've seen of Jasper if brute force was used on him he would become a brute!" Meg addressed her father imploringly; "Oh Papa could we put Jasper to Sally?" Her father answered; "Joe first then maybe Jasper somewhere down the road."

The banns had been called at the regimental chapel and Meg's parish church near the old barracks. Meg decided that she wanted to be married in the regimental chapel; "If I'm to be a daughter of the regiment it's only fit that I be married in the regiment." Letty, Jane and Hermione busied themselves helping Meg get ready for the wedding. As Letty observed; "This'll be good practice for when we have to organize Hermione's wedding." Hermione retorted with a smile; "Have you forgotten I've been married before? I don't think I'll require that much preparation." Although Jack was unaware preparations were also being made on his behalf. Sergeant Woodford informed SSM Meade that the lads of First Troop were requesting permission to provide a guard of honor. Meade scratched his head; "If they're gonna wear dress and 'ave lances they'll need The Colonels permission. I'll go and talk to the RSM."

The wedding day was slightly overcast and not as warm as might have been expected in late May, but the birds in the trees that surrounded the regimental chapel were in full song. Jack and his best man Chalky were inside the chapel waiting at the chancel steps when Meg arrived. A group of soldier's wives who were gathered outside gasped in unison as Jonathan handed her and Jane down from Letty's carriage. One loudly exclaimed; "Oh my Gawd, she's bloody beautiful!" A landau pulled up behind the carriage from which Jonathan handed down four bridesmaids in dark blue satin and lace gowns. Jane's gown was the same as the bridesmaids except the lace trim at her neck and wrists was white. Combined with Meg's white bridal gown the bridal ensemble was a not very subtle display of the regimental colors. As Jonathan took Meg on his arm, Jane took her place behind them with the bridesmaids following her two by two. When they entered the chapel to the strains of the wedding march Jack turned to look down the aisle. He gasped softly at the sight of Meg then his eyes scanned the congregation. In the front pews were Colonel Butler and Captain Barry sporting the latest male fashions, and with them were Cynthia, Letty and Hermione looking colorful and striking in their fashionable gowns and large lacy hats. In the back of the chapel were the RSM, Ned Perry and Sergeant Woodford in full dress uniforms; but no sign of Ginger or Paddy. He returned his attention back to Meg as she came up the aisle and his eyes remained upon her throughout the wedding service. At the conclusion of the marriage ceremony Perry and Woodford ushered the congregation from the chapel working from the back pews forward. The bridal party then proceeded down the aisle and just as they were about to exit the chapel they heard the familiar parade ground voice of the RSM; "Honor Guard present!" They walked out under an archway of lances formed by Paddy, Ginger and four other lads from 1ˢᵗ Troop in full ceremonial dress; that was when Jack realized why he hadn't seen Ginger and Paddy in the chapel. After passing through the honor guard they were showered with rice; then a line of well wishers starting with Colonel Butler began greeting them. After Jack saluted him the Colonel shook his hand and kissed Meg on the cheek, then Cynthia descended on them. She addressed Jack; "I know you'll take good care her of but I'm going to miss my little prude." She then smothered Meg with one of her stifling hugs, after kissing her frantically she moved back with her hands still on Meg's shoulders; "My Little Prude a married lady, who'd have thought?" Jack and Meg both noticed tears welling up in her eyes. After everyone had congratulated them there was another surprise in store. The four 1st Troop lads appeared each mounted and leading horses for Perry, Woodford, Ginger and Paddy; they were preceded by the RSM who was also mounted. When the bridal party had seated themselves in the bridal carriage and the landau Royce stationed himself in front of the carriage's team. He then gave the order; "Honor Guard take your stations!" Whereupon Perry and Woodford took up positions on the right and left sides of the bridal carriage; with Paddy behind Perry and Ginger behind Woodford. The four lads of 1st Troop formed up on the landau flanking it with two riders on each side. The RSM then preceded them at the walk and the bridal party progressed through the barracks and out of the main gate. They headed toward the Duke of York's Arms where Gus Davidson had prepared the upstairs banquet room for the reception. Meg had startled everyone when they were making preparations for the wedding, she had not only insisted that they hold the reception at the tavern but also that they have Gus serve his regular fare. Jane had exclaimed; "Pork pies, cheese and pickled onions at a wedding reception it's hardly proper!" Letty had chastised her; "It is Meg's wedding, whatever she decides is proper; will be proper." The bridal procession was impressive as they clattered along the cobbles with the RSM leading his saber at the carry, and the eight outriders with their lance heads gleaming and red and white pennants fluttering in the breeze. As they alighted from the carriage and landau in front of the tavern they were showered with rice once again. Upon entering the tavern Jonathan was approached by the landlord; "'Scuse me zur I want yew to know the barrel upstairs is fer the lads; it's free, them boys brings me lots uv trade." The tables in the banquet room were arranged in a U shape with the table for the bridal party at the head and those for the guests along the side walls. A separate table supported the large barrel of beer to which Gus had alluded surrounded by tankards. When the food was served Jane realized that Meg had been teasing about the fare; roast pork, mutton and beef were brought in with a great variety of vegetables. After everyone had finished eating Chalky stood to make the best man's toast; "'Ere's to Sergeant Spratt and Miss Meg. Wot most uv yer don't know is I give 'im 'is fust baff, I'm glad 'ee cleaned up good fer 'er sake." This brought roars of laughter from the guests and a cuffed ear from Jack as Chalky sat back down beside him. Jonathan then rose from his seat and raised his glass; "I make this toast with mixed feelings. I know my Meg could not be married to a better man than Jack but I hate to lose my little girl. To Meg and Jack may you both have a long life together full of the love you have for each other on this day." His toast was followed by Colonel Butler's then the Riding Master and finally Sergeant Woodford; who made the point that he was the first person in the regiment to become acquainted with Jack. When Jack arose to make his reply he had tears in his eyes; "When I say I'm the luckiest bugger on earth I challenge anyone to contradict me! I am going to address you in soldier's language because that's what I am; and I know Meg is going to make me pay dearly for it." This caused some laughter the loudest coming from Cynthia Butler. He looked around the room; "There are many people to whom I have to be thankful but I am going to thank some personally. The first person I would have liked to thank is the magistrate who had the Beadle drag me to the barracks instead of putting me in jail to be transported or hanged; unfortunately he died not long after I became a lancer. Then there's Sergeant Woodford who not only gave me the chance for a better life but saw to it that I got the first decent meal of my life, but he made me pay for it when he became my troop sergeant." This brought more laughter. Then he looked at Perry; "Riding Master, you were a right royal bastard! But you taught me all I know about riding horses and I thank you for it." He then turned Harry Butler; "Colonel Butler Sir, It was a great privilege to serve under your command and I wish you the best on taking up your new post." Looking past Meg he addressed her father; "Sir I have a great deal to thank you for: firstly for befriending me, then having Meg teach me to read and write; which as you know is still an ongoing task. And the one thing I have to thank you for the most is your beautiful daughter who has kicked me twice for my barrack room language." This caused the guests to laugh again, just as he was about to sit down six musicians from the regiment's band filed in and took their places on two benches at the end of the hall. In a state of surprise Jack addressed the guests again; "It seems that I owe thanks to yet another; someone has supplied us with music. Captain Barry Sir, would you convey our thanks to Colonel Hawkins? The Colonel declined his invitation although as you can see his lady Mrs. Hawkins and their lovely daughter have graced us with their presence. The Colonel's reason for his absence are in his own words; "With my Adjutant, RSM, four of my NCO's and half of First Troop 'A' Squadron gone, who the bloody hell is going to run the regiment?" This brought more laughter from the guests and another kick from Meg. He took her hand saying; "I was going to ask you to dance but I think my leg's too bruised." Meg led him from behind the table and the musicians struck up a Viennese waltz. After they led off, others joined them in whirling around the floor. At the end of the waltz Jack and Meg began mingling with the guests when Jane and Captain Barry approached them, Jane upbraided Meg; "You said we were going to have pork pies, pickled onions and cheese for the banquet." Then turning to Jack; "D'ye know what a tease she is?" Jack laughed; "I found that out a long time ago." Colonel Butler and Cynthia had joined them when Jane asked; "Where are you going for your honeymoon?" Jack answered; "We aren't going away, we're going to stay in the cottage Meg's father gave us. Besides, I couldn't afford to pay for us to go away and Meg's father has spent far too much money on us already." Jane nodded her approval; "How thoughtful of you Jack." Turning to Meg she added; "You married a thoughtful and considerate man." Cynthia gave a short laugh; "What he means is that he can't wait to be with his real true love." Jane's eyebrows shot up; "Whatever do you mean Cynthia?" Cynthia had a wicked twinkle in her eye; "Why, that bloody great big black stallion that's waiting for him." She looked at Jack; "And what about Nipper?" Jack answered defensively; "Corporal White and Private Weston are going to take care of him while I'm on leave. Nipper's the first horse I ever had and he'll always be first." Cynthia chuckled; "I'm sorry Sergeant I shouldn't be teasing you, I'm sure you get enough of that from Meg."

After the reception they were driven to their cottage in Letty's carriage which then went on to Letty's house with Jonathan and Hermione who were staying the night and Jane. When they entered the cottage; with Jack carrying Meg over the threshold, they found a lighted lamp on the kitchen table and one on the nightstand in the bedroom. Jack laughed when he saw it; "They couldn't have been more bloody obvious." Meg rounded on him; "D'ye want to be kicked again? No wait, my riding crop's right here, hanging on the wall." Jack cringed mockingly; "I'll go out and check on Sally before we turn in." Meg took the opportunity to go into the bedroom and undress, and then donned a revealing nightgown that Hermione had picked out for her when they had been shopping together. She climbed into bed and waited for Jack impatiently. It was over half an hour before he returned and Meg was fuming; "Where have you been all this time?" Jack gave a startled reply; "Sally's gone, Jasper's in there!" Meg relented a little; "Oh, I forgot to tell you Aunt Letty said she'd have Albert bring him down and take Sally up to her stables. There should be feed tack and a saddle in there also." Jack concurred; "That's all in there." Meg was not yet satisfied; "Why were you out there so long?" Jack was contrite; "I was just admiring Jasper." Meg gave an exasperated sigh; "This is our wedding night, you're supposed to be here making love to me not in the stable with that stallion." Jack deliberately misread her words; "I wouldn't give much for anyone's chances that tried to bugger old Jasper." Meg exploded; "Jack Spratt enough of the barrack room humor and come to bed or you'll be sleeping in the stable!" The following morning Letty and Jane stopped by the cottage during their morning ride. After they had secured their hunters they walked in on Meg who was in the throes of her third attempt at cooking breakfast. When she turned at the sound of the kitchen door they could see she was crying; "Oh! Aunt Letty I'm trying to cook breakfast but nothing is going right, what sort of wife am I going to be?" Letty gave a kindly smile; "You've been spoilt with servants all your life but never mind that, you and Jack can come up to the house for breakfast this morning. Later on I'll see if Cook will give you some lessons. What you'll learn from Cook will be a darn sight more useful than anything they teach you at that girl's school down the road." Meg face brightened; "Thank you Aunt Letty you're a dear. I have to leave the school anyway they don't permit pupils to stay when they marry. And I only went there to be near Jack." Letty gave a knowing smile; "And I suppose you thought nobody realized that was your motive. By the way where is Jack?" Meg nodded toward the stable he's in there with Jasper." Letty showed exasperation; "What's this? A brand new bride and he prefers the company of a bloody horse? Maybe we should get him gelded." This caused Meg to laugh; "Please no Aunt Letty! I want many more nights like last night." This caused Letty to laugh uproariously while Jane blushed furiously. The three of them walked to the stable and when their eyes were accustomed to the gloom they saw Jack with his arm over Jasper's neck talking softly to the big stallion. Jack looked up when they approached them and smiled; "After I talked to him for a little while he let me put the bridle on him." Meg gave an exasperated humph; "I woke up at five o'clock and you were gone from my bed. You had to be talking for a long while!" Letty poured oil on the troubled waters; "Why don't you two love birds come up to the house for breakfast and we'll concern ourselves with some more important affairs." Letty and Jane leading their horses walked with them toward the house. When they reached the stables Meg ran in; "I have to see Sally." As they entered Letty addressed the groom; "You won't need to walk these two Albert, We've just walked them up from the cottage." Meg was in a loose box stroking Sally's withers and cooing to her softly; "I've been neglecting you with the wedding and everything." Letty smiled; "If you'd like to go riding after breakfast I'll have Albert get her ready, and a hunter for Jack." Meg left Sally's side and went to Letty and hugged her; "You're the dearest, nicest aunt in the whole world." Letty held her at arms length; "Save your embraces for that new husband, maybe you can give me a grandniece or nephew before Jane gives me a grandchild." Jane's face turned crimson; "Oh, Mamma you are terrible!" This brought laughter from Jack and a comment from Meg; "And Cynthia calls me a prude!"

Their lives became an idyllic routine. Jack would ride one of Letty's hunters into Woolwich each morning where he had arranged with Gus to leave his horse at the Duke of York's Arms, he would then walk to the barracks. This had caused Mrs. Hawkins to remark to The Colonel; "Sergeant Spratt shows more tact than I've seen in some of your officers." Meanwhile Meg divided her time between housework, visiting with her aunt and cousin and learning to cook. When Letty had offered to let Jack have one of her horses "to get to work" until Jasper was ready he had declined; "Aunt Letty you have done too much for us already." Letty had bristled; "Tush boy, they have to be exercised anyway."

On Saturdays if Jack was not on duty at the barracks and if the weather permitted they would ride into Woolwich, leave Sally and Jack's mount at the Duke of York's then walk to the shops and make their purchases which Albert would pick up and take back with the supplies he picked up for Letty's household. Before they left for Woolwich one Saturday in July Meg said to Jack; "I think I should go back to riding side saddle." Jack looked puzzled; "Why darling?" Her reply startled him; "I think I'm carrying our baby." Jack took her in his arms and held her gently; "Oh Meg, will you be alright?" She laughed of course I will I'm as healthy as a horse, and you can hug me tighter than that. Now let's go and tell Aunt Letty and Jane." Letty was jubilant as she hugged Meg she told them I know a doctor in town who specializes in pregnancy care and child birth, we must go into the city on Monday and have him examine you." Meg's answer; "I thought I could have the regimental surgeon examine me to verify my condition, then get one of the wives who are experienced in midwifery to attend me at the delivery." Caused Letty to get angry in a way they had never seen before; "Meg Spratt you are my brother's only child and I refuse to have you attended by some army sawbones and a midwife. You are taking this daughter of the regiment thing too far!" Meg took the easy way out; "I will see your doctor if you insist Aunt Letty." Letty now calming down said I'll send Albert to tell your father straightaway." Jane with tears running down her cheeks was hugging her when Meg said; "We had better get ready if we're going into Woolwich." Jane stiffened; "You're going to ride in your condition?" Meg answered impatiently; "Of course I'm going to ride, but I'm going back to side saddle." Letty commented; "Good girl, you don't need to behave like an invalid, and you Jack don't treat her like one. And I suggest that you keep this news to yourselves until we know for sure."

The regiment was destined to stay in England until 1854 during which time Meg gave birth first to a boy and then a year later a girl. They named their first born Jonathan Francis Edward which resulted in his having two of his three namesakes Woodford and Perry as godfathers, with Jane who herself was pregnant at his christening as godmother. The girl who they named Elizabeth Leticia Cynthia Jane had three godmothers whose names she was given along with her deceased grandmother's, with Chalky as godfather. Elizabeth came as a blessing but also a disappointment. Meg had a difficult pregnancy and childbirth after which the doctor told them that she would be unable to conceive again. Jonathan who was still living in the house near the old barracks with Hermione who had moved in after their wedding visited often; spoiling the children. Meanwhile, Ginger and Molly had two more children in addition to the one Molly was carrying when they married. Simpkins had allowed Ginger and Molly; and Paddy and Binnie to move into two small cottages he owned in Woolwich for a minimal rent. Paddy and Binnie who had married a few weeks after Meg and Jack, and had two children during this time. It had taken Jack three months to break and train Jasper who he now rode "to work". One young officer who had seen Jack leading Jasper into the Duke of York's Arms protested to Colonel Hawkins; "Sergeant Spratt's got a better bloody horse than mine!" Hawkins put him in his place; "When you can ride as well as him maybe someone will give you a better bloody horse!" This brought gales of laughter from the other officers who were enjoying their after dinner drinks in the mess. Sally had given birth to two fine foals one by Joe and the other by Jasper; both them fillies which were housed in Letty's stables, Ned Perry had retired to live in Sergeant Major Capper's village. Much to Jane's chagrin Letty was now being courted by Hermione's first husband's brother; the Earl of Aldbourne. Meg had done her best to mollify Jane by pointing out that he had more money than even Letty. But Jane said; "I just can't bear the thought of Mamma being married to anyone after Pappa." Meg was impatient; "You have no right to be so selfish. Your mother is still a fine looking woman and she deserves to be happy!" Jane relented; "I know your right Meg, I just can't get used to the idea." Meg hugged her; "Dear Jane, I know you will in time."

When Meg had recovered from the birth of Elizabeth they began to go into Woolwich again on Saturdays. They would pay one of Letty's off duty maids to look after the children and resumed the routine they had followed before the birth of young Jonathan. One Saturday their usually uneventful ride was interrupted by a completely unexpected incident. When they were about halfway to Woolwich a ragged figure holding a pistol jumped out of a roadside thicket. As he pointed the pistol at them Jack perceived that his hand was shaking. In a quavering voice the would be highwayman demanded; "Stand and deliver." Jack laughing spurred Jasper forward, then; when he reached the intended robber swerved his mount around causing Jasper's hind quarters to slam into the ragged figure. The erstwhile highwayman fell sprawling onto the road his pistol flying from his hand. Jack quickly dismounted and still laughing picked up the pistol and turned to the prostrate figure; "Get up and tell me what you thought you were going to do." Jack was mentally jolted when he saw that the unsuccessful thief was a youth of about sixteen or seventeen in typical workhouse clothing. The boy was very frightened and pleaded in a whining voice; "Please zur don't turn me in I aint 'ad nuffin to eat fer free days, "an' I needed money to buy vittles." Meg had ridden up to them and was visibly shaken: "Darling, you could have been shot!" Jack laughed and waved the pistol; "Meg dear, it's not even loaded." Meg recovering from her fright became angry; "You could not possibly have known that!" Jack was still laughing; "I know, but I could see it was half-cocked, it couldn't be fired with the hammer in that position." Jack addressed the boy who was looking like he might make a run for it; "You take off and I'll run you down and next time you'll find out that Jasper can hit you a lot harder." The boy was quaking; "Wot er yer gonna do wiv me?" Jack took in the bare feet, the half-mast canvas trousers, ragged jacket and greasy cap;

"You'll find out, but for now you're going to walk in front of us until we get to town and remember what I said about running off." As they began riding along with the ragged boy walking ahead Meg asked: "What are you going to do with him Jack?" Jack answered with a wistful look on his face; "I'm going to see if the regiment will have him." Meg sighed; "You old softy, and he thinks you're going to give him up to the Beadle." Jack smiled; "Let him think that till we get to the barracks, some trepidation will be good for his soul." When they arrived at the barracks Sergeant Woodford was about to leave for the day when he saw them he stopped short; "Wot yer got there Jack?" Jack laughingly pointed at the puzzled looking boy; "If you and me don't know what that is who does? Who's orderly officer today?" Woodford remembered his manners and nodded to Meg; "Good day to you Meg, and 'ow's young Jonathan and that pretty little 'Lizabeth?" Meg smiled; "They're both very well and thank you Frank for asking." Woodford turned back to Jack; "Sorry Jack couldn't ignore yer missus. 'Anbury from 'B' squadron is OD I jes saw 'im go in the guardroom." Jack and Meg dismounted and Jack pointed the ragged boy to the guardroom. When they had secured their horses Jack ushered the boy through the door. Chalky who was now a sergeant was standing behind the desk and had just finished making his daily report to Cornet Hanbury. Jack who was in civilian clothes nodded to the officer respectfully. Sir I'd like to see if we could make a lancer out of this lad before he goes and gets himself hanged." Hanbury who was the officer who had complained to the Colonel about Jack's superior horse turned to Chalky; "What d'ye think Sergeant White?" As Chalky looked at the dirty figure memories came flooding back and Jack knew why he was smiling. He turned back to Hanbury; "We'll get 'im fed an' then see wot we can do wiv 'im." As Hanbury left the guardroom he gave Meg an admiring look; "Good day Mrs. Spratt." Meg returned the greeting while observing his envious glance at Jasper; "And good day to you Mr. Hanbury." She stepped into the guardroom without being noticed when Chalky was addressing Jack; "I bin pissed off since I pulled orderly sergeant but then yew brings this in fer me. Strewth, I'm buggered if this don't take me back a few years." Jack laughed; "When this young bugger tried to hold us up on the road he was shitting himself. See if you can't find out where he stole this pistol from and get it back to them without their knowing how we came by it." Then they both noticed Meg and their faces reddened Chalky greeted her; "Good day Meg" Meg answered with a curt good day, then; "So you're going to start this young man's first day by demonstrating the kind of coarse language you scoundrels are accustomed to using." Jack recovered his aplomb; "I know the kind of place this boy's from, believe me he's heard a lot worse."

Chalky had become a sergeant on Woodford's recommendation or rather; because of his insistent badgering of SSM Meade. When Woodford realized he had just months remaining before he was due to retire he felt he should have his successor in place. Despite Meade's attempts to point out that it was not normal procedure to promote a replacement prior to the predecessor leaving Woodford continued to insist. Finally Meade gave in and said; "I'll see wot the RSM sez." Royce took the matter to Colonel Hawkins who approved of the promotion saying; "I think Sergeant Woodford is showing initiative by planning ahead." The RSM smiled; "He has an ulterior motive, he doesn't want anyone other than White getting his troop, he thinks promoting him now will eliminate that possibility." Hawkins laughed; "Mr. Royce not only do you know every bloody thing that happens in the regiment; you even know how people think." It was Royce's turn to laugh; "I've known Frank Woodford for a lot of years and I'd be willing to bet that the old bugger will be well aware that I know he has an ulterior motive." The Colonel was now laughing with him; "Tell Meade to see to the paperwork and I'll approve it, he will have to be acting unpaid until Sergeant Woodford's off the regimental payroll."

Jack and Meg rode back to town and after they had stabled their horses at the Duke walked to the shops and made their purchases. After which they enjoyed Gus Davidson's fare before riding back to their cottage.

Although Jack's life might have been described as almost idyllic he silently suffered from a nagging confliction. His societal status put him in a virtual limbo. His father in law was of the gentry as were his wife's aunt and cousin both of which had married minor nobility yet he was a ranker who had been born in a workhouse and was in all probability a bastard. One night just after they had gone to bed Meg asked him why he sometimes seemed to have a pensive look about him. He felt that he owed it to her to be honest; "Meg darling, I know I should be more than grateful for everything I have but..." Then he went on to tell her about his musings. Meg was both angry and sympathetic; "Jack, why do you bother your head about such things? My mother was a baker's daughter and Papa was nothing but a glorified clerk when he first started with John Company, a well educated and well bred clerk but a clerk nevertheless. As for Aunt Letty and Jane well, you know about Uncle Jasper's origins." Jack sighed; "I'm sorry darling, you're right as always." Meg sat up and glared at him; "Jack Spratt, I am not always right and I don't need your apologetic condescension! What happened to the brave lancer that rode down a highwayman two weeks ago?" Jack smiled; "What I did was not particularly brave, he was just a frightened boy." Meg smiled lovingly; "And you saw yourself in that poor boy and saved him from prison or worse." Jack laughed; "He's with the recruits doing dismounted drill everyday from after first parade till suppertime, he might be wishing I'd never saved him right now. I'll wager he rues the day when Hansen got his hands on him!" Meg smiled wryly; "He'll probably rue the day when Sergeant Spratt gets his hands on him, I've heard he can be a right royal bastard." As he leaned over to put out the lamp he replied laughingly; "Such language from a baker's granddaughter, I think it's time we got to sleep." Meg giggled girlishly; "Sergeant Spratt I think you have one further duty to perform before you go to sleep." Jack could not help but think; "What a lucky bastard I am!"

The regiment under Colonel Hawkins was running like a well oiled machine. Major Sinclair- Johnson had been appointed 2i/c and Captain Barry had purchased the vacant majority to take over command of 'A' Squadron. At Woodfords request Ginger and Paddy were both promoted to corporal. When Woodford first told Meade he was considering Ginger to take Chalky's place as Troop Corporal; Meade was initially resistant; "Make Weston Troop Corporal? Yew must be out of yer bloody' mind Frank, ees got more stripes on 'is back than all the NCO's in the regiments got on their fuckin' arms!" Sergeant Woodford smiled; "And me an' yew aint got any? As I recall we wusnt no bloody saints wen we wuz privates." Joe Meade laughed; "Remember wen we tore up that knocking shop in Ireland? We both got twenty fer that." Woodford went on; "Ee's mended 'is ways, I 'erd ee stopped two fights at the Duke's an' ee don't get drunk no more." Meade finally relented; "Yer right Frank, can't expect 'em all to be like Spratt."

Butler now a brigadier visited the regiment frequently and Cynthia could always find a reason to ride out to the cottage and visit with Meg, where she would spoil the children by bringing them gifts and driving Meg to distraction. She would always insist on looking in on Jasper before she left, on each occasion while shaking her head she would make the same comment; "The General wanted to geld this beautiful creature. He must have needed his bloody head examined; senile old bugger!" This always brought the same protest from Meg; "I wish you would not use such language in front of the children." To which Cynthia would inevitably reply; "They don't take any notice of what I say, they just think their Aunty Cynthia's an eccentric old cow." All Meg could think to do was shake her head and sigh.

One Saturday when Jack and Meg joined the lads in the public bar after their dinner they were surprised to find Ginger and Molly with Paddy and Binnie among the crowd. Jack enquired of Chalky; "What are they doing here?" Chalky grinned; "One uv Simpkins drivers got a daughter that looks after their brats so's they can come 'ere for a drink. The girls wouldn't stay 'ome and let them buggers go to the pub without 'em. Probably thinks they'd be picking up 'ores." Jack laughed; "I don't know about Paddy but Molly's probably right about Ginger." At Meg's suggestion that they join them Chalky found a table where they could be sat together. After they were all seated Jack bought a round of drinks. Chalky started off the conversation by asking Meg how the children were. After assuring him that the children were happy and healthy Meg asked him; "And when am I going to be able to ask the same question of you Sergeant White? You're two years older than Jack and he's married with two children." Chalky shrugged; "There's a girl back 'ome I've bin askin' fer years, she says she likes me but can't make up 'er mind." Ginger chimed in; "Is that why yew never tried to pick up bints' wen we wuz out drinking? Strewth, that's a relief; I thought yew wuz one of them nancy boys." Meg cut the laughter short; "I think it's very commendable that Chalky has remained faithful to one girl." The men's conversation turned to matters of the regiment and the women were soon deep into discussing household matters and the rearing of children. On their way back to the cottage Meg raised the question of Chalky's unrequited love; "Darling how can we help Chalky win his ladylove?" Jack laughed; "So now you want to be a matchmaker." Meg bristled; "I'm serious, where's back home for Chalky?" Jack thought for a minute then named a small village in Wiltshire. Meg was elated that's where Hermione's from, she knows everyone there. I must go with her next time she goes home." Jack asked; "And who's going to take care of our children while you're gone? I have a better idea, why don't we ask Hermione if she could bring the girl back with her." Meg smiled knowingly; "Now who's being the matchmaker?"

CHAPTER 9

THE WINDS OF WAR

I N MAY OF 1853 the rumors began to circulate throughout the regiment about the possibility of war in south east Europe, as always the RHQ clerks were the source from where the rankers gleaned their information. The Saturday after the rumors first started to circulate Meg and Jack were sat in the public bar of the Duke with Ginger and Paddy and their wives when Chalky walked in with a pretty dark haired girl on his arm. They came over to the table and Chalky proceeded to introduce her; "This be Barbara but we jes calls 'er Barb back 'ome." After she was seated he named them all for her edification. When he got to naming Meg Barb smiled; "Me 'an Miss Meg's met already." Jack looked surprised. She went on; "Wen Lady Hermione brung me to Lady Aldbourne's 'ouse she wur there." Meg laughed at the look on Jack's face then informed him; "While Hermione was home she heard from Barb's father that they were trying to find a position for her. Hermione knew that Aunt Letty was looking for a maid to replace one who was leaving to get married, so she brought Barb back with her." Jack still looking surprised asked; "How long has she been here?" Meg still laughing said; "She commenced her duties last Sunday, she lives at the house now so she'll be our neighbor." Jack looking somewhat miffed enquired; "And when did you intend to inform me of this?" Meg laughed again; "I just did, silly. And what's even better Barb's going to get Saturdays off so that she and Chalky can see each other when he's not on duty." Jack's eyebrows lifted; "And how's she going to do that?" Meg smiled archly; "One of Aunt Letty's maids is some kind of religious zealot, Baptist or something like that. Aunt Letty said if Barb works for her on Sundays she can have Saturdays off." Jack turned to Chalky; "What have you got to say about this?" Chalky grinned; "I aint 'ad much say about anyfink, but I did ask her to marry me and she said yes." The women all started gushing and making suggestions about wedding preparations giving the men the opportunity to talk among themselves. Inevitably the topic of their conversation turned to the war rumors. The strange place names: Varna, Kulali and Sevastopol were bandied about the table with Ginger commenting; "What sort of name is Crimey?" This brought a laugh from Jack who'd been reading up on his geography since first hearing the rumors; "It's the Crimea, in the southwestern Russian empire." Then Chalky asked; "D'ye think we'll be going out there?" His question was answered two days later.

Monday morning every squadron was addressed by their OC before being dismissed after first parade. From his charger Major Barry cast his eye over the dismounted 'A' Squadron; "No doubt you lads have probably heard the rumors, well they're not rumors any more. There have already been some skirmishes in the Crimea and it seems likely we'll be joining the Turks and the French against the Russians, are there any questions?" Joe Meade raised his hand. Barry nodded to him: "What d'ye need to know Sergeant Major?" Meade cleared his throat; "When we leavin' Sir?" Barry replied; "No orders have been issued as yet, but we will commence practicing battle tactics tomorrow morning." Later in the stables while they were attending to their horses needs Ginger commented; "Wen the bloody 'ell did we get to be friends with the fuckin' Turks and the bleedin' Frogs?" Paddy smiled grimly; "When the politicians and the merchants decided where there best interests lay, laddie." Ginger shook his head; "'Ow did yew get to speak so posh yew bloody furriner? I can't understand 'af wot yew 'an Fishy sez sometimes." Paddy laughed; "Are you referring to Sergeant Spratt, Corporal Weston?" Ginger bristled; "Go get fucked you sodding bog trotter!" Paddy laughed again; "To be sure if we're going somewhere where there's no colleens I'll certainly keep me eye on you just to make sure that doesn't happen."

The regiment went into a routine of intense training in battle tactics. General Anderson and Colonel Butler were kept busy going to various stations to instruct officers in the latest recommended methods to be employed by cavalry units. In June Chalky and Barb were married in the regimental chapel with Jack as best man and Ginger and Paddy as ushers. Letty had a cottage which had become vacant on her estate in which she allowed Chalky and Barb to live at a minimal rent and Chalky got to ride with Jack "to work" on horses from her stable. The wives were now fast friends and whenever all of them were in Woolwich they would go shopping together leaving the men in the Duke's bar. One Saturday in November the men were sat drinking when Chalky brought up the question of their impending mobilization; "Yew erd anyfing in RHQ 'bout wen we're going Fishy?" Jack shook his head; "Nothing official but there's been talk about sometime in the New Year." Ginger chimed in; "Looks like we'll get to 'ave Christmas 'ere then." Jack then came up with an idea; "I wonder if Gus would let us have our Christmas celebration in the upstairs room? With the children and everything there's not enough room in any of our homes." Paddy agreed; "To be sure 'tis a great idea you have laddie!" With that Jack got up and walked over to the bar. The others watched as he and Gus discussed Jack's suggestion, when he rejoined them Ginger asked; "Wot 'e say Fishy?"

Jack replied; "He says the room will be available the Saturday before Christmas and for three pounds ten he'll serve us goose, mutton, vegetables, beer and a plum pudding. If you three boys come up with fifteen bob apiece Meg and I will come up with the other one pound five." They all started to protest that it should be divided evenly, then Jack held up his hand; "Call it our Christmas present to you, but I insist." Just then as the wives entered the bar Jack looked up and asked; "Are you ready to eat ladies?" Molly answered; "I don't know about yew gals but I'm bloody starving." Jack grinned as he saw Meg wince. While they were enjoying Gus's famous pork pies they discussed the upcoming celebration enthusiastically.

On the morning of the Saturday before Christmas Jack and Meg loaded the children into Letty's carriage and joined Chalky and Barb who were already seated inside. When she had heard about the party they had planned Letty insisted that they use her carriage to go into Woolwich. Chalky's first word to Jack were; "Bloody 'ell mate we're going in style today!" Meg glared at him; "Not in front of the children Chalky." Barb added her admonition; "Someone needs to 'ave their mouth washed out." Chalky looking crestfallen apologized. Then Meg rounded on their children; "You can both stop giggling and if I ever hear anything like that from either of you, I can assure you both there'll be some mouth washing in the Spratt household!" When they arrived at the Duke Paddy and Ginger were waiting with their families, after they had stepped down from the carriage Ginger felt compelled to comment; "Blimey we thought it wuz the Queen oo wuz comin' to 'ave a party wiv us!" Jack told the coachman when to come back for them then they all went up to the banquet room. After dinner gifts were exchanged and the older children played together while the wives cooed over the small babies and the men moved to another table. The other wives instinctively deferred to Meg and showed no resentment towards her. In fact she had become their leader from acceptance rather than feelings of inferiority. Meg brought up the subject of the impending war and the fact that their men would be away; "You know ladies we will need to help and support each other while our men are away." Molly who was always the most outspoken of the wives spoke up; "Wot 'elp er yew gonna need? Yew got money and yew lives near yer aunt." Meg addressed her directly; "I may be better off than you financially but I'll still need your love and friendship, in fact we'll all need those things from each other." Then Binnie piped up; "We should meet every week 'an talk about wot we bin doin' and 'ow the babes are." Meg was enthusiastic; "We can meet right here on Saturdays just like we do now, Barb and I can come in with Albert when he picks up the groceries for Aunt Letty." Then Barb had a question; "Wot about the other wives who stay home, wont they talk about us bein' in a pub wivout our blokes?" Meg startled them with her reply; "Bugger 'em it won't be any of their bloody business! In fact it wouldn't hurt for them to join us; after all we all belong to the same regiment."

Meanwhile the men were discussing the impending war and the intensified training they were undergoing. Jack made the point that he thought what Brigadier Butler had been teaching the regimental officers made a lot of sense; "It makes sense that we should charge at the full gallop straightaway. It means we can be on the infantry before they reload and get in under the shells before the gunners can depress their cannons. Ginger asked; "is it true the 11th Hussars aint bin doin' it like we 'ave?" Jack frowned; "Cardigans got 'em doing the charge like they're in a review; starting at the walk and then trot, canter and gallop. He claims by showing discipline and order this way; you intimidate the enemy." Chalky laughed; "I'm surprised ees not gonna scare the enemy by tellin' 'em eel ave 'em all flogged!" Then Paddy asked a question; "You said we could be on the infantry before they reload if they're formed up in a square won't the second and rear ranks be loaded?" Jack replied; "They don't normally use light cavalry against a square, that's work for the dragoons. But if they do use us to charge a square all I can say is God help us!"

Then Jack changed the subject; "How about the wives and children when we're away, I don't have to worry for my family but how about you blokes?" Chalky was the first to answer; "Lady Aldbourne is letting Barb stay in the cottage on the estate Then Paddy spoke; "Mr. Simpkins says Binnie and Molly and the kids can stay where we are now and he'll worry about the rent when we gets back, he's a broth of a man to be sure!"

Jack changed the subject again; "Ginger, you've got mates in 'B' Squadron; how's the highwayman doing?" Ginger laughed; "Yew means Turps; they tells me ees doin' good." Jack nodded his approval; "When I first got him from Hansen I heard one of the lads talking about Turps so I said who the hell's Turps? He said that's Reeves's nickname. They'd heard about him trying to hold us up on the Hemel Hempstead road and named him after Dick Turpin (a notorious 18th century highwayman). When we issued him his horse he was going to call it Bess, then one of the lads told him you don't give geldings girls names so he called it Dick." Jack looked thoughtful; "So he named him after Dick Turpin instead of Turpin's Black Bess." Then he smiled; "I don't think Dick Turpin would be flattered, that lad was a bloody poor apology for a highwayman." Ginger smiled; "Ee rides like one though, you did a fuckin' good job wiv 'im!" None of them had noticed Meg who had approached their table unnoticed and had heard the last part of their conversation; "I wish you'd all leave that foul language back at the barracks." Molly who was right behind Meg laughed; "Did yew know that 'er ladyship just said bugger and bloody?" Meg's face went scarlet; "Molly Weston you didn't have to tell them that, I thought you were my friend!" Molly laughed again; "I am yer friend, that's why I won't let yer get too far up on yer 'igh 'orse, in case yew falls off." It was Meg's turn to laugh; "You're a good friend Molly and I know you'll see that I keep my feet on the ground." Then Binnie and Barb joined them and the wives proceeded to tell their husbands about their plans for when the men were away.

Jack and Meg and children were invited to Letty's for the Christmas Eve supper after which they put the children to bed with Jane's toddler Robert before going to midnight mass at the village church. As they were walking to the village Letty's new husband addressed Jack; "What d'ye think about this Russian business young fella?" Jack answered; "Well your Lordship I don't know about the fighting capabilities of the Russian soldier, but I have heard their muskets and cannon are inferior to ours." Lord Aldbourne acquiesced: "Yes I heard the same but it wouldn't do to underestimate 'em, after all they did kick old Boney's arse." This brought an exclamation from Jane; "Oh Marmie such language, and us on our way to church!" This caused Major Barry to laugh; "Hope it doesn't fall in on us." The Earl had something more to say; "Jack I want you to stop being so formal from now on and address me as Uncle Marmie. Marmie is short for Marmaduke; I think my parents must have hated me giving me such a silly bloody name." This brought another exclamation from Jane; "Marmie you're incorrigible!" Then Meg commented; "Yes he's as bad as Cynthia." This brought further comment from the Earl; "You mean Harry Butler's wife? Damn fine woman, knew her as a gal. God! She was beautiful, I really fancied her but she only had eyes for old Harry." This brought a comment from Letty; "If I recall the girl you married was quite a beauty." The Earl answered reminiscently; "Yes Tabitha was beautiful, I thought the world had come to an end when she died. But I was lucky enough to find another beauty." Letty smiled in the darkness; "Why thank you Marmie I would like to think Tabby would have approved of me, you know we were friends as girls." Marmie answered; "Yes I was aware of that, and I know damned well she would have approved." Jane gave an exasperated sigh; "There really is no hope for him! Do you know I resented him when he was courting Mamma until Meg made me realize how selfishly I was behaving, now I think I love him in spite of his colorful language." Letty laughed; "Another twice married couple will be joining us tomorrow, Jonathan and Hermione are coming for Christmas dinner and to spend the week with us. I understand you men are going to be shooting pheasant after the holiday." Jack was curious; "How did the first Lady Aldbourne die? I'll understand if you find it too painful to talk about." The Earl replied; "She died giving birth to our son who is now a captain with the 16th in India. Last I heard he'd been seconded from his regiment to be an instructor. They're raising some new native cavalry regiments but I'm not sure it's a good idea." Major Barry interjected; "But Sir, haven't we had native regiments out there for years?" The Earl agreed; "Yes John Company raised 'em to start with but the ones my son is helping to form are of Sikhs and Punjabis and such and I've seen those buggers fight. With British style discipline and cohesion we could be in big bloody trouble if they ever turned on us!" Letty admonished him; "Enough army talk Marmie, we're almost at the church." As they entered the church they were greeted by the vicar; "A blessed Christmas to you Lord and Lady Aldbourne, Major and Mrs. Barry, Sergeant and Mrs. Spratt I see you have walked here on this fine frosty night. You know our Lord walked everywhere except when he rode a donkey into Jerusalem on Palm Sunday." Marmie couldn't resist; "Wouldn't have cut much of a figure in the cavalry I'll wager!" They all winced and Letty pinched his arm viciously as they headed toward the front pews. As they sat down the Earl had one final comment; "Sanctimonious old bugger, that'll give him something for his Palm Sunday sermon." Letty turned and glared at him; "I know you've had a few drinks tonight so I'm prepared to make allowances, but stop this hooligan like behavior right now!" The Earl hung his head in mock contrition and managed to constrain his ebullience through the length of the service.

On their way back to the house the Earl suggested they have one more drink before retiring for the night. Meg demurred;

"I'm sorry Uncle but we have to get the children and take them home to bed," Letty suggested they leave the children be; "You can leave them up there with young Robert I'll have a maid see that they're bathed in the morning; they can have breakfast here, in fact they might as well stay till dinner." Meg exclaimed; "Oh thank you Aunt Letty you are such a dear." After they entered the house Letty suggested they have their drinks in the library where they made toasts to Christmas and the regiment.

On Christmas morning Jack and Meg made their way up to the house for breakfast where they found that the children had been fed and were now playing in a room which Letty had had converted into a temporary nursery. When they were seated Marmie turned to Jack; "Well young fella, Letty's told me quite a bit about your background seems to me you've come a long way in a short time, what are your plans for the future?" Jack's answer surprised them all except Meg; "When my times expired Meg and I plan to start a home for waifs and strays, we intend to keep as many children out of those bloody workhouses as we can!" He looked at Meg; "I'm sorry for cursing darling I get so angry just thinking of those hell holes." The Earl asked; "How d'ye plan to pay for the upkeep of a home like that?" Jack replied; "We hope to find some wealthy patrons and we also plan to have a riding school where people will pay for lessons." Marmie seemed impressed; "I'm sure Letty and I can help if you persist with this plan, we know quite a few people with more money than they know what to do with, and the Earl of Shaftesbury is a friend of mine; he might be able to get someone interested in Parliament." Jack and Meg were both delighted with Marmie's approval and Meg expressed her feelings in her usual enthusiastic manner by getting up and going around the table and kissing the Earl on the cheek; "Uncle Marmie you are a darling." Then looking over at Jack she said; "Darling, we should name it The Earl of Aldbourne's Home for Children." As she sat back down by Jack he looked at her; "That would be the perfect name, but let's not forget its still some years away." She retorted; "There's no reason why I can't get started with fund raising and looking for a suitable location." The Earl had a suggestion; "We can set up a trust where donations can be deposited and gain some interest." Then Letty interrupted; "That's all well and good but we have to think about dinner and Jonathan and Hermione will be here shortly. Meg you and your Uncle Marmie can start making your plans another time, let's get Christmas out of the way first." Major Barry then announced that he was expected at the barracks by noon. Jane enquired anxiously; "Philip dear, you will be back for dinner?" Barry replied; "Yes darling we're feeding the lads at midday, you know it's tradition for the officers to serve the men their Christmas dinner." Jack stood; "With your permission I'd like to ride in with you and wish the lads a Merry Christmas." Barry was agreeable; "I'll get my horse and we'll meet down on the road." Letty gave them a warning; "Do not spoil your appetites for dinner." When they met on the road Major Barry regarded Jasper with admiration; "Whenever I think about what you did with that magnificent animal I'm still amazed. By the way, will he let anyone ride him other than you?" Jack's answer startled him; "Only Meg, Sir." Barry's expression betrayed his surprise; "How did you manage that?" Jack smiled; "I didn't, Meg would go in the stable and gentle him whenever I wasn't around. She got him to trust her and then to love her. Then one day after I'd been helping out up at Aunt Letty's stables she was up on Jasper and met me when I was walking back to the cottage. She didn't know that I was aware that she had been working with him so I acted surprised." Barry could not help but comment; "She's such a tiny little girl for such a large horse." Jack smiled; "Meg's a great horsewoman but she does have to use a mounting block to get on Jasper." Barry reflected; "Yes she does sit a horse well, I remember when she dead heated with the Colonel's wife on gala day." Jack laughed; "I'll bet Captain Portal does too, he was the finish line judge that day." This caused Barry to laugh; "Portal's still scared of Mrs. Butler but to tell the truth we all are to some extent." Jack agreed; "Meg and Aunt Letty are the only two people I know who'll stand up to her, and I think the only reason Meg can is because Mrs. Butler adores her." Their ride into Woolwich afforded them an opportunity to talk in a way which had never been possible before and they used it to get to know each other better. At one point Barry commented on Jack's statements at the breakfast table; "You know you sounded awfully passionate about the children's home!" Jack replied; "That's because I am, I lived in a workhouse the first sixteen years of my life and becoming a ranker in the regiment was like going to heaven that shows what kind of a place it was! There are far too many people living in poverty and Meg and I want to help however we can. This industrial revolution has forced too many people to dwell in want and misery while a few get rich. The reason I am here today is because I was starving and I tried to steal a loaf of bread. If it hadn't been for the kindness of the old magistrate I would have been transported or hanged." Barry sounded concerned; "I don't have any first hand knowledge of the social situation, d'ye think there could be a revolution like they had in France back in 1789?" Jack replied soberly; "I don't know Sir, I prefer to think that more of the upper class will come around to Lord Shaftsbury's way of thinking and prevent that possibility." During their ride Barry suggested that they address each other by first names when they were off duty and with the family. Jack demurred; "I'm afraid if we did I might forget at an inappropriate moment." The Major laughed; "You're probably right, I don't know if I could trust myself either." As they entered the outskirts of Woolwich Jack set Jasper's head toward The Duke of York's causing Barry to exclaim; "You can ride him to the barracks today your not in uniform, and hell it's Christmas!" As they passed through the main gate of the barracks the sentry saluted Major Barry then greeted them; "Merry Christmas Sir, and you too Sergeant Spratt." As they rode past the guardhouse Barry exclaimed; "Pity that lad has to miss out on the dinner." Jack smiled; "He'll do alright Sir, after he's done his two hours he'll have dinner with the cooks and you know those buggers always keep the best for themselves." Barry laughed then asked; "Where are you going Sergeant?" Jack who was riding off to the right replied; "I'm going to tether Jasper outside RHQ then I'll walk to the cookhouse." Barry was puzzled; "Why would you do that when there's a hitching rail at the cookhouse?" Jack seeing Barry's puzzlement explained; "I don't want to be seen as putting on airs and graces, you see I'm the only ranker who has his own horse." Barry smiled approvingly; "I'll go on then and see you there."

When Jack entered the cookhouse he went to the table where Chalky, Ginger and Paddy were seated and they all exchanged Christmas greetings. Then as Jack was sitting down Ginger exclaimed; "Look at 'im in those togs proper bloody gentleman aint ee, maybe we should call 'im Squire 'stead of Sergeant." Then Cornet Hanbury came to their table with a large tray on which was three steaming platters of goose, potatoes, parsnips' kale and stuffing. After placing the platters on the table he addressed Jack; "I'll be back with your dinner shortly Sergeant." Jack looked up; "No thank you Sir, I'll not be eating I just stopped by to the wish the lads a Merry Christmas. Oh, and a Merry Christmas to you too Sir." Paddy looked up from his platter; "Will you not be eating with us then boyo?" Jack shook his head; "Not this year lads, Meg's aunt insisted we have Christmas dinner up at the house and if I ate now I wouldn't do it justice tonight. I take it you'll be having your family dinners tomorrow as usual?" It was Ginger's turn to look up; "Me an' Paddy's family er 'avin ours togever." Then Chalky spoke up; "We're 'avin a Boxin' Day dinner wiv the Gamekeepers family at the lodge." Jack looked at his comrades with affection; "I think Lady Aldbourne wanted us to have Christmas dinner with her because she knows we'll be leaving for the Crimea in the New Year." Just then Barry came over; "Well all the lads have been served, are you ready to start back Sergeant?"

Jack stood up; "I'll see you lads the day after tomorrow." Glancing at Ginger and Paddy he said; "Wish Molly and Binnie and the children a Merry Christmas." Then to Chalky; "We'll come over to see you and Barb when you get back to the cottage."

As they left the barracks the Major commented; "D'ye know whenever I see the four of you together I think of the Three Musketeers." Jack grinned and said; "In the Alexandre Dumas novel? I never thought of me and those three rascals in that sense." Barry seemed surprised; "You've read the novel?" Jack replied; "That was part of the required reading when Meg taught me how to read and write. She would get me books that she knew I could relate too; the first one was Oliver Twist. I think I'm the most fortunate man on earth to have such a devoted beautiful teacher to become my wife. Although I'm now her teacher, once I mastered reading I got interested in mathematics which I'm now teaching her. Barry agreed with him on Meg's virtues then asked about his mates; "What d'ye know about your comrades?" Jack thought for a minute; "Well Weston came to the army from Newgate Prison. His father was jailed for debt and had to take the family to prison with him because they had nowhere to live. His mother got sick in there and when his father asked a jailer if he could get some physic for her, the jailer said only if he could have his daughter." The Major was visibly shaken; "You mean he wanted Corporal Weston's sister carnally?" Jack answered; "Yes Sir, then Ginger beat the jailer almost to death for which he got twenty-five strokes of the cat 'o nine tails and was given the choice of joining the army or being transported. Corporal O'Neill joined the army because of the conditions in Ireland; every so often he's able to send money home to his family. Sergeant White's father was a poacher and was killed by a game keeper's dogs, his mother died shortly afterwards and he couldn't get work around their village in Wiltshire because the gamekeeper and his squire made sure no one would employ him." Barry exclaimed; "What sort of a fucking rotten world are we living in?" Jack looked grim;

"Sir, I may be speaking out of turn but you should make a point of going out into that world to know what conditions are for the majority of people." The Major looked thoughtful; "I think I'm beginning to understand your passion for that home you and Meg are planning, Jane and I will support you in your endeavor, and we will make sure that young Robert grows up knowing that there are others in this world less fortunate than he."

When they reached the gates of the Letty's estate Jack turned to Barry; "After I've taken care of Jasper I'll walk up to the house." After the Major reached the stables he handed over his horse to a groom and walked into the house with a grim look on his face. As he entered the library Letty looked up; "My word Philip you look like thunder, what happened to you?" He then recounted what he had learned from Jack about social conditions; "I suppose I've always been aware of the existence of poverty but never thought about how it affected people who lived in those circumstances." Meg felt she should soothe his feelings; "It's not your fault Philip, you were raised in a beautiful house in the country with servants to serve your every whim. When you were old enough you were educated in an expensive school then your father purchased you a commission. You never really came into contact with the world to which Jack has opened your eyes." Barry looked uncomfortable; "I'll tell you ladies something that might shock you but I feel a need to unburden myself after Sergeant Spratt's revelation. On my sixteenth birthday my father said it was time I learned about women and he took me to a brothel in town. I realize now from what the Sergeant had told me about his mates that the girl I had that night probably came from similar circumstances as they. She was a prostitute because that was the only way for her to survive." Barry then realized that Meg's father and Hermione were present; "I am so sorry for barging in with a tirade like that, without even greeting you." Jonathan smiled grimly; "I think I speak for both of us when I say you are forgiven, it's obvious you're very agitated about what you've just learned." Letty rang for the butler, when he arrived she instructed him to bring the Major a whisky then turned to Barry; "Sit down Philip and have a good stiff drink." Then addressing Jane; "Take that stupid look off your face girl it took a lot of courage for him to make that admission!" Jack's entry into the library broke the tension somewhat as he informed them that he'd just seen Chalky take his horse into the stable; "I wanted to wish Barb a Merry Christmas so I thought I'd walk down to their cottage." Letty smiled up at Jack; "I'm sure she'll appreciate your felicitations, you'll also be seeing her tonight, she offered to help with dinner." Then Meg said; "I'll come with you darling." As they were walking to the cottage she told him about Barry's narrative and admission. Jack expressed his regret; "I never intended to make him feel guilty. You know I read about that Quaker Elizabeth Fry, the prison reform lady that died back in'45, she discovered that some poor families would sell their daughters to whoremasters to feed their other children." Meg smiled; "A little soul searching is good for everyone, but please never tell Jane or Philip." Although it does seem that you've got us another patron for the home."

Christmas dinner was a success with the traditional goose being served along with jugged hare, roast pheasant and a variety of vegetables all of which was followed by a huge plum pudding liberally anointed with custard. After which the men retired to the drawing room while the ladies watched over the children playing before being put to bed in the nursery. When the men were seated in the drawing room with their glasses of port and cigars, the conversation predictably turned to the approaching war. The Earl was the first to speak; "What d'ye think of the people they're talking about putting in charge, hardly any of them have any war time experience." Barry spoke up; "They're putting the Earl of Lucan in charge of a cavalry division and Cardigan's getting the Light Brigade." Marmie's eyes rolled back into his head God help those poor buggers!" Jack laughed; "The Major and I will be with the Light Brigade along with the rest of the Seventeenth." The Earl groaned; "Then God help you two poor buggers!"

After Boxing Day Jack, Chalky, Ginger and Paddy with the rest of the regiment went back to intense tactical training under the watchful eyes of their officers. The now Brigadier Butler would turn up unannounced to observe their progress offering both advice and criticism. On one occasion when he was observing "A" Squadron he called Woodford over, after the Sergeant halted in front of him and saluted he asked; "Is that Weston I see with two stripes on his arm?" Woodford smiled at the look on his former CO's face; "Yes Sir, ees me Troop Corporal." Butler shook his head; "He's handling his men very well, who'd have thought?" The Sergeant was now widely grinning; "I fink ee always 'ad it in 'im, jus' needed someone to bring it out." The Brigadier grinned back you've done a great job Sergeant." Woodford answered modestly; "Thank yew Zur, but Sergeant Spratt 'ad a lot to do wiv it." The Colonel's grin turned into a large smile; "Oh yes, we mustn't forget Sergeant Spratt, carry on Sergeant." Woodford saluted then curveted his horse and rode back grinning to 1st Troop.

Jonathan and Hermione stayed with the Aldbournes during the week following Christmas and the two men went pheasant shooting every day. When the Earl invited Barry to go shooting with them he had declined; "I'm sorry Uncle Marmie but we're in training and I'd feel bad about asking for leave even if the Colonel would give it to me." Marmie concurred; "You're right of course, wish all my squadron commanders were as conscientious as you when I had the Sixteenth!" Major Barry commented; "I heard they were a damn fine regiment under your command." The Earl said; "As far as I've heard they still are, I'll have to go visit 'em when they get back from India."

At breakfast on New Years Day Letty had made an announcement; "Tonight's dinner is going to be special New Years dinner and there will be a special surprise." While they were enjoying their pre-dinner drinks in the library Jane asked; "Where's Meg?"

Letty with something of a twinkle in her eye answered; "She's taking care of something for me, she'll be joining us after dinner." Dinner consisted of consommé soup, a fish course of trout almondine followed by roast pheasant with mushroom sauce and culminating with a soufflé for dessert. When everyone had finished eating Letty looked round the table; "Well, what d'ye think?" Jonathan commented enthusiastically; "That was a dinner fit for the Queen!" All present agreed also adding their compliments. Then Letty rang the bell which was used to summon the servants and Barb appeared. Letty smiling archly instructed her; "Please bring in the chef." Barb left then reappeared with a broadly smiling Meg. All at the table gave admiring gasps except for Jack who had been in on the plot. Jane exclaimed; "Meg dear when did you learn to cook like that?" Letty went on to tell the assembled company how much time Meg had spent learning the art of cooking. She looked over at Jane; "You remember that morning after their wedding when we found her crying because she didn't know how to cook breakfast?" Jane replied; "Yes Mamma, you told her you'd have Cook teach her." Letty beamed; "Yes and she took me at my word and you just enjoyed the fruits of three years hard study." Jack stood and walked over and kissed Meg after which the men all kissed her on the cheek and the ladies hugged her. Meg still standing thanked them with tears running down her face until Letty commanded brusquely; "Sit down girl and stop blubbering!" Jonathan had to comment: "Damn I wish we weren't leaving in the morning. I'd like to stay around and enjoy some more of my daughters cooking. She owes me a few gourmet dinners for the many times she's called me an ogre." This brought a laugh from Meg; Pappa, you are an ogre; a wonderful, generous loving old ogre and I wish I knew how I could repay you for all you've done for Jack and I." Jonathan looking misty eyed responded; "Just keep loving each other and raise my grandchildren to love their family and to respect and be generous to those less fortunate than they." This brought a comment from Jack; "I promise we'll do that Sir, for there was never a better example in that respect than you!" Letty cleared her throat; "Enough of this maudlin nonsense I want to see the children before we pack 'em off to bed. Meg you can collect Jonathan and Elizabeth in the morning." As she left the room for the nursery Jane nudged Meg's arm; "Did you see the tears in Mamma's eyes?" Meg smiled; "Yes, she tries to be such a tyrant but underneath it all she's just an old softy." As the rest of the women left for the nursery the Earl looked up from the glass of sherry he'd been enjoying; "Jack, Philip, I think the three of us are most fortunate to have married into this family!" Jonathan exclaimed; "On behalf of the family I welcome you. Gentlemen raise your glasses; to our family!"

The regiment continued rigorously practicing battle tactics. On one inspection visit Brigadier Butler was accompanied by General Anderson. After they had viewed each squadron they rode back towards RHQ; Hawkins turned to Anderson; "What d'ye think of 'em General?" The General nodded approvingly; "Harry and I are more than pleased with the regiments we've inspected, with the exception of one they've got their tactics honed to a fine edge. But right now Reggie I'd like to take advantage of your hospitality." The Colonel replied; "If you and the Brigadier will excuse me I have a couple of things to attend to in my office, but if you care to go on to the officer's mess for drinks I will join you for dinner." When they were comfortably seated with their glasses of scotch in the mess lounge Anderson addressed Butler; "You know Harry it's not the tactics that bother me, except for Cardigan's bunch. With maybe two exceptions, the general officers they have appointed for the Crimean expedition have no war time experience. The problem is going to be strategy and logistics!" Harry shook his head I know Sir, the only good thing I've heard is that Scarlett's getting the Heavy Brigade." The General nodded his approval; "Jimmy's what you call a Dragoon's Dragoon, but did you know Cardigan went wheedling to the Queen for a division?" Harry looked concerned; "He is a major general so he has the appropriate rank." Anderson replied; "Nevertheless the Duke of Cambridge got to The Queen and had it quashed, thank God!" Harry looked thoughtful; "Damn shame Wellington's gone he would be the one to lead the expedition." Anderson concurred; "With him in charge our boys would kick those Russian's arses'from the Crimea all the way back to Moscow!" Butler changed the subject; "Sir, did you forward my application to be with the expeditionary force?" The General's answer took Butler unawares; "No Harry for two very good reasons: You're too old to be in the fighting, and if they put you on the staff you'd be pointing out all the stupid bloody mistakes I know they'll make, and probably wind up being court martialled. And second but most important you can contribute more back here training the young officers in cavalry tactics. The word is that after this show is over there may be trouble in India." At that point Colonel Hawkins entered the lounge and sat with them then ordered a scotch from an orderly, he looked quizzically at Butler. Seeing his expression Harry enlightened him; "The General has just refused to let me go with the expeditionary force." Hawkins understanding his disappointment commiserated; "I know you'd like to be there with us Sir, but I think what you'll be doing back here will be more important in the long run." The General concurred; "Just what I told him Reggie, since he's been running this training program there's been a vast improvement in tactical skills in the regiments."

During the ensuing weeks the intense training continued and during their off duty hours all personnel who were married spent as much time possible with their families. Jack and his three comrades got together with their families whenever the opportunity presented itself. On a Saturday in February at the Duke of York after they had finished their repast Jack called for silence. Looking around the table he addressed Chalky, Ginger and Paddy; "Boys, I want us all to be clear about one thing. If any of us don't come back whoever's left will take care of their wives and families." Molly exclaimed loudly; "Bugger Jack, wot d'ye wanna bring up somefink like that fer wen we wuz all 'avin a good time!" Binnie who was usually the quiet one spoke up; "I think he's right it ud be good to know that we'll be looked out fer if somefink 'appens to our blokes." The three men looked at Jack as Chalky spoke up; "I fink I speaks fer all of us wen I sez that will be our sacred duty!" Jack placed his right hand palm down in the middle of the table: "To our sacred duty." They each placed their right hands atop of each others and repeated; "To our sacred duty." They then raised their tankards and repeated; "To our sacred duty." Then Meg spoke up; "Let's spend as much time together as we can until our men have to leave whenever that might be."

CHAPTER 10

DEPARTURE

DURING THE EARLY weeks of 1854 the four comrades and their families spent as much time as their military and domestic duties would allow. In March the regiment was officially informed that they would be leaving for Turkey in April. Colonel Hawkins called a meeting of his Squadron Leaders, his 2i/c Major Sinclair-Johnson, and Captain Metford who had been appointed Adjutant when Barry had become "A" Squadron's commander and the RSM. All agreed that they should have a full ceremonial parade prior to the regiment's departure; RSM Royce suggested two weekends before they left. His reasoning was that there would be a great deal to attend to during the last two weeks before they left therefore it would be better to have the parade earlier rather than later. After they had all agreed on the date for the parade the Colonel said wistfully; "I'd have liked to have a gala day like we did three years ago, but there's no place near the barracks to hold it." Barry smile archly; "There may be somewhere, could I get back to you tomorrow on this Colonel?" Hawkins who thought he knew what the Major was planning looked at him knowingly; "Thank you Philip I'll be interested to hear what you may come up with." Barry had one more request: "Colonel have I your permission to be absent from duty for the remainder of the day?" The Colonel answered: "Certainly just let your 2i/c know, I won't ask where you're going." After informing his 2i/c Captain Maxwell; Barry rode out of the barracks and took the Hemel Hempstead Rd. Half an hour later he arrived at the Aldbourne residence. At the stables he handed his horse to a groom then entered the house by a side door. He found Letty and the Earl in the library. After kissing Letty on the cheek he shook the Earl's hand. Letty exclaimed; "Well this is a surprise, what are you doing here at this time of day and where are Jane and Robert?" The Major explained: "I came here straight from the barracks; I assume they are home where I left them this morning." He then went on to explain what they had discussed at the meeting and the Colonel's expressed desire. Before he could continue Letty interjected; "There's those two fallow fields down by the lake it's far enough away from the woods not to disturb the nesting pheasants, although I don't suppose the ducks will be too happy!" The Earl cleared his throat; "Philip, for god's sake sit down and have a drink!" He rang the bell and when the butler entered he instructed him to bring the Major a scotch. When he was comfortably seated with a scotch in his hand Barry thanked them both; "That location will be perfect, as I recall those fields are separated by a hedgerow. The one is about three acres which will be ideal for the vendor's stalls, beer tent and the other functions that will need to be under tents. The six acre field will be more than suitable for competitive activities and the racing events." As he finished his drink Barry rose saying; "I should get back to Woolwich I would like to get this news to the Colonel before he leaves for the day." He kissed Letty on the cheek and shook the Earl's hand again; "Thank you Mamma and you Sir, I'll let you know when I have more details. When he arrived back at the barracks he rode straight to RHQ. He met Hawkins in the corridor who showed surprise; "Why Philip, I didn't think I'd be seeing you until tomorrow." Barry answered with a smile; "I couldn't wait to tell you what I've arranged. I talked to Lady Leticia and the Earl and they have a perfect location for our gala." The Colonel smiled back; "I thought that might be where you were headed, your news firms up what I'd been tentatively considering." The Major asked; "What might that be Sir?" The Colonel's answer delighted Barry; "We'll make it a two day event. With the parade on Friday morning, then open the mess to the ladies for lunch and dinner, and for the men we'll give them the rest of the day off after the parade. This'll give us a full day Saturday for the gala." The Major's enthusiasm elicited a schoolboy like exclamation; "Oh Sir, That'll be absolutely Top Hole!"

The Colonel sent letters to the Duke and General Anderson informing them of his intentions and requesting they meet with him to offer their suggestions. The meeting was held two day's later in the officer's mess, when they had decided what notaries would be invited to be seated in the reviewing stand the General had a suggestion; "I'd like to have a troop of Horse Artillery in the Parade, they could give a gun salute." The Duke and the Colonel agreed that it was a great idea. Then the Duke gave one of his customary harrumphs; "I know this would be contrary to protocol and I would normally defer to your senior rank Billy, but I would like to suggest we let Harry Butler take the salute." Anderson replied; "I'm in total agreement, Harry loves this regiment and maybe it might take some of the edge off the disappointment he's feeling about not going with them too the Crimea." At the conclusion of the meeting the Duke turned to the General; "It's lunch time Billy how about we sample the fare at this famous pork pie tavern of yours?" Hawkins suggested that as it was only a few minutes away that they walk to the Duke of York's Arms. As they entered the tavern Gus came rushing over to them. He knew the General as a customer and was acquainted with the Colonel but he did not recognize the Duke at first, he started to greet them; "Good day to yew gen'lmen welcome...Oh! Yer Grace I'm sorry I dint know it wuz yew, please fergiv me." The Duke har-rumphed; "They tell me you're an old cavalryman." Gus answered with some trepidation; "Yes Yer Grace, 3rd Dragoon Guards." The Duke harrumphed again; "I'm the Colonel in Chief of the 17th Lancers, a soldier just like you. So let's dispose of this bloody Your Grace nonsense, you may address me as sir. And your pork pies had better be as good as I've heard or I'll take that saber down that's hanging on your wall and I'll let you guess where I'll shove it." Gus who was now more at ease said; "Let me show yew to yer table gen'lmen." After they'd enjoyed their pork pies which at the General's suggestion they washed down with porter; "It's the only thing to drink with this food" Gus came over and asked them if the food was to their liking. The Duke laughed; "It seems that I won't need that bloody saber after all."

The following days were hectic. While the regiment con-tinued to practice field tactics work parties were sent to the Aldbourne estate daily to prepare the area where the gala would take place. Letty made sure the men had plenty to eat for their midday meals, when the Colonel rode out one day to see how the work was progressing he asked to see Letty and the Earl. He was shown into the library where he offered to pay for the men's meals. Letty exploded; "Why Reggie Hawkins how dare you insult me this way?" Hawkins was shaken; "It was not my intention to insult you Lady Aldbourne, it's just that their mid-day meals are accounted for in the regiments budget so there is no reason that you should bear that expense." Letty feigned fury; "Sit down and let me tell you two things: First you do not address me as Lady Aldbourne our families have known each other for years, and second if my feeding your men results in a surplus in your regimental funds you can send the bloody money to the regimental widows! Now sit down and have a drink." She rang for the butler; "Get Colonel Hawkins a scotch or whatever he'd like to drink." She then turned back to the Colonel; "Excuse me but I have to go and talk to Cook about tonight's dinner."

The Colonel and the Earl both stood while she left the room and as Hawkins sat back in his chair he let out a gasp. The Earl laughed: "Quite a spitfire isn't she?" When the butler brought his drink the Colonel downed it in one gulp; "After that I think I'm ready to face the Russians." They were both laughing when Letty returned, she glared at them both; "Giggling like two bloody schoolboys, do men ever grow up?" When he got back to barracks the Colonel rode straight to "A" Squadron, he walked into Major Barry's office sat down and proceeded to tell about his meeting with Letty. Barry laughed; "Mama's bark is worse than her bite." Hawkins sighed: "I would hope so; I thought Cynthia Butler was a virago but I think your mother in law could give her a run for her money."

When the day before the parade arrived all ranks of regiment heaved a collective sigh of relief. While they had still continued their tactical training, they had daily parade rehearsals and were also sending work parties to the Aldbourne estate. The sergeants major had had to draw up schedules to rotate the men in their squadrons in order; so that they all could be fully rehearsed for the parade while the other duties were addressed. Also, the inclusion of the horse artillery troop had necessitated some changes from their customary ceremonial parade drill.

The Friday morning two weeks prior to the regiments scheduled departure saw the squadrons ride on parade in their usual order except this time a troop of horse artillery brought up the rear. When the 17th turned into line the artillery wheeled their teams with their guns and caissons into line then dressed them back so that the front pair of each four horses dressed on the front rank of "D" Squadron, then their troop officer took his station front and center. When the inspection was complete the RSM gave the order and the 17th turned into columns of three while the artillery troop formed their teams into file behind "D" Squadron with their mounted officer at their head. As they trotted past the reviewing stand with head and eyes right Jack who was riding with "HQ" Squadron took in the scene on the reviewing stand. Brigadier Butler in a scarlet tunic with a fore 'n aft plumed hat on his head; stood returning the salute. Behind him was General Anderson wearing a similar uniform but with larger gold epaulettes. The General was flanked by the Duke and Colonel Hawkins with the Colonel of the Royal Horse Artillery regiment who had provided the artillery troop and Major Sinclair-Johnson. The reviewing stand presented a riot of colors created by the dress uniforms of the many high ranking officers. Just before "HQ" Squadron was ordered "eyes front" he glimpsed Meg's father with little Jonathan on his shoulders and Meg and Hermione who were both holding up Elizabeth, they were all waving frantically. After passing in review the columns halted at the far side of the parade ground; then the RSM gave the order: "Parade turn left into review order!" The artillery officer with his saber fully extended above his head made an anti-clockwise circular motion and gave the order; "Guns wheel left, at the gallop to the rear!" The gun teams followed the officer at a thunderous gallop to the far corner of the parade ground where they halted line abreast with the guns facing back towards the reviewing stand. On his command the team's drivers dismounted, uncoupled the teams from their caissons, remounted and galloped another fifty yards taking them well off the parade ground. Once halted the drivers dismounted again then held the heads of their teams lead horses. After this maneuver was completed the RSM gave the order; "The regiment will advance in review order, at the walk forward!" As they were about to give a royal salute the Duke being the only member of the royal family present was now on the saluting rostrum. As the regiment came to a halt at the customary ten paces and the band stopped playing the RSM gave the order; "Royal salute, Salute!" The officers saluted with their sabers, and then the artillery officer's order carried across the parade ground; "Troop will fire Royal Salute, number one gun Fire!" The guns fired in succession twenty-one times and smoke rolled across the parade ground. Little Jonathan waved and shouted with delight while Elizabeth covered her ears and cried. After the last echo had rolled away the officers brought their sabers up to the carry and the RSM gave the order; "Officers will return swords." Upon which the officers sheathed their weapons. The RSM then curveted his mount to face the reviewing stand, addressing the Duke he asked; "Are their any further orders, Sir?" The Duke replied; "Mr. Royce you will lead the regiment in three cheers for Her Majesty the Queen." Royce wheeled his horse around to face the regiment; "The 17th Lancers will give three cheers for Her Majesty the Queen!" He paused to allow time for the unbuckling of chinstraps then; "Three cheers for Her Majesty the Queen, Hip Hip!" On each Hurrah all ranks in the regiment raised their helmets high above their heads. After the last Hurrah had echoed away the RSM ordered; "Regiment will replace headdress, replace headdress!" He then wheeled again to face the reviewing stand where Brigadier Butler was back on the saluting rostrum, sheathing his saber then saluting he addressed the Brigadier; "Sir, have I your permission to dismiss the regiment?" Harry Butler with a wistful look on his face said; "You have my permission to dismiss the regiment Mr. Royce and may I also add, well done everybody!"

Later in the officer's mess while nursing his drink the Duke asked the Colonel; "Does everyone know about tomorrow's gala?" Hawkins replied; "Yes Sir, the provost staff handed everybody a broadsheet at the main gate as they left." This brought a contented grunt from the Duke; "I'm beginning to think I made the right decision in giving you the regimental command." Cynthia Butler could not restrain herself; "Oh really Your Grace, was there a time when you had some doubts?" The Duke harrumphed; "That was a figure of speech Cynthia, and you'd do well to confine your teasing to Meg Langsbury." Hermione felt the need to correct the Duke; "Her name is Spratt Your Grace she's now a married lady with two children." The Duke who was not very tolerant of being corrected looked from Harry to Jonathan; "Can't you two keep your womenfolk in hand?" Harry laughed; "Keep General Willingham's daughter in hand, I'd like to meet the man who could do that." The Duke's demeanor began to soften; "I've heard about old Marty Willingham, quite a tartar they say. And as for Hermione's father; I served under him when I was a wet behind the ears cornet. I'd say you've both got your hands full with these two ladies. Speaking of that pretty little daughter of yours Jonathan; is she going to join us for dinner?" Jonathan replied; "No Your Grace, she and Sergeant Spratt are taking the children to town for the afternoon. Then I believe they will be having supper with a bunch of rankers at the Duke of York's this evening." Cynthia laughed; "D'ye think Queen Meg will be holding court with her regiment?" It was Harry's turn to laugh; "No one concerned themselves with the regiment more than you did darling, could it be you're a little bit jealous?" Cynthia responded with a hint of regret in her voice; "I do miss the regiment but I could never be resentful of Meg, I love that girl." Jonathan then told them how Meg had got Chalky's, Ginger's and Paddy's wives to form themselves into a mutual aid group and then started recruiting other wives; "I believe they're now about thirty strong." The Duke harrumphed; "That gal's one hell of an organizer maybe we should have made her an officer. That lot that's going to be in charge of the expeditionary force couldn't organize a piss up in a brewery!" Cynthia could not let the opportunity go by; "I understand Your Grace will have a division." The Duke glared then chuckled; "And how bloody intelligent d'ye suppose I am?

The following morning at 7o'clock a column of cavalry accompanied by assorted wagons proceed along the Hemel Hempstead road to Letty's estate. The vendors who had set up during the week had arrived earlier with there wares and various mouthwatering cooking odors were being carried on the breeze. As the column progressed down towards the lake some of the house servants and estate workers stood waving and cheering. Meg, Jane and the children stood waving on the front steps of the house, there were tears in the eyes of both women. As the end of the column disappeared through the trees on down the track that lead to the lake they turned to each other and embraced, they were both visibly sobbing. Meg was the first to pull away saying; "I have to go down to the cottage and get my riding clothes out of mothballs and we both need to pull ourselves together." Jane replied; "I know but I'm going to miss him so." Meg squeezed Jane's hand; "When they left the old barracks for Woolwich Cynthia told me if you're going to be a soldier's wife you'd better get used to goodbyes, I don't think I'll ever get used to it." Then Meg brightened up; "Why don't we meet up with the girls when we go down to the gala?" Jane looking puzzled asked; "The girls?" Meg now smiling replied; "Yes silly, Molly Weston, Binnie O'Neill and Barb White. I guarantee Molly will bring a smile back to your face, in fact I'll be surprised if she doesn't put you in hysterics." Jane had now regained her composure asked; "Are you going to ride today?" Meg laughed yes and this time there won't be a questionable dead heat, I'll be up on Jasper." Jane gasped; "That big stallion, Oh Meg! Are you sure you can handle him in a race?" Meg laughed again; "I'd say we're about to find out."

The day was a resounding success with Turps coming in second to Jack in the chota pegs and the rings. Before the lady's race was due Jack rode Nipper down to the cottage and came back leading Jasper. As he was tying him to a hitching rail Cynthia approached; "What are you going to do with that big black bugger Sergeant?" Saluting Jack looked at her with a smile on his face; "Why nothing Ma'am." Cynthia showed exasperation; "Then why the bloody hell is he here?" Jack's reply caused Cynthia to become speechless momentarily: "Meg's riding him in the ladies race." Cynthia recovered her composure enough to let out a loud; "Bugger me!" Jack had a huge grin on his face which caused Cynthia to glare at him; "Sergeant Spratt you're laughing at me and I'll be damned if that little minx hasn't pulled a ringer."

Just then Meg approached; she was dressed in the same jodhpurs and vest exactly as four years before. When Jane had reproached her about wearing the same riding attire as she had at the old barracks Meg had responded; "They're still good and they still fit so why should I waste money on new clothes?" Cynthia glowered down at Meg; "What d'ye mean by this young lady?" Meg put on her bewildered little girl smile; "Why whatever do you mean Cynthia?" Cynthia was still glowering; "You know damned well what I mean, riding that bloody great stallion in the ladies race." Meg now had a more knowing smile on her face; "Well I thought this time I'd win fair and square." Cynthia tried unsuccessfully to feign anger; "What d'ye mean you won fair and square before." At Meg's rebuttal Jack could no longer refrain from grinning; "I won because you browbeat poor Captain Portal into declaring me the winner, when in fact you probably won by a nose; he was terrified of you." Cynthia gave an exasperated sigh then drew Meg into her arms; "So that's why you had the trophy placed in the regimental trophy room, and by the way Portal was a cornet back then. All subalterns should be browbeaten frequently and mercilessly." Meg was laughing with her head pillowed in Cynthia's bosom; "Let me go Cynthia or you'll suffocate me." Cynthia held her at arms length; I love you Little Prude, and by the by he's still terrified of me." As she walked away she turned to Jack; "Make sure you always take care of her, and wipe that bloody grin off your face!"

Jack cupped his hands for Meg's left foot as she stepped into his hands he lifted her and she swung her right leg over the saddle. As she slid her feet into the stirrups Jack looked up at her; "Do you really want to do this darling?" Meg looked down smiling; "Next to marrying you I don't think I've ever wanted to do anything more in my life."

The course was longer and wider than the one they had made back at the old barracks; one circuit was four furlongs. It had been decided that the length of the ladies race would be one mile which was two circuits. As the starter was getting them lined up there were audible gasps from some of the lady riders when they saw Meg's mount. Jasper appeared even larger with his diminutive rider in the saddle. At the sound of the starter's pistol they were off with Meg kicking Jasper into an easy gallop. For the first circuit the field was bunched behind Meg and Cynthia with Meg and Jasper a length ahead of Cynthia and her grey mare. At the half mile point Meg allowed the reins to go completely slack indicating to Jasper it was now his race to win. His reaction was electrifying; his stride lengthened and with clods of turf flying from his hooves he pulled away. Coming into the final furlong they were ten lengths ahead of Cynthia and the grey and fifty yards ahead of the rest of the field. As they came thundering towards the finish line the spectators were cheering wildly, the rankers were loudest of all; cheering on a daughter of the regiment. Meg and Jasper crossed the finish line handily, when she pulled him up Jonathan grabbed the bridle and as she jumped down Jack caught her in his arms; "You were magnificent, you handled Jasper perfectly." Meg shook her head; "No, Jasper won the race." Once I let him have his head he did it on his own, I just happened to be in the saddle." Jack laughed; "I remember your father lecturing me about self deprecation so why don't you put that false modesty away and accept the credit which you so richly deserve?" Just as they were kissing Cynthia came up to them; "Bugger! Once again there's no bucket of water handy." She looked hard at Jasper; "Well I'll be damned, he's not even blowed and there's hardly any sweat, and that bloody old fool The General was going to geld him!" Harry who along with General Anderson and the Duke were now all standing around Jasper felt he had to comment: "Now Cynthia that's no way to talk about your father." Cynthia bristled; "Silly old coot, I'll talk about him anyway I want." She then clasped Meg in one of her formidable embraces; "My dear Little Prude you rode magnificently, now walk with me and we'll cool 'em down." As they walked off leading their horses the Duke harrumphed; "Give those two lances and sabers and send 'em out to the Crimea. I wager they'd run those bloody Russians all the way back to the Kremlin. I can see Cynthia ramming her saber clean up the Tsar's arse!" General Anderson laughed; "Aren't you related to the Tsar Sir?" The Duke harrumphed even louder; "Distantly and only by marriage, and we don't talk about Charlotte's side of the family, bunch of bloody Prussians." Anderson could not resist; "But didn't the Prussians win Waterloo for us?" The Duke gave a glare which softened into a grin; "One day you'll go too bloody far Billy."

As they were walking the horses Meg's children and little Robert who had been watching the race with Letty, Jane and Hermione descended upon them. Little Jonathan was calling Mamma! Mamma! Elizabeth was saying something that seemed to resemble Mamma and Robert was uttering something that sounded like A'hegg. The children hung round Meg's legs while the women took turns in hugging her. Cynthia questioned Letty; "Where's Marmie?" Letty's response: "He's in the officer's tent doing what he does best, drinking and telling lies." Caused Cynthia to laugh: "He used to be quite a Casanova; the General had to run him off more than once." Letty joined in with her laughter; "He still thinks he's a Casanova but he's not quite the young blade he used to be." Cynthia could not resist; "Keeps the old blade sheathed more now eh?" Jane was blushing furiously; "Oh Cynthia! Meg's right you are incorrigible." Meg addressed the children; "Stay with your grandmammas' while Aunt Cynthia and I take care of the horses." As they walked on Cynthia turned to Meg; "You've got yourself a wonderful family Little Prude." Meg's reply caused Cynthia to dissolve into uproarious laughter; "And I've also got the best bloody horseman in the regiment!" Cynthia suggested that they take Jasper and her mare to the officer's picquet lines where a groom could take care of them.

On their way to the officer's picquet lines they were confronted with a completely unexpected sight, Riding Master Perry,

Gus Davidson, Capper and Teddy. The four of them were walking abreast with their arms draped over each others shoulders. It was very obvious all four of them were exceedingly mellow from drinking. Perry was the first to recognize Meg and Cynthia he drew up short causing the other three to stumble to a halt. Perry tipped the wool cap he was wearing; "Good day to you Ma'am and Miss Meg that was a great race yew won." Cynthia glowered at him accusingly; "You're drunk Mr. Perry!" Perry was swaying slightly; "Yes Ma'am we've bin drunk since arter the parade yes'day. Me, Jake an' Teddy 'ere come up frum the village to see the parade. Arter the parade we went to the Duke of York's fer a drink and Gus ad zum wiv us an' let us stay there fer the night. S'mornin we 'ad brekfus and then come 'ere." Cynthia was smiling; "I know Mr. Davidson but who are these other two reprobates?" Perry had a drunken grin on his face; "This 'ere be Jake Capper ee wuz Major Barry's father's SSM in India. An' this be Teddy Jackson ee's landlord uv our pub back at the village, ee wur in 11th Hussars." Just then Jack rode up on Nipper; when he saw Perry he dismounted and shook the Riding Masters hand; "It's so good to see you sir, how have you and Mrs. Perry been?" Perry slurred his answer; "We bin good an' I see your lady's looking as bonnie as ever, an' 'ow is them babies?" When Jake Capper realized who Meg was he exclaimed; "No wonder w'enever I saw that young bugger ee allus 'ad a great big bloody smile on 'is face." Jack laughed and looking at Perry asked; "Whatever happened to the six pint rule?" Perry drew himself up; "They rules be fer young buggers like yew not us'ns oos served our time." Meg castigated Perry; "Mr. Perry I was going to let you see the children but what with your being drunk and the language I'm not so sure." Perry was contrite; "Miss Meg I promise yew I wont 'ave no more ta drink till arter I seen them babes, an' I'll watch me mouf." Meg smiled grimly; "They're down by the race course with their grandmother and Major Barry's wife, and behave yourselves around them!" The Riding Master looked at his three companions; "C'mon lads an'

'member watch yer moufs." As they walked off still slightly swaying Jack laughed and looked at Meg; "And I used to be scared of
him." Cynthia also laughing could not help commenting; "I never
saw Ned Perry cowed like that except by his wife Nancy." Jack
made a suggestion; "I'm sure you ladies want to get back with
the others, with your permission I'll lead your horses down to the
picquet lines." Meg kissed him on the cheek; "Thank you darling,
see me before the men's race." As they walked back towards the
lake Cynthia observed; "You two seem to be as madly in love as
you were four years ago." Meg smiled archly; "What can I say?
Jack's an amazing lover!" Cynthia laughed; "What happened to
my Little Prude?"

Jack arrived at the at the picquet lines riding Nipper without reins; leading Jasper with one hand and Cynthia's grey with
the other. One of the grooms looked at his mates; "Now ee's jus'
bloody showing off!" Jack leaned over giving Jaspers bridle to
the groom then dismounting and handing the grey over; "Mrs.
Butler said you'd take care of these, see they're fed and watered
and rubbed down." The groom looked at Jasper; Ee aint a orficers 'orse, we only takes care uv orficers an' orficers wives 'orses."
Jack glowered at the groom; "Well Private I suggest you discuss
that with Mrs. Butler." The groom took on an alarmed look; "Not
bloody likely! We'll take care of 'im Sarge." After remounting
Nipper, Jack rode away with a huge grin on his face.

Down by the lake everyone was gathering for the men's race as
Jack rode towards the ladies he saw Ned Perry holding Elizabeth
and making her laugh by making funny noises. When he drew up
to them he heard Cynthia comment; "I hope she likes the smell of
beer fumes." Jack could not resist; "Well her mother likes her beer
so she's probably used to it." Meg swung round her copper tresses
flying as the daggers shot from her green eyes. Cynthia laughed;
"I think you touched a sore spot Sergeant." Jane prompted by the
sight of Meg's hair said; "Why don't you wear your hair shorter
now you're a married lady?" Jack had a hint of alarm in his voice;

"If ever she cuts her hair short I'll give her the horse whipping she's been promising me for years, now I have to go down to the starting line." Cynthia was laughing as Meg stared at Jacks back saying as he rode away; "So you'll horse whip me, well we'll just see about that!"

The men's race presented a large field and as they exploded from the start line Harry Butler on Carrington took the lead with Jonathan up on Joe close behind. Jack knowing both horses were powerful and would not be handicapped from running on a tight course as they had been at the old barracks had planned a strategy. He had reasoned that once they took the lead he and Nipper would get in behind them. Following his plan he brought Nipper in behind Joe who was about half a length back from Carrington. The men's race was a mile and a half or three circuits. Jacks plan was to stay in behind them until the last hundred yards or so then make a run for the finish; he was relying on Nipper's ability to come up with the extra effort as he had done so often before. As they came round the final turn they were leading the rest of the field by several lengths with Carrington still leading Joe now by a full length and Nipper half a length behind Joe. Jack gauged they were now at the point where they should make their move, he pulled Nipper over and dug his spurs in at the same time. Just as they were pulling up on Joe both Joe and Carrington put on a spurt. Clods of turf flew as the two powerful stallions pulled away from Jack and Nipper, Nipper seemed to sense that there was yet more required from him and Jack's knees could feel his sides straining. Jack lay across Nipper's neck trying to give him as much encouragement as he could but the two stallions continued to pull away. About fifty yards from the finish Jack felt Nipper stumble he pulled him up and they crossed the finish line at a canter a distant third to Carrington who had beaten Joe by half a length. Jack dismounted quickly and started to check Nippers fetlocks and pasterns. Harry Butler came up behind him; "Hope we aren't looking for an excuse Sergeant." Jack couldn't hide the look of annoyance on his face; "No sir you had the race won before Nipper stumbled; I was just looking to see if he'd torn anything." The Brigadier was feeling guilty; "I'm sorry, I should know you well enough by now to know you wouldn't be looking for excuses." Jack softened his visage into a smile; "Thank you sir." Cynthia who had overheard everything grabbed Harry by his sleeve and pulled him out of earshot; "Harry Butler you should be ashamed of yourself accusing that boy of looking for excuses! He's never given an excuse or looked for an easy way out in his life. He gave you both a good run for your money and with you and Jonathan both up on two thousand guinea pure bred hunters and him on a fifteen guinea remount. And don't forget Jack and Nipper beat you both handily back at the old barracks." Harry Butler was duly contrite; "I know dear, and had he been up on Jasper he would have won handily today, in fact I'll ask him why he wasn't riding him." With that he walked back to where Jack was still examining Nipper; "Sergeant Spratt, why weren't you riding Jasper?" Jack's expression conveyed a look of disbelief that the Brigadier should ask such a question; "Why sir, the other rankers had to ride their remounts, it wouldn't have been fair." Harry couldn't resist pursuing the subject; "But the officers in the race were all mounted on well bred horses." Jacks reply brought a chuckle from Cynthia who was stood with her husband; "Sergeant White and Private Reeves came in right behind me and they too were on their remounts, you were the only officer that beat us; the others didn't even place." As they walked away Cynthia couldn't help herself; "Reminds me of their engagement party, he got you again." Harry shook his head; "I may have created a monster by taking an interest in that young fella." Cynthia laughed; "May I call you Mary Wollstonecraft Shelley?"

After the awards were presented, people mostly spent their time going around to the various vendors' stalls or drinking. The officers and their wives gathered in the officers mess tent, while the rankers and their wives mingled in the beer tent. Meg had buttonholed Jane and steered her away from the officer's mess. Pulling her towards the beer tent Meg was telling her; "Jane darling, you have to have a drink with the girls." Jane was reluctant; "The last time I saw them was at your wedding, I'm not sure how I should behave around them." Meg heaved an exasperated sigh; "Just be you, no try to be more down to earth." Jane was offended; "whatever do you mean?" Meg heaved another sigh; "When we get in there order a half of beer and try to keep your eyebrows from disappearing into your hair every time you hear a cuss word or a ribald comment." After her eyes had become accustomed to the gloom Meg spotted "the girls" sat at a table laughing; no doubt at one of Molly's jokes. She steered Jane over to them; "Girls, I think you all know Major Barry's wife." Molly looked up; "Please sit down Ma'am, Binnie go get the Major's lady a drink." Jane sat down and getting her cue from the look on Meg's face said; "Please call me Jane." Binnie came back from the long table that served as a temporary bar and placed half pint mugs in front of Jane and Meg; "All we've got is beer but it's the best; good, ol' Gus giv' it us." As Jane sipped her beer daintily Meg glared at her across the table; "Dammit Jane drink it don't play with it!" Molly laughed; "Meg 'ere usually 'as a pint mug, must be trying to be a lady today." Meg glared at Molly; "Tell it to Binnie, she brought me the half." Jane began to drink with more abandon and was soon beginning to feel more at ease with the girls. Philip Barry was looking around the officers tent; "Has anyone seen Jane?" Lavinia St Claire-Johnson had a mischievous gleam in her eye; "Last time I saw her she was going towards the beer tent with Meg Spratt." The Major strode out of the tent door and headed in the direction of the beer tent as he entered he spied Jane sat at the table with Meg and the girls. When Jane saw him she called across the tent; "Come and have a drink with the girls' darling." Barry, feeling he had little choice; walked over and sat at the table. Molly greeted him; "Good uv yer ta jine us Major, Barb go get the Major a pint." By the time Barb returned with his beer Philip had surmised correctly that Jane was tipsy. He mentally shrugged his shoulders and thought; "Might as well go along with it, who knows I might even enjoy meself, Jane certainly seems to be happy." Cynthia was stood with Brigadier Butler in the officer's mess holding a glass of wine in her hand. Looking at her husband she asked; "Where're Philip and Jane?" Overhearing, Lavinia could not resist; "I think they're over at the beer tent." Harry looked at Cynthia; "I've got to see this!" They walked from the officer's tent and entered the beer tent; after their eyes became accustomed to the gloom they spotted Philip and Jane with Meg and the girls. Harry looked at Cynthia saying; "Well I'll be damned, let's leave before they spot us." As they turned and left the beer tent Cynthia exclaimed; "I would have thought Jane was too bloody stiff necked to mix with the ranker's wives." Harry laughed; "Yes and you also thought Meg was a prude." Laughing they headed for the vendor's stalls. Just after Harry and Cynthia left the tent the RSM entered when he saw the Major and Jane sat with Meg and the girls a look of disbelief crossed his face, he quickly got himself under control and roared in his parade ground voice; "Your attention please!" After the noise died down he addressed the revelers; "Just in case some of you have had too much to drink and might have forgotten; I'm here to remind you of The Colonels requirements. As he informed you at the awards ceremony he wishes to address everybody at half past four. You will be at the registration tent at the stated time that means everyone; there will be no exceptions!"

Promptly at half past four the Colonel stepped onto the raised platform located at the side of the registration tent he was followed by the Duke, General Anderson and Brigadier Butler. Royce who was stood at the side of the platform bellowed; "Silence for the Colonel!" As the crowd quieted down Hawkins cleared his throat; "Your Grace, Lords, Ladies and Gentlemen, officers and men of the 17th Lancers, I hope everyone has enjoyed the festivities. As you know the regiment will be sailing for the

Crimea in two weeks and we will be leaving Woolwich with much regret. I think I speak for all ranks of the regiment when I say that the hospitality we have been shown by the civilian residents of Woolwich and the surrounding communities will always be among our fondest memories." Turning to the Duke; "I believe you wish to say a few words Your Grace." The Duke stepped forward; "I too will be sailing with the expeditionary force, in fact they've given me command of a division. Would you believe my own regiment will not be part of that division? I'd feel a bloody sight safer with my own boys around me!" This caused much laughter especially from the rankers. He continued on a more serious note; "We are going to war to prevent the Russians from gaining a foothold in the Mediterranean and eventually turning their attention towards India; a part of our empire they have been eyeing hungrily for years. We have no way of knowing how many will return but we do know that we leave to fight for our Queen our country and the empire!" A voice in the crowd shouted; "God save Her Majesty the Queen" The crowd responded as if it were a single voice; "God Save the Queen!" Then another voice in the crowd shouted; "And the 17th Lancers!" The crowd responded; "God save the 17th Lancers!" The Duke had one more comment; "Up to now I've drank very little today knowing I was going to get up and talk to you lot, well bugger it now I'm going to bloody well catch up!" The crowd dissolved into laughter. As the Duke and the others stepped down from the rostrum the RSM stepped up and walked to the front; "Those already detailed to return to barracks with the wagons will start loading at seven o'clock, those who have to return with their horses will form up at half past seven under their troop sergeants prior to proceeding back to barracks accompanied by the wagons. The officer's tent and beer tent will be struck and transported to the barracks by the allocated work details tomorrow that will be transported here by wagon after church parade, to clean up and restore the area to its former condition. Beer will cease to be served after eight o'clock and I strongly emphasize that you do not return to barracks in a drunken state if you do it will earn you a flogging."

When the "Musketeers" as Major Barry had christened them; strolled back to the beer tent with their wives Meg had a question; "How are Nipper and Chalky's horse going to get back to the barracks?" Ginger answered; "Me an' Paddy er gonna lead 'em back and take care of 'em, we got Major's permission an' we got jes a short walk to 'ome frum the barracks." Meg turned to the two corporals; "Thank you lads, Jack has good friends." Paddy laughed; "He's a good friend to have; now let's be having some beers together like friends should, that's if you colleens haven't had too much already." Molly rounded on him; "Bugger yew Paddy, us girls u'll drink yew bloody pansies under the table any day!" Ginger chimed in; "If we're bloody pansies wur did all them brats come frum?" Molly's answer brought much laughter from the other girls: "Now that's somefink you pansies can never know fer sure." They were all laughing as they sat at a table in the beer tent. Ginger, Paddy Molly and Binnie left the beer tent at seven the girls hugging each other just a little longer, a little harder and more emotionally than usual; Molly and Binnie were riding back on one of the wagons. After they had gone the laughter became muted, just before eight o'clock Jack uttered the thought that had been on everyone's mind; "Bugger this bloody war! It's taking us away from our families." Chalky looked across the table at him; "I know and I prob'ly wont be 'ere wen our baby's born." A stunned silence was broken by Meg as she went round the table and hugged Barb; "I don't know what to say, I'm so happy for you but it's so sad that Chalky's leaving at a time like this." Jack looked over at Chalky; "Congratulations mate and you Barb. Tell you what I've got some pull with the RSM; I'll get him to see if the Colonel can keep you back to help with the regimental depot they're forming." Chalky shook his head; "They pays me fer bee'en a sojer not fer skivin' frum me duty! 'sides it wouldn't be fair to the uvvers." Meg still hugging Barb asked; "When are you going to tell Molly and Binnie?" Barb with tears in her eyes replied; "Wen we're all togever next Saturday, but yew gotta look surprised like it's the fust time yew erd it or they'll kill me! Meg laughed; "Oh Barb darling, I promise you I'll be appropriately surprised."

The following Saturday saw the girls as they now referred to themselves gathered in the Duke of York's. Barb had come in with Albert and Meg rode alongside them on Sally. Meg and Jack no longer dined in the back room preferring to be with the others in the Public Bar. When Meg and Barb entered the bar Molly and Binnie were already waiting. When Molly saw them she said; "The blokes will be 'ere later, they're keepin' 'em busy at the barracks." Meg nodded her head; "I know Jack's been getting home late every night and he's on duty tomorrow." Binnie commented; "Looks like they're gonna keep our blokes busy till they leaves, yud fink they'd give us more time wiv 'em now." Molly laughed; "Maybe it's a good fing, if we 'ad more time wiv 'em we might be getting' in the family way 'fore they leaves." This gave Barb her cue; "One uv us 'as!" Molly and Binnie looked startled while Meg made a feeble attempt to emulate their looks of surprise. The girls smothered Barb hugging and kissing her then Molly rounded on Meg accusingly; "Yew knew about this already!" Meg braced herself ready to make her denial when Barb spoke up; "I'm sorry girls I told Meg last Saturday arter yew left the beer tent." Molly exploded; "Barb White I may never speak to yew agin!" Barb wrapped Molly in a tight embrace; "I'm sorry darlin' but I wuz so worried abaht Chalky goin' off to war an' me wiv a baby, I spose I wuzn't finkin straight." Molly held her off at arms length; "We fergivs yew but don't never do nuffin like that agin." Meg thought she'd lighten up the mood; "Let's have a beer." Gus who was behind the bar looked up; "Wot can I get yew luvly ladies?" Meg's answer brought a smile to his face; "You know damned well what you can get us Gus Davidson, four pints of your best." This caused him to laugh; "It took me awhile to get used to a lady like yew drinking pints of beer now yew swears like a trooper and

I saw yew ride like one last Saturday, wot's the world comin' to?" Meg glared at him; "I'm buggered if I know but why don't you get those bloody beers?" Gus busied himself pulling the handle drawing the beer and chuckling all the while. The girls who were sat at a large table had almost finished their first pints when their men came in. After they had all finished embracing and were seated Gus came over with four pints of beer for the men; "Can I get you some vittles and are you ladies ready for more beer?" They all nodded, Jack laughed; "Maybe we should take a cartload of Gus's pies to throw at the Russians that'll put 'em on the run." He had his back to the door so he hadn't seen Gus's wife come in the room. Nell Davidson was a large woman and she pulled herself to her full height and addressed Jack's back; "Sergeant bloody Spratt why are you insultin'my vittles? I seen you put two of my pies down at a sitting, that with bread an' onions an' all. Yew aint nothin' but an ungrateful bloody donkey walloper!" Gus broke in; "Eh steady Nell, I wuz a donkey walloper meself." Nell came back; "Yew wuz a dragoon, them's mounted infantry." This caused the whole barroom to rock with gales of laughter. Jack got up and walked over to Nell and hugged her; "I'm sorry Nell you know I was only joking, we're going to miss your pies. Nell's reply caused the bar to explode with laughter again; "Yew better bloody well be joking!" Looking over Jack's shoulder she said to Meg; "'ow d'ye live wiv this young bugger, let alone 'ave babes wiv 'im?"

As the afternoon went on the lightheartedness around the table began give way to pensive retrospection and eventually as they prepared to leave there was much hugging and kissing and copious tears on part of the girls. As they were riding back in the twilight behind Barb and Albert in the wagon, Chalky on one of Letty's hunters and Jack and Meg on Jasper and Sally; Jack asked Chalky what he was going to do about Barb and the baby. Chalky informed him that Letty was going to let Barb stay in the cottage. Jack looked at Meg accusingly; "Did you know about this?" Meg owned up; "Yes I did but when Barb told me the arrangements hadn't been finalized, and what with you boys being on duty so much lately she didn't even tell Chalky 'till yesterday." Jack made a noise that sounded like "humph." Meg laughed; "You're beginning to sound like the Duke." Jack asked; "What about when the baby comes?" Meg replied: "when it's close to her time Barb will move in with me and Aunt Letty will have Jonathan and Elizabeth up at the house. When Barb goes into labor Aunt Letty will stay with her while Albert and I drive into the village and get the midwife." Jack felt he had to ask; "What if the midwife is attending another birth at the time?" Meg smiled in the gloom; "There are three midwives two sisters; and one of their daughters's who is also skilled at birthing." Jack's reply brought a chuckle from Chalky; "I wish I could believe those bloody generals that's going to the Crimea with us are going to be half as well organized as these women." Meg could not resist; "Don't expect too much from them after all they are just mere men."

The regiment left Woolwich in the morning of the 14th April headed for their port of embarkation where they assembled preparatory to boarding and sailing on the 17th.

CHAPTER 11

THE HOME

JACK AND JOHN Beaconsfield were sat in The Royal George on a Friday afternoon concluding one of their many interviews; Jack had drawn on his many memories for Beaconsfield to weave into his biographical account; which the newspaper was running as a weekly serial. John looked across the table at Jack; "I found out something interesting after our last meeting." Jack looked at him with a knowing grin which twisted the scar on his cheek; "Oh and what would that be?" Beaconsfield was obviously put out; "You're not the poor old survivor of the charge you pretended to be." Jack laughed; "I don't remember pretending to be anyone." Beaconsfield glowered; "You let me believe you were down and out." Jack was clearly playing with him; "I didn't think I had any control over what you believe, and what made you think you could follow an old light cavalryman on horseback without being noticed?" Beaconsfield was still put out; "That beautiful stallion you were riding should have tipped me off, I always thought you walked here till the last time." Jack smiled; "Jasper was his grandsire. You were upwind on a mare, Perry gave you away." John gasped; "Well I'll be buggered, you knew I was there all the time! But I did get to see that children's home you said you were going to found. When I saw that board at the gates of that beautiful house I remembered what you had told me about your breakfast announcement on Christmas morning in '53, The Earl of Aldbourne's Home for Children." Jack smiled proudly; "Why don't you visit us sometime? I could show you around and I know Meg would love for you to dine with us." Beaconsfield was enthusiastic; "As a matter of fact I'm staying here until Monday, at the risk of being presumptuous I'd like to take you up on your offer tomorrow!" Jack was agreeable; "How about twelve o'clock tomorrow noon? That will give me plenty of time to give you the dog and pony show before dinner." They both stood and shook hands Jack saying; "Tomorrow then, good evening to you John."

Saturday at twelve o'clock saw Beaconsfield standing in front of the big oak door of the grey stone manor that housed the children's home. As he was about to grasp the bell pull the door opened to reveal a petite woman with long copper red hair streaked with a slight trace of grey; looking up at him with bright green eyes. Although he knew this had to be Meg he also knew she had to be in her forties. Knowing that flattery usually worked with older women he asked; "Would you be Riding Master Spratt's daughter Elizabeth?" Meg gave one of her tinkling laughs; "You must be Master John Beaconsfield; and you certainly know how to flatter an old lady." John feigned astonishment; "You mean you're Meg? Meg decided to tease him; "We have only just met young man, isn't it a bit soon for you be addressing me by my first name?" Beaconsfield was nonplussed; "I'm sorry Ma'am I meant no offence I'm just so used to Jack referring to you as Meg." It was now obvious she was teasing him and as she looked past him towards the hitching rail he mumbled; "I should have been prepared." Meg looked up at him; "I'll get someone to stable your horse. And for what should you have been prepared? And do come inside." John stepped into the hall and saw Jack standing at the bottom of a large spiral staircase, Jack smiled; "I see you have already become a victim of Meg's teasing." Meg addressed Beaconsfield in a sharp tone; "I asked you a question Sir!" John not knowing whether she was serious or not said in a low voice while removing his hat; "I should have been prepared for your teasing." Meg started to laugh; "Oh and what has this reprobate of a husband of mine been saying about me? But let's go into the parlor and sit down before you reveal all the lies he's been telling you." When they were seated in the parlor Meg rang a small bell and a young girl dressed as a maid came through the door; "Joanie please get the gentlemen whatever they want to drink and I'll have a sherry. Also, have Jimmy take care of his horse." As the maid left the room Beaconsfield could not resist; "You're not having a pint of beer ma'am?" She flashed the daggers of which Jack had told him and Jack laughed; "You had that coming darling." Just at that moment a young woman walked into the room. She was dressed in tan jodhpurs and a green waistcoat; flame colored tresses cascaded down her back; she was a mirror image of Meg but without the grey streaks in her hair or the subtle traces of the years in her face. John jumped to his feet as Jack said; "John this is our daughter Elizabeth, Elizabeth meet John Beaconsfield." John stood momentarily transfixed then finally managed to utter a garbled; "It's a pleasure to make your acquaintance Miss Spratt." He thought he detected mockery in her eyes as she said; "It is my pleasure sir." Then turning to her father; "Where did you find this handsome young fellow Papa?" Jack was smiling broadly; "Now Bess, you've got enough young fellas' down in the village at sixes and sevens please don't add John to your herd of moon eyed swains." Elizabeth turned back to John; "Please sit down sir, standing there with your mouth open you look like a tree that might contain an owl's nest." As John sat down Meg exclaimed; "Bess Mr. Beaconsfield is our guest, please refrain from being so discourteous!" Elizabeth feigned contrition; "Please accept my apology if I have offended you in any way sir." When the maid returned with Meg's sherry and scotch for Jack and their guest she turned to Elizabeth; "Can I get you something to drink Miss Bess?" Bess declined; "No thank you Joanie I was drinking at The White Hart earlier, maybe later." Jack looked at his daughter; "Who were you drinking with Bess?" Bess sounded just like her mother when she laughed; "Oh the usual crowd Papa." Jack looked over at Beaconsfield; "She means half the eligible young men in the county." John who was obviously smitten replied; "It's easy to see why they seek her company." Bess gave her tinkling laugh again; "You really know how to compliment a girl John Beaconsfield." Jack looked at Meg; "I remember the first time I heard those words." Meg still in a teasing mood returned his gaze with a mischievous twinkle in her eyes; "On that occasion I do believe you had just been commenting on a portion of my anatomy." Bess laughed with her parents, she had obviously been told the story of the threatened spanking. Jack looked at his wife affectionately; "I still may carry out that promise." Meg shot back; "And you might still get a horse whipping." Bess addressed John; "If you have finished your drink you may come with me and help me take care of Perry." Meg protested Mr. Beaconsfield is a guest, you can't put him to work!" Bess's reply indicated she would brook no interference; "Mamma, I understand he is going to dine with us, in that case he can work for his supper." John saved the day; "I will be happy to assist Miss Bess and I still have my own horse to attend to." Jack smiled; "When you two have done with the horses I'll show John around."

When they arrived at the stable John saw a small boy struggling to remove Perry's saddle he quickly strode over; "Here young fella let me help you with that." The boy turned giving him a look of defiance; 'I allus 'elps Miss Bess wiv 'er 'orses." He was looking past John at Bess with eyes that shone with devotion. Bess laughed; "Come here Jimmy." The boy ran over to her and she wrapped her arms around him; "This is Jimmy, Papa found him outside of The Royal George one night begging, so he brought him home to join the others." John was curious; "How many children do you have here?" Bess thought for a moment; "Eleven girls and nine boys. They are all runaways from abusive homes, squalid orphanages or workhouses. The numbers of workhouses are beginning to diminish but the progressive institutions are not increasing quickly enough to take in all the children in need. Dr Barnado has been doing wonders with the home he founded in London and apparently he has plans to open others, but raising money is always a problem. William Booth has also opened a children's home under the auspices of his Salvation Army, but he seems more involved with proselytizing than making sure that he has the right kind of people taking care of the children." Beaconsfield shook his head; "You seem to have considerable knowledge of the charitable institutions." Bess had a grim look on her face; "Until our society develops a conscience the burden of charity will continue to fall on the shoulders of people like my parents and Dr Barnado. To the everlasting shame of the English people it took an Italian immigrant to acknowledge the plight of our homeless children!" Then looking at Jimmy; "You may finish taking care of Perry." Jimmy gave her a look of adoration; "Yes Miss Bess, I took care of the genl'man's orse wen ee got 'ere." Just then Jack appeared; "Well John let me give you that dog and pony show I promised." Bess looked at her father; "Please may I accompany you Papa?" Jack smiled indulgently; "Of course you may darling."

After the tour when they were sat in the parlor with drinks John was effusive in his praise; "This is a wonderful thing you're doing here, how do you finance it all?" Jack smiled; "Between Philip Barry's family's contributions and the Earl twisting the arms of everyone he could cajole or threaten Meg, was able to build a considerable trust fund while I was in the Crimea. Then while we were in India, Meg's father and Lady Hermione managed the fund. The house was donated by Lord Sanger. After his wife died Marmie persuaded him that he'd be better off living with his son in Devon, and then coerced him into signing the

house over to the trust. As its Saturday the children have the
half day off except for Jimmy and Joanie, two others will be on
duty next week. Although if Bess is out riding; Jimmy will insist
on being available to take care of her horse." Bess laughed; "As
long as Jimmy is here I know I'll be taken care of." Meg added;
"I've never seen such an intense case of puppy love." Jack went
on; "As you saw from the farm and the dairy we're pretty well
self-sufficient. We sell the milk, pigs, eggs and the crops we grow;
except that which we need for our own use, and the children take
care of the labor on the farm. They also see to the day to day running of the house and periodic maintenance. This has a twofold
advantage it keeps our labor costs at a minimum while enabling
us to teach the children skills which hopefully they will find mar-
ketable when they leave here as young adults. I shouldn't take too
much credit for teaching them, Bess and Meg school them and
our foreman deserves as much or more credit than anyone, Mr.
White is an excellent teacher when it comes to running a farm."
John looked at the smile forming on Jack's face; "You mean…"
Jack's smile was now fully formed; "Yes it's Chalky." Beaconsfield
felt he had to ask: "What happened to Ginger and Paddy?" Jack
enlightened him: "Well we all came back, all four of us survived
the Crimea and three of us India and that was a bloody miracle in
itself! Ginger bought Teddy Jackson's tavern and Paddy went to
work for Molly's father at the blacksmith's shop and Chalky and
Barb live here in the estate farmhouse." John was curious; "Do
you see anything of them now?" Jack's replied in the affirmative;
"We get together twice a year in June and at Christmas either
here or at Ginger's Tavern. John changed the subject; "After
you introduced me to the children and showed me their living
quarters, which are a credit to you and Meg, I noticed another
dormitory at the back of the house. Who was that for?" Bess
interjected; "That's for the old soldiers." John gave her a quizzical look. She continued; "Every so often an old soldier who is
down on his luck wanders through these parts. We offer them a

meal, a bath and a nights lodging, some of them stay for a few days and we have them work for their keep. Others stay the night and move on. Our society is so corrupted by individuals in power whose only concern is amassing wealth, that these men are given a pittance and cast aside when they leave the army." Jack burst out furiously; "These men have been cast aside like so much rubbish!" Then tracing the scar with his index finger he continued; "This is what I left the army with, many of them left with limbs or eyes missing. Some of them are blind and others have lost their minds and yet we have MP's in the commons talking about vagrancy some have even suggested putting them in the penal system. These vile bastards are dancing to the tune of the big industrialists; many of them have their constituencies in the northern mill towns and cities or the factories in the Midlands, and bow to the industrialists in order to keep their seats in Parliament. The irony is that many of the mill and factory owners are originally from the working class; the very people they work to death and under pay." Meg looked at John; "Now you've got him on his soapbox." Jack addressed Meg; "Don't make light of this dear." Then turning again to John; "Because most of the old soldiers do not own any land they do not have the right to vote. So please tell me how is it that men who go abroad to fight for their country and in many cases come back maimed; are regarded as criminals and are not allowed to participate in choosing the government of the country for which they sacrificed so much?" Again Meg interjected; "It was not my intention to make light of the condition of the poor unfortunates of whom you speak darling, but Mr. Beaconsfield is our guest and I think conversation on a lighter subject would be more appropriate." Jack was contrite; "You're right dearest, it's just that I get so angry when I think about the way our old soldiers are served." Meg glanced from John to Bess; "Dinner is four hours away and as Cook is off today I'll be preparing the evening meal, so why don't you young people go off and do what young people do these days." Bess beckoned John;

"Come let me introduce to my moon eyed swains." Then she led him out to the stables. John had noticed earlier that the stables contained a larger number of horses than three people would normally require asked; "Why do you have so many horses?" Bess laughed; "Because my father is a hypocrite." John was puzzled; "I don't understand. Bess explained; "These industrialists which my Papa so detests have sons and daughters, and they think they can use their money to make their children into young ladies and gentlemen, and one of the things young ladies and gentlemen do is ride horses, so my father panders to the neavue riche by taking their money to teach their brats to ride." John laughed; "I don't think your father is a hypocrite at all. I think it's the absolute irony that he takes their money to help deprived children and old soldiers." Bess shrugged; "I suppose you could look at it that way. I'll take Cynthia this time you can ride one of our hunters." Jimmy appeared from nowhere; "I'll get 'er ready fer yew Miss Bess. "Then turning to John with a look of hostility; "I'll show yew yer 'orse an' wur the tack room be." Bess glared at him; "You will prepare Mr. Beaconsfield's horse, and take that hateful look off your face!" Jimmy showed minimal remorse; "Orlright Miss Bess if yew sez so." John spoke up; "If he shows me to my horse and where to get the saddle and harness I'm sure I can manage." Bess concurred; "Yes I suppose it will make things a little quicker."

As they rode towards the village and The White Hart Inn John commented on Beth's chestnut mare; "Is it safe to presume that Cynthia is named after Mrs. Butler?" Beth smiled reminiscently; "Yes she died in a hunting accident some years ago the mare she was riding shied at a badger and crashed into a five bar gate instead of clearing it. The name of the mare she was riding was Little Prude. Oh, and by the way she was Lady Butler, the General was knighted in sixty-three." John was genuinely concerned; "I'm so sorry Miss Bess, from what your father has told me your mother loved her very much." Bess had a trace of sadness in her voice; "Yes she was mother to Mamma and grandmother to Jonathan and I. But we get some consolation in knowing she went out in a way of which she would have approved. And please call me Bess and I will call you John." John nodded in agreement; "I gather that Perry was named after Riding Master Perry. Bess smiled again; "Yes Perry is really Papa's horse but I like to ride him sometimes just to irritate the county set, none of them has a horse as magnificent as Perry." John was laughing; "I think that you and Cynthia Butler would have made a good pair." It was Bess's turn to laugh although wistfully; "Just for a little while Cynthia, Mamma and I were a trio, but I was just a little girl then, d'ye know what her last words were "Give Little Prude my riding crop." John could not help choking a little with emotion; "Is that the one I saw on the wall above the parlor fireplace?" Bess nodded; "Yes and Mamma will not let anyone touch it, she takes it down every so often to wipe it off and oil it but she and only she ever handles it." Then John asked the question that he had intended to ask Jack and Meg; "Where is your brother nowadays?" Meg's answer baffled him; "He's with the Corps of Guides cavalry in India." John exclaimed; "But aren't their rankers all native troops?" Meg's reply was; "Yes with the exception of a few senior NCO's, but Jonathan's a captain." John was even more baffled; "He holds a captains commission?" Meg smiled broadly; "I know it's unusual for someone with his origins to get a commission, but when people such as The Duke of Cambridge, The Earl of Aldbourne and General Butler use their influence, well unusual things can happen. Besides the Guides are not as class conscious as the traditional cavalry regiments; they recruit officers for their skills and aptitudes." As they rode their horses at a walk along the village high street; John saw The White Hart Inn had lines of horses tied to two hitching rails. He turned to Bess; "This seems to be a popular gathering place." Bess gave an exasperated sigh; "It's the same crowd of wastrels that I left here earlier." When they were close enough to dismount John jumped down quickly and went to assist Bess to alight. She glared down at him and dismounted brushing his hands aside; "Do I look frail to you Mr. Beaconsfield?" John nonplussed mumbled an apology then saw a smile starting at the corners of her mouth; "Bess Spratt you are a minx!" she was laughing while they secured their mounts then grabbed his arm; "Come and see the county zoo." When they entered the tavern Bess guided him past the door with Public Bar etched into its glass to a room further back in the tavern identified as the saloon bar, from which loud conversation emanated. As she pushed open the door and they entered; the room was momentarily silent then a voice exclaimed; "Why it's Good Queen Bess!" Bess glowered at a tall good looking young man leaning on the bar; "And you Geoffrey Armstrong are a base varlet!" They were quickly surrounded by a crowd of young men all curious about John. The questions came; "Where d'ye find this one? Is he another one dying from unrequited love? D'ye mean this is what you turned me down for?" Bess raised her hand commanding silence; "This is Mr. John Beaconsfield, he works for The Daily Messenger." This brought a comment from Geoffrey Armstrong as he said in a disparaging tone; "Oh, a newspaper man." Bess shot daggers from her blazing green eyes; "Sorry Geoffrey I forgot how much the mention of work frightens you." One of the young men was laughing; "Geoff, when will you learn you are no match for Bess when it comes to matching words?" Another one spoke up; "Or matching wits for that matter." Bess then commenced to introduce each one to John, when the introductions were completed she remarked; "And not one of them is worth the powder it would take to blow them to hell." They tarried at the White Hart for two hours during which time Bess and the young men engaged in constant verbal jousting while she drank beer from her own pint mug. Eventually Bess turned from her victims and addressed John; "I would like leave now I'm tired of these buffoons and there's some people I'd like you to meet on the way back." As they were leaving one of the group by the name of Nigel Marston called out; "Goodbye Your Majesty." To which

Bess replied; "You may kiss my arse Nigel!" This brought much laughter from the group above which Geoffrey's voice was heard; "Oh Bess darling, when are you going to make me such an offer?" As they left the tavern Bess looked at John whose face wore a look of disbelief; "Did I shock you? Well that's the only way to deal with those insufferable boors." John asked; "If they are such insufferable boors why do you associate with them?" Bess shrugged I really don't know, maybe it's because I enjoy humiliating them." John had another question; "Have any of them ever asked you to marry them?" Bess laughed; "No their families would disown them if they considered marrying a retired ranker's daughter. Their thoughts are with bedding rather than wedding." On their ride back John realized that he had fallen hard for this petite copper haired spitfire of a girl and practically choked on his own words; "Bess would you think it remiss of me if I were to ask your fathers permission to call on you?" Bess feigned a scowl; "Yes Master Beaconsfield I would think it very remiss! If you wish to call on me you will seek approval from both my parents." She was laughing as John trying not to stammer asked; "And if they grant permission would you acquiesce? Bess edged Cynthia over so that their mounts were flank to flank, reached out, pulled on the lapel of his riding jacket and brought his face down to hers then kissed him on the lips. As she pulled away she smiled at him; "Will that serve as my answer?" John was blushing and spluttering and Bess was laughing at him as they approached the gate at the entrance to the mansions drive. Bess gave him a look of mock disapproval; "Now pull yourself together we're going to meet the people I told you about." She rode up to the hitching rail in front of the lodge just inside the gate dismounted and secured Cynthia, John followed suit. Before he had finished tying off his mount a tall beautiful blonde girl came flying through the lodge door, she threw her arms around Bess and almost lifted her off her feet. She was hotly followed by another who was identical to her in looks and dress; and they all joined in a triple embrace.

Bess finally broke loose and called John over; "John please let me introduce you to my dear friends Pamela and Patricia Sanger, ladies please meet Mr. John Beaconsfield." John doffed his cap and gave a slight bow; "It is with the greatest of pleasure that I make your acquaintance ladies." The two girls giggled then looking at Bess asked in unison; "Where have you been hiding this delightful young man?" Bess smiled; "I only found him today." Looking at John she exclaimed; "And you sir, do not make it too great a pleasure!" The twins were both dressed in jodhpurs and riding jackets that were identical in color and style. Bess looked at John who was regarding the statuesque twins with open admiration; "I am going up to the house to ask Mamma if she can seat two more for dinner, can I safely leave you till I get back?" The twins chorused together; "Oh he will be safe with us Bess darling." Bess looked over her shoulder as she mounted Cynthia; "I wish I could be sure of that." As Bess rode off John turned to the twins; "I'm not going to give you ladies the satisfaction of trying to tell you apart so I'll address you jointly. Where on earth did you come from?" One twin fixed John with deep blue eyes; "We have been friends of Bess since we were twelve, I'm Patricia but you may call me Patty." The other regarded him with equally deep blue eyes; "I'm Pamela and you may call me Pam, why don't you come inside while we wait for Bess." When they were inside the lodge John asked; "I understand Mrs. Spratt is preparing dinner without any help, won't this be something of an imposition?" He was unable to be sure which twin answered; "We're already invited. When Bess's mamma found out we were back from London this afternoon she made a point of inviting us." John was in a quandary: "But why did you let Bess ride up to the house to ask?" They both laughed and answered him in unison; "This way we were able to have you to ourselves for a little while to see if you meet with our approval." John was blushing profusely and words came out that he would not normally have uttered; "I'm sorry ladies but your scrutiny is making me feel like a prize bull in an auction pen." This sent the twins into peals of laughter which reached Bess's ears as she was tying Cynthia to the hitching rail; as she entered the lodge she glared at John; 'What have you been up to with these wantons?" One of twins answered through their laughter; "He told us he can perform like a prize bull." Bess asked; "Is that what you told these two trollops?" John was now totally off balance, blushing and spluttering he tried to extricate himself; "On my honor I said nothing untoward." Finally Bess could contain herself no longer as she joined with the twins in laughing at a thoroughly discomfited John she looked at him through tears of merriment; "Oh John I'm sorry, I should have never left you alone with these two." John's reply conveyed his irritation; "You do not appear very sorry!" Still laughing Bess took his arm; "Come, let's go up to the house; Mamma will be waiting." Outside as John and Bess were mounting their horses the twins came around from the other side of the lodge riding identical mounts which made John gasp; "Blonde horses, well I never!" Seeing the look on his face one of the twins enlightened him; "They are called Palominos our grandfather had them brought over from America. He has the stallion and he let us have these fillies on the understanding that he can put the stallion to them when they are ready." John thought; "How did I manage to meet the four most outspoken, attractive and unabashed women in my life all in one day?" When they reached the stable Jimmy was outside waiting. After they were dismounted the twins took turns in lifting Jimmy off his feet and kissing him on the cheek but he never took his eyes off Bess. She instructed him; "Take care of Miss Patty's and Miss Pam's horses until they go back to the lodge, I'll send Joanie down to let you know when to get Mr. Beaconsfield's horse ready." They entered the house with the three girls chattering animatedly and John trailing behind them. Jack noticed the look on Johns face; "Why so serious John? I would have thought a man blessed with such a bevy of beauties would be ecstatic." John shrugged his shoulders; "If I

ever was on a high horse they surely brought me down from it."
As they were sitting at the dining room table Meg entered the
room: "Tell Joanie what you'd like to drink." When she turned to
leave the room Jack said; "Wait Meg, guess who's the latest victim
of Bess and the terrible twins." Meg smiling looked over at John:
"Oh you poor fellow, you never stood a chance." Jack looked at
John in mock sympathy; "Don't feel badly, no doubt you saw what
Bess can do to those young layabouts in the White Hart. You
should hear some of the stories Taffy has told me of when the
twins and Bess are in there together. Taffy Griffiths is the landlord; formerly a sergeant-major with the 24th of Foot, I'm sure I
don't have to tell you he's Welsh."

After dinner while they were sat round the table drinking
wine Jack addressed John; "I suppose you must be wondering
how I come to be living in the vicinity of not just two beautiful women but four. Well these two beauties are Lord Sanger's
granddaughters, when he donated this house to the trust he made
one condition, that the lodge be available for his family, right now
Pam and Patty are fugitives from London society." One of the
twins looked at Jack; "Oh Papa, you make it sound like they ran
us out of town." John interjected; "If you were treating the men in
London anything like you treated me that would not be surprising!" Meg laughed; "It would appear John that you received the
full treatment." Johns face took on a serious look; "Sir, Ma'am,
there is a matter I would like to discuss with you in private." Jack
looked around the table we're all friends and family here I doubt
that you have anything to say that cannot be said in front of us
all." John took the plunge; "Sir, Ma'am, I would like to have your
permission to call on Bess." Jack looked at Meg and they both
nodded in agreement, Jack replied; "I know I speak for both of
us when I say we feel that if Bess desires your company; knowing her good judgment it is definitely acceptable." Almost before
Jack had finished both twins were out of their chairs and hugging
Bess. One was heard to comment; "Oh Bess darling now you have

your very own beau!" John thanked Jack and Meg and thinking that now was a good time to leave said; "I hope you will forgive me but I'd like to be on my way before dark. Meg called Joanie and told her to see that Jimmy had John's horse ready. Jack got everybody's attention declaring they should have a toast to celebrate the evening's event. Everyone's glasses were refilled then Jack stood and indicated to Bess and John to remain seated, the others stood and raised their glasses as Jack declared; "To Bess and John." Then looking at John and laughing; "May God have mercy on his soul!" As they all prepared to leave Bess addressed Meg; "Mamma, could John not come to church with us tomorrow?" Meg replied; "Splendid idea, if we all meet here at nine o'clock we can eat breakfast first, it looks like we'll be having nice weather so we can walk into the village." One of the twins suggested they leave with John and see him as far as the lodge. Bess looked at them both accusingly; "That had better be all you'll be doing." As John rode down the drive flanked by the two beautiful young women on their blonde horses he could not help thinking that from Jack's description of Cynthia Butler; "She must have looked a lot like them when she was young." When they arrived at the lodge one of the twins taunted him; "You have been very quiet since we left the house, were you savoring that kiss Bess gave you in the stables?" John reddened; "We thought we were being discrete." Both twins laughed as they watched John canter his horse towards town.

The following morning John arrived at the lodge just as the twins were headed for the house. As he dismounted he took note of their highly fashionable identical dresses as he greeted them; "Good morning ladies, may I escort you to breakfast?" They answered him together; "Indeed you may sir, we would be most appreciative of your company." When they arrived at the stables Jimmy came out to meet them. He took the reins from Johns hand after giving him a baleful glare then turned his back and led the horse through the stable door. One of the sisters turned to the other; "It would appear we weren't the only ones who saw that kiss last night."John now had one twin on each arm and they were both laughing merrily as the trio approached the house, Bess came bustling out through the French windows of the solarium; "I hope this behavior is not indicative of what you two were up to with him last night."Then she stood on her tip toes and gave John a chaste kiss on the cheek. One of the twins exclaimed; "Oh Bess we know you can do better than that!" The other laughingly added; "You certainly did better than that last night." Bess blushed: "Oh Pam, you saw?" Pam laughed; "And so did Jimmy." Bess was downcast; "He'll be devastated." It was Patty's turn; "John should steer clear if he sees Jimmy with a pitchfork in his hands."Then they were all laughing as Bess hugged each twin in turn. Jack and Meg were regarding the group through the French windows Jack could not help commenting; "John is beginning to look like a stallion in a pasture full of mares in heat." Meg scowled; "I hope you are not going to be using any more of those barrack room comparisons around the girls." As the foursome entered through the French windows John looked at Bess and said; "Thank you dear." Bess regarded him with a puzzled expression. He continued; "It was obvious last night that you all avoided addressing Patty and Pam by name in order to keep me guessing. Well this morning I noticed one of these ladies had a small freckle just below the lobe of her left ear and when Bess called them both by name I was able to ascertain that she was Patty." Patty exclaimed; "Why Mr. Beaconsfield how observant of you!" John smiled; "I'm a newspaper reporter it goes with the job but there is one thing I haven't been able to fathom, why do you both address Bess's parents as Mamma and Papa?" Pam explained; "Our parents died from cholera in India when we were twelve. We were in school at Cheltenham and Bess was our friend there, she brought us to her home on school holidays and her parents took on the task of being our parents." John needed to know more; "What about Lord Sanger?" Patty answered; Grandpapa was having too difficult a time trying to cope with Grandmamma being sick to be any good at parenting." John looked from one to the other; "Forgive me ladies for prying into your personal lives." Pam spoke again; "Dear John, no apology is necessary if you're going to be Bess's beau that makes you our friend." At this point both twins kissed him on the cheeks, one from each side. Bess grasped his hand; "Let's go in to the dining room; they're ready to serve breakfast." While they were sat eating breakfast Meg had a question for John; "Where will you be headed when you leave tomorrow John?" John replied; "I'm going to cover a potential mill strike in Yorkshire Ma'am." Bess gasped; "Might that not be dangerous?" Jack interjected; "It will be dangerous for those poor bastards when the Yeomanry is ordered out to disperse them." Meg reprimanded Jack; "Please darling, watch your language in front of the girls." Looking around the table she said; "Please let's change the subject else he'll be on his soap box again." Jack persisted; "I consider myself to have been a good soldier and loyal subject of the Queen. But I would never have obeyed an order that would require me to ride down and saber my own unarmed countrymen, men who are just asking for a fair wage on which to raise their families." John looked up from his plate; I mean this with no disrespect sir, but do you consider yourself to be a socialist?" As Jack fixed John with his gaze, the scar on his face seemed more livid than usual; "I have no time for political labels, I just happen to believe that people should respect and treat one another fairly and that everyone should be able to live with dignity." Meg spoke imploringly; "Jack I have warned you, if your views were to get back to some of our patrons we could lose funds for the home." Although intended to soothe, her words inflamed Jack all the more, his response was impassioned; "Yes, they send us money and sometimes they visit the home when they ooh and ah over the children and tell us what a wonderful thing we're doing, and yet they support the very system that oppresses these children. I know this is not an ideal subject for breakfast conversation but I have one more thing to say before we discuss more pleasant matters. In a short while we are going to take a pleasant walk to a beautiful ancient church that was built by a brutal baron on the backs of his serfs. No doubt he thought it would ensure him of a place in heaven despite the many atrocities he had committed against his fellow man. The Vicar will no doubt preach to us about the son of God that lived in poverty and healed the sick and succored the poor, even though he is part of an establishment that is only second to the Roman Catholic Church in possession of land and money. And ironically I will put money in the collection plate. There, now I will step down off my soap box." Meg heaved a sigh of relief; "Thank goodness!" Then looking at the twins she asked; "Did you get those lovely gowns in London?" They chorused; "Yes." Bess smiled; "And who are you planning to dazzle with your beautiful attire today?" The two young women had conspiratorial smiles on their faces, then Patty spoke; "We thought we might go to The White Hart for luncheon after church." Realization came to Bess; "You're going to bait the zoo creatures." Jack spoke up; "Why don't we all go? We can have some pork pies in Taffy's back room, and then these two can go and torment those poor lads." Bess chimed in; "They're not going to have all the fun, I want to be part of it." Meg brought them all down to earth; "Before we talk about luncheon let's get breakfast and church out of the way." Just as they were about to leave the house a handsome middle aged man with one arm and his empty left coat sleeve pinned up to the shoulder appeared at the door and addressed Meg; "Mornin' Miz Meg, me an' Barb's come ta get the young'ns fer church." Jack propelled John to the door and introduced them; "John Beaconsfield please meet Albert White better known as Chalky, and the man who saved my life." Chalky grasped Johns hand; "Pleased ta meet yew zur." And then with a mischievous grin; "I give un 'is fust baff too." John laughed; "I've heard the story, please call me John." Chalky still grinning replied; "An' yew must call me Chalky and I'll bet my story be better than 'is." An attractive dark haired woman appeared behind Chalky; "This be me missus, 'er name be Barb." John gave a slight bow; "It is my pleasure Mrs. White. Barb looked at him with her brown eyes; "Pleased ta meet yew zur, and yew best be callin' me Barb if'n we're gonna get along." Meg laughed; "Barb doesn't say much but when she does its right to the point." Meg addressed Chalky; "If you get the children we can all walk to church together."

After Matins they were all gathered outside the church as Barb was getting the children lined up Jack turned to Chalky; "How about a pint mate?" Chalky shrugged; "Me an' Barb's gotta get that lot back to the 'ouse." Barb overhearing turned to Chalky; "Yew go on an' 'ave a drink I'll see to these'ns; "Bess spoke up no you won't Barb White I'll take 'em up to the house." And then indicating the two oldest; a girl and boy; "These two can take care of the others when we get there." Barb asked; "'Ow 'bout yew?" Bess who was already leading the crocodile of children back toward the home called over her shoulder; "I'll be back soon." When they entered the White Hart the women walked through to the dining room at the back of the inn while Jack, Chalky and John went into the Public Bar. Before they ordered their beers Jack instructed the barman; "See that the ladies in the dining room get whatever they want." They were drinking their second pints when Bess who had changed into riding clothes breezed in; "I thought I'd find you rascals here." When the men stood up Bess chided them; "Sit down, we're in the public bar and I don't intend to be a lady today." They sat back down at their table laughing. Jack nodded to the barman; "Bring this "not a lady today" a pint of the best." Bess informed Jack that Cook was feeding the children when she left then asked; "When are we going to eat?" John suggested they take their drinks to the back room and join the ladies. Bess feigned offence; "Am I not a lady, John Beaconsfield?" The three men laughed as John answered; "You just finished telling us you were not a lady." On their way to the back room they encountered Geoffrey Armstrong returning from the men's privy, he stopped and turned to Jack; "Ah Mr. Spratt, do you intend to enter Perry in the steeplechase next Sunday?" Jack replied; "Yes Geoffrey, but why do you ask?" Armstrong smiled; "I have just purchased a hunter from Ireland that has one of the finest bloodlines in Britain and I can't wait to try him out against Perry." Bess laughed; "You mean your papa bought his little boy a pony." An irate Armstrong rounded on Bess; "Your manners ill become those of a lady!" Bess laughed even more; "How would you know Geoffrey? No self respecting lady would be seen in your company so you have no standard by which to make a comparison." Jack was pushing Bess towards the back room; "That's enough daughter you and the twins can torment those poor fellows all you want after we have eaten." While they were eating pork pies, cheese and pickled onions Jack looking at Meg commented; "Whenever we eat here it brings back memories of Woolwich and The Duke of York's Inn." Meg added; "Whenever the O'Neill's and the Weston's visit they insist on eating here sometimes more than once." After they had eaten Bess and the twins left for the saloon bar from where loud voices and laughter could be heard. John had a question that had been on his mind; "Do the twins not have beaus?" Meg answered; "Our Jonathan and Patty are betrothed, when he comes home from India next year they are to be married." A look of realization came on Johns face; "That diamond ring she's wearing today, I thought it was a heirloom." Meg continued; "Pam is seeing a young guard's officer presently on palace duty in London. According to Patty their betrothal is imminent." On their way out of the inn Meg opened the door of the saloon bar and informed the girls they were leaving and someone was heard to say; "Another beautiful woman, I think I've died and gone to heaven." Meg's comment brought a wry smile to Jack's face; "I'm old enough to be your mother Geoffrey Armstrong." Geoffrey was not to be silenced; "If you were my mother I might be inclined to commit some unspeakable sin." As Bess was leaving with the twins she turned; "Oh Geoffrey so you have incestuous tendencies, is that why they call you a mamma's boy?" After they exited the tavern the laughter at Armstrong's expense could be heard coming from the saloon bar all the way out to the street. Meg looked up at Jack; "Your daughter has a sharp edge to her tongue Sir." Jack laughed; "I wonder where your daughter inherited that trait from Ma'am?" Bess and John were walking behind them, and John was leading Cynthia, seeing how they held hands and laughed together John said; "It's easy to see they're still very much in love." Bess sighed; "Yes and it was love at first sight with them." John looked down at Bess; "That's the way it was for me." An impish gleam showed in Bess's eyes; "Oh when and where and with whom did this occur?" John gave an exasperated growl; "You really are a minx Bess Spratt!" Behind them the twins were observing how close they were pressed to each other. Patty turned to her sister; "Maybe we'll be invited to a wedding soon." Pam answered; "If they get married without inviting us there will be bloody hell to pay!" When they arrived at the lodge Meg looked back at John; "Will you join us for dinner tonight?" John declined; "I'm sorry Ma'am I'd really love to but I have to get everything ready for an early start tomorrow. I have to take a train to London for a meeting with my editor after which I'll be taking a train to Bradford." When they reached the house Jack invited them all to the drawing room for drinks. While they all relaxed with their drinks sitting in an eclectic hodge podge of overstuffed leather arm chairs Jack stood and proposed a toast; "To brighter future for all children." To which they all stood in response. When they were reseated Jack addressed John; "I think one more session should take care of the story. When will you be able to return?" John was hesitant; "It depends on how long this Yorkshire thing takes and whether or not my editor has another assignment for me. I'd really like to get back here for the steeplechase next Sunday." Bess glared across the room at John; "I hope that is not all that will bring you back sir." John mumbled apologetically; "I thought you'd take it for granted that seeing

you would be the most pressing thing to expedite my return."
Bess's reply did nothing to relieve his discomfort; "Take it for
granted, take it for granted? I'll have you know sir I take nothing
for granted. And you would be well advised never to take me for
granted!" Jack looked at Meg; "That poor boy has a lot to learn."
Meg smiled; "I think he's going to learn the hard way just like
someone I know." Bess rang for Joanie, when she appeared she
was instructed to tell Jimmy to get Mr. Beaconsfield's horse ready.
John finished his drink then made the rounds of the room saying his goodbyes. The twins hugged him and kissed him on the
cheek, Meg and Barb hugged him and he got firm hand shakes
from Jack and Chalky. Bess took his hand; "Let me see you to the
stables." Then, glancing at Pam and Patty she exclaimed; "Before
those two vixens get their hands on you again." They left through
the French windows followed by the twin's laughter. When they
reached the stables Jimmy was stood holding Johns horse, he
thanked him as he took the reins. As Jimmy slouched back to
the stables he gave John a murderous look over his shoulder. John
gave a half hearted laugh; "D'ye think I should check the girth
strap?" Bess stood on her tip toes and kissed him. Startled John
exclaimed; "Isn't this being a little indiscrete?" Bess laughingly
replied; "I think it's a bit late for discretion." As he rode away
Meg and Jack appeared seeing the look of sadness on Bess's face
Meg put her arm around her saying; "I know what you're feeling,
but you've only known him two days." Jack cleared his throat;
"And we are just the right people to lecture her on the ill advis-
edness of falling in love at first sight." As they walked through
the French windows with Bess between her parents their arms
linked laughing, the twins, Barb and Chalky wondered what the
joke was.

CHAPTER 12

FOREIGN SHORES

HE HARBOR WAS full of ships some steam and some sail. Some
were tied to the docks and some were stood off in deep waters
being loaded by lighters. The docks were alive with soldiers
and horses and appeared to be in a state of chaos. As far as Jack
was concerned appearances were not deceiving. There were young
officers' running back and forth giving orders and countermand-
ing orders. Cargo was being loaded and sometimes unloaded and
an atmosphere of mayhem prevailed. Jack cursed under his breath
as he thought; "Bloody jumped up young pricks! Why don't they
let the NCO's handle things?" RHQ, HQ and B Squadrons had
been assigned to the steamer on which Jack had been detailed
to supervise the loading of the squadrons' mounts and pack animals. As one of the horses hanging in a sling around its belly
was swung over the hold the dock worker whose job it was too
position the animals for lowering into the hold let out a bellow; "Bloody thing bit me! I'll giv' yer bite 'ere take this!" He
then began beating the frightened horse with a marlin spike. Jack
jumped down off the crate he had been standing on and ran over
and wrenched the spike from the dock worker's hand saying; "If

you hit another horse you'll be going for a fucking swim!" The dock hand took a swing which Jack easily dodged and countered with a right hook to the dock workers jaw. Standing over the dazed prostrate worker he addressed him with a menacing tone; "The next one to be loaded is mine and if you don't behave yourself I'll make you kiss his arse!"

Jack reflected back to the day before they had left barracks. He had been summoned to Colonel Hawkins's office. The Colonel ordered Jack and the RSM who had marched him into The Colonels presence to stand at ease; "Sergeant Spratt I am about to make you an offer for which there will be very little time for consideration. General Butler, Mr. Royce and I feel that you would be a great asset as riding master at the regimental depot. It would mean official promotion to the rank and the accompanying pay increase. It is more than likely that we will need more trained troops to fill the inevitable gaps in our ranks when the regiment returns." Jack was torn between being home with Meg and the children and fighting alongside his mates, after brief consideration he gave his answer; "Sir, I greatly appreciate your confidence in me but I think my place is with the lads. If there's going to be fighting I should be there with them." Hawkins looked at Jack with a slight smile on his face; "So you think the Musketeers will vanquish the enemy eh?" Royce gave a chuckle; "Major Barry is an admirer of your little group, he often talks about D'Artagnan and his comrades." The Colonel turned again to Jack; "I know how devoted you are to your family and that it could not have been an easy decision to make so quickly." Jack addressed The Colonel with some alarm in his voice; "Sir, can we please keep this from my wife?" His apprehension faded with The Colonel's reply; "No word of what just transpired will leave this office." Hawkins then turned to the RSM; "Leaves us with something of a quandary Mr. Royce." Jack spoke up; "Sir, may I make a suggestion?" The Colonel nodded and Jack continued; "Could the regiment not hire a civilian with the requisite skills?" Royce spoke up; "Like we hire civilians for the commissary. We should have no trouble requisitioning the funds." The Colonel looked at Jack with a knowing smile; "Seems you have solved our problem Sergeant, you wouldn't have someone in mind?" Jack was grinning; "I thought maybe Mr. Perry Sir. Private Reeves has been working with me on his own time; if you promote him to corporal he could be Mr. Perry's assistant." Hawkins asked; "Is that the one they call Turps, your highwayman?" Jack laughed; "Yes and he's probably the best horseman of all the rankers." Royce interjected; "Present company excepted." The Colonel looked at the RSM; "D'ye think Perry'll accept?" Royce laughed; "If I know Ned when we send for him he'll get back here ahead of the messenger."

Jack turned his attention back to supervising the loading and saw that Nipper was being lowered towards the hold in a series of jerks. He ran to the side of the ship and leaned over the rail glaring down at the two gantry operators; "Pay that winch out smoothly; you're scaring the horses, no wonder your bloody mate up here got bitten." One of the men looked up; "We don't take our fuckin' orders from you." They had dropped the pawl into the teeth of the winch cog suspending Nipper in midair. At that moment Lieutenant Hanbury appeared on the dock, looking up he asked; "What's going on Sergeant Spratt?" Jack saluted; "These men are scaring the horses and making them difficult to load into the hold Sir." Hanbury glared at the two on the winch; "Who's in charge of the loading of these animals?" One of the men indicating the chandler's warehouse behind them answered; "Our foreman, ees in there." At that point a bustling figure wearing a bowler hat came out through an office door in the warehouse. He glared at the two winch operators and asked; "Wot the bloody 'ell's goin' on 'ere?" The man who had defied Jack was truculent; "These soddin' sojer boys er tellin' us 'ow to do our job." Hanbury asked the foreman for his name. The foreman informed him that his name was Suggs. Hanbury then instructed him; "Well Mr. Suggs, from now until all the animals are loaded your men will take their orders directly from Sergeant Spratt." The foreman exploded; "Not fuckin' likely we got a contrac', this is civilian bizniss!" The lieutenant's voice took on a menacing edge; "Do you know who owns these docks?" The foreman was belligerent; "Cawse I does, The Earl of Milford." "Well what d'ye think will happen when I tell my uncle the Earl about your lack of cooperation?" Suggs was showing signs of servility; "I don't know zur." Hanbury now had the upper hand; "Well I'll tell you Mr.Suggs. The Earl will contact your employer and you and these layabouts will be dismissed. So I suggest you instruct your men to take their orders from the Sergeant." With this Suggs turned to the men on the winch; "Frum now on yew takes your orders frum the Sergeant or yew'll get sacked." He then shouted the same orders up to loader on the ship. Hanbury strode up the gang plank and addressed Jack: "I think that should take care of things Sergeant." Jack expressed his gratitude; "Thank you Sir, I didn't know the Earl was your uncle." The officer smiled conspiratorially and in a lowered voice said; "He isn't, I only met the old goat once and I wouldn't want him for a relative at any price; but I'll have the old bugger in the family until this ship is loaded. By the way is that pretty little wife of yours going to be coming with the regiment?" Jack shook his head; "No sir, my mates and I decided to leave our wives home, they'll take care of each other." Hanbury smiled; "I see now we have lady musketeers, would Mrs. Spratt be the female equivalent of D'Artagnan?" Jack smiled back; "I suppose you could say that sir." As Hanbury prepared to depart Jack's salute was returned by the officer who was still smiling at the thought of female musketeers.

After they had been at sea for two days conditions on board became very arduous. Jack was constantly below decks doing what he could to make life more bearable for the horses, making sure their halters and leg ropes were secure and that the barrier boards that separated the animals remained firmly anchored to the deck. He recalled the stevedore that supervised the placement of the horses in the hold saying; "If yew runs into ruff wevver yer 'orses is gonna be scared and they'll start tryin' to rear and kick. If'n them ropes aint tight and them boards aint secure some uv um ull get 'urt." Jack was constantly rounding up corporals and privates and ordering them down into the holds to tend to the horses. This task was not made easy by the fact that much of the time the men and Jack himself were seasick. None of the rankers on board had ever been to sea prior to the voyage and a few were so debilitated by seasickness as to be incapacitated. On one occasion when he was rounding up a working party he spied a private hanging over the rail that he ordered below to help with the horses. On hearing Jack's order the private turned his head and exclaimed; "Fuck yew! I'm fuckin' dying 'ere." The effects of seasickness combined with weariness had caused Jack to become short tempered and he shouted; "If you don't do as I say you will be guilty of disobeying an order. You are already guilty of insolence and insubordination which I'm prepared to overlook if you get your miserable arse below decks and help with the horses." The private shouted back at Jack with defiance; "Fuck yew agin!" Jack turned to see a sailor who was observing the scene amusedly and shouted over the wind; "Go and get me one of those ropes ends your bosun likes to use on you tars." The sailor thinking to enjoy some more fun at the expense of the landlubber soldiers walked off swaying with the ships motion and returned grinning with a knotted ropes end that Jack took from him, then glaring at the disobedient soldier he growled; "I haven't got time to find an officer and have you arrested so you either get down that hold or I'll give you a taste of this." The private made no attempt to move and as Jack raised the ropes end his arm was grasped from behind. He spun round starting to utter an oath when he found himself face to face with the Adjutant. Captain Metford asked accusingly; "Just what d'ye think your doing Sergeant Spratt?" Jack's reply was defensive; "I need men down with the horses to make sure they're secure, and this one refused to get down there when he was ordered." Metford turned his attention to the private; "Did you refuse to obey the Sergeants order?" The private started to whine; "I be sick zur." The Captain shouted above the wind; "Over half the men on this bloody ship are sick but they're not shirking their duties! Now get down in that hold or I'll have you put in irons until you come up before the Colonel." As the private staggered toward the hold Metford turned back to Jack; "Sergeant you do not administer punishment. He has to be charged and the Colonel decides on the appropriate penalty. I take it you'll be charging him with insolence and insubordination as well as refusing to obey an order?" Jack's reply took the Adjutant by surprise; "I don't wish him charged Sir and I'm sorry I lost my head, it wont happen again." Metford shook his head; "I suppose you know what you're doing but let him think he'll be on orders until tomorrow. Some trepidation will be good for his soul." Jack smiled while he replied; "I recollect using those same words myself once; in a different situation."

After they left the Atlantic and passed through the Straits of Gibraltar entering the Mediterranean; where the weather was less severe, they sailed eastward until they entered the Aegean Sea then through the Dardanelles Straits, east across the Sea of Marmora and through the Bosporus Straits to the Black Sea, then north where they finally docked at the port of Kulali in Turkey. They unloaded and disembarked only to load and embark for Varna in Bulgaria a few days later. Conditions at Varna were bad; there was a shortage of forage and water and there was an outbreak of cholera. The Light Brigade was formed up and in June the Heavy Brigade under Sir James Scarlett arrived at Varna but the divisional commander Lord Lucan was still back in Kulali with the expedition's commander Lord Raglan. While they were waiting to get all of the division's elements including headquarters assembled Colonel Hawkins came down with cholera. On the morning of their fourth day at Varna as Jack was contemplating his breakfast of salt pork and brackish water an orderly from RHQ entered the makeshift mess hall and brought him a summons. When he arrived at the rickety dining table Jack looked up at him; "I haven't had to eat shit like this since the fucking workhouse! What's your business Private?" The private tried to be officious; "Colonel wants to see yer right nah." Jack looked down at the right sleeve of his tunic; "Are you bloody well blind Private?" The private quickly became more respectful; "Sorry Sergeant." Jack asked; "Isn't the Colonel sick? I'll come right away." When he entered the colonels tent Jack was shaken by his appearance. He was propping himself up on his campaign bed with one elbow and wheezing painfully and hardly able to acknowledge Jack's salute. His face was drawn and had a grey/green pallor, the Colonel spoke painfully; "Sergeant Spratt when Divisional Headquarters arrives you will be transferred to Lord Lucan's staff until further notice." He observed the look of combined anger and disappointment on Jack's face and went onto explain; "They wanted an expert horseman to carry dispatches and as far as I'm aware you're the best bloody horseman we have in this fucking hell hole. Look at it this way; you'll get better rations and you aren't likely to be in any fighting." Jack struggled to get his feelings under control before speaking; "Permission to speak frankly Sir?" The Colonel nodded at the same time admonishing him; "You have my permission but I won't tolerate insolence." Jack asked the question that was uppermost in his mind; "Did General Butler or Mr. Langsbury have anything to do with this?" Despite his obvious distress Hawkins managed to sit upright, his voice was angry; "If you're trying to suggest that I was given instructions to find you a safe berth to protect your arrogant arse you flatter yourself. You're the best bloody horseman I have and that's all there is to it. Then he softened his tone; "They're shipping me home on the mail packet the day after tomorrow, if you wish to write a letter to that pretty little wife of yours I'd be happy to see that she gets it." Jack's demeanor became less resentful and he thanked Hawkins; "I'm very grateful for your offer to carry a letter to my wife and I'm sorry if I spoke out of turn. I've been lucky enough to serve under the best two CO's anyone could ask for and I had no cause to say what I said." The Colonel lay back down before he spoke again; "If someone overhears you they'll think you're kissing my arse." Jack's reply was heated; "If they think that; they can kiss mine!" The Colonel uttered a gurgling sound; "If you make me laugh in my condition I'll have you bloody well court martialed. Bring your letter to my orderly tomorrow and make sure you report to Divisional Headquarters as soon as they arrive, if ever they arrive." Jack saluted then wished his Colonel a safe voyage and a speedy recovery. When he passed Hughes on his way back to HQ Squadron the clerk who was now a corporal remarked; "You look pretty down in the mouth Sergeant." Jack glared at him; "I've just been detached to fucking Divisional Headquarters." Hughes asked; "Aint that a piece of luck? You'll get good vittles and you should be clear of any fighting." Jack rounded on him; "I came out here to fight not to be a fucking postman for some jumped up generals!" Taking advantage of Divisional Headquarters tardiness Lord Cardigan took command of the whole cavalry division and moved the Light Brigade eight miles inland to Devna. Jack was ordered to remain at Varna Where he was to take up his new post.

Six weeks later Meg heard the sound of hooves after which came a knock on the front door of the cottage. Upon opening the door she beheld Turps now Corporal Reeves holding his horse's bridle. Masking her unease she asked; "What can I do for you Corporal?" He replied; "I have a letter for you Ma'am." Needing some time to collect her thoughts she instructed the corporal to take his mount around to the stable, tie him to the hitching rail and enter the back door. When Reeves respectfully knocked on the back door Meg bade him enter and sit down. When they were both sat at the kitchen table Meg containing her anxiety asked; "And where's this letter Corporal?" Turps slid his cartouche belt round, extracted a letter from the pouch and handed it to her. When she saw it was addressed in Jack's handwriting she heaved an audible sigh of relief. Guessing what had been going through her mind Reeves spoke up; "Colonel 'awkins was shipped 'ome sick 'an ee sent this letter to Mr. Perry at the depot "an ee giv' it to me 'an zed get it to Miz Meg an' make sure you puts it in 'er 'and." Meg smiled; "While I'm reading this why don't you sit and I'll get you a beer, in fact I'll get us both a beer." Turps was apprehensive; "If I'm gone too long Mr. Perry is gonna skin me alive. Meg set him at ease; "If Mr. Perry has any problem with you resting and refreshing yourself and your horse; tell him Mrs. Butler and I will pay him a visit." This brought a smile to Reeve's face; the two ladies had a reputation in the regiment for putting people in there place. He had a request: "Ma'am, I'd like to see to Dick before I takes me ease." Meg smiled; "Oh yes your horse, you couldn't name him Bess because he's a gelding so you named him after Dick Turpin himself. There's a bucket by the pump for water and there's oats and a feed bag inside the stable." Reeves expressed his gratitude; "Thank you ma'am but I brought me own oats an' feed bag." Meg showed her approval; "My husband taught you well." Turps smiled: "Yew don't fergit nothin' Sergeant Spratt teaches yew, ee drives it in wiv an 'ammer." Meg nodded; "While you're out there look in on Jasper please." Meg took the opportunity afforded by the corporal's absence to read Jack's letter, she opened it with trembling hands and proceeded to devour the words:

My Darling Meg,

I cannot express the words that would tell you how much I miss you and our children, it's only been eight weeks but it seems more like five years. I am well and have just been informed by Colonel Hawkins that I have been detached to Divisional Headquarters so it doesn't look like I'll be involved in any fighting, (at this Meg heaved another big sigh of relief) and I should get some edible vittles. I heard that Chalky, Ginger and Paddy are fair to middling over at "A" squadron so you can pass that on to the girls. If you get the opportunity to see The Colonel and Mrs. Hawkins please thank him and tender my respects to them both. I would like to make this letter longer but I'm still in this wind blown rag of a tent at regimental HQ and these conditions are not conducive to writing well. Give my respects to all and give our children a big hug and kiss from their Papa. I miss you so much that the pain is physical; please know I love you with all my heart.

Yours forever
Jack

When Reeves entered after knocking and saw the tears running down Meg's cheeks he enquired; "Not bad news I 'opes."Meg looked up; "No Corporal, I just miss him so." Turps commiserated; "Your bloke's the best there is even if ee did knock me on me a… backside wiv that gurt big b… beautiful stallion the first time I set eyes on 'im." This made Meg laugh; "You could have expressed yourself freely, I've been around soldiers long enough not to be offended, but thank you for being so respectful." Reeves continued; "When I knowed ee'd saved me frum 'angin' I fawt ee wuz Jesus Christ. But wen 'ansen 'an 'im got me in the trainin' troop I weren't so sure. Now I knows 'ansen made me into a sojer and your bloke tawt me to ride good." Meg interjected; "From what I've seen you're a bloody good horseman."When she saw his eyebrows lift and his face redden she thought somewhat guiltily; "Now I understand the satisfaction Cynthia gets from shocking people." She stood and telling Reeves to remain seated crossed the kitchen to the larder, when she returned she placed a plate of cold roast beef, cheese, newly baked bread, farmhouse butter and pickled onions on the table together with a knife and fork; "Here Corporal as your horse is eating so must you." Reeves protested; "Ma'am, I can't accep' this." Meg's eyes flashed; "If you don't eat this food I will tell my husband that you refused my hospitality!"

When Divisional Headquarters finally arrived the expeditions commander Lord Raglan had already decided to invade the Crimea. Jack followed his regiments progress from information gleaned from his excursions to Light Brigade Headquarters and his occasional contact with the regiment's headquarters staff. He witnessed the incompetent handling of the landings at the ironically named Calamita Bay. There were major actions such as Alma and many smaller engagements when eventually it became certain that the key to defeating the Russians would be Sebastopol. Sebastopol was a fortified coastal town on the Black Sea located in the Crimea which was joined to the mainland of the Ukraine by an isthmus. The Russians had set up defenses on its inland flank consisting of artillery batteries at the end of a valley with redoubts on either side of the valley's entrance. This valley and the surrounding area guarded the Woronzoff Road which would permit access to Sebastopol itself. When the Cavalry Division arrived at Balaclava as the area was known, their ranks had been considerably reduced by disease and malnutrition. The horses were in poor condition due to insufficient and poor quality fodder and being required to stand for long hours in cold and rain. The 17th along with the rest of the Light Brigade stood too at first light after which they were ordered to take up a position in support of Sir Colin Campbell's Highlanders. When Lord Cardigan finally joined his brigade, after having had breakfast on his yacht in which he had sailed from England Raglan ordered the Light Brigade to return from supporting Campbell and take up a position to the left of the second line of redoubts.

After some indecisive actions involving the infantry and heavy cavalry highlighted by the epic "Thin Red Line", when the 93rd Highlanders literally rose up out of the ground putting the Cossack cavalry to flight, the first cavalry action of consequence was by the Heavy Brigade under Brigadier Sir James Scarlett. Scarlett leading the brigade consisting of the Royal Dragoons, Inniskillen Dragoons, 4th Dragoons and the Royal Scots Greys charged uphill; fell on the Russian flank then ran the crews off the guns in the northern redoubt. After the Heavy Brigade had put the Russian cavalry to flight no order was given to pursue and thereby turn their retreat into a rout. The 17th was on the left flank of the front rank of the Light Brigade and sat there impatiently while Cardigan out in front of his command fumed visibly and vocally. Finally an officer and a sergeant rode down from Divisional Headquarters. Jack rode a little behind Captain Nolan who was charged with imparting Lucan's orders to Cardigan. When they pulled up in front of the Brigade Commander it was obvious to Jack that these two men disliked each other intensely. Cardigan despised Nolan of the 15th Hussars for being an "Indian officer" despite the fact that he was one of the finest horsemen in the British Army and had an exemplary record of service. Nolan had an issue with Cardigan because he'd made no secret of his contempt of Indian officers and Nolan in particular. The Captain saluted then gave Lucan's order; "Take the guns." Cardigan asked sneeringly; "What guns?" Nolan threw out his right arm and gestured into the general direction of the valley saying in an insolent tone; "There are your guns My Lord!" As they started back to Divisional Headquarters Jack addressed Nolan; "Sir, have I your permission to join my mates of the 17th?" Nolan still seething from his exchange with Cardigan ignored protocol and answered; "You might as well, their strength is down from cholera and God knows what other diseases that dwell in this fucking hell hole." Jack wheeled Nipper and galloped up to Captain Morris who was now commanding officer of the sorely depleted 17th Lancers, he saluted and made his request; "Permission to join 1st Troop "A" Squadron Sir." Morris asked; "Were you granted permission to relinquish you duties at Divisional HQ?" Jack answered knowing full well that Nolan did not have the authority to detach him and thinking poor bugger's going to catch hell from Lucan; "Yes sir." Morris smiled; "Go join your Musketeers and find a lance if you can." As Jack rode towards 1st Troop's place in line; a trooper he was about to pass fell unconscious from his horse, his stirrup bucket swiveled forward and his lance fell across his mount's neck. Jack grasped the lance and set it in his own stirrup bucket. When he reached 1st Troop Chalky who was now acting troop officer nodded towards the former owner of Jack's lance who was now being carried to the rear; "Poor bugger, anuvver one dahn to that fuckin' cholera." As Jack was edging Nipper between Ginger's and Paddy's horses Ginger asked: "Wot yew doin' dahn 'ere wiv us peasants?" Jack gave a hollow laugh; "I'm here to make sure you clowns don't fuck up." Then Paddy had a question; "Why aren't you up front with Chalky boyo? " Jack answered; "The troop's his command I'm just along for the ride." Then Captain Morris shouted back; "Quiet in the ranks!" At the same instant Cardigan drew his saber and brought it up to the carry with the order; "Brigade at the walk advance." The bugler sounded the command and the officers and hussars and light dragoons also brought their sabers up to the carry. Ginger muttered loud enough for Jack and Paddy to hear; "Stupid owd bastard's gonna get us all kilt!" Just as the order to trot was sounded Captain Nolan appeared and galloped to the front of the brigade gesticulating agitatedly. Cardigan was waving his saber violently and pointing behind himself. Just as Nolan started to place himself to prevent Cardigan's progress a half spent round from a Russian cannon bounced off the ground and tore into his chest. He fell from his horse screaming then lay on the turf quivering; a gaping cavity pumping blood where his chest had been. Cardigan could no longer control the pace of the advance, so he ordered the bugler to sound the charge and the brigade broke into a gallop. Those armed with sabers held them at full arms extent pointing towards the enemy, the lancers lifted their weapons out of their stirrup buckets and couched them under their arms. Cardigan spurred his white charger Roland to retain his place at the head of his command and the sole intent of every soldier was to get into the guns as quickly as possible and out from the withering salvos from both flanks and to their front.

They not only had cannon and musket fire to contend with there were also panicked riderless horses whose herd instinct caused them to gallop alongside the others jostling the mounted troopers. Finally they were into the guns and what could only be described as hell on earth. A hell of wreathing gun smoke, the pungent smell of gunpowder and the screaming of wounded horses. Men were shouting oaths as sabers flashed and lances stabbed, added to this was the boom of the cannons and musket fire. They were almost through the artillery positions when Nipper set himself to jump the tongue of an ammunition caisson. Just as his front feet left the ground a wounded riderless horse crashed into the caisson causing the tongue to swing upwards. Nipper's left fetlock struck the tongue which caused him to stumble and go down on his front knees on landing. Jack's lance went point first into the ground and the shaft snapped in two. He instinctively threw himself off Nipper and landed on his feet in a crouching position. As he was straightening up he saw a Russian gunner running towards him holding a cannon's ramrod like a quarterstaff. He drew his saber just as the artilleryman changed his grip on the ramrod and swung it like a huge club, Jack thought; "You stupid bastard now I've got you." He ducked and the ramrod swung harmlessly over his head. With the Russian off balance and his right side facing towards him, Jack drove the point of his sabre into the gunner's armpit. The Russian screamed as he turned and Jack could see the terror in the Russian's eyes when he realized he could not draw his saber with his useless right arm. Jack remembered the admonition he'd heard from both Hansen and Perry; "Never 'esitate cos that's wen yew gets to be dead!" He swung his saber bringing it down into the place where the gunners shoulder and neck were joined. The Russian collapsed with blood spurting from his neck. Then he heard Ginger scream out; "Be'ind yer Fishy!" Jack spun around in time to see a Cossack riding at him saber at the ready. He jumped to the horse's left forcing the Cossack to bring his saber over his mount's neck. However the rider was close enough for the point of his saber to slice down from the corner of Jack's eye to just above the corner of his mouth. As the Cossack curveted his horse to make a second run, Jack with blood running down his face stuck his saber in the ground and pulled his lance from the turf. Even though the shaft was broken in two there was still four feet left. The Cossack rode at the bloody faced Jack determined to finish him off. When Jack judged him to be close enough he feinted to the Cossack's left causing him to anticipate the same move as before. As the Cossack leaned over to his left Jack jumped back to the right side of the horse and drove the lance head into the rider's right hip. The Cossack swung back to his right screaming with his saber poised. Before he could bring his saber down Jack thrust the lance head up under his chin. The Cossack fell from his horse with the lance still protruding from his head. Ginger who'd had his horse shot out from under him ran over to Jack after dispatching the Russian infantryman who was still reloading his musket. He looked from the Cossack to the gunner and exclaimed; "Bloody "ell! I'm fuckin' glad yew an' me is on the same side." Jack looked around and asked; "What about Chalky and Paddy?" Ginger answered; "They wuz on their 'orses las' I see 'em, I fink they wuz goin'arter the cav'ry be'ind the guns." Just at that moment Chalky appeared staggering through the smoke supported by Paddy. Chalky's left arm hung limply down his side a dirty rag soaked with blood was tied around his sleeve at the elbow. Paddy looked at Jack and said; "Bloody musket ball so it was. And we both had our horses shot from under us." As Jack moved toward Chalky a Russian infantryman with a musket and fixed bayonet came running out of the smoke and seeing Jack ran at him full tilt. Chalky and Paddy had just reached the spot where Jack's saber was stuck in the ground; Chalky pulled it out with his good right arm grasped it under the guard then drew his arm back and threw it like a javelin. The saber struck the Russian in the back hung for a moment then fell to the ground; Chalky then broke from Paddy's grasp ran to where the saber lay and picked it up. As the infantryman turned Chalky with what was left of his strength ran him through and then collapsed. Jack stood transfixed, and when he was finally able to speak he looked down at Chalky then back at his two other comrades and said in a choking voice; "You're the best bloody mates anyone ever had!" Meanwhile Paddy revived Chalky with some water from a discarded canteen and now had him back on his feet. When the color returned to his face Chalky looked around at his fellow lancers and gave his orders; "As actin' Troop Orficer I orders us all back to our own lines, now let's git our arses out of 'ere." Their progress up the valley was slow and they were in danger from some isolated Russian cannon that were still manned and random musket fire. Jack was leading Nipper who was favoring his left front leg and trying not to put his weight on it; when they came upon an officer trapped under his dead horse. The horse had him pinned to the ground by his right leg, when he saw them approaching he waved his left arm feebly. When they reached him he ordered; "Get me out from under this fucking animal!" Jack and Ginger lifted the carcass off his leg while Paddy pulled the officer clear. When he was able to stand the officer addressed them; "I am Major Lord Chesham of the 13th Light Dragoons then looking at Nipper he ordered; "Help me up on that horse." Jack protested; "Sir, you can't ride him he has an injured foreleg if you ride him the injury could become permanent." Chesham shouted angrily; "I don't fucking care! My bloody leg was almost broken, and if you disobey my order I'll have you broken and flogged." Jack who was holding a piece of dirty cloth up to his cheek to stanch the blood from his wound was hesitant to disobey the officer's order but reluctant to cause Nipper anymore suffering; was spared from having to make a decision by a shout from up the valley. A private of the 13th was galloping towards them leading a horse. When he was close enough he called to the major; "Lord Chesham Sir, I have a spare horse for you." Chesham turned to Jack; "I've a bloody good mind to have you flogged for even considering disobeying me!" As he rode off on his new mount neither the Marquis of Chesham nor Jack was aware that they were father and son. This circumstance would be revealed in another place at another time. Ginger said; "If yew'd 'ave give me the word I'd a run the bugger through an' they'd uv thought the Russky's ud done 'im in." Jack smiled and replied; "I was thinking about it myself. That trooper might have saved his fucking Lordship's sorry arse." As they continued their labored progress up the valley Jack leading Nipper walked beside Chalky, looking around at the devastation of the battlefield at the dead riders and horses, with the wounded being carried off and stricken horses thrashing and screaming, Jack said to Chalky; "Where's the bloody reason for this, why?" Chalky turned his pain drawn face to Jack saying; "There aint no reason to it and it aint a rankers place to be asking for a reason why, ower job is to get out there an' do it; an' if we dies doin' it, it's just too fuckin' bad!"

After they reached their lines Jack spied the Farrier Sergeant and called him over; "Hey Bill can you take a look at Nipper?" Woden strode over to where Jack was stood holding Nipper's bridle and stated; "Aint got much time gotta get back out an' finish off zum more uv 'em poor buggers." Jack asked; "How many horses did we lose?" Woden gave his estimate; "I reckons abaht 'alf of wot went in." As the Farrier Sergeant was examining Nippers foreleg Jack commented; "I saw you riding in the charge with that bloody great pole axe, are you fucking crazy?" Woden laughed; "There's at least fower Russky"s that's tellin' Old Nick 'ow crazy I am." Then he looked up at Jack; "Soak a rag in cold water and wrap it round 'is fetlock an' keep it wet 'til the 'eet's gone, it's a sprained tendon, good job yew dint ride 'im arter ee did it." Jack looked peeved; "You know I wouldn't do that!" Woden laughed again; "I know, the way yew luvs this'n and that big black bugger yew got back 'ome I wonders if there's any luv left fer that pretty lil missus o' yourn. Now I gotta get back out there and take care uv zum more." Jack watched him go back and mount his horse after which a private handed him his pole axe. The trooper's horse had two large canvas bags slung pannier style behind the saddle; the bags were soaked red with blood. He thought about the grim task they were about; chopping off the left front hooves of the dead horses so that a tally could be taken from their regimental numbers. The horses that were badly injured would be dispatched with a blow between the ears from the spike of the pole axe, he shuddered. His thoughts were interrupted by Ginger; "Eh mate, the surgeons done wiv Chalky let 'im take a look at yer face." Jack asked; "How's Chalky?" Ginger looked grim; "They took 'is arm off, ee'l be going dahn to the orspital at Scutari tomorrer." Jack had another question; "How did he take it?" Ginger grinned; "Ee dint make a sound." Jack smiled knowingly; "Chalky's a tough bugger if anyone could take it; it would be him." Ginger startled Jack by laughing loudly; "Ee dint make no sound cos ee passed out wen ee see the saw comin'at 'im." Jack shrugged; "Well, at least he'll be going home. " By now they had arrived at the barber-surgeon's tent identified by its red and white spiraled pole as Jack entered a corporal in a blood spattered apron waved to a chair and told him to sit. The surgeon who'd just finished removing a bullet from the thigh of a trooper who lay groaning on the table came over to him and asked; "What's your injury Sergeant?" Jack removed the rag which he had been holding against his cheek. The surgeon examined his wound then uttered; "Um, that'll need some stitches." Jack reacted; "D'ye mean you're going to sew it up?" The surgeon nodded his head; "If we don't it will never come together and heal. Jack asked: "Will it leave a scar?" The corporal laughed; "Wot is ee, a pretty girl er one uv them nancy boys?" The surgeon glowered at the corporal; "That's enough Corporal, there's some softened catgut in that bowl on the table and bring me a curved needle." Jack saw the needle which reminded him of those he had seen the upholsterers plying in a furniture workshop. The surgeon threaded the needle talking as he did so; "They call it catgut but it's actually from sheep's guts but it does the job." When he first pierced the skin Jack flinched and groaned. The surgeon admonished him; "You have to keep still if I'm to get this done properly. " Jack replied through barely open lips; "This hurts more than that bloody Cossack's saber." When the surgeon had finished he gave instructions to Jack; "Let me look at that in two week's time and maybe we can take the stitches out." Jack asked is there anyone at Divisional Headquarters, that's where I'm assigned." The surgeon nodded; "Yes Lucan's got a doctor with him, tell him Surgeon Riley sent you." Just as Jack left the surgeon's tent holding a clean rag to his cheek a corporal from Divisional HQ rode up and addressed him; "Lord Lucan said if yew're still alive you gotta report to HQ, 'an the way ee 'is yew might be better off dead. Jack smiled grimly; "I've got to walk my horse; he's lame." As the corporal turned his horse to head back he said to Jack; 'I fink yew're about to get fucked Sergeant, good luck." When Jack finally arrived at Lucan's tent he found a captain in the uniform of the 8th Hussars waiting. After he saluted the captain he tethered Nipper to the hitching rail then stated; "I believe Lord Lucan is expecting me, Sir." The captain's smile was grim as he said; "Follow me Sergeant." Jack removed his lance cap and placed it under his left arm as they entered the tent. Lucan was sat behind a rickety looking desk with a general officer stood to his right. The captain saluted the officers and announced to Lucan; "Sergeant Spratt reporting as ordered Your Lordship." Lucan glared at Jack: "What've you got to say for yourself Sergeant?" Jack feigned ignorance; "Is there something amiss Your Lordship?" Lucan exploded; "Yes, there is something amiss Your Lordship! There is a great fucking deal amiss, where the fucking hell have you been?" The general officer who by his epaulettes was a brigadier took in the sight that Jack presented: battle dress torn and stained with mud and blood and a bloody rag held to his left cheek while trying to keep his lance cap under the same arm, and yet his weary eyes still showed fight. He thought to himself; "And Wellington called 'em the scum of the earth." Lucan roared again; "Where were you dammit?" Jack replied; "I joined my mates in the charge, Sir." Infuriated even more by Jack's answer he asked; "And who gave you permission to leave your assigned duties Sergeant?" Jack answered; "Captain Nolan, Sir." Lucan's tone was quieter but no less menacing: "Convenient, Captain Nolan was killed and can neither verify nor negate your story. But that aside, Captain Nolan did not have the authority to grant you permission. Sergeant, you are guilty of leaving your post, neglecting your duty and insubordination. Is there any reason why I should not have you shot?" The brigadier noted a gleam of defiance in Jack's otherwise weary eyes as he answered; "None that I can think of Your Lordship." The tent was filled with an ominous silence for what seemed to Jack like an eternity, and then Lucan burst into a fit of laughter. When he regained his composure he turned to the brigadier; "Toby, do you believe this cheeky bastard, he defies me by agreeing with me; what the hell shall I do with him?" The brigadier spoke up for Jack; "By the look of his face he was definitely in the fighting, maybe that's punishment enough." Lucan looked back Jack; "How many d'ye kill Sergeant?" Jack tried to seem nonchalant; "Two Sir, a gunner and a Cossack." Lucan relented; "Get your arse over to the mess tent you look like you could use something to eat. Take the rest of the day to rest up and report for duty at six o'clock tomorrow morning." Jack had a request; "Permission to report to the surgeon Sir." Thinking Jack wanted to get his wound tended to Lucan said; "When you get outside ask the Captain to direct you to my doctor's tent." After getting directions from the 8th Hussar captain Jack led Nipper to a tent which had a sign attached to a stake in front of its entrance displaying the words: R.J. Sutton MD. When Jack entered the tent he saw an elderly grey haired man dressed in a black frock coat sitting behind a table, the doctor looked up and addressed Jack; "What may I do for you Sergeant?" Jack answered; "Sir, could you spare me a bandage about three feet long?" The doctor looked puzzled as he walked over to Jack and pulled the hand holding the cloth away from his face; "Well I see it's been stitched, but you need a pad for this wound not a bandage." Jack's reply bought a look of surprise to the doctor's face; "It's for my horse Sir, he sprained a tendon and the farrier sergeant told me to keep a cold compress on it." The doctor smiled; "You must be Spratt I've heard about you, there's a white chest behind the tent you'll find what you need in there. And if you tell a soul I gave you medical supplies for a horse I'll cut your balls off!"

Jack rode a spare remount until Nipper was healed, and for the rest of the campaign he attended to his duties at Divisional Headquarters and saw no further action. Ginger and Paddy stayed with the 17th which mostly performed vedette and foraging duties until the regiment sorely depleted from disease, the action at Balaclava and the battle of Inkerman Heights where although they were stood to in reserve they received heavy fire and sustained more casualties, sailed for Ismid on the Bosporus in November 1855 and thence to England, then on to Ireland in May of 1856. Nearly all of the regiment's senior officers including Major Barry had been sent home early in the expedition's campaign mostly due to diseases such as typhoid and cholera. One surgeon was heard to remark; "The rankers have got more resistance to disease coming from where they do, if they live past five years old they're almost immune to anything. Now these bloody bluebloods, they've never been exposed to anything like a workhouse or a prison and that's why they're more susceptible!"

CHAPTER 13

HOMECOMING

F RIDAY MORNING SAW John Beaconsfield outside of the Royal George unloading his baggage with help from the carter who had driven him from the railway station. The twins who had been in town for the purpose of mailing some letters saw him as they rode away from the post office. Pam turned to Patty saying; "Ride for the house and tell Bess he's back I'll keep him entertained 'til you get here." Patty turned her horse and spurring the filly into a gallop headed for the home. Pam rode up to the cart and as John turned at the sound of hooves said: "Good morning John, welcome back." After which she dismounted and secured the palomino to the hitching rail then turned and gave John an enthusiastic hug and kissed him on the cheek. John laughed; "That was one of the best greetings a man could wish for." It was Pam's turn to laugh; "Wait 'till Bess sees you, she's been like a mare in heat all week." John grimaced; "I don't think it would be a good idea for me to call her a mare, in heat or otherwise." Pam laughed again; "Let's go inside and you can buy me a drink." Turning to the carter she tossed him a shilling and said; "Josh be a dear and take Mr. Beaconsfield's luggage inside." The carter looked up with a grin; "Anyfink yew sez Miz Pam." They walked into the inn and headed for the bar with Private etched in the door glass, when they were both seated John asked Pam what she would like to drink. She asked for sherry and John ordered a pint of porter. As they were savoring their drinks John asked; "Where's your sister?" Pam looked up from her sherry;" She was headed for the house when last I saw her, I expect she'll be back." They had just finished their second drink when Bess burst through the door; "Oh there you are, you finally return and I find you drinking with another woman." Patty came through the door behind Bess laughing; "She even led a horse here for her beau and here he is consorting with a wanton trollop." John stood and Bess flew to his arms. As they kissed hungrily Pam smiled at Patty saying; "And you called me a wanton trollop." When they left for the home John and Bess were flanked by the twins as they rode four abreast down the high street; two town workers who were resetting some loose cobbles in the road looked up. One turned to the other commenting; "Strewf, zum blokes gets all the bloody luck!"

When they arrived at the stables Jack and Meg came out of the house to greet them while Jimmy and another boy took the horses. Jack strode over to John and shook his hand energetically saying; "Why is it whenever I see you you're surrounded by beautiful women?" Seeing Meg approaching John said; "Here comes another beauty." Meg stood on her tiptoes and gave John a kiss on the cheek while hugging him tightly saying; "That gets you a kiss from an old lady." John held her at arms length exclaiming; "No more of this old lady nonsense, you are a vision of loveliness and a most desirable woman!" It was Bess's turn to exclaim; "Mamma if you steal him from me I will never forgive you!" Then Jack joined in the teasing; "And if you cuckold me I shall be forced to challenge you to a duel John Beaconsfield." Patty turned to Pam saying; "By the looks of things there won't be much for us to enjoy." They all entered the house laughing gaily. When they were seated in the library Meg rang a small bell and a young girl dressed as Joanie had been the week before came through the door and addressed Meg; "Yes Miz Meg?" Meg looked around at Jack and the guests; "Sarah would you be a dear and fetch whatever drinks our company may require, I'll have a sherry." As Sarah went around the room asking each one what they wished to drink; Meg looked at John saying; "How now sir, no remarks regarding a pint of beer." This caused a renewal of the laughter for which John waited to abate then made an announcement; "My editor has given me the whole of next week off which will give Mr. Spratt and I ample time to finish the last episode of his story which will be published in the Messenger a fortnight from Sunday. And speaking of publishing my editor says he knows a publisher who would probably be inclined to publish the story in book form and he would be happy to go fifty- fifty on the royalties, which could bring in some extra funds for the home." Bess launched herself on John forcing him back into the overstuffed chair and smothering him with ardent kisses saying; "Oh John I love you so much, and thank you for being so wonderful to Papa." Meg smiled: "If Cynthia were with us she'd be looking for a bucket of water right now." After Bess had released him Jack addressed John; "How did it go with the mill worker's strike?" John's answer brought a look of approval to Jack's face: "Well sir from the point of view of a sensational headline it was a failure, but from a humanitarian point of view it presented a shining example." Jack was on the edge of his chair; "Well come on man tell us what happened!" John continued with a smile on his face; "The High Sheriff of Yorkshire and the Mayor of Bradford decided against calling out the Yeomanry and had the city police force there to keep order. The Mayor addressed the strikers telling them they had an hour to air their grievances after which they would be required to disperse peacefully, and it worked." Jack was now smiling like the proverbial Cheshire cat, his comment was; "Thank God someone has finally come to their senses. I just hope other municipalities will follow Bradford's example." Meg interjected; "Enough of politics I have some news I've been keeping for when we were all together." Then looking at Patty; "Jonathan is coming home from India early he should be here in February." Patty jumped out of her chair and flew across the room, wrapped her arms around Meg and began kissing her while saying; "Oh Mamma you have made me so happy I love you so much!" Meg freed herself and held Patty at arms length; "You'd do well to save some of that love for our son and it's just as well you don't paint your face like so many women, with those tears you'd be a mess." John could not resist; "I've heard it said that beautiful women don't need makeup and ugly women don't deserve it." Everyone began laughing except Bess she looked at John accusingly; "So you think Patty's beautiful? First Mamma and now Patty, I'm beginning to think you're some kind of philanderer. Isn't the name John Juan in Spanish? That's what I'll call you; Don Juan." This brought still more laughter with Jack looking at Meg saying; "He's definitely going to learn the hard way." Then it was Pam's turn; "I too have some news; "Simon will be here tomorrow." This took everybody by surprise except Patty. Bess turned on Pam; "How long have you known?" Pam looked at Bess archly; "Since Wednesday, he went down to Devon to ask Grandpapa for my hand in marriage and he doesn't have to be back on duty at the palace until Tuesday." Bess feigned anger; "Pamela Sanger you are a secretive vixen, how dare you keep such news from me for two days?" Pam laughed; "I just had to see the look on your faces." Bess's retort caused more laughter; "You deserve a good spanking!" Then Patty made a suggestion; "Let's go to the White Hart for lunch, I'll wager we can find plenty of volunteers in the saloon bar to administer that spanking."

As they rode toward the village Jack up on Perry and John riding the hunter Bess had led to the Royal George; Jack looked over his shoulder at the four women following them. Meg on Sally III, Bess on Cynthia and the twins on their palominos, he shook his head; "I was never on parade with a prettier troop!" John laughed;

"I wonder what the Duke would have done had the 17th paraded a pretty troop like that?" Jack smiled back; "That randy old goat would have chased 'em all around the parade ground." Behind them Meg asked the girls; "What d'ye think they can be laughing at?" When they drew close to the White Hart John spotted a dapple grey heavy hunter tied to the hitching rail. He turned to Jack; "That grey's a beautiful animal he's as big as Perry." Jack answered; "That handsome piece of horseflesh must be Geoffrey Armstrong's latest acquisition." After they were seated in the back room Geoffrey Armstrong came through the door looking at Jack he asked; "Did you see my grey outside?" Bess spoke up; "Yes the talking horse." Armstrong glared at her; "Whatever d'ye mean?" She answered with a mischievous smile on her face; "He asked me the way to the glue factory." Armstrong tried to ignore their laughter and asked Jack to see him in the saloon bar after their meal. Jack looked up saying; "Yes Geoffrey I think we'll all join you." Geoffrey left not feeling too happy at the prospect of having to contend with Bess and the twins once again. After their meal they all repaired to the saloon where Geoffrey addressed Jack; "Well are you entering Perry Sunday?" Jack gave him a mysterious smile; "Yes he'll be there." Armstrong wondering what the smile indicated asked; "Will you be riding him?" Jack replied; "No not this year." This evinced another question from Armstrong; "You bringing in a professional jockey or something like that?" Jack's answer left him hanging; "No nothing like that, but why don't you wait 'till Sunday to find out?" For the next two hours they enjoyed drinks in the saloon bar where Jack, Meg and John enjoyed the entertainment provided by Bess and the twins baiting the county zoo. On their way back to the house Jack turned his horse went back to where the women were walking their horses and pulled alongside Bess, he smiled at her; "I have a favor to ask you darling." Bess who could read her father almost as well as Meg asked; "Is this to do with what you were talking to Geoffrey about?" Jack's reply was not a complete surprise to her;

"I would like you to ride Perry on Sunday he's getting on in years and he'll be carrying less weight with you up. I've decided this will be his last time and I'd like him to go out a winner, but that grey of Armstrong's looks like he'll be hard to beat." Bess smiled at her father fondly; "Of course I will Papa but I so hope I won't let you down." Jack smiled back; "You could never do that!"

Saturday morning as John was making his way to the inn's dining room for breakfast he spied a tall handsome young man dressed in the height of fashion talking to the landlord. He overheard him asking the way to the home. Despite the civilian apparel his military bearing gave him away. John strode over to him and held out his hand saying; "May I safely presume that you are Simon Hawksworth of her Majesty's Coldstream Guards?" While shaking his hand Simon replied; "You may Sir, and whom do I have the pleasure of addressing?" John introduced himself; "John Beaconsfield a recent acquaintance of a young lady who I believe is about to become your fiancée." Simon nodded; "Pam has told me about you, I understand you are calling on her friend Bess." John smiled; "Yes I am currently enjoying Bess's company. Would you join me for breakfast?" Simon assented and after they were seated and had placed their orders John commented; "I thought Pam was expecting you on the one o'clock train this afternoon." Simon smiled archly; "I took an earlier train, thought I'd surprise her." After breakfast John directed Simon to the livery stables saying; "I'll get my horse from the stable in the back and meet you over there." As they were riding towards the home John and Simon became better acquainted and just before they reached the lodge John made a suggestion to which Simon agreed enthusiastically. Simon dismounted and stayed hidden behind the mansion's wall. While John rode up to the lodge leading Simon's horse but before he could dismount to pull the door bell Patty appeared she looked at the riderless horse then as Pam emerged she asked; "What d'ye have there John?" John replied I found this horse wandering along the road. Would you know to whom it belongs?" Upon his cue Simon strode through the gateway saying; "I think that may be my horse." Both girls were momentarily frozen and dumbstruck then they launched themselves at Simon. After they had both been hugging and kissing him for what seemed to John like hours Patty stood back leaving him to Pam who continued kissing him for a while then addressed him accusingly; "Whose idea was this? You weren't supposed to be in 'till one o'clock and I was going to meet you at the railway station." Simon reached into his pocket then took Pam's left hand and slid a ring onto her ring finger saying I couldn't wait to give you this." Pam looked down at the ring which had a large blue sapphire surrounded by diamonds, she gasped; "Grandpapa said yes?" John smiled; "Yes darling we have his blessing." Pam started to kiss him again when Patty said: "Let's go up to the house and tell Bess and Mamma and Papa." As they approached the house the young men leading their horses with Pam on Simon's free arm and Patty on John's. Bess saw them through the French doors and exclaimed; "It's Simon, and that minx Patty is flirting with John again." Bess flew through the doors, ran up to Simon, stretched up on her tiptoes to kiss him on the cheek then turned and addressed Patty; "Let go of my man you trollop!" Then to John; "I was so looking forward to your return and I find you once again philandering with one of my best friends." Simon who'd only met Bess briefly on two occasions stood rigidly a dumbfounded look on his face. Jack who with Meg had come out behind Bess looked at his wife saying; "Simon obviously doesn't know our Bess." Meg laughed as Bess stood on her toes and began to smother John with kisses. She then turned and hugged Patty and Pam in turn kissing them both on the cheek. Then the girls linked arms and entered the house laughing. Simon and John were left holding their horses and Simon exclaimed; "Well I'll be damned!" Then looking at Jack and Meg he lifted his hands and said; "I don't understand!" Jack laughed saying; "Don't try Simon, if you marry Pam you may be together for fifty years; and you still won't know her completely." Just as Simon was about to inform them that he and Pam were now officially betrothed Bess came flying through the French doors once again; she addressed her mother breathlessly; "Mamma, you must come and see Pam's ring!" The two young men handed their horses to Jimmy then walked toward the house with Bess and her parents. Inside Pam was showing her ring to two of the girls who were wards of the home; they gasped audibly at the sparkling diamonds and the large blue sapphire. One of the girls commented; "Why Miz Pam that big blue un matches yer eyes." Jack looked at Simon; "I take it it's now official." Simon smiled yes the old boy gave us his blessing yesterday." Jack asked; "How is Lord Sanger?" Simon's answer caused Jack to smile; "He's fit as a fiddle, Pam's and Patty's brother Miles told me he's seeing a lady." Meg chimed in; "Isn't he seventy-five or something?" Simon replied; "Yes, but he doesn't look or act a day over fifty." As the women were gushing over Pam's ring she addressed Bess teasingly; "It appears you're the only lady present that doesn't have a ring on the third finger of her left hand." John seeing this as an opportunity addressed Jack and Meg; "Sir, Ma'am with your permission I would like to rectify that situation post haste." As Bess moved to John's side looking up at him adoringly, Jack and Meg looked at each other, when Meg nodded her head in assent Jack turned to the couple; "You have our blessing, although it seems that everything has been so sudden!" John turned to Bess there's a jewelers just down the High St. from the Royal George let's go and get you a ring." Bess kissed him saying; "Give me time to change into riding clothes." Then turning to one of the young girls who had been watching bemusedly she instructed her; "Tell Jimmy to have Cynthia and Mr. John's horse ready." As Bess left to change Simon spoke up; "This calls for a celebration." John came up with a suggestion; "While Bess and I are in town why don't we arrange for us all to have dinner at the George, the rest of you folks can meet us there." Bess came back dressed in jodhpurs and riding jacket exclaiming; "I know this is rather informal but I'm too excited to spend time changing into a riding habit and it's been so long since I've ridden side saddle I can't remember where the damn saddle is, and it's probably not been soaped for ages." As the couple disappeared through the door Jack feigned a stern look at Pam saying; "I suppose you know you're responsible for this young lady!"

John and Bess rode to town in an exhilarated mood. When they reached the jewelers they could hardly wait to secure their mounts before hastening through the door. As they peered through the plate glass at the rings displayed on the counter John let out an exclamation of triumph; "There it is!" Bess looked to where he was pointing and saw a ring that closely resembled her mother's engagement ring, she gasped: "John it's just like Mamma's, I really love it!" John addressed the store assistant; "D'ye have the emerald ring in the lady's size?" The assistant bustled off then came back with a red felt lined tray containing a number of rings just like the one John had selected. When Bess had found one that fit John asked the assistant its price. As the assistant was putting the ring in its velvet lined box he said; "That'll be seven guineas Sir." Bess looked at John with some concern: "Papa told me he paid four guineas for Mamma's ring." John smiled indulgently; "That was twenty-six years ago darling, we've just experienced what the economists refer to as inflation." The assistant spoke up; "If you're talking about the ring Mrs. Spratt wears with her wedding ring that would fetch seven guineas today." John thanked the assistant then turned to Bess; "Let's get over to the George and see the landlord about the dinner arrangements." After they entered the Royal George John went to find the landlord while Bess waited in the dining room sipping a sherry. When John returned with a tall middle aged man about her father's age he introduced him; "Bess this is Tom Naismith the landlord of this fine establishment." Bess and Tom both laughed together, then Tom enlightened John; "Why bless yew zur I knowed Miz Bess since 'er wuz in pigtails." John laughed at his own faux pas; "Of course,

I should have known." Tom smiled at Bess; "I unnerstans congrats is in order." Bess smiled up at him saying; "Thank you Tom d'ye think you'll be able to feed us all at such short notice?" Tom asked; "'ow soon will the uvers be 'ere?" Bess answered; "They'll be here shortly but I'm sure we'll sit around and have some drinks for a while." Tom said; "Give me an hour and me and the missus ull 'ave zum roast beef an' Yorkshire pudden wiv zum egg custard ta foller." He then addressed John I erd yew talkin' to Mr. 'awksworf, yew zed ee wuz in the Coldstreams, I served under a Major 'awksworf in the Guards, d'ye fink they're kin?" John shrugged; "I only met him for the first time this morning, but you can ask him yourself when they get here." When the others arrived Tom bustled out of the kitchen and told the barman; "See these folks gets whatever they needs 'till dinner." Then turning to Simon; "Zur, excuse me but is Major 'aksworf uv the Colstreams kin uv yourn?" Simon smiled saying; "Major Hawksworth formerly OC of 'A' Company, Second battalion of Her Majesty's Coldstream Guards is my father." Tom beamed then said; "Well I'm buggered I wuz 'is color sar'nt. Simon's smile grew even bigger as he extended his hand; "It's an honor to know you Color Sergeant Naismith." As they shook hands Jack looked on thinking; "Us soldiers are all brothers under the skin." Simon felt the need to say more; "My father often mentions your name when he recalls being in command of 'A' Company, he's a general now." They were still grasping hands as Tom said; "An' a bloody good'n if I knows anyfink!" They finally released each others hands as Tom said; "I gotta get back to the kitchen if we're gonna get yew folks fed." Simon sat down with the others and sighed looking around the table he said; "The Regiment's like a family." Jack smiled at Simon; "I know exactly what you mean." Then John stood up and addressed them; "I would like to make the betrothal of Bess and myself official." Then turning to Bess while sliding the ring onto her finger he said; "Dearest Bess will you marry me?" Bess had tears in her eyes as she answered; "I don't know what to say except yes darling." She stood and they kissed while the others applauded. Meg looked at the ring and exclaimed; "It's just like mine!" John smiled at her; "I had to get one that would match the beautiful eyes she inherited from her mother." Meg got up from her chair and as the twins were admiring Bess's ring she went up to John and pulled his head down and kissed him full on the mouth saying; "You are one smooth talking rascal John Beaconsfield and I think I could fall in love with you myself." Bess heaved an exasperated sigh; "Between Mamma and these two vixens my John is never going to be safe." During dinner the talk turned to the twin's upcoming nuptials. When Patty mentioned that Jonathan was coming home in February Pam suggested a double wedding. Simon told them as he was only a subaltern he would have to get his Colonel's permission and then added; "But it's really just a formality, Lord Sanger's and the Colonel's families are connected." After they had finished their dessert and the pot boy was clearing the table Tom's wife came out, she looked at Simon; "Be yew Mr. 'awksworf?" when Simon nodded in affirmation she continued; "Wen I wuz laid up arter 'avin our Joey yer mammy cum by every day wiv food an' medsin, 'er be a saint!" Simon thanked her saying; "My mother was always concerned about the welfare of the soldier's families." Jack looked at Meg and smiled as they both remembered Cynthia. Mrs. Naismith had one more thing to say; "Mr. 'awksworf Zur, yew tell your mammy Cora Naismith blesses 'er evr'y day uv 'er life." After Simon assured her the message would be passed on Jack looked at the grandfather clock standing at the foot of the stairs that led up to the guest rooms saying; "I think we should be leaving I'd like to make it an early night, we have the steeple chase tomorrow. Simon and John escorted them out to where the horses were tied where John asked of Jack; "Where's Perry?" Jack replied I let the old fella rest today, he's running his last steeplechase tomorrow." After the two younger men had shaken hands with Jack, hugged Meg and Patty and kissed their fiancées' and Jack's party were mounted on their horses John said; "I recall someone commenting that I always seem to be surrounded by beautiful women." Meg laughed saying: "One day that silver tongue of yours is going to get you in trouble John Beaconsfield." Both the twins were now laughing and the young men could not tell which one of them said; "Like when he told us he could perform like a prize bull!" As the party rode away down the High St. Simon looked at John questioningly; "What was that all about?" John smiled saying; "Let's go into the bar and I'll tell you over a night cap." After John had told Simon how the twins had twisted his words they were both laughing heartily, overhearing them Cora asked Tom; "Wot be they laughing at?" Tom's answer brought him a scowl from his wife; "If I wuz gonna marry one of them beauties I'd be laffin' me bloody 'ed off too."

Sunday morning after breakfast at the house they all rode to the White Hart where everyone was gathering for the steeplechase. Geoffrey's father Squire Armstrong, a big florid faced man was organizing the event from the back of a large heavy hunter. He cast a look around saying; "Looks like everyone's here, let's go round to the yard and get this thing ready." When they were assembled in the yard at the back of the inn he gave them instructions; "You'll line up right here and be off when I fires me pistol. You'll head for St. Marks whose steeple you can see clearly to the west." He pointed at the distant church with his riding crop then continued; "You will stay on the roads and bridle paths, the marshals will show you where you can cross pastures, you will not encroach on private property where the owners have not given their permission! Upon reaching the church you will touch the milestone on the side of the road in front of the church then head back here for the finish. There will be marshals' all along the course to make sure that there's no cheating; if you cheat you'll be disqualified. We have half an hour before the start so you can all have a drink before the off, and as it's against the law I'm sure there'll be no betting." The last was said with a huge wink.

When they were gathered in the saloon bar Geoffrey came up to Jack and said; "I see you rode Perry here how about we have five guineas on Perry against my Grey Billy?" Jack looked at Meg who nodded her assent, after they had shaken hands on their wager Geoffrey asked; "Which of those fellas that came with you are riding Perry; Beaconsfield or the other chap?" Bess who had been standing behind Armstrong throughout the transaction spoke up; "That fella would be me." Geoffrey spun round and spluttered; "You, you, but you're a woman, a woman has never competed in the steeplechase, I'll talk to the Squire about this!" Bess laughed; "Let's both go and see him." They both walked across the room to where the squire was stood with a glass of whisky in his hand deep in conversation with two local farmers. The Squire glared at Geoffrey when he interrupted their discourse and blurted out; "Bess here says she's riding in the steeplechase, she can't do that can she?" The Squire still glowering answered; "Don't know of any reason why not, there aint no rule against it." Geoffrey started spluttering again; "But she's a woman!" The Squire his face even redder than usual shouted above the saloon's hubbub; "If you're afraid a woman's going to beat you, bloody well withdraw!" Geoffrey stamped back across the room followed by a laughing Bess. He addressed Jack angrily; "This is not fair she weighs less than you." Jack responded; "And Perry's three times Grey Billy's age so I think that should make things about even, but no, Bess is a better rider than you; I suppose that put's you at a disadvantage." As Armstrong turned away angrily he muttered; "We'll see about that!"

When the Squire was satisfied that the competitors were lined up properly he raised his arm and they were off at the report of his pistol. A quarter of a mile down the road from the inn there was a five bar gate where a marshal indicated they could cross the field behind it. Geoffrey cleared it easily followed by Bess. Across the field was another gate where a marshal would direct them back to the road. Jack watched Bess and Perry clear it through a telescope he had brought with him, and then they were out of sight. Bess and Geoffrey crossed three more fields that were part of the course Bess and Perry clearing the gates with ease as did Geoffrey and Grey Billy. Bess held Perry behind Grey Billy until they reached the milestone in front of the church Geoffrey reached down to touch it then looked over his shoulder at Bess and Perry as he turned for the backstretch. Bess whose arm was not long enough to reach down from the back of Perry touched the milestone with the end of her riding crop. The congregation leaving the church cheered the riders on as they started the second leg of the race. Halfway back it became obvious that it had become a two horse race with Bess still two lengths behind Geoffrey, then at the final furlong Bess gave Perry his head. Geoffrey looked over his shoulder to see Bess and Perry gaining on him and started giving Grey Billy the spurs and laying on with his riding crop, but Perry was inexorably closing the distance. A hundred yards from the finish line Bess moved up on Perry's neck and appeared to be whispering in his ear, he then increased his already considerable stride to beat Grey Billy by a length. As the Squire was declaring Bess the winner with the spectators wildly applauding Geoffrey strode over to his father declaring; "I'm the winner, she cheated!" The Squire turned on his son angrily saying; "What the bloody hell are you talking about?" Geoffrey equally angry replied; "She didn't touch the fucking milestone." The Squire still angry said we'll see what the marshal says, and watch your language we have ladies present." The marshals were slowly coming in when the squire spotted a small dark man riding a nondescript bay and called him over; "Hey Mickey weren't you at the church?" Mickey answered in a thick Irish brogue; "Aye sor I was an' all." The Squire then asked him; "Did Miss Spratt touch the milestone?" Mickey's reply infuriated Geoffrey; "Yes sor she did so, I seen her with me own two eyes so I did." Geoffrey in his fury shouted; "With her bloody riding crop, not her hand!" The Squire went face to face with Geoffrey and with a low menacing growl said; "There's nothing in the rules that says she can't touch it with her riding crop, or you with your pecker for that matter." Geoffrey stalked off towards the back door of the inn sulking; as the Squire once again announced Bess as the winner. John was hugging Bess ecstatically saying; "You were magnificent darling." Bess smiled and looking at her mount said; "Perry deserves the credit." John looking at Perry blowing with sweat lathered on his muzzle and withers asked; "How did you get that final burst out of him?" Bess's smile got even wider; "I reminded him that Jasper and Sally were two of his grandparents" Jack who had overheard them said; "A horse with his bloodlines is bound to have a great heart." When Bess was able to break away from those congratulating her she removed Perry's saddle, then after wiping him down draped a horse blanket over him and said to John; "Come walk with me while I cool Perry down." The Squire announced that the prize presentation would take place in half an hour after the contestants had cooled down their horses, and then went into the inn to tell Geoffrey to get outside and take care of his horse. As John and Bess were walking away from them with John leading Perry, Meg with tears rolling down her cheeks said; "I wish Cynthia could have been here she would have been so proud." "Jack agreed; "I know darling."

When all the contestants were assembled and the spectators that could squeeze in found a place to stand in the saloon bar; the Squire presented Bess with a huge silver cup with the figure of a galloping horse on its lid. As he handed it to her with John helping her to hold it up he said; "When Mr. Spratt brought the cup back to me last week little did I dream that his daughter would win it. Miss Bess you ran a great race. I know your father was a riding master in the 17th and I've seen your mother ride, it's definitely in your blood." When they were all sat down with the cup on the table between them Jack looked at the engraved plates on its ebony base. The six which bore his own name above the blank one which would soon bear Bess's name along with the year then he smiled, and looking around the table he said; "It's all in the blood, Bess and Perry, it's all in the blood." They were all surprised when Geoffrey came over and banged his tankard on their table calling for everyone's attention then addressing the room; "I wish to apologize to you all and especially to Bess and my father. Today I behaved like a spoilt child and was guilty of extremely poor sportsmanship." Then turning to Bess he said; "Congratulations Bess, you ran a great race and beat me fair and square. Please forgive my boorish behavior." Bess got up from her chair went to Geoffrey then stretched up on her tiptoes and kissed him on the cheek saying; you're forgiven Geoffrey." Then the twins and Meg followed suit as Jack approached to shake his hand Geoffrey said with huge smile; "Damn, that was great I should make a fool of myself more often!" As he shook his hand Jack said; "Good for you, it takes a man to admit he's at fault." After shaking John's and Simon's hands and being introduced to Simon, he looked at the ring fingers of Pam's and Bess's left hands and shook his head saying; "Now there's no one left at whom I can set my cap." Meg looked up then nodding at John said; "If you'd like to take some lessons from that silver tongued young devil; I guarantee you'll be a lot more successful with the young ladies." This caused laughter all around the table as Jack invited Geoffrey to join them. On their way back to the home Simon commented on Perry's performance; "You don't very often see a horse come from behind like that, he and Bess were fantastic." Jack responded; "When he was the same age as Grey Billy he would have done the same thing without blowing and sweating, now the old boy's going to be time expired." Bess showed alarm; "You're not going to put him out to grass Papa?" Jack smiled at his daughter; "No darling, we can still use him for hacking around but we're not going ride him to hounds anymore and he's done with racing." Bess heaved a sigh of relief then looked at her father mounted on Perry saying; "It would have been nice if you could have been up on him for his last race." Jack replied; "Even though I think he could have won had I rode him, I think the extra weight would have taken a lot more out of him, and he has too much heart to know when to hold back." When they reached the lodge Jack addressed the twins; "Why don't you girls come up to the house for dinner? Jimmy can take care of your horses and then take them down to your stables." Everyone was agreeable and after they reached the stables Jack gave his instructions to Jimmy then they all repaired to the library for drinks before dinner.

As Christmas approached the children of the home were beginning to get excited although some of them had never before known the joy of celebrating the season. Jack had erected a large fir tree in the great hall (a custom introduced to England by the Prince Consort in 1841) and the gleeful children helped with the decorations. Jack and Meg however experienced two minor disappointments: Bess had accepted John's parent's invitation to spend Christmas with them as an opportunity to get to know one and other and Simon's parents had also invited Pam for the same reason. While Meg and Patty were commiserating together Meg lamented; "I'm not going to have any of my daughters with me for Christmas." Patty corrected her; "You'll have one, me." Meg taken by surprise asked; "But won't you be going down to Devon to spend it with your grandpapa?" Patty laughed sardonically; "No Mamma, Miles's mousey little boor of a wife will be there and neither Pam nor I can stand her." Meg hugged her and said; "Then you will get three times as much of my love to make up for the absence of the others."

Christmas Eve saw the O'Neill's and the Weston's descend on the home. As the carter who'd transported them from the railway station handed down Ginger's youngest, a pretty girl who resembled her mother but in a much more refined way; Chalky's and Barb's son James came running over. He took her other hand telling the carter; "I'll take care of Miss Annie." They'd been writing to each other since they'd met in June when his regiment had returned home after a five years posting in India and James was completely smitten. They kissed causing Ginger to shout; "Oy, wot yer fink yer doin', yer intentions better be proper!" Jack looked at Meg and they both smiled at the irony. After the hugging, kissing and hands shaking were dispensed with two boys from the home brought the luggage inside and they all retired to the library. When everyone had drinks in their hands they started to catch up on all the latest events in their families. Ginger and Molly had two sons in the army: one had joined the 17th and the other was in the Royal Engineers as Ginger put it; "Ee wuz good at maffmatics an' ee wanted to use 'is lernin'." Both young men were now sergeants and their parents did nothing to conceal their overweening pride in their boys. One of the O'Neill's boys was a corporal in the 17th and the other had obtained a midshipman's berth in the Royal Navy. When Paddy's youngest son had expressed his desire to join the navy Paddy had gone to the Crown and sought Gunner Wilson's advice. Gunner had contacted an admiral with whom he'd served when the admiral was a midshipman. Holding his finger up alongside his nose Gunner said; "I knows someone that owes me a favor." Paddy found out later from one of Gunner's old shipmates that when they were serving under a particularly brutal captain, the captain had ordered a midshipman up the rigging for some minor infraction. Despite the fact that the midshipman was deathly ill, the captain would not relent. When the captain was back in his cabin Gunner had climbed the rigging and told the midshipman to give him his hat, go to foc'sl and rest in his hammock while Gunner served out his punishment. As only Gunner's head wearing the midshipman's hat could be seen in the crow's nest no one on deck detected the ruse. Gunner had explained to Paddy; "That young bugger wuz so grateful ee told me if ever I needed a favor to call on 'im. Well now ee's an old bugger an' a admiral so I'll claim me favor." Paddy was particularly proud this Christmas as they had received news from their son that he had just passed his lieutenant's exam.

Ginger looked up from his drink with a suggestion; "Let's go to the White 'art an' 'ave zum uv Taffy's pork pies." Then looking around the room he asked; "Wur's everyone?" Chalky answered him; "The wimmen er in the kitchen, reckon they be plannin' tomorrer's dinner an' Annie's walkin' wiv James." Ginger feigned disapproval; "Out walkin' wiv a bloody dragoon, wot yew let 'im jine the dragoons' fer?" Chalky shrugged; "I tried to get 'im ta go in the 17ᵗʰ but ee wanted the dragoons an' Barb said let 'im go in wot ee wants, an' yew asks me that same damn fool question ev'ry time I sees yer." Ginger laughed; "I does it just to remind ev'rybody 'ow 'enpecked yew are." Ginger hadn't seen Barb come back in the room; she came up behind him and cuffed his ear saying; "It's 'igh time Molly reined yew in Tommy Weston!" Jack managed to get heard over the good natured ribbing; "Let's get everyone together and we can walk to the village for dinner."

They were all sat in the back room of the White Hart enjoying Taffy's fare when Meg let out a gasp, Jack looked to where Meg's gaze was directed then he himself gasped. Entering the room were Jonathan Langsbury with Hermione on his arm. Meg flew across the room flinging herself at her father repeating; "Oh Papa, oh Papa!" Then while hugging him looked up accusingly and said; "You old ogre you didn't let me know you were coming." Jonathan looked down at his daughter with a doting smile on his face; "We wanted to surprise you and if I should be punished for that well, knocking the stuffing out of me should be punishment enough." Meanwhile Jack after hugging and kissing Hermione on the cheek; turned to Jonathan and as they shook hands Meg began hugging and kissing Hermione. Jack asked; "How are you Sir and you Ma'am?" Jonathan replied with feigned anger; "Dammit Jack we're Papa and Mamma!" Jack looking contrite said; "I'm sorry Papa I was so surprised to see you both, please come and sit down." When they were seated the rest of the company came over to greet them, then when everyone was seated once more Jonathan looked at Jack and said with a smile;

"I see D'Artagnan is together with his Musketeers once again. Meg asked; "How did you know where to find us Papa?" Her father answered; "When we got to the home Cook told us where you were and the carter that brought us from the railway station was kind enough to bring us here. Now how about we order some of these famous pork pies?"

On Christmas morning all the women helped prepare the food for the feast and by three o'clock in the afternoon the women along with the children of the home were sat at the big table in the great hall. Jonathan had insisted that he and the rest of the men bring the food from the kitchen declaring that the ladies had done enough and Christmas was for the children. After the table was laden with four geese, two huge platters of roast beef and a vast assortment of parsnips, carrots, potatoes and other vegetables the men sat down, Jonathan at the head of the table at Jack's insistence. During the course of the meal Jack expressed his regret at not knowing that his in laws were going to join them for the holidays; "You brought gifts and we have nothing for you." Jonathan looked around the table saying; "Seeing us all together is the greatest gift we could wish for." Hermione nodded her head in agreement. Jonathan went on; "Besides the gifts we brought were for the children only." Jonathan who had been particularly disappointed by the absence of Bess stood up and lifted his glass; "To absent loved ones." They all stood and echoed the toast. After dinner the ladies and the children cleared the table while the men went to the library to relax with port wine and cigars. When they had finished in the kitchen the ladies joined the men leaving the children to enjoy their Christmas gifts. Jack made a point of thanking them all for the gifts they'd brought for the children then added; "As you all know, it's been our policy since the beginning that we only give presents to the children. Looking around I see a wonderful group of friends and family that have the greatest gift of all, each other!" His statement brought applause from the group and an outbreak of hugging and kissing all round.

After everyone was seated again Jonathan addressed Patty; "Well young lady what do you and my grandson have planned for when he comes home?" Patty smiled; "We are going to have a double wedding with Simon and Pam but Jonathan doesn't know yet." Jonathan had another question; "Have Jonathan and Simon ever met?" Patty looked thoughtful saying; "No but I'm sure they'll get along." At this point Meg interjected; "I know they'll get along, Simon's a fine young man and he has a lot in common with our Jonathan." Meg's father smiled; "As always daughter I bow to your instincts."

In the second week of February Jack, Meg, Bess and the twins took the train to London's Paddington station then took a hackney cab to Victoria station where they boarded the train for Southampton. As they waited on the quayside for the P&O steamer to dock Patty was jumping up and down trying to spot young Jonathan among the passengers leaning over the ship's rail. When she finally spotted him she let out a girlish squeal saying; "Oh Mamma, Oh Papa, there he is!" Jonathan was frantically waving from the ship and as they waved back Patty was still jumping and squealing Meg turned and admonished her; "Get control of yourself Patty you're acting like a silly schoolgirl!" Jack turned to Bess remarking; "You should have seen your mother when I came home from the Crimea." Bess laughed; "I was still very young then but I do remember some squealing, didn't Cynthia have to quiet her down?" Meg glowered at them both; "When you two have quite finished ganging up on me let's find a spot where we'll be close to the gangplank when he comes down." After the gangplank was lowered an officious young man in a P&O 3rd officer's uniform strode down and standing at its foot cautioned everyone on the dock not to crowd the disembarking passengers. As they waited for what seemed like hours to Patty as the passengers came down the gangplank, many of them being greeted and embraced by those waiting on the dock she gave another squeal; "There he is, there he is!" A tall young man was striding down the gang plank toward them wearing the grey/green uniform of the Corp of Guides carrying two large leather valises. Behind him was an equally tall figure dressed in flowing robes with a turban on his head bearing a large sea chest on his shoulders. Jack immediately identified him from his dress as a Pathan from northwest India. Jonathan reached the dock and Patty was hugging and kissing him before he could put down his valises. Jack took the valises from Jonathan and after shaking his hand while they hugged, then turned him over to the tender mercies of the ladies. When the hugging and kissing frenzy was over Jonathan asked for their attention; "Before we start catching up I wish to present my loyal companion Risaldar Major Saif Ali Khan." Leaning on the upended sea chest the Pathan smiled saying in a sing song voice; "I am pleased to meet you all; Sahib and Memsahibs. I feel I should make it clear that I am now retired from the Guides and you may call me just plain Ali." Jack stepped over to where Ali stood and shook his hand; "Welcome to England Ali." When Jack was able to get their attention he suggested they hire two cabs as there was now too many in the party for one to hold them all. When they reached the cab stand Jack instructed the first two hackney cab drivers to take them to Black Horse Inn. He then explained to Jonathan that they would be meeting his grandfather, Hermione and John there and that they would be having dinner and staying the night, then travel home in the morning. When they entered the inn Jack asked the doorman where they would find the Langsbury's, on entering the Private Bar they found not only Jonathan, Hermione and John but also Simon wearing his guards patrol uniform. After prying Pam away from Simon and Bess from John Jack managed to introduce the three younger men to each other. Then Jonathan introduced Ali to Simon, John and his grandparents. Jack called for their attention; "Now everyone let's all sit down and have a drink and we can start catching up." The elder Jonathan acquiesced; "Best damn suggestion I've heard all day." Meg looked over at Hermione; "I see you've been no more successful than I to get him to stop cursing." When they were seated Jack addressed Ali; "I served in India for seven years." Ali replied; "I know Sahib, you were with the 17th Lancers your son has told me a great deal about your family, I understand your Memsahib was there also;" The elder Jonathan interjected; "Meg was born there I brought her home when her mother died." Ali looked at Meg with a gleam in his eye; "It would seem Memsahib we are the only two Indians at this table." This caused some laughter at which point a pot boy came to their table for their drinks order. Jack's raised eyebrows at Ali's order did not go unnoticed; he looked at Jack amusement showing in his brown eyes; "You are surprised that I a Muslim ordered scotch? I acquired many bad habits serving with the Guides a taste for alcohol was one of them. May Allah in his infinite mercy forgive me." Jack had a question that had been on his mind since he had first set eyes on Ali; "I had you pegged for a Pathan but your beard and moustache nearly threw me." Ali stroked his neatly trimmed pointed beard that was complimented by his military moustache with its pointed waxed ends; "Ah yes another bad habit, many of my own people find it hard to accept that I do not wear the full beard as is their custom, but there is nothing in the Koran that says one must, and this way is more comfortable. Jack turned his attention to his son; "How did you come by this interesting fellow?" Jonathan replied he was a daffadar when I joined the Guides as a wet behind the ears subaltern, and he taught me all I know. Ali interjected; "I did not have to teach him to ride, but he did teach me to speak proper English" The younger Jonathan smiled; "I can take little credit there, Papa taught me to ride and Ali was an excellent pupil. When he was time expired I asked him to be my paid companion and he accepted." Ali laughed; "The Captain feels that the term servant is demeaning, but that is what I really am."

When they arrived at the end of their railway journey Jack suggested that everyone go to the Royal George while he found a carter to haul the baggage, and hire a horse from the livery stable so that he could ride to the home to get the ladies transportation. Jack was back in less than a hour; he strode into the private bar and informed them he had a carriage outside for the ladies but the men would have to ride with the carters. When they emerged from the inn they were greeted by Chalky and Barb who had brought the carriage, then Jonathan saw James mounted on a large hunter, he was almost running towards James when he dismounted. They clasped each others shoulders then shook hands with almost violent enthusiasm. There were tears in both their eyes as they stood with their hands on each others shoulders. Jack seeing the look on the faces of Simon and John explained; "They grew up together, they're like brothers." James spoke first; "Look at you a bloody captain; I'm glad I wasn't in uniform I would've had to bloody well salute you." Barb admonished him; "James, mind yer language there's ladies present." The younger Jonathan laughed and looking at the twins and Bess said; "We knew these ladies when we were all children, they can cuss with the best of 'em." Barb frowned at Jonathan; "That don't mean yer muvver an' Lady 'ermione as to listen to it." Then she walked over to him and embraced him while kissing him on the cheek saying; "I wuz there wen yew wuz a baby so don't be givin' me no cheek Jonathan Spratt." Jonathan smiled down at her; "You're still as beautiful as you were on the day I left for India." Barb looked up at him with tears streaming down her cheeks; "And yer still the biggest liar since Tom Pepper!" Chalky pushed between them to shake Jonathan's hand saying; "Yew'd better listen to 'er, I fink 'er ud still use the copper stick on yer both." Jack had led Perry back with him and after he had returned the hired mount to the livery stable he mounted Perry saying; "Let's get up to the house, I've warned Cook; and dinner will be about two hours." As they headed for the house Jack rode alongside the carriage containing the ladies while James rode beside the cart which the younger Jonathan was riding; they remained in animated conversation until they reached the house. When they reached their destination the ladies went into the house while Ali helped the carters unload the luggage. When everyone was seated in the library with drinks in their hands, Jack looked around asking; "Where's Ali?" His son replied; "I told one of the children to show him to his quarters, he would be uncomfortable in our company." Jack was insistent; "But he seemed perfectly at ease in Southampton, so I insist that he join us at dinner time." Jonathan smiled at his father; "Still the old equalizer eh, I'll appeal to his Pathan aversion to giving offence by refusing a host's hospitality." Ali appeared at dinner together with Jonathan and looking at Jack said; "I am here because I did not want to insult you by refusing your hospitality Sahib, but it is not customary for servants to sit with the sahibs in India." Jack's eyes went steely; "First of all we are not in India." Then after looking at Meg; "And second of all we decide who we break bread with in this house, and our son's friends will always be welcome in our home and at our table." Meg had thoughtfully had a finger bowl with an extra table napkin set at Ali's place at the table and after sitting down he looked down the table at her; "I am humbled by your consideration but rather than make your guests uncomfortable I will eat with a knife and fork as you do Memsahib." Jack looked down from the head of the table; "Ali, you will eat in whatever way you are most comfortable and there will be no more Sahib or Memsahib. You will address my wife as Miss Meg and me as anything but Sahib."

The conversation around the dinner table soon turned to wedding plans and the twins got into an argument as to who should wear their mother's wedding gown, Pam insisted that Patty should wear it as she was the oldest. Patty's reply was; "Don't be ridiculous it was only by three bloody minutes." The younger Jonathan saw his chance; "There I told you, she can cuss like a sergeant- major." Patty kicked him and Meg looked down the table toward them; "Has your grandmother's gown been kept in good condition?" Pam answered; "Yes, Mamma got married in her mother's gown, so Grandmamma Sanger's was put away in mothballs." Meg smiled; "Problem solved, Patty's the oldest so she will wear their grandmother's gown and Pam will wear their mother's." Both twins left their seats and ran to where Meg was sat, as they hugged and kissed her they told her how wise she was. Hermione smiled and looked at her husband; "Meg must have inherited her wisdom from Elizabeth." Jonathan smiled back; "I had enough wisdom to marry you, didn't I?" As Jonathan had to be back with the Guides by early May they decided on a March wedding. From that point in time the days until March were filled with frantic preparations.

CHAPTER 14

NEW BEGINNINGS

HE CHURCH WAS in London close to St James Palace and the Guard's barracks. When Simon had told Jonathan that his Colonel insisted they have an honor guard Jonathan suggested they find a church close by the barracks for the convenience of the officers who would be in the honor guard. Jack had written a letter to the Colonel of the Kings Dragoon Guards which resulted in James being granted leave to fulfill Jonathans wish to be his best man. At the insistence of the twins Meg was matron of honor and Bess maid of honor. The twins had asked Jimmy to be their ring bearer a request he refused emphatically; "I aint dressing up in no cissy clothes an' 'ave everybody laff at me!" After the twins had pleaded with her Bess had managed to talk a very reluctant Jimmy into accepting. His reluctance faded somewhat after enjoying two trips to London for wedding rehearsals. Annie Weston and Simon's sister Penelope were the bridesmaids.

On a cold day in March with a late winters sun looking down on them four young men stepped out of a carriage in front of the church: Simon in the full ceremonial uniform of the Coldstream Guards, Jonathan wearing his Guides uniform, John dressed in a morning suit and James in the full-dress uniform of the Kings Dragoon Guards. As they entered the church they each handed their headgear to a guardsman inside the porch: Simon his bearskin, Jonathan his side hat, James his brass helmet and John his grey silk topper. The four strode up the aisle of the church to the chancel steps where the best men took their positions on the grooms' right-hand sides. James had been a natural choice for Jonathan and Patty together with her sister had wheedled Simon into asking John to be his best man. The congregation enthralled at the vision of the four young men three of them resplendent in military uniforms was soon to be treated to another feast for the eyes. Less than two minutes after the grooms' party had arrived; the organ struck up the bridal march and as the congregation turned to see the bridal procession they gasped in unison. Lord Sanger in morning dress walking erect, his full head of snowy white hair the only indication of his age strode up the aisle with a twin on each arm. The beauty of the statuesque sisters in white lace carrying their yellow rose bouquets was complimented by the petite figures of Meg and Bess in dark green with their red tresses flowing down to their waists. Following Meg and Bess were Annie and Penelope in white satin carrying red carnation bouquets similar to those of Meg and Bess. Leading the party was Jimmy in a specially tailored morning suit carrying a red velvet cushion bearing four gold rings. After Lord Sanger had given the brides away and the rings had been exchanged the bridal couples followed the priest from the chancel steps to the altar for the conclusion of the ceremony. Then when the congregation had exited the church the bridal party proceeded back down the aisle, as the men were retrieving their headgear in the porch Jonathan spoke to Simon; "You and Pam go first, it's your guard of honor." As they emerged into the watery sunshine the crowd that had gathered gave a collective gasp at the vision presented to them. First there were Simon and Pam: he resplendent in his guards uniform and she a vision of stately beauty in her white lace gown with headdress and veil; set off by her bouquet of yellow roses. Following them through the arch of swords held by eight officers of Simon's battalion were Jonathan and Patty. The comparative drabness of Jonathan's uniform was somewhat offset by his ornate Indian style saber hilt and scabbard, and the colorful ribbons suspending the two medals on the left breast of his tunic, Patty presented an identical vision of beauty as her sister. Behind them came John with Meg on his arm followed by James and Bess, James now sported the four inverted chevrons of a riding master on the right sleeve of his dress uniform. Bringing up the rear were Annie and Penelope with Jimmy walking between them. Outside they posed for photographs; which had become a customary ritual at weddings in recent years, then after the wedding party had left for the reception the guests found their own ways to the hotel where the wedding breakfast was to be held. When everyone was assembled in the banquet room the guests were instructed by the Master of Ceremonies to take their seats at the designated locations. Jack was walking from table to table unable to find a place with his name when Lord Sanger called to him; "Get over here Jack, you belong at the head table, you and Meg have been parents to my girls for eleven years." After the speeches and the meal the guests repaired to the ballroom to dance and mingle. As Jonathan and Patty whirled past Jack and Meg; who were talking to Simon's parents, Meg remarked; "Aren't they a beautiful couple, and Jonathan seems even taller in uniform." Jack laughed; "He must have inherited his height from his grandfather." Simon's father commented; "Your daughter obviously inherited her beauty from her mother." Meg adopted her coy little girl pose and batted her eyelids; "Why General Hawksworth, are you flirting with me?" The General answered with a laugh; "I know better than to flirt with a 17th Lancer's lady, they're a bunch of tough buggers." Jack answered also laughing; "You Coldstreams are such hulking great blokes we have to be bloody tough before we take you on." Meg turned to the General's wife; "Have you noticed when soldiers get together they seem to have this compulsion to curse?" The General's wife shrugged; "If your husband is anything like mine he'll curse without being around other soldiers. And by the way, please call me Marjorie and I'll call you Meg if you've no objection." Meg smiled her assent as the General turned to Jack saying; "And you may call me Charles Jack, you're not in the army anymore so you don't have to call me sir nor salute nor kiss my arse for that matter." Just then Simon and Pam came whirling past, Meg nodded toward them; "And there's the other beautiful couple. Later as the guests gathered outside to see the two couples off Meg looked at Jack with tears in her eyes saying; "Things have come a long way darling; our daughter will be leaving us soon." Jack kissed his wife gently and replied; "Yes darling but we'll always have each other." As they were turning to re-enter the hotel Jack paused; he had spied a figure across the road that seemed familiar. Jack told Meg to wait saying; "I've a feeling I may know that fella." He hurried across the road and accosted a ragged, bearded figure with a wooden leg walking with the assistance of a crutch. Taking in the torn and dirty overcoat and the greasy cap Jack asked; "Don't I know you?" The ragged figure answered; I knows yew, yew becomed Riding Master Spratt an' I be Kershaw of "C" Squadron." Jack's memory was coming back; "You were in one of my training troops when I was Perry's assistant." Kershaw nodded in agreement; "Yeah, an' a right royal bastard yew wuz!" Jack laughed then asked; "What's your Christian name Kershaw?" The one legged man replied; "They christened me Fred'rick, but evr'yone calls me Fred." Jack was curious; "Where do you live Fred?" Fred shrugged his shoulders; "I don't ave a 'ome, I sleeps where I'm at when it's night." Jack was horrified; "You mean you live on the streets?" The old soldier looked at Jack with weary eyes and said; "Wen I got 'ome frum the Crimey me owd lady and the babes wuz all dead frum dipferia. I can't get no job wiv me one leg so I 'ave to beg." Jack looked at Fred's wooden leg; "How did that happen?" Kershaw grimaced; "Cannon ball smashed it 'an killed me 'orse." Jack let out a shout of rage; "The fucking bastards!" Fred looked startled saying; "They wuz only fighting fer their country like usn's." Jack looked at Fred a grim scowl on his face; "I don't mean the Russians, I'm talking about the bastards that cause people like you to have to beg on the streets." Fred looked at Jack with a smile that was more of a grimace; "I wuz wiv that bunch that wen an' talked to the bloke oo rit that bloody poem 'bout us, 'ad that bugger bin there ee'd uv rit summut difrnt." Jack took a sovereign from his pocket and placed it on Kershaw's palm saying; "Take this and get a good meal inside you, then find a decent place to sleep tonight. Be here tomorrow morning at nine o'clock." Fred was puzzled; "Wot yew want me 'ere fer tomorrer?" Jack explained; "I have just attended our son's wedding with my wife and daughter and we're staying here tonight. Tomorrow you're coming home with us." Fred uttered one word; "Why?" Jack answered; "Because you're an old comrade down on his luck." As they shook hands a gleam came into Fred's eye; "Be that missus of yurn still as pretty as er wuz?" Jack laughed looking over his shoulder as he walked away; "I think so, but then I'm prejudiced." When Jack rejoined Meg she asked; "What was that all about?" Meg had been talking to Jonathan and Hermione in Jack's absence so Jack enlightened all three of them. When he had finished his narrative Jonathan gave a short laugh and commented; "Just like a little boy bringing home a stray puppy." Jack's face darkened; "With all due respect Papa that man is my comrade, he lost his leg fighting for his country. He then came home and found his family had died from diphtheria, a disease that's rampant in our cities and towns because of the lack of sanitation." Jonathan looked contrite saying; "I'm sorry Jack I shouldn't have made light of it." Jack held his hand out to Jonathan and as they shook hands he addressed his father in law; "I may have been a little prickly; I just get angry when I see how our old soldiers are treated." Meg smiled at her father; "He's still an old softy when it comes to his mates." Jack laughed; "When he asked me if you were still pretty I told him you were a wrinkled old crone." Meg shot her daggers at him; "You're not too old for that horse whipping Jack Spratt!" The four of them arms linked went back into the hotel and as doorman saluted them he wondered what they were laughing about.

The following evening back at the home Meg and Jack were sat in front of the fire in the library enjoying after dinner drinks. Jack spoke; "John said his editor wants him to write about the rest of my time in the army, but I think he might have had something to do with talking the editor into the idea." Meg laughed; "He's going to be around here a great deal of the time anyway." Then Meg asked; "How's Fred?" Jack replied; "Well he's bathed and shaved and he ate well. He insisted on eating with the children."

Meg looked at Jack adoringly; "I was just thinking, I know it must sound strange but it's seems that I owe everything to that blackguard of the 47th." Jack smiled back at Meg; "Fate's a funny thing, if the Beadle hadn't caught me stealing from your uncle's bakery we might never have met." Meg got up from her chair, walked over and kissed him; "Let's go to bed darling. " Jack laughed; "If you're trying to seduce me you've just succeeded."

EPILOGUE

F OR THOSE READERS not familiar with British military history and customs some of the situations in the preceding chapters may seem unlikely or impossible. However, although the incidents may be fiction the situations could and probably did occur.

In the late seventeenth century the English army was organized into a centrally controlled and cohesive entity by Oliver Cromwell and remained so after the restoration of the monarchy. Regiments tended to recruit from particular cities or counties so that many of the officers and rankers had a place of origin in common. The eighteenth and nineteenth century practice of increasing the army's manpower by forcing felons to join the ranks reinforced regimental loyalties. The former felons found that despite the harsh discipline; their lives in many cases were far better than they had been previous to entering the army. In most cases they would be receiving three meals a day, be paid weekly and have a place to live and sleep, something many of them had never known before. As most rankers were either in the army to escape poverty or to avoid prison, transportation or hanging; their regiments became their homes and their families. In the latter part of the nineteenth century as social conditions improved for the working classes, those joining the army

335

often did so because their father, an older brother or other family member had served and they usually chose to serve in the same regiments. Commissioned officers were predominately from the aristocracy and upper middle classes. They also tended to follow family members into the same regiments as a matter of tradition. At the height of Britain's imperial prominence a large standing army was needed along with the navy to defend and control its territories, providing considerable employment opportunities for many who would have been otherwise unemployed.

It should be noted that the British armies of the eighteenth, nineteenth and twentieth centuries rarely lost a battle unless they were outnumbered or outgunned. Most battles that were lost were due to incompetence at the general officer level, rather than lack of courage or determination on the part of the rankers; as in the American Revolution. An often quoted anecdote attributed to Napoleon states: "Give me French officers and English soldiers and I will conquer the world!"

My vehicle for this novel was the 17th Lancers although I most confess I have taken considerable liberties with their history however, it would be impossible to overstate the esprit de corps of this and other traditional units of the British army.

During the last two centuries there have been many changes in the structure of the British army. Massive cuts in military expenditure in 1922; called for severe reductions in the number of standing regiments. Many regiments avoided disbandment by being amalgamated with other similar units; the 17th Lancers were amalgamated with the 21st Lancers, thus becoming the 17th/21st Lancers. These amalgamations allowed the traditions and customs of the combined regiments to remain alive. Since World War II there have been successive reductions through the years and in 1993 the 17th/21st Lancers were amalgamated with the 16th/5th Lancers, the new regiment's title is now The Queens Royal Lancers.

THE LAST OF THE LIGHT BRIGADE

RUDYARD KIPLING

There were thirty million English who talked of England's might,
There were twenty broken troopers who lacked a bed for the night.
They had neither food nor money, they had neither service nor trade;
They were only shiftless soldiers, the last of the Light Brigade

They felt that life was fleeting, they knew not that art was long.
That though they were dying of famine, they lived in deathless song.
They asked for a little money to keep the wolf from the door;
And the thirty million English sent twenty pounds and four!

They laid their heads together that were scarred and lined and grey;
Keen were the Russian sabres, but want was keener than they;
And an old Troop Sergeant muttered, "Let us go to the man who writes
The things on Balaclava the kiddies at school recites."

They went without bands or colours, a regiment ten file strong,
To look for the Master-singer who had crowned them all in his song;
And waiting his servant's order, by the garden gate they stayed
A desolate little cluster, the last of the Light Brigade.

They strove to stand at attention, to straighten the toil bowed back;
They drilled on an empty stomach, the loose knit files fell slack With
stooping of weary shoulders, in garments tattered and frayed,
They shambled into his presence, the last of the Light Brigade.

The old Troop Sergeant was spokesman, and "Beggin' your pardon," he said,
"You wrote o' the Light Brigade, sir. Here's all that isn't dead.
An' it's all come true what you wrote, sir, regardin' the mouth of hell;
For we're all of us nigh to the workhouse, an' we thought we'd call an' tell."

"No thank you, we don't want food, sir; but couldn't you take an' write A
sort of 'to be continued' and 'see next page' o' the fight?
We think that someone has blundered, an' couldn't you tell 'em how?
You wrote we were heroes once, sir. Please write we are starving now."

The poor little army departed, limping and lean and forlorn,
And the heart of the Master-singer grew hot with "the scorn of scorn."
And he wrote for them wonderful verses that swept the land like flame,
Till the fatted souls of the English were scourged with the thing called
Shame.

O thirty million English that babble of England's might,
Behold there are twenty heroes who lack their food tonight;
Our children's children are lisping to "honour the charge they made"
And we leave to the streets and the workhouse the charge of the Light
Brigade

CPSIA information can be obtained
at www.ICGtesting.com
Printed in the USA
FFOW01n1605211016
28687FF